CU00645794

# POKER FACE

**THE BEAUFORT POKER CLUB BOOK ONE**

MAGGIE GATES

Copyright © 2021 Maggie Gates. All rights reserved

No part of this publication may be reproduced, transmitted, or distributed in any form or by any means including photocopying, recording, information storage and retrieval systems, without prior written permission from the publisher except in the case of brief quotation embodied in book reviews.

This book is a work of fiction. The characters and events in this book are fictitious. Any similarity to real places or persons, living or dead, is purely coincidental and not intended by the author or are used fictitiously.

The author acknowledges the trademark status and trademark owners of various products, brands, and/or establishments referenced in this work of fiction. The publication/use of these trademarks is not associated with, or sponsored by the trademark owners.

This book is intended for mature audiences.

ISBN-13: 979-8-9908378-0-5

Cover Design by Melissa Doughty - Mel D. Designs

*To the asshole chef who said a little girl couldn't run a kitchen.*

*I ran the damn kitchen.*

# POKER
# FACE

# CONTENT WARNINGS

While my books are generally upbeat and uplifting, each story can delve into heavy topics. This book is intended for mature audiences and contains explicit language and sexual content. I encourage you to read the content warnings made available at www.maggiegates.com/content-warnings

TREAT YOURSELF WITH CARE.

WITH LOVE,
   Maggie Gates

# 1

## MADELINE

"What a pompous ass," I muttered as I choked down the bile bubbling up in my throat. One short clip of Chef Luca DeRossi on my phone was enough to snap me out of my mindless scrolling. The way he sneered at the competitors from his throne of judgment made me throw up in my mouth a little bit.

*Ugh.*

Life was unfair. Why were complete jackasses always handsome and rich? Why couldn't they be as ugly on the outside as they were on the inside? Being struck with the Pinocchio effect would go a long way.

My stomach growled. *Maybe I was just hangry.*

I looked down at my leather purse and wondered how far removed it was from beef jerky. The bag of pretzels and Coke on the cramped flight from North Carolina to Los Angeles did nothing to cure my growling belly. The complimentary air-condition-on-the-fritz made the middle seat feel like a microwave. Luckily, the old man asleep by the window next to me didn't stir once after take-off. The floppy-haired teen in the aisle seat was too engrossed in his phone to notice the sound of my stomach collapsing in on itself like a dying star.

*Hotel, food, gym, shower, meet and greet.*

I mentally ticked off my to-do list as I spotted my ride outside the airport. I loaded my suitcase and slid into the back seat.

Palm trees lined the sidewalks, tourists snapped selfies, and I swore that every hot guy in sunglasses looked exactly like Ryan Gosling. There had to be something in the water out here in California, because these beach boys looked nothing like the ones on my stretch of sand. I yanked the elastic ponytail out of my hair and gave it a run through with my fingers. Pulling my phone out of my pocket, I fired off a quick text to my neighbor–slash–landlord–slash–best friend.

MADDIE

Made it to L.A. How's Heather?

STEVE

Same ol, same ol. Mel's gonna drop by to check on her while I'm on duty. Have fun out there, Mad Dog. The left coast isn't gonna know what hit them.

MADDIE

See you Monday night. It's your turn to bring the beer to poker.

STEVE

Good luck tomorrow. Give 'em hell.

God bless Melissa Jacobsen. She was a saint. Even after pulling a twelve-hour shift at the hospital, I had no doubt that she'd show up at Steve and Heather's house with some kind of takeout and a baked good. Probably some of the pastries I kept stocked at Queen's Coffee.

The poker club, as we called it, was my group of friends who met every Monday to blow off some steam, get a little tipsy, lose a few dollars to each other, and make sure everyone had somebody to lean on.

That last thing was more of an unspoken agreement.

At the moment, it was all-hands-on-deck to make sure Steve could keep his schedule as a detective with the Beaufort Police Department while Heather went through chemo again.

Sometimes life didn't make sense. Steve and Heather were high school sweethearts. They were the picture perfect couple—the football star and the head cheerleader living happily ever after. He spent his days protecting and serving and she shaped young minds as a second grade teacher at Beaufort Elementary. Well, she did up until the beginning of the year when her cancer came back with a fiery vengeance.

I felt guilty for flying to California for a few days. But if I was able to win a little prize money and bring home bragging rights to Revanche, it would be worth it.

The driver pulled up to the front of the hotel and gave me a dismissive nod. "Thanks," I said with a smile as I got out and dragged my bags onto the sidewalk. California wasn't nearly as humid as North Carolina, but the May heat was sweltering to say the least.

A chilly blast pummeled me in the face as I walked into the air-conditioned lobby, and I flashed the front desk clerk a smile. "Madeline Dorsey. I have a reservation for two nights. It's reserved in the group for the *Pastry Throwdown* competition."

The clerk began furiously typing, searching for my

reservation. I didn't understand why it took so long. I could have an FBI-level dossier drawn up on my friends' exes in the time that it took for the front desk to pull up a reservation.

My phone vibrated in my pocket and I pulled it out to read the message.

HANNAH JANE

> Good luck, Mads! You got this! Don't be nervous. Just think of all the things you say when you rant about He-Who-Must-Not-Be-Named.

I had the best friends a girl could ask for.

Hannah Jane was the event coordinator at the Taylor Creek Inn. The name made the inn sound quaint, but it was a luxury hotel on the Carolina coast that sat right on the water.

She handled everything from luxury weddings to corporate retreats. We didn't grow up together. But seeing as Revanche, the restaurant I practically lived at, was right next door to the inn and I did most of the wedding cakes for her events, we were thick as thieves.

She was another part of the poker club. Dealing with insane brides for a thousand hours a week earned her the right to a few stiff drinks every Monday.

Hannah's mention of He-Who-Must-Not-Be-Named had me thinking that it had been a while since I had thrust my personal opinion into the internet stratosphere. I tapped on the screen and opened up my feed, firing off the first thing I could think of.

@XOMaddieLeeDee - 05/27 - 2:46 PM
*At least Chef Luca DeRossi has a nice face and lots of*

*money. That helps hide the fact that he doesn't know the differ-
ence between a bouquet garni and a bouquet of flowers.*

Okay, so it was childish. But before I had the sense to delete the post, the desk clerk slid my room key across the counter and pointed me in the direction of the elevators.

Hotel room: *check*. Now, onto the rest of my to-do list.

# 2

## LUCA

**M**y feet slapped hard against the treadmill. I punched up the incline and increased my speed. I nearly tripped when the music pulsing through my ears faded and the robotic chirp of Siri's voice echoed in my head. "New mention. At-Chef Luca DeRossi, maybe if you spent as much time in the kitchen as you do taking selfies in expensive suits, you'd be a better cook."

*Kiss my James Beard Award-winning ass,* I thought to myself. I didn't even know why I still looked at social media. The whole thing was a cesspool of cowards who hid behind their phones because they were too scared to say things in person. I wanted to delete my digital presence entirely, but Astrid—my agent and overpaid gopher—would butcher me faster than I could say *mise en place.*

I slowed down to an easy jog to gently lower my heart rate before moving to the free weights. As much as I wanted to go take a fucking nap, I knew Astrid would chew me out if I didn't maintain the image that got me a spot in *30 Under 30.* Seven years after making that list, I managed to double my net worth and began acquiring boutique, fine dining restaurants for my restaurant group rather than starting them from the ground up. Work smarter, not harder? I did both.

Suck it, Twitter assholes.

I'd barely caught my breath when ten miles of blonde hair in a reckless ponytail waltzed by me, carried by long legs with an ass like a dream. She stepped onto the treadmill directly in front of mine, and bent in half to tie her shoe. *Hell-fucking-yes.* I could run another mile—or twenty—with a front row seat to that view.

She flashed me a smile over her shoulder and all the blood rushed away from my head. I licked my lips as she set her water bottle in the cupholder and turned on the treadmill, gradually increasing her speed. I lowered the incline on my machine and ran faster. Her blonde hair swished back and forth like a metronome, and I matched my speed to hers. She glanced back at me again and grinned as she picked up her pace.

*So that's how you wanna play it.*

I adjusted my ball cap and grabbed my towel to soak up the sweat on my face. I wasn't about to be shown up by a damn mermaid.

———

"IMPRESSIVE," I said with a grin as I slumped over the front of the treadmill at the end of my cool down.

Blondie laughed as she began to wipe down her machine with sanitizer.

"My endurance or my cleaning skills?" she asked.

I watched with rapt fascination as she tossed her hair to the side, nudging a bead of sweat off her neck.

I would have licked it off for her.

*Damn. I really need to get laid.*

"Little bit of both," I said with a wry laugh.

She gave that thing a white glove treatment. It was so clean a health inspector would eat off of it without a second thought.

I cleaned mine thoroughly—*I wasn't a total asshole*—and draped my sweat towel over my shoulder. "I smoked you on that last mile, though."

"Um, my incline was all the way up and you were running flat, thank you very much," she said with the slightest southern drawl. It was irresistibly adorable.

"Maybe, but I was already five miles in when you showed up. So I win."

I followed her across the gym toward the locker rooms. Sure, I could afford to work out somewhere private with a trainer, but with as much as I traveled, a nationwide membership to a chain gym made more sense.

She smiled and I caught a glimpse of her dimpled cheeks. "And what is it that you won exactly? This was just a little friendly competition with a stranger."

"Well, you could give me your number and we could lose the *stranger* bit. I mean, I did win and all. I think that'd make us square."

She lingered outside the door of the women's locker room and crossed her arms. The motion pushed her sports bra-covered breasts up and I wasn't subtle with the way I watched.

She didn't cower away, instead choosing to rake her eyes up my shirtless torso. "I'm not local," she soothed. "Wouldn't do you much good."

"How long are you here for?"

"Three days," she said, "But I'm here for work, not pleasure."

"Do you have time for a drink? Maybe turn your work trip into a little bit of work *and* pleasure?"

She tapped the screen on her phone to check the time and I stole a peek at the photo. She was with a brunette on the beach. They each had an arm wrapped around the other. she was flashing a peace sign while wearing a smile that made her look like she didn't have a care in the world.

Her silvery blonde hair was almost white against her tan skin and hung all the way down to her hips. It didn't quite hide the teeny black bikini that left very little to the imagination.

My dick stood at attention. I shifted my weight between my feet and held my towel in one hand over my crotch to hide my raging hard-on.

"Any other time I'd say yes, but I have a prior engagement tonight," she said, looking back up at me with a smile. "I should probably head back to my hotel to get ready."

I nodded and backed away. I wanted to see her again, but I didn't want her to think I was a creep. "Alright, fair. How 'bout your number? If your schedule frees up, shoot me a text and we'll get that drink or a slice or something."

"You from New York?"

"Grew up in Brooklyn. Why?"

She smiled, "Because you called it a *slice*. I've only ever heard New Yorkers and folks from Jersey call pizza that."

"Perceptive," I said, cracking a smile. *Beauty and brains.* I respected that. "So, what do you say, out of towner? Give me your number? I'll make it worth your while."

Uncertainty hung in the hair until she finally typed in her passcode and relinquished her phone. My fingers brushed hers as I took it from her and filled in my contact information.

"Hot Guy from the Gym in LA?" She laughed when she read the name I'd entered. "I don't get a name?"

"Luke," I said, extending my hand.

"Maddie," she shook my hand and held it for a moment, turning my hand left-to-right and assessing my sleeves of tattoos. "I like your ink."

"You got any?"

From the picture I saw on her phone, there weren't many places she could've been hiding a tattoo, but I'd be lying if I said I didn't want to search every square inch of her just to see for myself.

"Wouldn't you like to know," she teased. Her lips curled into a devilish smile. She had a wild gleam in her eye that should have scared me off, but it didn't.

"Well, Maddie-who's-not-a-local. I gotta work the next two days," I said. "But I'm free tonight."

She wasn't much shorter than me, which was surprising considering I was six-two.

I stepped forward until our tennis shoes hit each other and leaned down, my voice dropping into a low rumble. "I'd like to collect on my winnings. So, if you're up for it, I know a little spot not too far from here that has great late night food. My treat, even though I won our little race."

Her eyelashes fluttered shut as my lips brushed the corner of her ear. She placed her hand on my chest and took a step backward. "I'll think about it, Hot Guy from the Gym in LA"

"Luke," I corrected as she turned to go into the women's locker room.

"Luke," she confirmed with a pointed finger gun and a smile I wouldn't soon forget before disappearing around the corner.

I trapped my lower lip between my teeth and scrubbed the beard along my jaw. I loved her confidence. Self-assurance was sexy. I wasn't usually one to get wrapped up in a girl, but hell—I'd give my left arm to see her again.

# 3

## MADELINE

I followed the producers through the studio kitchen like an obedient puppy, taking note of where all the equipment was, what types of ovens they had for us, and where the blast freezer was hiding.

I was thankful that production allowed the contestants to scout out the competition space the night before, rather than flying blind when the clock was ticking.

The older lady to my left was pawing through the dry ingredient shelf.

*What a sweetheart.* She looked like Betty Crocker reincarnated. *She would be eliminated first. The sweet ones never survived.*

I sized up the loudmouth to my right and rolled my eyes.

*Never mind. Betty Crocker will make it to round two. The stand-up comedian will probably get stuck in the walk-in fridge if he doesn't shut his mouth and pay attention.*

I rolled my shoulders back and forth to get the nerves out as I took it all in.

*Pastry Throwdown* was a televised baking competition that had a cash prize of fifty grand. I never cared much for cooking shows, but one of the producers had reached out and recruited me.

I was going to turn it down, but only a fool would say no to a one-in-four chance to win that much cash, right?

The poker club practically signed my name on the dotted line for me. Steve and his detective partner, Chase, threatened to escort me to Los Angeles to make sure I actually got on my flight. Of course, when I put up a fuss, Hannah Jane went and said those three little words that I never said no to.

*I dare you.*

And that's how I ended up on a film set, side-eyeing and mean-mugging the other three competitors. Sweet Betty and Loudmouth didn't stand a chance. If I had to put money on it, I'd say that Charissa Miles and I would be going head to head in the final round.

I would win, of course. If you don't enter a competition thinking you're going to win, you've already lost.

I knew Charissa from pastry school. Every semester we'd be top two in the in-house showcases. To say the two of us were competitive was an understatement. If it wasn't competing in school it was competing for internships. After we graduated, the competition moved to industry accolades.

It wasn't going to be easy, but the prize was worth it. Rubbing my win in Charissa's smug little face would be the icing on the cake.

The producer quickly marched us out of the kitchen and into the large dressing room. Sets of chef whites embroidered with each of our names and branded with the competition logo were waiting for us.

While she droned on and on about tomorrow's schedule, what to expect, and passed out stacks of papers with all the pertinent information, my phone buzzed in my pocket.

I pulled it out and quickly glanced at the screen.

HOT GUY FROM THE GYM IN LA

Still at your prior engagement?

I smiled and quickly texted back.

MADDIE

I see you called yourself from my phone so you'd have my number. Pretty presumptuous, Luke.

HOT GUY FROM THE GYM IN LA

You're exceptionally beautiful, so I'd be a dumbass not to press my luck and hold you to your word. So how about that drink?

MADDIE

Smooth. You know who else was smooth? Ted Bundy. How do I know you're not a serial killer? This is California after all. Did you know that California has the highest number of serial killings in the country? Over 1,500.

HOT GUY FROM THE GYM IN LA

Let me paint you a picture, beautiful: You. Me. Cervezas, carnitas, and ceviche. Maybe some tostones. The place I go to is open real late. I can meet you at your hotel as soon as you're done. I'll show you a good time.

MADDIE

You never said you weren't a serial killer.

HOT GUY FROM THE GYM IN LA

You willing to take a risk, Maddie? Go out with the handsome stranger you just met on your three-day work trip to Cali. You might just have the time of your life.

MADDIE

I'm here for work and you're distracting me.

HOT GUY FROM THE GYM IN LA

I dare you.

I groaned and cursed my resolve as I slid my phone back into my pocket. I never *not* took a dare.

Truthfully, I was a bit of a wild child. Live on a houseboat? Sure. Climb up to the roof of my houseboat and jump off? Done. Skinny dipping? Not even a challenge. Taking shots? Pour me another. Sit on the beach and watch a hurricane come in? Yes, please.

The producer started talking about the judging panel, but it was in one ear and out the other. All I could think about were those tattoos that wrapped around his muscular arms. That dark stubble that seemed a bit like a two-day beard. Those brown eyes that looked like the finest chocolate. His jet black hair that was both effortlessly messy and totally stylish at the same time.

It was clipped short on the sides—just a light buzz of hair, but left longer on top. He had a cocky grin that curved up at the corner of his lips and—*God*—his thick lashes.

I had never been jealous of a man's eyelashes, but holy hell—those things were like bat wings. They put my cheap falsies to shame. Luke was every bit tall, dark, and handsome with a dangerous edge that had my spine-tingling.

That didn't even cover his muscles...

Today must have been my lucky day. I was half tempted to go buy lottery tickets. Seeing him shirtless and glistening with sweat did all sorts of things to my lady parts.

Luke had sculpted arms and a chest that was made for admiring. He had those two hard lines that started on either side of his abs and dipped below the waist of his shorts. And that package I'm almost one hundred percent certain was hard? That thing could annihilate a woman.

I bit my tongue as a string of profanities raced through my head. Without completely thinking it through, I yanked my phone back out and stabbed the letters on the screen with an excited fury.

MADDIE

> Fine. I'll text you the address of my hotel when I'm done.

HOT GUY FROM THE GYM IN LA

> See you soon, beautiful.

———

I PUSHED the close button on the elevator over and over again. Finally, the doors slid shut and it began to rise. The meet and greet went smoothly. I couldn't complain. Charissa and I were cordial, but I knew that tomorrow all those professional manners would go out the window.

I shoved my keycard into the door and practically ripped the handle off as I barreled into my hotel room, leaving a trail of clothes in my wake. I traded my trim trousers and breezy, professional blouse for my denim cut-offs and my favorite concert tank that read, *God is great, beer is good, and people are crazy*.

I tossed my black pumps back in my suitcase and swapped them for the strappy leather sandals that wrapped around my ankles. The perfect mix of cute and badass. They were on the verge of falling apart after wearing them day in and day out.

A few layered necklaces, my favorite rings, a quick smokey eye, and I was ready. I flipped my hair over and doused it in a cloud of dry shampoo and hairspray, just to give my blonde beach waves a few more hours of life.

Just as I coughed and waved away the fog of noxious fumes, my phone vibrated against the bathroom counter.

HOT GUY FROM THE GYM IN LA

Here. What's your room number? I'll come up and meet you.

MADDIE

Not a chance, Ted Bundy. See you in the lobby.

Another glance in the mirror and I was good to go.

My style wasn't exactly what people called *proper.* I lived in denim shorts that were shorter than some people's undies. I preferred band shirts that I cut down to loose tank tops.

Miss Jackie, one of my least favorite nurses at my mom's care facility, once told me *to my face* that I looked like a tramp and that a nearly thirty-year-old woman should dress like a lady.

So I wasn't joining the Junior League any time soon—sue me. I slung my purse over my shoulder and headed out the door.

———

"Damn." Luke grinned when I spotted him sitting on a couch in the lobby, his ankle was kicked up, resting on his knee.

To say he was a big man was an understatement. He stood up and I swear the ceiling raised itself just to accommodate him. I was tall, but he was at least a head above me.

He was wearing the same hat he had on at the gym. The

Yankees logo was bright white against the navy blue of the flat-brimmed snapback. His white t-shirt hung loosely off his broad shoulders, disguising what I knew was the most jaw-dropping six-pack I had ever seen. His jeans were ripped and faded in a way that said, *I definitely paid big money for these.* And God, did he smell good. Warm and spicy. I wanted to wrap myself up in him and take a big whiff.

"Hi." I smiled as I bounced toward him.

"Hey, beautiful. You ready to go?"

"Where are we going exactly?" I questioned as I glanced down at my bare legs, "This is fine, right? Cervezas and carnitas made it sound kinda casual."

"You look like a million bucks," he said with a cocky grin. His hand slid to the small of my back as he led me out the lobby doors.

"Would you like me to bring your car around, Mr.—"

"No thanks, we're walking," Luke said to the valet before the kid could finish his sentence. He took my hand and led me down the sidewalk. I raised an eyebrow, but didn't say a thing. "It's not far from here," he explained. "Besides—I, uh, I kinda figured you wouldn't wanna ride in a car with a serial killer." He flashed me a confident smile and winked.

"Ah, so you *are* a serial killer." I laughed as he took my hand and led me down the sidewalk. "But hey, if you're gonna be a psychopath who likes chopping innocent women into *tartare a la blonde*, at least you're honest about it."

"Well, I am good with knives." The growl of his low timbre sent a zip of excitement down my spine.

"A serial killer with a sense of humor." I snorted. "That's new."

"How 'bout this." He halted mid-stride and raised his

hands in surrender. "I promise I won't go all Jeffrey Dahmer on you until *after* our date. Happy?"

"Well, if you decide to turn me into a skin sweater—" I snapped a picture of him with my phone and sent it to the poker club "—at least now my friends will be able to pick you out of a lineup."

"Fair enough." Luke laughed, twisting a lock of my hair loosely around his finger and tugging on it playfully. "But, uh, I don't think the rest of the mermaids will put up much of a fight."

"I'll have you know—" I swatted his hand away and resumed our walk "—two of my friends—one being my next door neighbor—are cops."

"Cops?" He raised an eyebrow and casually shoved his hands in his pockets. "I'm not afraid of cops. Crazy girl-friends, however... let's just say that I've learned that a girl's best friend is more ruthless than the CIA."

"Believe me, you don't wanna get on my friends' bad side."

"Oh yeah?"

I opened up the group text and handed him my phone.

## THE POKER CLUB

HANNAH JANE

OMG! HE'S HOT! LIKE H-O-T HOT! That's gym guy? Way to go, Mads!

STEVE

Want me to run his photo and see what I can find?

CHASE

I'm already at the station. Give me a name and consider it done.

MELISSA

Wait! What am I missing? I just got off work. (Btw, I'm on my way over with dinner for Heather, Steve. Food will be in the fridge for you).

HANNAH JANE

Maddie picked up a west coast hottie is what happened! WELL DONE, SISTER.

STEVE

I hate this conversation. So much. Be safe, Mad Dog.

CHASE

WHAT IS THIS DICK'S NAME?

KRISTIN

WE DON'T KNOW THAT HE'S A DICK, YET. GIVE HIM A CHANCE! (Especially if he looks like that. YUM. He looks like he has abs. Does he have abs? Can I see a picture of the abs)?

CHASE

Any dude with a face like that is a dick.

BRIDGET

You mean a HOT face?

CHASE

I said what I said.

HANNAH JANE

I second the ab pic.

BRIDGET

Lol, Kris—he's not a doughnut. And he's
Maddie's. Cool it. But yes. We need
photographic evidence of any and all abs.
Please and thank you.

HEATHER

I'm just saying, an ab pic would make me
feel better.

STEVE

Hey now, married woman. I have abs too.
(Well, I used to. It still counts).

HEATHER

Love you, babe. (Draw me a picture,
Maddie).

CHASE

We need more dudes in this group. There's
way too much estrogen coming out of the
phone and it's getting all over my uniform.

Luke's lips went from a frown to a thin line to a cocky
smirk. He stepped under a streetlamp, lifted the hem of his
shirt and trapped it between his teeth before he held my
phone out and—*hell yes*—took a selfie showing off his glorious, glorious abs.

*Note to self: save that photo and frame it. Pass it down to my
daughters and granddaughters. Luke's abs will be the family
heirloom.*

I let out an involuntary whine when the fabric fell back
down, covering his stomach. Luke's thumbs flew over the
screen before he finally handed my phone back and let me
read the text.

> Contrary to your very beautiful friend's belief, I am NOT a serial killer. I consent to being fingerprinted and DNA tested. Also, yes. I have abs. See below for proof of six pack. - L

"Oh my God." I cracked up reading the message. "You're so full of yourself."

We laughed, lingering beneath the streetlamp. Luke slid his hands on my hips and backed me up against the pole.

"Now that your friends know who I am," he said as his voice dropped into a tantalizing rasp. "Is it too forward of me to kiss you right now?"

I tilted my chin up until I was only a breath away from his lips. "Do you think I'm the kind of girl that kisses on the first date?"

"You make it sound like you'll give me a second." His nose brushed the tip of mine as he shook his head. "You don't strike me as the kind of girl who waits to be courted. You seem like the kind of woman who takes what she wants and doesn't apologize for it."

I draped my arms around his neck and leaned in.

# 4

## LUCA

The moment my lips met hers, it was magic. They were soft, warm, and tasted like vanilla. Maddie was sugar and spice. Heavy on the spice. Her fire was sexy.

I dug my fingers into the curve of her ass, and she plastered her hips to mine. Her ripped-up denim shorts barely covered her round ass, and I didn't mind one bit. My dick tensed against my jeans, and I knew that if I didn't end the kiss right then, I'd throw her over my shoulder like a caveman and haul her back to her hotel room. Pulling away was a feat of superhuman strength.

I rested my forehead on hers and grinned from ear-to-ear as our chests heaved against each other. "I do plan on buying you dinner, but I haven't been able to stop thinking about you all day and I couldn't help myself." I pressed the pad of my thumb against her lip and wiped away the sheen left from our kiss. Her cheeks turned soft pink as she bit her lower lip when my thumb left it.

"Remember that work thing I had earlier?"

"Yeah?"

"I hardly paid attention. All I thought about was whether I was going to let you take me to dinner or not."

"And?"

Maddie leaned in as if to kiss me again and whispered, "I'm starving," against the corner of my mouth.

I took her hand and kissed the center of her palm. She laced her fingers through mine, as I pulled her down the sidewalk.

We walked a few blocks without saying much of anything at all. Feeling so comfortable with a stranger was odd, but there was something about Maddie that put me at ease. She didn't strike me as one of the media darlings that I was used to meeting—the kind of girl who was on a green juice cleanse to drop five pounds that didn't even exist.

No, Maddie was strong. Her arms and thighs had the kind of muscle tone that only came from hard, back-breaking work—from living the kind of life other people wish they had the courage to do.

She was light and brilliant and warm. I loved her laugh. She had a smile that could drive away a storm. The way she was unafraid to look directly at me was intoxicating. The depth in her eyes made me want to know everything about her.

"This is us," I said as I pointed to the row of food trucks that surrounded a neighborhood entrance. People milled around with styrofoam plates in hand. Families crowded around picnic tables. Latin music wafted through the air from an old-school boombox that was set up in the pass-through window of one of the food trucks. The smell of garlic, chilis, and cumin mingled in the air. I watched Maddie take in the scene.

"Where do we start?" Maddie nodded toward the row of trucks.

That made me smile—*my kinda girl.* "I like the way you think. How 'bout you grab us a table, and I'll go order."

"I dunno." She gave me a hesitant look. "I don't usually trust other people to order for me."

"You'll like it. Trust me."

She held up her hands in surrender and headed toward an empty picnic before pointing at me and yelling, "Better not let me down, Hot Guy from the Gym in LA"

---

"Oh, God." Maddie moaned as she dragged a tostone through the sofrito ranch sauce and popped it in her mouth.

*I knew food.*

Little Miss Mermaid would never admit it, but no palate stood a chance against the delicious mountain of food I provided. The wonderful thing about the spot I took her to was that each truck represented a different region of Latin America. We had a little bit of everything at our table: Mexican food, Puerto Rican food, some Peruvian, and a little Columbian.

Maddie let out another involuntary groan of satisfaction. I could watch her eat all day long. Watching Maddie's pink lips wrap around the mouth of her bottle of beer bottle was doing all sorts of things to my head. *And my dick.*

"So." I cleared my throat and looked away in an effort to relieve the tension in my jeans. It did not work. "What exactly brought you to LA?"

"Work," she mumbled in between bites of ceviche. She stabbed another piece of fish and popped it in her mouth. "This is so good. That prior engagement I had—you know what they served instead of dinner? *Charcuterie boards.*" She pursed those pink lips and frowned in displeasure as she pointed her fork my way. "Adult Lunchables is what that is. You know what is not an appropriate offering when you're told that dinner will be provided? A meat and cheese platter that everybody's grubby, nasty hands have been all over."

I finished off my beer and cracked open my second, taking a minute to slide a lime wedge in the neck of the bottle. I raised my eyebrows and smirked, tilting my drink toward her in silent toast. "I see you have strong feelings about this."

"You have no idea," she muttered between bites. "This is seriously the best ceviche I've ever had. I would never eat raw fish from a truck. So if I get food poisoning tomorrow, I'm blaming you."

I popped a bite of fish in my mouth. "Well then." I grinned as I chased it down with a swig of beer. "That'll make two of us and I'll just have to come hang out at your hotel until we're both on the mend."

"You're awfully confident, aren't you?" She giggled and took a sip of beer. Maddie may have sounded like Reese Witherspoon, but she was hell on heels—*er*—flip flops.

"So do I get a last name, Maddie? Where you're from? Some grid coordinates to help me track you down when you go back home?"

"What are you, a Navy SEAL or something?" She laughed again and it made me smile. The sound was infectious. "You're gonna *track me down*?"

"Nah, nothing that exciting."

"So what do you do?"

"Acquisitions." I shrugged. "I oversee business consolidations." It wasn't a lie. It was slightly more misleading than the whole truth, sure. But it wasn't a lie. I'd be traveling to the East Coast at the end of this week to do just that.

I was having one of those days where I wanted to be anyone but *Luca DeRossi.*

Astrid had been all over my case about going out and being seen at events and openings while I was in town. She was still livid that I had ended things with my ex.

Apparently, my public image mattered more to her than my personal happiness. Astrid's opinion was a non-issue, though. She was excellent at her job and I had thick skin.

When Maddie came prancing into the gym and immediately showed her competitive side, I was hooked.

I liked it when she called me Luke. It felt like the most normal thing in the world.

She didn't see me as a rich guy with coattails she could ride. By my guess, Maddie had no fucking clue who I was. When she busted my balls for potentially giving her food poisoning, I couldn't help but laugh. No one except my family had ever ragged on me that way—not in a long time, at least.

The food truck owner was previously an executive chef at one of my restaurants. He ran such a tight ship that his garbage cans were probably more sanitary than some of the city's top restaurants.

"So you're a suit," she teased. "I gotta say, I'm a little surprised, Luke."

"What do you do? What brought you out here?"

She trailed the tip of her finger around the rim of the glass bottle, and for once, seemed a little nervous. "I'm representing the...*company* I work for at an event tomorrow and Friday."

"And then?"

She smiled. "And then I'm going to LAX and catching a flight back to North Carolina."

"Reaaalllllyyy," I drew out. "What if I said I'd be out your way for business soon. Any chance I'd get to see you again?"

Maddie shook her head and it gutted me. "Probably not. I live in a little town on the coast. When I get back it'll be Memorial Day weekend and that kicks off my busy season. Lots of tourists and all that."

I shrugged like it wasn't a big deal and I understood. But truthfully, I wasn't going to give in that easily.

Someone had turned up the salsa music and people began to pair off. I reached across the picnic table and offered my hand, "Dance with me?"

Maddie knocked back the rest of her beer and slid her palm into mine as I led her out onto the asphalt. She rested one delicate hand on my shoulder and I put mine on her waist, leading her as we matched our steps to the swift rhythm of the bongos.

With her pelvis glued to mine, she rolled her hips like she'd been dancing all her life. With one hand, I spun her away from me before dropping her down into a low dip. She had an unparalleled smile when I brought her back to her feet and kept us moving to the beat.

I leaned down and captured her lips with mine. My hands skated up and down her sides. When she breathed a quiet moan, I slid my tongue up against hers. We stopped dancing and I sensed her grip tighten on my bicep. I thrust my hands into her thick waves of hair, wrapping the silver and gold threads around my fingers, as kissed her like I was starving.

I held on to her hips as I walked backward, guiding her to the picnic table, and pulled her onto my lap as I sat down. She straddled my hips and settled the thin strip of denim between her legs up against my cock.

"You're a fucking dream, Maddie," I growled softly as I

tucked my head beneath her chin and kissed the dip of her collarbone. I felt the vibration of her laugh against her skin, and it sent sparks skittering between us.

The market lights overhead began to dim and I knew that the clock was about to strike midnight.

I wasn't ready for my Cinderella to turn into a pumpkin.

"I have an early morning," she said as she rested her forehead on mine. "And you have to work the rest of the time that I'm here." She rested her forearms on my shoulders and ran her fingers over the buzzed hair at the back of my neck. "But you have my number."

"I'll call you," I said as I pecked her lips one more time and slid her off my lap. I adjusted myself without shame and cleared our empty plates off the table.

I looked back at Maddie and saw her pull up a rideshare app on her phone. I took the phone out of her hands and slid it into the back pocket of her shorts, stealing one more squeeze of her ass. "And I'll walk you home."

"I'm not letting you in my room, Luke," she said as a coy smile pulled at the corner of her mouth. She leaned in a little closer and teased, "No matter how much I want to."

I leaned down and brushed my lips against the curve of her ear. My beard tickled her cheek and it made her giggle. "I will walk you home and kiss you goodnight."

And I did just that. We made our way back to her hotel, took the elevator up, and stalled just outside the door to her room.

"I had a great time with you, Mad."

"I did too." Her cheeks were rosy and she looked down at her painted toes that were the same light blue as the sky. "Do you wanna..."

I was a little disappointed when she didn't offer to let me

in, but the alternative was the most fun I'd had with a woman in a long time.

An hour passed as we sat on the floor outside her hotel room door and played twenty questions. Another hour went by and she fell asleep, curled up in my arms, resting against my chest.

I knew her favorite color was black. I knew that her eyes were gray like her mom's—and that gray eyes were a rare genetic trait. I knew that she liked to bake and that she enjoyed falling asleep to serial killer documentaries. She told me that she was an only child and her dad left when she was young.

I told her about my two older sisters and their obnoxiously large broods of very loud children. I told her how my parents had been married for nearly sixty years and that it both intimidated and inspired me. I told her about my Nonna, who I loved more than anything. And when we ran out of words to say, we just sat there.

*And it was perfect.*

She'd mentioned that she had an early morning, so somewhere around three in the morning, I broke down and found her room key in her bag. I scooped her up into my arms, and carried her inside.

She barely stirred, and I doubted that she would even remember me bringing her in. I found a pad of paper on the bedside table and scribbled down a note, plugged her phone into the charger, and kissed her on the forehead before letting myself out.

## 5

# MADELINE

Even though I had participated in culinary competitions before, *Pastry Throwdown* was the first televised baking challenge that I had ever competed in.

Still, I wasn't a stranger to working under pressure. I lived for it.

I loved the rush of a slammed dinner service at Revanche. I loved the pressure of the wedding season when we cranked out massive tiered cakes that would be served to thousands over the course of a single weekend. Time management was my superpower.

It didn't matter that I was running on very little sleep and had a slight hangover. I'd grab a catnap on the sofa in the dressing room between rounds while the judges did their thing.

Round one was a piece of cake. *Literally.*

The challenge was to create a plated dessert that incorporated savory spices from a table full of secret ingredients. The saffron and chili powder spoke to me. Maybe it was the memory of gorging myself on incredible food with Luke last night, but those were the first two things I snatched off the table.

I took another look at the clock and went back to the dishes that I was wiping with a dry towel before I plated my spread. I lined up my flawlessly clean plates and swapped out my dirty gloves for a new pair.

The pistachio sponge was the first thing to go down on the white porcelain. I had cut the light green cake into a delicate rectangle before topping it with a ribbon of saffron-honey mousse.

The dark chocolate petals that I jazzed up with cayenne and chili powder swooped over the cake like a wing. I picked up the feather-light strands of cotton candy that I'd made from chili-infused caramel and placed them around the cake like a nest.

When the judges tasted the heat and the sweet, they wouldn't know what hit them.

As the clock counted down the last ten seconds of the first round of competition, the judges filed in and took their seats at the table across from the kitchen.

I gave each plate a discerning assessment before tossing my gloves in the trash and stepping away from my work table at the exact moment the final buzzer blared. Production assistants dove in like madmen to tidy up each one of our kitchens so they were neat and clean for the next round.

I felt the crinkle of a slip of paper in my pocket and smiled.

*Maddie,*
*I hope I get to see you again.*
*That was the best night I've had in a long time.*
*I'll call you soon. Sleep well, Beautiful.*
*-L*

I had read it at least forty times before finally rolling out of bed, savoring the memory of dancing with Luke under the string lights.

*Kissing Luke while his hands were tangled in my hair. Talking with Luke until the night turned into morning. The vague memory of being carried into my hotel room and tucked into bed.*

Assistants grabbed two of the plates that I had prepared and took them for close up shots before delivering them to the judging panel. I grabbed the third plate and joined the other three contestants in the line-up.

My eyes scanned across the room from the host to the judges.

*And then I saw him.*

Every girl dreams about meeting her celebrity crush— running into them on the street and snapping a selfie. Maybe even being saved like a gorgeous damsel and having said celebrity crush sweep her off of her feet.

Me personally? Let's just say that me and the Hemsworth boys have had our fair share of imaginary meet-cutes.

The thing is, every girl dreams about what they would do if they got to meet their celebrity crush, but no one dreams about what they'd do if they met their celebrity nemesis.

And let me tell you—I have a celebrity nemesis.

*Luca DeRossi.* Celebrity chef, restaurateur, and grade-A asshole.

And he was sitting in front of me wearing a scowl that could be seen from space.

*And ten hours earlier I had been sitting on his lap, clinging to him like a koala while his tongue was down my throat.*

The tic in his jaw was flexing like one of those blow up

creatures that undulate outside of used car dealerships. If he was thinking anything other than hatred, he did a damn good job of not showing it.

Our eyes met for the briefest of seconds and his lips pursed into a thin line.

Okay, to be fair, he didn't *look* like Luca DeRossi when I met him yesterday, and he very clearly introduced himself as *Luke*.

The dark hair that he covered with a snapback last night was now impeccably styled—gelled and moussed to perfection. He had traded his casual ripped jeans and t-shirt for his signature tailored Italian suit that probably cost more than my house. Gone was the beard and covered were the tattoos.

The Rolex on his wrist hid the first pieces of the sleeve of tattoos that I now knew was there.

Why didn't he show off his tattoos more? They were hot.

*Dammit, Maddie—get your shit together. You do not like this man.*

I'd go on an axe throwing date with Jack the Ripper before I'd ever let myself be alone with Luca again.

He had shaved his beard, leaving only a thin shadow in its place. I could see the sharp edges of his jaw and the cheekbones that made models everywhere weep with jealousy.

Worst of all, that smile that turned my insides to a puddle of goo was nowhere to be found. In its place was a scowl that had the room on pins and needles.

From the end of the line, Charissa cut her eyes over at me. For the first time, I realized that Luca's vicious gaze was still locked on me.

Sensing the awkwardness, the host cleared his throat to begin his recap of the challenge and introduce the judges.

I stood in line with a death grip on my plate. Luca sat stoically with his hands clasped on the table. His momentary surprise and vile reaction to my presence was quickly replaced with a snooty air of indifference.

One by one, each competitor presented their plates to the judges. Sweet Betty Crocker—Patty—went first, followed by Jeff the loudmouth, then Charissa.

When the host called me forward, I walked to the judging table, set my plate in the middle, and stepped back to the patch of tape that marked where I was supposed to stand for the critique.

"My name is Chef Madeline Dorsey. I'm the executive pastry chef at Revanche in Beaufort, North Carolina."

Something akin to shock or horror flashed in Luca's eyes, but no one noticed.

To everyone else, He was *the* Luca DeRossi—judgmental asswipe and belligerently critical dickhead.

To me, he was Jekyll and Hyde.

I had seen the good person underneath, but it was all an act. He fucking played me, and for what? Just to see the embarrassment on my face the next day when he inevitably ripped me a new one? *Not today, Satan.* Two could play that game.

Jenna Lachlan, the editor in chief of *Patisserie Magazine*, smiled and motioned to the plate. "This looks divine. Tell us about what you've created, Madeline."

I took a shallow breath and steeled my nerves. "For round one I was inspired by the bold flavors of the chilis and the luxurious saffron on the secret ingredient table. On your plate you have a pistachio génoise with honey-saffron mousse, a spiced dark chocolate wing, and chili-caramel fairy floss." I plastered on a polite smile. "Enjoy."

Jenna dug right in while food blogger, Winston Nacey,

picked up his plate and examined the aesthetic design of the dish.

I forced myself to look at Luca. I wasn't going to be scared off by a grumpy asshole the size of Alaska. He had his fork in his hand and was poking at the dessert like the mere presence of it in front of him was a disappointment.

After what seemed like an eternity, he cut the tiniest slice of cake and mousse, broke off a shard of the chili chocolate, and sprinkled on a few strands of the spicy caramel cotton candy. He gave the bite one more look before deeming it worthy of going in his mouth.

Jenna and Winston were making indecent moaning noises as they scraped their plates clean. Luca chewed his one bite slowly, his jaw flexing with each motion. His Adam's apple bobbed as he swallowed it down and chased it with a sip of water. He pushed his plate away ever so slightly to signal that he would *not* be going back for seconds.

"Wow, Madeline—just wow." Jenna beamed. "Do you have another plate hiding back there because I'd eat this for breakfast, lunch, and dinner! The sponge was the *perfect* texture to contrast against the creaminess of the mousse. The saffron balanced the sweetness of the honey, and the dark chocolate with the chili and cayenne was the perfect mix of sweet and spicy."

Winston leaned over the table and looked down at Jenna, "You didn't even mention the best part–that cotton candy! What a concept! How did you do it?"

I let out a nervous breath and smiled for the cameras. "I made the chili infused caramel, cooled it on a silicone sheet, and then ground the hardened caramel into a fine powder in a food processor before spinning it in the centrifuge to get the caramel grains to form cotton candy strands."

"Ingenious and impressive that you were able to put

together such a well formed dessert in just forty-five minutes. Phenomenal job, Madeline," Winston said as he popped his fork in his mouth one more time to savor the last traces of the dish.

All eyes turned to Luca, who was seated in the middle of the panel. He took one last look at the plate in front of him before turning his full focus to me. He cleared his throat, and I felt my pulse beginning to race.

I looked down to make sure my knees weren't locked. The last thing I wanted to do was pass out in front of his nemesis-ness. I shifted my weight from foot to foot just in case.

"*Madeline,*" he began, saying my name as if the concept of it was totally foreign to him. "Tell me, what inspired you to use the chilis?"

I knew what he was doing. He was trying to get in my head and make me lose focus, all while pretending he didn't have a care in the world.

*Well, guess what. I wasn't falling for it.*

"The chilis are a versatile ingredient. They pair well with a lot of different sweet components. If part of my dish didn't work in production, I wanted to make sure I had chosen secret ingredients that would allow me to quickly reorient the direction of my dish to keep from losing any more time."

"So what I'm hearing is that you couldn't make up your mind and went with the easiest ingredient to work with," he clipped.

I cracked a smile. "Work smarter, not harder. With the clock ticking, I didn't want to back myself into a corner."

There was a twitch at the corner of his mouth and, for a fleeting second, I thought that maybe he would smile.

That hope was crushed because he stifled any show of emotion—positive or otherwise.

Luca sat back in his seat and bore into me with his gaze. "It was nice, Madeline," he said in the most patronizingly placid tone possible.

*Yep. I was going home in round one because I just so happened to make out with the cranky judge.*

———

CHARISSA WENT HOME after the first round. To say I was shocked was an understatement.

Sweet Betty Crocker and Jeff with the big mouth survived to battle it out in round two.

Patty was a surprisingly fierce competitor. She had the charm of a grandma mixed with the venom of a copperhead. Out of the three of us, she was the one cussing up a storm.

Round two was much of the same. Jenna Lachlan and Winston Nacey sang my praises and Luca looked at me like I was a piece of gum stuck to the bottom of his very fancy shoes.

At least Jeff got eliminated after his macarons cracked in the oven.

*What that moron was thinking, trying to make macarons in thirty minutes, was beyond me.*

I barely beat the clock in round two, but my hazelnut gelato with a crispy tuile cookie and warm pear compote won the judges over.

*Well, at least the two that weren't the devil in the flesh.*

"Man, that Chef DeRossi sure has it out for you, cupcake," Patty said as we walked back to the dressing room for a short break before the last round.

I ripped the ponytail out of my hair and scratched the sore spots on my head, then unfastened the first two buttons on my chef whites to give me a little more breathing room. Two rounds of competition, both thirty minutes each, was actually *hours* of filming.

The constant resetting of the kitchens, having us say the same damn thing over and over, listening to the host practice his stupid zingers—it was enough to drive a sane woman mad.

"Don't I know it," I groaned as I sunk down into the couch and put my feet up on the coffee table. "He's an asshole."

Patty snorted, "A good looking asshole if there ever was one."

That made me giggle a little, "I guess you're right."

"What fresh hell do you think they're gonna spring on us for the last round?" she asked as she grabbed a bottle of water out of the mini fridge and guzzled it down. "Bake a cake in a coffee pot? Cut all the cords to the stand mixers and force us to make buttercream with a hand whisk?"

"Diabolical is what it is," I said as I wagged a finger her way. "I'm starting to wonder if the prize money is worth it. I'm just gonna have to use it for a double knee replacement when this is all over."

The top of my bag was open and my phone was laying on top. I had used our lunch break to take a cat nap after I inhaled a turkey sandwich, so I hadn't had time to look at it since I left the hotel this morning.

I picked it up and tapped the screen. The poker club group chat was full of well wishes and good luck texts, but a stray message that had been sent just over two hours ago caught my attention.

HOT GUY FROM THE GYM IN LA

We need to talk.

The way the words jumped off the screen had me reading it in his disgusted tone of voice.

I knew I shouldn't respond. If anyone found out that Luca and I had been—shall we say—*previously acquainted*, I would have been thrown out of the competition. And whether I liked it or not, I needed that prize money.

Still, my pride beat out any common sense I had left and, before I knew it, my fingers were flying over the screen.

MADDIE

Kiss my ass.

HOT GUY FROM THE GYM IN LA

Real mature. This isn't over, Madeline.

MADDIE

Ooooh, you think using my full name scares me? Guess what, Luca DeRossi. It doesn't. You think you're going to one-up me by screwing me over with the judges? Guess again.

Luca didn't text back right away. Either the judges had been summoned from their break or he was ignoring me. We only had a few minutes before Patty and I went head to head in the final round. So I did the only thing I could do.

**@XOMaddieLeeDee - 05/28 - 3:55 PM**

*@ChefLucaDeRossi wouldn't know a good dessert if it hit him in the face.*

# 6

## LUCA

*So, this was the Maddie who was the perpetual thorn in my virtual side.*

I sat in the green room and strangled my phone so hard that I thought it would crack. I swear the girl devoted her online existence to bashing me. It wouldn't surprise me if my picture was somewhere in her house with devil horns and scratched-out eyes.

I knew what my role was. *Always the grumpy asshole judge.*

Jenna was the nice one, Winston was the loose cannon of positivity, and me? I believe the exact description the executive producer gave when he pitched the gig to me was, "I need you to act like the lovechild of Simon Cowell and Gordon Ramsay. There's a bonus in it for you if you make one of them cry."

I wasn't going to make anyone cry—I wasn't a sadist. I would be fair and firm. No bullshit.

But that was before I saw Maddie standing in line, holding a flawlessly plated confection.

After that, all I could think about was licking that saffron-honey mousse off of her naked body.

Like I said, I knew what my role was. But my dick? He didn't get the message. And neither of us knew what we were going to do about Little Miss Mermaid.

After tucking her into bed the night before, I'd gone back to my LA condo and jerked off in the shower to the thought of her mouth wrapped around my cock.

Watching her work in the studio kitchen during the first half of the competition had been a test in self-restraint. Her desserts could make a monk orgasm and test his resolve with a single bite, and I had to sit there and be the cold picture of indifference.

One of the assistants stuck her head in the room and summoned us back to the judging table for the last round. I fired off one final text to Maddie and shoved my phone back in the pocket of my suit jacket.

LUCA

Good luck, Madeline.

———

THE FINAL ROUND of the competition was brutal.

I didn't envy Maddie or Patty in the slightest. They had four hours to create a tiered cake that represented the theme of opposites.

I'd judged enough of these TV specials to know that vague challenges were the worst. It gave the competitor too much room to play with the concept. Usually, they dabbled too much in the planning stage, trying to narrow down an idea rather than jumping in with both feet.

*But not Maddie.*

She was a beast in the kitchen. While Patty was fumbling her way through sketching a design, Maddie had already scooped her cake batter out of the industrial-size mixer and was double-checking the temperature on the convection ovens. *Smart girl.*

The last round was long, so the other judges and I got up and meandered around the set to observe the competitors. Maddie and I were going to have it out eventually, but I tried not to spook her in the middle of the competition.

*Much.*

I rose from my seat and smoothed out the suit that Astrid had delivered to my condo this morning. She didn't bother asking why it looked like I hadn't slept all night. She knew better than that.

I stopped at Patty's station first and asked some open ended questions to feign interest as I poked around her table. I was talking to her, but my eyes were on Maddie.

Winston Nacey was pestering her with stupid comments, and she looked like she was three seconds from throwing him in the blast freezer and jamming the door shut.

I didn't blame her. I hated food critics with a fiery passion. They were the culinary version of WebMD. They thought they knew everything, but they were all frauds wrapped in a user-friendly package.

Commentators shouldn't get credit for what competitors do.

I gave Patty a curt, "Best of luck," and made my way over to Maddie's station.

"Chef Dorsey," I said as I craned across her work table to see what she was up to.

"Chef DeRossi," Maddie said with practiced neutrality before pursing her lips into a thin line. She bit back whatever resentment she felt and busied herself by whipping up a blackberry gelée.

I crossed my arms and stood tall. "Tell me, Chef, how are you incorporating the concept of opposites into your final creation?"

"I decided to go with the two greatest opposites there are," she said as she ripped off a sheet of plastic wrap, let it kiss the surface of the gelée, and set the bowl to chill in an ice bath.

"And what are those?"

She paused a beat and a devilish smile quirked at the corner of her pretty mouth. "Heaven and hell."

"Ah, the great divide," I said with a grin. I knew what the long-legged devil was up to.

She looked ready to career over the table and throttle me, but I cut my eyes toward the boom mic that hovered over us. Either she decided I wasn't worth it, or took the hint and kept her mouth shut.

I lingered by her table. A minute passed, and then another. Truthfully, I had nothing else to say to her. I just liked watching her work.

She was lightning fast on her feet; smooth and efficient in her motions, and her brain was three steps ahead of where her hands were. Seeing her in action left no question in my mind as to why Madeline Dorsey was one of the most sought-after pastry chefs in the country.

It was peculiar that she was content working in a sleepy fishing town on the Carolina coast when she should have been working in a Michelin star restaurant. Preferably one of mine.

"Anything else I can do for you, Chef DeRossi?" she asked dismissively, her voice tinged with irritation.

*Kiss me. Make love to me. Let me shove all those bowls and spatulas off the island and lay you out, strip you bare, and kiss every inch of you.*

I cleared my throat and stepped back to put a few necessary feet of space between us. "That'll be all. Best of luck, Chef."

————

MADDIE WON. Because of course she did.

Conflict of interest aside, it wasn't even a fair fight. She kicked Patty's granny ass and she kicked it *hard.*

Her "Heaven and Hell" cake was genius. Layers of dark chocolate devil's food contrasted the light angel food cake. Her blackberry gelée and white chocolate ganache gave the cake the most immaculate tang and creamy sweetness.

As I sampled the filling of her tiered masterpiece, I realized that I was tasting *her.*

When I kissed her underneath the street lamp, I thought she tasted like sugar and vanilla. Now, I realized, she tasted better than that. Maddie was complex and smooth and sweet and delicious.

I wanted to devour her.

When the confetti fell and Maddie was handed that oversized check, I stifled my grin, but still applauded her. Her brilliance in the kitchen aside, she was just one surprise after the other.

So she thought I was the devil. Honestly? I'd been called worse.

I could live with that—maybe even change her mind.

When I shook her hand after she'd been crowned the winner, I was surprised when she smiled politely and muttered a terse *thank you* before turning her attention to the rest of the judges.

I guess that was preferable to her smacking me clean across the face. Maybe I probably should have been a little more forthcoming about who I was.

Then again, she had a few things to 'fess up to as well.

I packed my things and high-tailed it back to my condo to change. I could have called Astrid and had her bring me a change of clothes, but I didn't want her knowing about Maddie unless absolutely necessary. Astrid was a great assistant and a kick-ass agent, but she never took well to my lady friends. Especially the ones she didn't vet herself.

I leaned against the hallway outside of Maddie's hotel room and closed my eyes as the exhaustion of the day weighed on me.

Being a judge was definitely better than competing, but the days were still long. I knew she had to be feeling the exhaustion of an eighteen hour competition.

It never failed to amaze me how long it took to film something that would be condensed into a neatly packaged hour special.

I knocked quietly on the door. Either she was asleep or she was ignoring me.

I checked my phone again and let out a groan.

*No new messages.*

She never texted me back after the day wrapped.

I knew she had another day of work ahead of her. Tomorrow all the contestants had to watch the footage back and give little interviews that they'd sprinkle into the episode.

I knocked against the door again, then opened my mouth and almost called her name.

But I stopped myself. I didn't want to risk anyone hearing me and poking their nosey heads out and recognizing me.

I didn't know if the other contestants were staying in the same hotel, but getting made wasn't something I was willing to risk. I pulled my ball cap lower over my eyes and slumped against the door before plopping pathetically on the floor.

I must have dozed off, because the next thing I heard was her raucous laughter as she said goodnight to someone. *Did she go out on a date? Was he walking her to the door?* I scrambled to my feet and crossed my arms as her voice carried down the hall.

I scrubbed the twelve hour scruff that covered my jaw. I had the beard growing ability of Sasquatch.

I kept my facial hair in check, but when I'd met Maddie at the gym, I had been coming off a three day stretch without any public appearance commitments and let it get a little unruly.

If I had been clean shaven, we never would have been in this predicament.

I couldn't fault her for not recognizing me. If she had known, she probably would have told me to fuck off the minute she spotted me.

Maddie rounded the corner, tossing her long waves over her shoulder.

During filming, she had taken her hair down before she and Patty came back onto the set for the results of the final round.

As the annoying-ass host droned on and on, all I could think about was running my hands through it instead of maintaining my composure and cranky screen personality.

"Night, Patty. Thanks for the drinks. See you in the morning," Maddie said as the elevator doors closed. She fished through her bag for her room key and pulled it out with a victorious, "Aha!"

Her smile immediately fell when she saw me waiting.

Instead of turning or keeping her distance she picked up her pace and pushed me out of the way when she got to the door.

Maddie jammed her keycard in the slot and yanked the door handle until it gave way. The door flew open and she darted inside, shoving it back in my face.

"We need to talk, Madeline," I growled as I stuck my foot in the room to keep her from locking me out.

"Nope."

"Will you just let me in? We have to talk about this."

She dropped her shoulder and rammed into the door.

I hissed and jerked my foot out of the way, "Dammit, Maddie—you're gonna break my fucking foot! Just let me in."

"Get lost, *Luke,*" she spat, throwing the name I had used when I introduced myself at the gym back in my face.

"Hey, you're not off the hook here either. You didn't tell me who you were or why you were here."

"I didn't lie," she countered. "I said I was here for work. I just didn't tell you what that work was."

"When we came back here after dinner you said you liked to bake!" I shouted as I stopped dicking around and pushed my way inside, slamming the door behind me so we could have it out face to face.

Maddie threw her hands in the air, "Not a lie! I like to bake!"

"That's like Lebron James saying he likes to play basketball or Simone Biles saying she's *kind of* into gymnastics!"

Maddie tossed her bag onto the bed and turned back to me. "You said you were in acquisitions and oversaw business consolidation, so excuse me for not giving a shit about semantics."

I lifted my ball cap and ran my hand back through my

hair. "It wasn't a lie—I have a restaurant group and that's mostly what I do now."

She took two long strides and, before I could blink, Maddie was nose to nose with me. "You didn't tell me you were *Luca DeRossi*." The vile way she hissed my name was laced with poison.

"I just have one question for you, Madeline," I sneered as I crossed my arms over my chest. "Do you hate me because I'm rich and successful or because I'm a better chef than you?"

Hate flashed in her eyes and the freckles on her cheeks tensed as she wrinkled her nose. "Fuck you, DeRossi."

I looked down and saw the dip in the neckline of her tank top. Just like the one she had on last night for our date, the lettering across her chest made me laugh. *Way Too Pretty For Prison.*

Accurate.

Her full breasts strained against the lacy bra that peeked through her tank top.

"You didn't think that when you thought I was just Luke," I countered as my voice dropped into a low, seductive tease and I grabbed a fistful of her tank.

"You tried to sabotage me all fucking day," she said as she stabbed my chest with her finger.

I raised my hands in defeat and took a step back. "Maddie, listen to me. You won. Fair and square. I didn't take it easy on you, and I didn't try to screw you over."

"You were ten times more harsh with me than any other contestant and you know it. You were *trying* to make me lose."

I scoffed, "So, what? The great Madeline Dorsey can't take a little heat? I wasn't trying to make you lose. I wanted to see what you could do under pressure."

She walked past me and opened the door. "You need to leave."

"Mad—"

"Lose my number, Luca."

I turned to face her. "I meant what I said—I had a great night last night. But here's the thing I can't figure out. Why didn't you tell me who you were?"

She locked her jaw, nostrils flaring with seething rage. Her voice trembled with adrenaline and anger as she said, "Get out," through gritted teeth.

I edged closer and pushed the door shut. "Why didn't you tell me who you were? Why didn't you tell me what you were doing here?"

Maddie's hand shook like a leaf against the door handle, "What, so you could get me thrown out of the competition after we made out last night?"

"Is that what this is about? That stupid contest?" As soon as the words were out of my mouth I regretted it.

Maddie looked like I had punched her in the face. And honestly, I kind of felt like I had.

She was still riding high off her win and I came in and pissed all over it.

"Maddie—" I began, my voice dropping into a gentle tone.

She wouldn't even look at me. Her eyes were trained on the floor. "Please leave."

"Maddie, I didn't mean it like that."

"I said please."

"Mad—"

"Do you always make it a habit to be a jackass?" She'd choked down the hurt and replaced it with unfettered hatred.

"Why didn't you tell me who you were?" I pressed again.

"Why would it have mattered?"

I laughed at the ceiling and shook my head. "I know who you are."

"I'm nobody."

"You're not nobody, Madeline," I said as I trailed my fingertips down her bare arm. "I know exactly who you are."

She crossed her arms and held the door open with her foot. "You don't know me at all."

"Maybe not as well as I want to, but I *do* want to know you, Maddie."

Maddie shook her head. "There's no reason for you to be here. Go."

"Mad—"

"Go, Luca." Her lips pursed as the corner of her mouth began to quiver. "Whatever this was? It never happened."

I straightened out my ball cap to shadow my eyes and shoved my hands in my pockets. I walked out and lingered in the hallway, waiting for her to slam the door in my face. "This isn't over, Maddie. Not by a long shot."

"Goodbye, Luke."

It was the most cutting possible thing she could have said. She wasn't saying goodbye to me. She was saying goodbye to who she thought I was.

My phone dinged with a notification as the valet pulled my car around. I tapped on the screen to see what it was about.

@XOMaddieLeeDee - 05/29 - 2:02 AM
   *When someone is two faced, just know that you can't trust either of them.*

Okay, so maybe I had created a fake account so that I could follow Maddie without her knowing.

I didn't want to reveal that I had put two and two together and knew she hated my guts. Why she hated me—I had no idea. It definitely went further than a little harsh critique from across the judging table. That was for damn sure.

One thing was certain. I'd be seeing Madeline Dorsey again, whether she liked it or not.

# 7

# MADELINE

I had never been so thankful to be back in North Carolina.

Back to the grind. Back to being myself. I craved my routine.

Whatever had come over me in California was a thing of the past.

At least for a short time, I was $50,000 richer and was home just in time for Memorial Day.

I rolled my windows down and let the smell of the salty air fill my senses as I crossed the bridge from Morehead City to Radio Island.

There was nothing quite like living on the coast. Traffic came to a crawl as soon as I got into Morehead. I cranked up the radio and sat back in the seat of my Jeep, thankful that I had put the top down for the three hour drive from the airport to Beaufort.

My phone lit up, and I grabbed it out of the cupholder.

Ignoring a text from he-who-must-not-be-named, I swiped across the screen and pressed it to my ear. "Hey,

Chase. I just got back to town. I'm coming through Morehead now."

There was an unusual pause before Chase spoke up,
"Have you passed the hospital yet?"

My brows furrowed. "No, not yet. Why? Mel need lunch
or something?"

"Not Melissa." Chase sighed. "Steve's there with Heather
again. It's, uh, it's not looking good, Mad." He cleared his
throat and switched from sounding like a concerned friend
to a police officer. "She doesn't have much time. You should
probably head over there and say goodbye."

Car horns blared as I whipped around a median and
took a shortcut to Carteret Presbyterian Hospital.

"Did you just run a red light?" Chase chirped in my ear.

"It was yellow."

"Don't be getting yourself killed on the way over there.
Stop speeding."

"I'm not speeding."

"Liar. Stop speeding."

"I was not speeding," I said as I eased off the accelerator.
"I was driving with purpose."

I heard Chase groan on the line. "You just admitted to
speeding. Please don't ever get arrested. You'll incriminate
yourself in three seconds flat."

"Good thing I've got an in with two cops in the department," I sang. I pulled into the emergency entrance of the
hospital and threw the gearshift into park. "I'm here. You
heading over?"

"I'm covering for Steve down at the precinct, but I'll be
down as soon as I get off."

My sandals hit the pavement and I slammed the door
shut. "Thanks for giving me a call."

"Anytime, Mads. I gotta go. Give Heather a hug for me."

"I will." I hung up, my finger lingering for just a second over the unread text message that was taunting me.

I could open it.

I could read it.

He'd never know.

I could read it and then delete it, and it would be like it never happened.

I chickened out and shoved my phone in my pocket as I stormed through the doors of the emergency department. I waited, resting my palms on the front desk until a nurse caught a glimpse of me.

"I need to see Melissa Jacobsen. Can you let her know that Maddie Dorsey is here?"

The lady gave me a critical look before rolling her eyes and disappearing through a door. I paced in front of the double doors before Melissa finally came into the waiting room and gave me a tired smile.

"Hey."

Skipping the pleasantries, I asked, "Be straight with me. How bad is it?"

Mel cut her eyes to the other people waiting in the lobby. She lowered her voice and said, "You know I can't give you that information."

"Melissa Renee Jacobsen, I just flew clear across the country, I'm exhausted, and I need to know."

She fingered her ID badge and looked at the ground. "She caught some kind of infection. The chemo isn't doing her much good this time around. It's just making her immune system turn to crap." She paused while a group of EMTs passed by before adding on, "It'll be a miracle if she makes it through the night."

*Fuck.* I swallowed the lump in my throat. "Is—is she conscious?"

"She was the last time I went up there. Steve hasn't left her side. Everyone else has stopped by. Chase is gonna try and come by again when he gets off duty." Mel cocked her head toward the elevators. "East wing. Room 312."

I gave her arm a squeeze. "Thanks Mel."

"Hey," Melissa called as I stabbed the arrow button to the elevator. "You never told me if you won."

I pasted on a grin and tossed my hair over my shoulder. "You know I had to sign an NDA. I can't tell you until it airs."

Melissa rolled her eyes. "What are we gonna be drinking in a month when it airs?"

"Tell Bridget to have a bottle of Macallan Twelve on hand."

Her eyes widened. "You're serious?"

I grinned like the Cheshire cat as she bolted over and threw her arms around me.

"Oh, I knew you could do it! How do you feel, big shot?"

I sighed. Honestly, it felt like I could breathe a little easier. The championship title was cool, but the prize money was going to go a long way. "Pretty damn good."

Melissa glanced at her watch. "I gotta go. Tell Steve I'll be up to see them when I get a break."

————

"SOMEONE TOLD me there was a party in here," I joked as I tiptoed into Heather's hospital room.

Steve looked up from his seat beside the bed and offered a weak smile, "Hey, Mad."

"You look like hell."

He turned his eyes back to Heather. She laid completely still, swallowed by the hospital gown that was four sizes too big for her emaciated frame. Her chest barely rose, but the lines on the monitor off to the side seemed unconcerned.

"I'm in it," he admitted quietly. His rumpled polo looked like he had slept in it. His brown hair was mussed—probably from constantly dragging his fingers through it. He looked much older than his thirty years.

I blinked back the tears that welled up in my eyes and slapped on a smile as I walked in.

After all, I was the life of the party. I wasn't the crying shoulder. I was the one who could turn anything into a good time.

I was YOLOs and peace signs and daredevil antics.

I sat in the empty chair beside Steve and placed my hand on Heather's blanket-covered knee.

"She can hear you," Steve mumbled.

I nodded and let out a tremored breath. "Hey, Heather. It's Maddie. I, uh, I just got back from California. Thanks..." I swallowed the lump in my throat. "Thanks for texting me before the competition." A tear slid down my cheek and I quickly wiped it away before laughing it off. "I won."

Heather's lips curled up around the oxygen tube that was threaded into her mouth. Steve nearly jumped when her hand listlessly squeezed his. He grabbed a small white board from the rolling table and uncapped a dry erase marker. He wedged the marker into Heather's fingers and laid the white board on her stomach.

Her movements were pained. Heather's grip on the marker made it seem like it weighed a thousand pounds. Finally, her hand stilled and she closed her eyes again. Steve took the marker back and handed me the white board.

I cocked my head and studied the picture. "Heather, you know I'm shit at Pictionary." I laughed reluctantly. It looked kind of like a rocket. A rocket with two—"Oh my God. You drew a dick!" I couldn't help but keel over with laughter.

Steve cracked a smile and shook his head. "A dick and a question mark?"

Heather gave us a thumbs up.

"The guy Mad met in California?" Steve guessed.

She grimaced as she nodded carefully.

I sighed and ran a hand back through my hair before faking a smile. "Heather, you're not going to believe this. Settle in, sweet cheeks. Because I've got a story for you."

———

I TOLD Heather and Steve everything from meeting Luca in the gym, to him ripping into me during the competition, to having it out with him in my hotel room.

By the time I was done, Heather was barely responsive and Steve was looking more and more hollow.

I went down to the cafeteria and brought him back a depressing looking chicken salad sandwich and a Coke.

I said my goodbyes and hurried out to my Jeep, avoiding the ER and Melissa entirely.

When I sunk into the driver's seat I allowed myself to cry for a solid two minutes before grabbing a wad of fast food napkins from the glove box and drying my eyes.

I wasn't expected back at the restaurant until Tuesday, but I didn't exactly want to be home either.

Steve and Heather would be at the hospital for God knows how long, Chase was on duty, Melissa was at work, and Hannah Jane's Sundays were always booked with events.

The holiday weekend meant that Kristin was slammed

turning over rooms at the inn and Bridget would be working double shifts at the bar.

I guided my Jeep into the back parking lot at Revanche and ripped the keys out.

I was angry, and dammit—I was going to take it out on some dough.

The upside was that I'd get a head start on my Tuesday production schedule.

I held the elastic tie between my teeth as I spun my hair into a blob on top of my head and secured it.

I unlocked the back door and dropped my bag into my locker, trading it for the soft headwrap I preferred rather than my chef's hat. I kicked off my sandals and grabbed the spare pair of socks I kept for this exact occasion. I slipped my feet into my orthopedic clogs and grabbed an apron off the hook before stomping down the stairs to my dungeon of sugar and carbs.

The pastry kitchen at Revanche was in the basement of the three story restaurant. The rooftop dining space was opulent and luxurious with an outdoor fireplace, string lights, and an unmatched view that looked out over the water. I loved the view of the wildlife reserve where wild horses roamed.

The second floor was ground level and housed the main dining area, our private event rooms, and the main kitchen.

I was perfectly happy being sequestered in my cave of solitude.

I passed a few of my interns and pastry cooks on my way down. They were used to me popping in at all hours of the day and night, even when I was supposed to be off.

It was the beginning of dinner service, so final preparations were in full swing to send plate after plate of carefully curated desserts up to happy guests.

I opened the door to the walk-in freezer and propped it open with a doorstop. It always took the newbies a little getting used to, but I'd been around the walk-ins for over a decade now. Stepping into a freezer that was ten below didn't phase me.

I checked the stash of shaped croissants and danishes to see what we were low on before sealing the door shut, heading to the walk-in fridge, grabbing a block of dough that had been resting in the chilly air, and piling a few pounds of butter on top. I loaded up my arms and went to work.

I caressed the yeast dough into a rectangle before smearing on the butter, folding it over three times, and then beating the shit out of it with a rolling pin to thin it out.

"Heard you were down here," Scott hollered over the racket I was making.

Croissants were hard work, but they were cathartic. Turning a fifty pound block of dough into light, flakey, perfectly laminated pastries was a noble task.

The fact that I could take out my anger, rage, and sadness by wielding a rolling pin made it bearable. Everyone knew that if *I* was the one who was making the croissants, that I was not to be fucked with.

"Didn't have anything to do," I grunted as I hefted the sheet of dough over on itself before adding another layer of butter and stretching it out again. A few more turns and then it would go back into the fridge before being sent through the sheeter. I wiped my hands on my apron and turned to face him. "Shouldn't you be upstairs?"

Scott Christensen was the executive chef at Revanche. He had twenty years of experience to my ten, but still treated me as an equal.

"Just came to see how California went. If you're down

here beating the sweet dough like it pissed in your cereal, I'll take that as a sign that it didn't go that well."

I shook my head and laid the ruler down against a finished sheet of dough and began to cut perfectly identical triangles. "California was fine."

"So why are you down here when you have PTO, kid? Other than the fact that you're a workhorse and don't know how to take a day off."

The smooth motion of the pizza cutter slicing through the dough was calming. My pulse slowed and my voice quieted. "Heather Pelham is back in the hospital. Doesn't look good. I said goodbye."

Scott's brow furrowed and he gave me a sympathetic nod. "That..." He shook his head and sighed again. "That sucks, Mad. I'm sorry to hear it." He glanced at the clock overhead and jerked his thumb back toward the stairs. "I better head back up before Carol loses her shit with the rush, but, uh, I'll pack something up for you to take to Steve when you're outta here. 'Aight?"

I forced a smile and turned back to my dough. "Thanks, Chef."

"Anytime, Chef," he retorted as he started up the stairs. "Hey, don't forget about the managers meeting tomorrow. Ten in the morning."

I gave him a thumbs up and he disappeared back into his kitchen.

———

MY ARMS WERE ACHING and my lower back was throbbing, but at least I had worked out some of those pesky emotions.

I stayed well after dinner service ended and went back behind my staff to give the kitchen an extra thorough clean.

Robert Mullon—the owner of Revanche—and Scott pretty much left me alone. I ran a tight ship and both of them were happy to sit back and watch us make top ten lists, win awards, and rack up soaring sales with my desserts.

On top of regular restaurant service, my team supplied breads, pastries, and other a la carte goods to a few local coffee shops and grocers. Our neighbors at the Taylor Creek Inn went through hundreds of our croissants and danishes every day.

With Memorial Day officially kicking off the summer tomorrow, wedding season would be in full swing. That meant that most of my time would be devoted to my brides and grooms and making their cake dreams happen.

Robert liked to have a managers meeting once a month with me, Scott, and Carol Hong—our front of the house manager. After thirty years of growing the restaurant, Robert was slowing down and just showed up to sign the paychecks. We were okay with that.

I locked up and finally mustered the energy to head home. The headlights of my Jeep flashed across the trees as I drove further inland and circled around the bay.

I cut the wheel and bumped down Steve and Heather's driveway. Their house was dark, but Steve's Challenger was parked up by the garage.

It was a nice car, but since it doubled as his unmarked vehicle, he never parked it in the garage, claiming that in an emergency it would take too long to pull out. I circled around to the side of their property, eased up to park beside the boat ramp, and killed the engine.

That's when I saw him.

Steve was sitting by himself on the end of the dock, still in the clothes he had been wearing at the hospital.

These were the moments in life that being the quarterback and the homecoming king didn't mean shit in the grand scheme of things. Steve and Heather had everything. They were the golden couple that *should* have had fifty more years together. But time was cruel.

I pulled my suitcase out and shut the door.

"Hey, I didn't think you'd be home tonight. Figured you'd still be at the hospital." I lifted the brown paper bag that flaunted the Revanche logo. "Scott sent y'all a buncha' boxes of something that smells like heaven."

His eyes never left the water.

The lights from my houseboat reflected off the surface. Our shadows curved and twisted in the glassy blackness as I sat down beside him. "You hungry?"

Steve stroked the thick stubble on his face and shook his head. Sure, he wasn't the most talkative person in our friend group, but this wasn't like him.

"Need something to drink?"

There was a twitch of his eyebrows. He laid back on the dock with his feet flat on the boards and his knees bent in the air. "Something strong," he mumbled.

I pushed off the creaky wood and walked onto the deck of my houseboat, lugging my suitcase over with me. When I came back, I had a bottle of Jack in my hand. I didn't really want to wash anymore dishes and tonight wasn't the night for messing with glasses.

I sat down beside him again and nudged his knees with my elbow. "Cheers." I took a swig from the bottle and passed it over.

Steve pushed up on his elbows, took the bottle from me, and drank a long pull.

"Wanna talk about it?" I offered quietly when he handed the whiskey back. I took another sip and set it aside. I traded downing the rest of the bottle for mindlessly picking at a loose thread on the hem of my tied off t-shirt. This one said *Momma tried.*

He sat up and hunched over, resting his forearms on his knees. "How much liquor you got stashed in that boat of yours?"

I forced a wry smile. "That bad, huh?" I made the string worse as I pulled at it, but I didn't do well with these kinds of conversations. I never knew what to say. I either ran away or I made things awkward—there was no in between. "Do they think she's gonna come home anytime soon?"

Steve choked down his answer, but I looked over and saw the tear sliding down his cheek and disappearing into his beard.

"Steve?"

"She's already gone, Mad," he croaked out.

Silence hung heavy between us.

I had known Steve since we were in diapers. Ever since the first day of third grade when Heather Daniels walked in with her Lisa Frank backpack, he had been head over heels for her.

Like any couple that fell for each other at a young age, they'd had their fair share of breakups and fights, but they never lasted long enough for either of them to start seeing anyone else.

Eventually Heather Daniels became Heather Pelham and, I swear, all of Beaufort and half of the Crystal Coast turned out for their wedding.

The way Steve looked at her when they said "I do" was the same way he looked at her that August when they met in Mrs. Phillip's classroom at Beaufort Elementary. It was the same way he was looking at her when I had seen them at Carteret Presbyterian just a few hours earlier.

It was the way he was staring at the water now.

Grief was a wicked thing to bear. It was the price of having too much love and no one to give it to.

I had always been just a little jealous of Heather. Not because I wanted Steve for myself—he was like a brother to me.

It had been written in the stars for the two of them to spend their lives together, but I couldn't help but be jealous of the way he looked at her.

All my life I wanted someone to look at me that way. The kind of way that you knew when they said, "Til death do us part," they meant it.

Steve's shoulders sagged like the life had been drained straight from his veins. I picked up the bottle and sucked down a few ounces before handing it over to him. He took it and stared at the glass rim for a moment before setting it aside and closing his eyes. I scooted closer, draped my arm around him, and rested my head on the corner of his shoulder.

He was fit, but not like Chase. Steve was soft and comforting. I wrapped my arm around his back and leaned against him like a life-sized teddy bear.

For an hour we sat there while the crickets chirped a gentle dirge and the water lapped against the shore.

Steve laid back on the dock again, lacing his fingers together and slipping them behind his head. When he closed his eyes, I pulled my phone out of my pocket and opened up the poker club group text.

Melissa had already rallied the troops to get a meal train going and make sure that Steve had someone to stay with him until his family could make it in.

MADDIE

I've got tonight covered. FYI—he keeps a spare key under the blue gnome by the garage in case any of y'all need to get in the house. Gotta be at the restaurant by 10am if someone can swing by then.

HANNAH JANE

How's he holding up?

MADDIE

He lost her. How do you think?

CHASE

A bunch of us from the department are gonna come by tomorrow. I'll be there by 9 AM so you can get to work. We'll cover dinner too.

MELISSA

Chase, repeat after me: I will bring Steve a well rounded meal and not takeout from Ed's diner.

HANNAH JANE

You can stop by my place and grab a casserole out of the deep freezer.

CHASE

I'm a grown ass man. I'm perfectly capable of feeding myself and/or others. Besides, Ed's has salads. I think.

KRISTIN

We had a last minute cancellation at the inn. I'll block it off in case he wants to stay here instead of his place.

MELISSA

I'm off the next two days, so I can go with him tomorrow to start the funeral arrangements. Bee— do you think we can have the wake at the bar?

BRIDGET

Shouldn't be a problem. I'll see what we've got on the schedule. Mad, how is he really?

STEVE

I'm fine.

CHASE

Cut the crap, dude. We know you're not fine. None of us are.

HANNAH JANE

What Chase is trying to say is that we love you, Steve.

MADDIE

We love you, but you're not getting out of bringing the beer to poker club. It's still your turn.

STEVE

Thanks.

# 8

# LUCA

Robert led me down the stairs from the rooftop dining space to the main floor of the restaurant.

I wiped the beads of sweat from my forehead and basked in the wave of cold air from inside.

*Thank God for air conditioning.*

The humidity here was no joke. I'd been in North Carolina for—I glanced at my watch—just shy of five hours, and sweat was already pouring from places I didn't know it could.

Revanche was impressive. No doubt about it. From the reclaimed wood floors to the exposed brick walls. The vines that ran up the many trellises and pergolas on the roof, the outdoor fireplace, the kitchen that was a chef's wet dream— it was a sexy restaurant and I was still kicking myself that Robert wanted to sell.

"So, that's uh, that's just about it, Mr. DeRossi." He waved his hand around the space. "Mad's kitchen is downstairs. But between you and me, she doesn't like anyone touching her space except for her staff. So, I stay out of her way. Girl works hard and kicks ass. The folks around here can't get enough of her desserts. I just sit back and let her do her thing."

"Call me Luca, please." I grinned, shrugging my shoulders casually.

I was more than a little giddy to see Maddie's kitchen. I'd been dreaming about it ever since I put the pieces together.

This business deal had been in the works for a while, but Robert had kept it on the down-low to avoid spooking his staff. It wasn't just the restaurant that was valuable. It was the people who made the magic happen.

A restaurant was just a building. I could build a hundred restaurants just as nice as Revanche, but the people in it were what made it valuable to me.

A lot of restaurateurs in my position liked to overhaul the staff as soon as they had the keys to the door in hand. They'd clean house and then bring in their own people to run things. That wasn't how I preferred to do business. At least not now. I tried my best to keep everyone on.

I glanced to the doorway that I assumed led to Maddie's lair. "I'd like to see the pastry kitchen. Just for a minute."

Was she down there? Her reaction to seeing me again was going to be less than optimum, but I couldn't help myself. I held my palms up and away in a show of good faith. "I'll keep my hands to myself. Chef Dorsey won't even know."

Robert snorted and just shook his head. "Maddie'll know. But it's gonna be your place soon, so she'd best be gettin' used to someone else calling the shots. Girl's a damn good pastry chef, but she's stubborn as a mule. You'll have your hands full for sure."

*Yes fucking please,* I thought. There hadn't been a minute since our date in LA that I hadn't thought about having my hands full of her particular brand of ornery beautiful.

I chuckled and followed him down the narrow staircase.

Going up and down, over and over again, must be a bitch for the servers and pastry team during dinner service.

Briefly, I contemplated if putting in a dumbwaiter would be an option. I'd have to call in a contractor, but it might be worth the hassle.

The steep stairs opened up to a brightly lit kitchen that was so clean I wanted to weep.

Stainless steel tables sparkled. The three-compartment sink was spotless. Rolling pins, spatulas, whisks, and other utensils were in uniform rows on hooks and shelves. Everything was labeled, and everything had a process. The meticulous organization was enough to give me a semi.

Robert motioned for me to have a look at the kitchen, and I didn't hesitate to poke around. I yanked open the handle to the walk-in freezer and shivered.

Rows of Cambro bins lined the shelves. I snooped a little further and pawed through the bins of shaped and frozen croissants that were ready to proof and bake off. Containers of house-made gelato were lined up like soldiers. I poked around the walk-in fridge. Health inspectors probably bowed to her organizational and sanitary prowess.

I glanced at my watch again and knew that we needed to head up to Robert's office before his management team showed up for the big news. I secured the door to the walk-in and followed him upstairs, flipping the lights off behind me.

When we made it into the office, a short lady with jet black hair pulled into a tight bun was already waiting. "Carol, good to see you," Robert settled into the chair behind his desk, then looked up at me. "This is Carol Hong. She's my front of house manager. Been with me since the early days."

A man just a little older than me knocked on the door-frame and gave me a cursory glance. "Scott Christensen," he said with obvious confidence.

I offered my hand and shook his. "Luca DeRossi."

Scott turned to Robert and said, "Mad called me and said she's running a few minutes late. Heather Pelham passed last night. She's on her way. Stayed with Steve last night until someone could get there to be with him this morning."

The room suddenly felt heavier. Carol and Rob both grimaced at the news.

Maybe that was why Maddie hadn't returned any of my texts. I wasn't trying to annoy her into talking to me, but I figured she'd at least want a heads-up that I was about to buy Revanche.

*It would be fine.* At least, that's what I hoped.

Maybe Maddie had cooled down since the competition. Maybe she'd even be glad to see me. The thought of that made my heart do funny things.

I rarely stuck around when I acquired restaurants as successful as Revanche. Typically, I'd put in a general manager to oversee the day-to-day and make sure that things were running smoothly. I liked making the existing staff feel confident that I wouldn't come in and bulldoze the place or make changes left-and-right.

*Not this time.*

The *Pastry Throwdown* competition had been kismet. Apart from the fact that I had one hell of a date with Maddie, I got to watch her in action.

When I put two and two together and realized that the girl from the gym was the pastry chef who had grown Revanche's reputation enough for me to take notice and put a generous offer in, I knew I'd stick around and oversee the transition myself.

"Here she comes," Rob said, nodding toward the entrance.

*Here we go.*

I turned to face the door and crossed my arms as it swung open. I hardened my expression to reinforce the grumpy judge face I'd practiced for this very occasion.

"Hey, sorry I'm running la—" Maddie stopped dead in her tracks and locked eyes with me. She looked three degrees away from boiling over.

Carol, Rob, and Scott exchanged confused looks. The tension was as thick as the humidity outside.

"Hey, sweetie." Robert cleared his throat and waved Maddie inside. "How's Steve holdin' up?"

Maddie never took her eyes off me. She locked her jaw and hissed through gritted teeth. "He's hanging in there."

"Well, let's get on with this so y'all can go enjoy your Memorial Day," Robert said, sighing as he pressed his hands to the desk and rose to his feet. "I'm selling the restaurant."

*Well, he ripped that Band-Aid right off.*

Robert scratched his bald spot nervously before continuing. "Y'all know me and Sandra have been wanting to move to Greenville so we can be closer to the grandkids. And, well, Mr. DeRossi made me an offer I can't refuse. We'll sign the papers once we're done here, and he'll take over from there. Effective immediately."

Everyone in the room shifted uncomfortably.

"Just like that?" Scott asked, eyebrows raised.

Robert nodded and looked at me. "As far as I know, Mr. DeRossi and his group are planning to keep the whole team. Might even bring in some new staff. His plans look solid, and I trust that Revanche will be in good hands."

Maddie's temper went from boiling to lava. She stomped across the office in those tiny denim shorts of hers and grabbed a sheet of paper out of the printer tray.

"Maddie—" Scott cautioned.

She grabbed a pen off the desk and scribbled a few lines across the blank sheet of paper. Silently, she looked at the calendar, wrote down a date and then another, signed her name at the bottom, and handed it to Robert.

"What's this?" He asked.

"That's my notice," she snapped. "Just pretend I gave it to you two weeks ago." She leveled me a searing look and stormed out the door.

I didn't waste a second.

I was on her tail like smoke on fire. "Maddie," I called after her as I followed her through the empty dining room, snaking around the tables that had chairs flipped with their legs in the air. "Maddie, stop."

*She didn't.*

Then again, I didn't know why I actually expected her to listen to me.

She cut through the main kitchen and went out the back door. The daylight was blinding, and I tripped on the gravel as she stomped out to the back parking lot.

"Maddie!" I shouted.

She stabbed her key into the lock of her Wrangler and twisted so hard I thought for sure it'd break. I closed in on her and grabbed the door handle to stop her from getting in.

"Mad—"

"Don't fucking touch me, Luca," she spat.

Those gray eyes that had been haunting my dreams were anything but docile.

I had no intention of backing down.

*If she would just speak to me, we could fix this.*

Before I could say anything else, the rough grip of a hand on my shoulder pulled me backward.

"Look, boss," Scott Christensen said as he turned me around, "I don't plan on losing my job, so don't do something stupid that'll make me have to punch you in the face."

He was loyal to his team, even if it put him in the crosshairs of the person paying him big bucks. I respected him for it. That was the type of guy I wanted on my team.

I gave him a curt nod and took a step back, my hands raised in defeat. "I tried to text you, Maddie. I tried to give you a heads-up. You never responded."

"Wait," Carol piped up, "You two know each other?"

"Yes," I said, realizing that she and Rob had followed us outside as well.

"No," Maddie countered.

I turned my attention back to her and eased forward slowly. "I don't accept your resignation."

"Well that's not my problem. I tendered my resignation to Mr. Mullon."

"Maddie, you're one of the reasons I looked at buying Revanche in the first place." She opened her mouth to retort with something undoubtedly snarky, but I beat her to the punch. "*Before* California."

I was shouting and I knew I needed to reign it in. Coming from a big, Italian family, it wasn't uncommon for the DeRossis to shake the windows when we got into it.

Still, I needed her to respect me as much as I respected her.

"I told you in Los Angeles—I know who you are."

The three pairs of ears behind me were probably chomping at the bit for a morsel of juicy gossip to sink their teeth into, but I wasn't going to give it to them.

I pressed my hands together and took a breath to keep

from saying something stupid. When my temper lowered to a simmer, I looked at her and dropped my unamused judge's face on.

"You have twenty-four hours to decide if you want to keep your job or move forward with your resignation." I glanced at my watch and noted the time. "I'll expect to hear from you by 10:34 tomorrow morning. I want you on my team, *Chef Dorsey*, but the choice is yours." I let a sly smirk slip up the corner of my mouth before I added on, "You have my number."

Maddie didn't say a word. Rage radiated from her body as she slid into her Jeep and slammed the door.

*That went well.*

Maddie spun tires and kicked up gravel on her way out. I turned and headed back into the restaurant to finish signing the papers with Robert.

Maybe I had been going about this thing with Maddie all wrong. Maybe I should have tried harder to hunt her down before I went to meet with Robert. Hell, maybe I should have told her about the buy-out when she was in California. Maddie had a short fuse and, apparently, I had lit it a long time ago.

# 9

# MADELINE

I tore out of the Revanche parking lot and didn't even think about where I was going. I just drove until the familiar ramshackle building came into sight.

From the outside it didn't look like much, but that was the point. Jokers was a locals-only bar. It was far enough inland that the summertimers never bothered to scout it out. The whole place looked like one big health code violation, but that was just part of its charm.

It didn't matter that it was only eleven in the morning. It was a fucking holiday, and I'd day drink if I wanted to.

Because *I* wanted to. *Not because seeing Luca DeRossi again had pushed me to the brink.*

The creaky screen door let out a shriek, slamming behind me as I stomped in. Apart from a few barflies, Jokers wasn't busy. The soles of my sandals snapped as they pulled against the inexplicably sticky floor.

Behind the bar, Bridget was talking to some regulars who were in for lunch. She smiled at me and I did my best to return the gesture, despite my recent encounter with Satan.

"Hey, babe," she said, wiping the oak counter clean with a bar towel. "Didn't expect to see you in this early. How's Steve?"

I shrugged and saddled up on a bar stool. "Quiet. People are over at his house, but he's not really talking all that much." I tossed my hair to one side to keep the sweat building up on my neck at bay, and rested my elbows on the bar. "Funeral's gonna be the day after tomorrow."

Bridget pulled her phone out of the bedazzled back pocket of her jeans and smiled at a text before stowing it away and pouring me a tall glass of whatever she had on tap. "So, is there a reason you're here before noon on a Monday, or did you just wanna see me and tell me about Abs?"

"Abs?"

Bridget pulled up the hem of her shirt just an inch and did her best smolder before breaking out into a laugh. "You know—*abs*. Hot guy from California who took you out on a date and crashed the group text? You never told us what happened with him."

As she finished teasing me about Luca, her phone buzzed again. She was answering the text before I could blink.

"Seems like you have some news," I said in between sips of the IPA. I nodded toward her phone. "Seeing someone?"

"It's new," she mumbled coyly.

"Uh huh," I grinned. "Who is it?"

Bridget smiled sheepishly as she shoved her phone into her pocket and grabbed a plate from the kitchen window. She set a platter of chicken fingers and mozzarella sticks in front of me and I groaned in delight.

"Marry me."

Bridget snickered. "I'll have to let Abs know that fried food is the way to your heart."

"I pretend to be fancy, but I'm really trash," I said with a laugh.

Being a professional chef didn't mean jack shit. I still loved pecan waffles from Waffle House, chicken fingers, mozzarella sticks, and Cosmic Brownies.

"If things don't work out with your hottie, I'll take the left side of the bed," Bridget said with a wink. "I'll even let you let you leave your socks on the floor. Won't even nag you about it."

I snorted and nearly choked on a mozzarella stick. Coughing, I clutched my chest, fully prepared to throw myself against the bar to self-administer the Heimlich maneuver.

She shoved my beer toward me and I took a grateful gulp, gasping as stale bar air finally filled my lungs. "That was some serious topic avoidance," I pointed out. "Spill it, Bee. Who is he?"

She blushed and fingered the bar towel. "You, um, you remember Kyle Kingsley back from when we were in high school?"

The name sounded familiar. "I think so. Doesn't he own a car dealership or something now?"

Bridget nodded, "Yeah. The dealership on the corner of 70 and 101 in Havelock."

"So, you're seeing him?"

She shrugged as she wandered over and brought one of the other patrons another round. "Like I said—it's new."

"Well, good for you," I said as I inhaled another chicken finger. "'Bout time you got some."

Bridget smirked and tightened her blonde ponytail. "What about you? You getting any?"

I shoved another bite into my mouth.

"Did you hook up with your west coast beach boy?" she asked.

I stabbed a mozzarella stick in marinara sauce and brought it up to my lips. Before I could take a bite, Bridget snatched it out of my hand and popped it in her mouth.

"Tell me everything, Mad," she mumbled.

I took a long sip of my beer and slammed it down. "Hot Guy from the gym ended up being a judge for *Pastry Throwdown*. And his name is Luca DeRossi."

Bridget froze. "Luca DeRossi as in *the Luca DeRossi*?"

"One in the devilish same."

"Oh my God. Did you sleep with him?"

"No!" I shouted a little louder than I meant to. The sparse lunch crowd stared at me and I gave them a middle finger. "I did not sleep with him."

"But..."

"But I may have made out with him a little... Or a lot." *Okay, so maybe we were dry humping. Whatever.*

"You made out with your mortal enemy."

"Just dig a hole, toss me in, and let me die in peace," I groaned.

Bridget rapped her fingers on the bar before speaking up again. "Why do I feel like there's something that you're not telling me?"

"What? There's noth—"

"Spill it, Maddie Lee."

"Mr. Mullon finally sold Revanche," I said with a huff. "To Luca."

Bridget froze in place. Her eyes widened until they were as big as my plate. She reached over, grabbed my beer, and gulped it down, draining the glass dry.

I wrinkled my nose in disappointment, but Bridget filled my glass again and slid it back to me.

"I'm pretty sure bartenders aren't supposed to drink on the clock."

Bridget rolled her eyes. "You just told me that your arch nemesis, also known as the hottest man on the planet, is your new boss."

"I quit."

"What?"

"I quit. I walked out of the manager's meeting and quit."

"And what did Rob say? Better yet, what did *Luca DeRossi* say?"

"Stop saying his name like you'll bow at his feet if he walks in the door," I said.

Lord knew I couldn't handle tall, dark, and asshole-y being conjured again.

I sighed. "He said he wants me to work for him and I have until tomorrow to decide if I actually want to quit or not."

Bridget looked over my shoulder toward the door. "And what would you do if he-who-must-not-be-named just walked into the bar?"

My rage went from a hot summer's day to the surface of the sun in an instant. "What?!" I hissed as I whipped around.

But it wasn't Luca. It was Chase.

He smirked and pulled at one of my waves like he had when we were kids. "Is Bee messin' with you, Mad Dog?" He shot Bridget a wink. "Seems like someone's gotten under your skin." He hopped up onto the bar stool beside me and stole a chicken finger off my plate.

Bridget leaned over the bar and eyed the gun and badge clipped to his belt. "I thought you were off duty."

Chase shook his head. "I'm covering for Steve. Just some water, darlin'."

Bridget slid the glass across the wood toward him. He caught it, giving her a flirtatious smile.

"Thanks, Bee." After taking a long drink, he turned on the stool to face me. "So, I heard about you raising hell at the restaurant this morning. Wanna talk about it?"

I raised an eyebrow. "Do I look like I wanna talk about it?"

"Fair enough," he said, finishing off his water before stealing another bite off my plate. "So, is it true?"

"Is what true?"

"Oh, you know—all that shit the rumor mill's spinning these days. Did, uh, did that chef guy actually buy the restaurant from Rob Mullon?"

Sometimes I forgot just how fast news traveled in small towns.

I nodded. "That he did."

"And?"

"And, what?"

"And, what about you? You hate the guy."

"I quit."

Chase cracked a smile, but it disappeared when he noticed Bridget behind the register, texting someone with a dopey smile on her face. "Not surprised," he muttered.

I looked from Chase to Bridget and back again. "What? About Bee dating Kyle Kingsley or me quitting the restaurant?"

He frowned. "How, uh, how long has Bee been seeing him?"

I mumbled something noncommittal as I finished my food.

He glanced at his phone and got up, pulled a couple dollars out of his wallet, and tossed them down on the bar.

"Chase, you just had water. That's free," Bridget said as she shoved the money back at him.

Chase shook his head, pushing the bills toward her again. "That's for the excellent service, darlin'."

Bridget rolled her eyes, but took the cash and tucked it into the pocket of her waist apron. Her voice was soft, and her eyes were dreamy as she smiled and said, "Stay safe out there, Chase."

He gave her a wink. "Thanks, Bee. See you two ladies later."

Chase left Jokers and got into his unmarked police car. When my plate was reduced to crumbs and all that was left of my beer was a light line of foam around the glass, I rested my elbows on the bar and put my face in my hands.

"What do I do, Bridge?"

"About what?"

"My job."

Bridget grabbed my dishes and tossed them in the bus bin. "How was the date?"

"What do you mean?"

"You know, before you knew who he was."

I sighed. "Amazing. We had the best time." I hated admitting that, so I took it out on the paper napkin, tearing it into tiny bits of lame-ass confetti.

"So, you don't wanna work for him because you have feelings for him?"

I pointed a defiant finger at her. "I don't have feelings for him."

Bridget rolled her eyes. "Sure you don't."

My phone buzzed on the bar-top with another text from Hot Guy from the Gym in LA.

I shoved my phone away without looking at it.

Bridget, however, didn't have such qualms about contact

with the devil. Without skipping a beat, she grabbed it and opened it up.

*I really needed to change my passcode.*

Her eyebrows raised as she read whatever the devil had texted. "Mads, he's looking for you."

I raised my empty glass toward her. "Well then pour me another, barkeep. He's new in town. No way he'll look here."

Bridget shook her head, took my glass, and tossed it with the rest of the dirty dishes. "I'm cutting you off. You're acting like a child."

"You're the one who gave me chicken fingers."

"Madeline Lee Dorsey, you're the best pastry chef I know. Don't let one jackass take that from you."

"I can go work anywhere. The inn, Queen's Coffee—hell, I'll work here. I can mix drinks."

Bridget shook her head, "I love you, but I'm not hiring you. And you're too overqualified to be baking muffins and making lattes at Queen's."

"I hate him."

"Do you? Or do you just think you hate him?"

That was the million-dollar question, wasn't it?

———

IT WAS the first Monday in a long time that we hadn't played poker. Still, we all got together and crowded into Steve's house for dinner.

It had been a week that felt like a century. No one asked about Luca taking over Revanche, but they all knew. There were no secrets between us.

Melissa and I tackled the dishes while Bridget, Chase, and Steve shot the shit.

Kristin and Hannah Jane snuck through the house while

Steve was distracted, tidying up, throwing in a load of laundry, and cleaning as much as they could.

Kristin was the first to leave. The rest of us lived in Beaufort and Morehead, but she commuted to work at the Taylor Creek Inn all the way from Havelock.

Chase and Hannah Jane were next. They lived two doors down from each other and usually rode together.

Kyle Kingsley showed up right before Chase left. I swore he was going to blow a gasket when Kyle escorted Bridget to his car and drove her home.

Melissa lingered, making sure that Steve had everything he needed, even asking if he wanted her to stay longer. Steve shrugged off the offer and disappeared into his garage.

"You going to work tomorrow?" Melissa asked as she followed me down the path from Steve's house to the water, where my houseboat was tied off.

"Haven't decided yet."

"Cutting it a little close, aren't you?"

I shrugged. "It's embarrassing."

She rolled her eyes as she hopped onto the deck of my houseboat. "Since when does anything embarrass you?"

"Mel, we were bordering on public indecency in a parking lot after eating food truck tacos."

She giggled and sat down in one of the deck chairs.

I plugged in the string of market lights and sat across from her. "Even if I didn't want to see him eaten by a shark, I can't look at him every day and go on like nothing happened."

"Why do you hate him so much?"

"You know why."

"That thing with the restaurant in New York? Girl, that was *years* ago. Forgive and forget, Mads. It had nothing to do with you."

"I stand up for my friends. I'm not working at Revanche if Satan is signing the checks."

Melissa leaned forward. "Maddie, you're loyal to a fault. Maybe it was just bad luck. Maybe there was more to it. You don't know. Luca DeRossi buying out the restaurant could be great for you. You won the competition and a big-name chef sees you as a valuable asset. For once in your life just think about yourself."

## 10

---

## LUCA

I leaned back in the leather office chair and stared at the clock.

*10:29 AM.*

I tapped my phone again just to make sure I hadn't missed a text from Maddie.

Nope. *Nada.*

My foot tapped anxiously on the floor. Her employee file was on the desk in front of me. She had an impressive resume. I scanned it again to take my mind off the possibility that maybe she wasn't going to show up.

Maddie had studied at the Culinary Institute of America right after high school and graduated at the top of her class. After that, she did a year-long internship in New York City with one of the country's top cake designers, then did a stint as a pastry cook at my flagship restaurant in Manhattan.

*That was news to me. I never knew Maddie worked for me.* I made a mental note to shoot the restaurant's general manager an email and get a copy of her file.

After two years in New York, she returned to Beaufort and took a job as the pastry chef at Revanche.

Though it initially began as a one-woman show, Maddie had grown the pastry program here into an entire team of people that had her basement kitchen running nearly twenty-four hours a day. The wholesale accounts she'd landed brought in a huge chunk of profit.

Even though my accountants had done a bang-up job, before Robert handed over the keys, we went through the books with together one more time.

Besides standard restaurant service, Revanche produced breads, pastries, and individual desserts that were resold in coffee shops and cafes all along the coast.

Scott and Maddie also teamed up to provide five-star catering for weddings and other events.

Selfish desires aside, there was no way replacing Maddie was going to be a simple task.

I looked at the clock again. *10:33 AM.*

I pushed out of the chair and let out a muttered string of profanities. Scott made it clear that the staff was loyal to Maddie and vice versa. Replacing one person was one thing, but replacing an entire team was another.

I wandered through the dining room where Carol was double-checking lunch and dinner reservations. Her servers were doing a meticulous inspection of every place setting and table. I ducked my head into the main kitchen. Scott wasn't there, but his sous chef and line cooks were busy preparing for the lunch crowd. I rounded the corner and passed the storeroom, hoping Maddie would be in there.

But she wasn't.

My phone buzzed in my pocket with the timer I had set. *10:34 AM.*

I didn't want to believe that Maddie would quit, but I steeled myself for the worst as I headed down the stairs to the pastry kitchen.

Scott and Maddie were hunched over one of the stainless-steel worktables, pouring over spreadsheets and menus. Her team of bakers and pastry cooks worked in a near-sprint as pan after pan of croissants went from the proofer to the oven. Mixers whirred and bowls clattered. It was organized chaos, and it was beautiful.

I cleared my throat. Scott looked up, Maddie did not.

"Chef Dorsey, a minute, please," I said.

Maddie's eyes never left the menu she was working on.

It looked like they were working out the seasonal dessert pairings for the summer menu.

I stood off to the side and watched for a moment before piping up and saying, "The flourless chocolate torte—you should add some of the chili-caramel cotton candy you made for the competition. It'll be a big draw, especially after the episode airs."

Finally, she looked up at me. Her face was completely devoid of any expression. "We don't have a cotton candy centrifuge here."

"Rush order it. I'll approve the expense," I said.

Maddie paused a beat, growing the tension before she finally said, "Yes, Chef."

Her chilly demeanor was unnerving. Wanting to avoid the cold, I caught her eye once more and motioned up the stairs. "My office when you have a moment."

Her eyes turned back to the menu placed between her and Scott. "Yes, Chef."

―――――

THERE WAS a knock on the doorframe before Maddie poked her head in. "You wanted to see me, Chef?"

I waved her in. Maddie closed the door behind her, and I motioned for her to have a seat.

"I didn't think you were going to be here today," I admitted as I peeled my eyes away from her body.

The way her Rolling Stones t-shirt peeked out of the undone top buttons of her chef's coat made my heart race. Her long, silvery blonde waves were in a massive bun. Covering her head was a bright teal head wrap that screamed *beach hippie*.

Those gray eyes pierced into mine with relentless ferocity. "I'm taking a day off tomorrow. My sous chef, Rae, is covering."

"Okay."

"Oh, I—" she stuttered.

"Thought I'd say no?" I asked, cracking a smile. "You probably had a ten minute argument planned, didn't you?"

"Something like that."

A flicker of amusement ticked at the corner of my mouth. "Would you like me to pretend to fight with you, so you can get it off your chest?" I teased.

Maddie rolled her eyes.

I leaned back in the chair and crossed my arms. "Are we gonna be able to make this work?"

"Are you going to stay out of my kitchen?"

"I think it's *my* kitchen now," I countered.

Smoke rose off the top of her head, and she balled her fingers into tight fists.

"I'm joking, Maddie," I said with a sigh. "Look. I'm not coming in, riding roughshod all over the way you all do things around here. There will be some changes, but nothing drastic. You, Scott, and Carol run the show."

Her little lips turned into a frown. "What kind of changes?"

"Some new equipment. I'm talking to a contractor to see if we can put a dumbwaiter in, so your staff and the servers don't have to keep hauling ass up and down the stairs during service. Eventually, I'll bring in a GM to be my eyes and ears when I'm not here and I'm hiring a third-party HR firm to make sure that staff issues are handled properly. I know that sometimes employees don't feel comfortable bringing up problems if they have to tell them to the superior they have a problem with. I take care of my staff."

That last thing piqued her interest.

I lifted my hands. "Does that sound reasonable to you?"

"Yes, Chef," she said. Her expression was pulled into a hard line. The flirty, free spirited girl I met at the gym in LA was nowhere to be found.

"Do what you want in front of your staff, but when it's just us—call me Luca. We don't have to pretend like we're strangers."

"I'd prefer if we did."

I rose from my chair when she made a move for the door. "Maddie—"

"My staff want to know if there's going to be a delay in getting their checks this pay period," she asked in the same calm tone she used during the competition—a far cry from what I knew her to actually be like.

It wasn't the raucous laughter when we had dinner or danced, or the quiet murmur she used when we sat on the floor outside her hotel room and swapped personal facts.

Madeline Dorsey was anything but cold, but her voice was frigid.

I shook my head. "No. I'll make sure everything's done on the same schedule."

"Okay." She made a reach for the doorknob, but I

stepped in front of the door. "Is there something else you need, *Chef DeRossi*?"

The condescension that dripped from her words made me want to choke her. *The fun way.*

"Yeah, I want you to stop acting like a fucking robot, Mad." There was a flare in her eyes, and I knew I had pushed a button. "I know there's a person in there," I said as I trailed the tip of my finger along the middle edge of her pristine chef's coat. "I just don't get why you're so hellbent on us hating each other. Because I'm not."

Her chest rose and fell, and I searched for something— some inkling of what was going through her head. For some idea of what she felt.

But I came up empty.

I took a step back and traced my tongue across my lip. "For what it's worth, I'm sorry about the loss of your friend. I hope you got to spend some time with her when you got back from California."

Maddie's eyelids fluttered as she looked down at the floor and blinked back tears. She took a steadying breath and put her hand on the doorknob again. "Anything else you need, Chef?"

"That's all. I'll pop down during service to observe."

She gave me a nod and opened the door.

"Hey, Mad—"

She turned and looked over her shoulder, raising her eyebrows.

"If you need anything, just let me know," I offered with a pathetic smile.

"I'll be sure not to need anything." And with that, she dipped into the main kitchen and headed down the stairs.

## 11

## MADELINE

Grief and loss were lawless and vile things. I hated them.

It was the opposite of everything I wanted in life, and yet I found myself constantly surrounded by them.

It was rare for me to take a day off, but I had learned that there was no avoiding grief—only acknowledging it and continuing to move forward.

I stood at the graveside in between Melissa and Bridget. Chase, Kristin, and Hannah Jane were in the row behind us. One by one, we stepped forward and placed a rose on top of Heather's casket.

The preacher was saying something that was supposed to be comforting, but it was all in one ear and out the other. Even for it being a Wednesday morning, the cemetery was packed with mourners saying their goodbyes to Heather.

The moment I saw the headstone, it made me angry.

*Heather Catherine Pelham—loving wife, daughter, and friend.*

How could someone's life be summed up on a headstone that way?

That was it?

Wife, daughter, and friend?

Everything in me wanted to leave, but I couldn't abandon Steve like that. I wouldn't abandon the rest of my friends.

Maybe Melissa was right. I was loyal to a fault.

My eyes gazed across the sea of black suits and dresses, but one figure stuck out to me. He stood slightly outside the crowd, but was no less attentive to the funeral proceedings.

*And he was looking at me.*

When the service ended and the crowd dispersed, I milled around for a moment, making promises to meet everyone at Jokers to drink in honor of Heather.

Still, he lingered.

I crossed the grass and headed for my Jeep. I was too focused on being careful to walk parallel with the burial plots to notice that Luca had caught up to me.

"You look nice."

I looked down at the black dress I pulled out of my closet this morning. It hit just above my knees and had a conservative neckline. I'd left my hair down even though the temperatures were going to crack triple digits in just a few hours.

"Thanks," I mumbled politely. "You, um... You didn't have to be here. You didn't even know her."

Luca shook his head and opened my Jeep door. "Maybe not, but I know you."

"Is this what you meant when you said that you care for your staff?"

"Yeah. I would've shown up if it was Scott or Carol, but I wouldn't have walked either of them to their car," he said with a chuckle.

"Luca, I'm not in the mood to fight with you today. I need to get going."

He cracked a smile and rested his arm on the hood. "Good, because I don't enjoy fighting with you." He gave me a curious look when I sat in the driver's seat and took off my black heels. I tossed them in the passenger's seat, then traded them for my favorite sandals.

"You wore those in LA," he mused. "On our date."

"Don't think you're something special, Luca. I wear these every single day." I grabbed the pair of denim shorts I had stashed in the back seat and shimmied them up and under my dress.

His smile grew into a devilish smirk. Suddenly, the North Carolina heat had nothing on the fire I felt deep in my belly.

"I didn't think I was special, but then you went and called me Luca instead of Chef." He pressed his hand over his heart and leaned in a little closer. "I like hearing you say my name, Madeline."

I caught a whiff of something spicy and expensive.

*God, his cologne was going to be the death of me.*

Goosebumps flooded my bare arms. "Stop it," I said as I stuck my key into the ignition, and my Jeep roared to life.

Stifling air blasted out of the vents, but it quickly began to cool and I was grateful—I didn't think I could stand any more heat between us.

"You're making me forget that I hate you."

"Good. Because *I* don't hate you." He slammed the driver's side door shut. Just when I thought I had gotten rid of him, he rounded the hood, opened the passenger's side door, tossed my shoes into the floorboard, and got in. "Now, where are we going?"

"Get out of my car," I snapped.

I looked around for Chase or Steve. Hell, even Melissa at five-foot-nothing would help get this interloper out of my vehicle, but everyone had already left.

*Dammit.*

Whatever. I reached around and lowered the zipper on the side of my dress.

Whatever Luca had been looking at suddenly became unimportant because his eyes were glued to me.

"I'm not giving you a striptease," I snapped as I lifted my dress over my head, leaving me in my jean shorts and black bra. I snatched the tank top from the back seat and yanked it on as fast as I could.

He reached over and pinched the side of my shirt so he could read it. "Blame it all on my roots?"

I shot him a contentious glare. "If you haven't heard of Garth Brooks, get out of my Jeep right here, right now."

Luca looked relaxed as he loosened his cufflinks because *of course* he was wearing cufflinks that probably cost as much as my car.

He was Luca DeRossi, and I could *not* let myself forget that.

*No matter how much I wanted to straddle him in that seat, hike my dress up, and sink down onto the impressive package I'd gotten a teasing sample of in Los Angeles.*

"And if I have heard of him, you'll let me stay?"

"Probably not, but I'll hate you a little less."

"Wanna tell me why you hate me so much to begin with?"

"Nope."

"Great. Then where are we going? I heard someone mention something about Jokers. It's a bar, right?"

"Get out of my car, Luca."

"I'm new in town," he said with a self-righteous smirk.

"Isn't this the perfect opportunity for that southern hospitality that I've heard so much about?"

"Out," I snapped.

Luca looked like he wanted to come across the center console, but he stayed rooted to his seat. Still, I could see the growing turmoil in his mind.

"Maddie, listen to me," he began, his voice low and raspy and calm. "You lost a friend and, for that, I'm very sorry. But you and me? This thing between us? Whatever happened in California *happened*. We can't pretend that it didn't, or we're not gonna be able to work together. I won't push you, but I'm not letting this go. And I'm sure as fuck not forgetting about it."

Assuming that he wasn't getting out of my car anytime soon, I eased on the accelerator and headed down Highway 101 to Jokers.

Luca reached to fiddle with the radio dial, and I swatted his hand away.

"My car, my music. Don't touch."

"Yes, ma'am."

I wanted to strangle him. *Why did his voice have to sound so damn sexy? Why did he have to look so comfortable in a three-piece suit?*

"So, where are we going, Chef Dorsey?"

I rolled my eyes. I knew he was just calling me that to get under my skin, and unfortunately, it was effective. "Not here."

"What do you mean, *not here*?"

"I mean, when we go to Jokers, you call me Maddie. Not Chef Dorsey."

He licked his lips, and the memory of my mouth latched onto his washed over me like a tidal wave.

I shifted in the driver's seat, nearly swerving off the road.

Luca reached over and put his hand on the wheel to steady the Jeep. "And I thought California had terrible drivers," he muttered. His eyes cut over to me again. "So, *Maddie*, are you gonna call me Luca or Chef DeRossi?"

His hand moved away from the wheel, but instead of keeping to his side of the Jeep, he rested his arm on the center console and trailed his fingers along the frayed hem of my shorts.

I wanted to swat his hand away, but I didn't. I just leaned back in my seat and kept driving.

"Or you could call me Luke."

I cut my eyes in at him, "You lied to me."

"I didn't—"

"You said your name was Luke, and when we met you didn't look like—" I waved my hand toward his rather sexy suit "—that."

"So, what? I have to show a pretty woman my birth certificate and two forms of ID before taking her on a date just because I didn't shave that morning?"

His sleeve had gotten pushed up as he continued to ghost his fingers over my thigh, his ink peeking out from behind his Rolex.

"I never knew you had tattoos."

"Most people don't. I keep them covered when I'm being *Luca DeRossi*," he said, mocking the way I had differentiated between his two personas.

His hand skated down to my knee, and I whimpered instinctively, wanting him to move it back up my thigh again.

"And to be fair, my family calls me Luc. Just not L-u-k-e."

I was thankful when the gravel lot that the bar sat on came into sight. Luca was slowly chipping away at my defenses, and that just wouldn't do.

I pulled into a spot beside Steve's Challenger and cut the engine. Turning to Luca, I said, "Lose the jacket."

"Excuse?"

I waved my finger around his torso. "Jacket off. You look like money."

"And the problem is?"

"This isn't the place you go to flash your wad of hundreds. Jacket off, watch off."

Luca cocked his head and flashed me that perfect smile. "Anything else you want to come off?" he teased, looking around the tight interior of my Jeep. "I mean, it's a little small, but we can have a good time in here. You just say the word, beautiful."

I swatted his chest, and my hand ricocheted off it like a ping-pong ball against a brick wall. "Keep your pants on."

I got out and locked the doors behind me. Thankfully, Luca took my advice and stepped out onto the gravel in his perfectly tailored pants and white button-up. He had loosened his tie and rolled up his sleeves.

I sucked in a shallow breath as sweat and lust lingered in the valley between my breasts.

I remembered what it felt like for him to hold me. To hold my hand. To kiss me. To pull me close and whisper sweet nothings in my ear. Those memories were the only things I could think about ever since he showed up in Beaufort.

I felt his hand slide onto the small of my back, and I jumped back instinctively. "What are you doing?"

If my reaction put him off, he didn't show it. He simply moved his hand higher to rest between my shoulder blades. "Walking you inside."

"Luca—"

With two quick steps, he turned and had my back

pinned to the door of my Jeep. The handle bit into my spine, but I didn't dare move. His hips pushed against mine and his eyes zeroed in on me. "Why do you hate me so much?"

"Because you're an ass."

He clicked his tongue and gave me a terse shake of his head. "You can do better than that, Mad."

"You're not as good as you think you are."

"In the kitchen or in bed?" he asked as he took a chance and rocked the bulge in his pants between my thighs. "Because I never got to show you the latter."

I sucked in a sharp breath, and it caught in my throat. My eyes fluttered shut, and Luca chuckled quietly, knowing that he had won that round. I wasn't letting him take the win that easily.

"Both," I croaked out breathlessly.

Luca leaned in, cocked his head, and brushed his lips against the outer shell of my ear. "Did something happen when you worked at my restaurant in New York? Is that it, Madeline? Because I would have remembered you, and I don't." His hand slipped under the hem of my tank and dug into my hip. "Tell me what I did so we can put it to bed."

I didn't want to talk about it because I knew that as soon as I did, I'd have to admit how much I wanted him. It wasn't just that he was my boss now. I didn't like admitting that I was wrong.

*And maybe I had been entirely wrong about Luca DeRossi.*

Before I could decide whether or not I was going to talk about New York, a deep voice came from the direction of the bar.

"Hey," Steve bellowed.

I looked over Luca's shoulder and saw Steve and Chase on a warpath toward us.

"Get off her, shit dick," Chase shouted. Melissa, Kristin,

and Hannah Jane stood crowded in the bar's doorway, watching the action.

Luca took a wise step back and raised his hands. I stepped forward to block Steve from taking a cheap shot at Luca. I hated when the two of them went all big brother on me.

"Steve, stop."

"Who the fuck do you think you are, putting your hands on Maddie?" he spat.

Catching a break between customers and not wanting to miss the action, Bridget had joined the girls in the doorway, and the four of them were heading toward us.

I cursed the fact that I would have to play devil's advocate and took a step back to stand shoulder to shoulder with Luca.

Melissa had already put two and two together and was tapping her fingers together like a mad scientist. Chase looked like he was three seconds from leaving a Luca-shaped dent in the hood of Steve's car. Steve looked like he was about to rip Luca limb from limb.

Melissa took a step forward, putting her hand on Steve's arm and tugging him backward.

*"Fuck me,"* I groaned under my breath.

Either I fed Luca to the wolves, or played the southern belle.

I huffed and looked around at my friends. "Y'all, this is Luca DeRossi."

# 12

# LUCA

**W**ell. That could have gone worse.

Steve could have flattened my face like he wanted to. Maddie could have hung me out to dry, but she didn't.

*Fuck me.*

Watching her change out of her little black dress in the front seat of her Jeep had been a test of self-restraint that I nearly failed.

Now, I was punishing myself by staying at the hole-in-the-wall bar with her, rather than calling myself an Uber and heading back to my beach rental.

My phone lit up with Astrid's name and I ignored it. It would piss her off, but she worked for me—not the other way around.

Maddie was swinging around the filthy dance floor like she owned the place with the bartender, Bridget. With the number of drinks Maddie had sucked down in just a few hours, she should own stock in the place.

"Oh my God!" she squealed in drunken giddiness as she

made a beeline for me. She let out a gasp. "Did you know that you're *Luca DeRossi?*"

I chuckled and rested my hand on her waist to keep her from tipping over. "That I am."

"I hate you, you know," she admitted much too cheerfully for my taste as she rocked back and forth.

"I know."

"But you," she began as she stabbed me square in the chest with one pointed finger, "Don't know whyyyyyy!"

"Alright, Mad Dog," Bridget said as she rounded the bar and slid Maddie a glass of water. "Why don't you sit down by Mr. DeRossi and drink that while I get you something from the kitchen."

"Fried pickles!" Maddie shouted.

Bridget gave her a searing assessment. "Have you eaten today?"

Maddie rolled her eyes. "Yes, mother."

"What," Bridget pressed.

"Cereal before the funeral." At the sound of the last word, Maddie sulked. I couldn't tell if it was the alcohol-induced petulancy, or her stifled grief finally working its way to the surface.

Bridget disappeared into the kitchen and returned a few minutes later with a plate covered with French fries surrounding a mammoth turkey sandwich, and set it in front of Maddie.

"Make sure she eats all of that," she instructed me as she refilled Maddie's glass with more water. "You need anything?"

"No, ma'am," I said as I shook my head and reached across the bar to offer her my hand. "Luca DeRossi."

Bridget laughed. "Oh, I know who you are, Abs."

I smirked and brushed off Bridget's teasing. "Right, the text when I was in LA."

She glanced over at Maddie as she wolfed down the sandwich. "Do me a favor and look after her, will ya?"

Before I could respond to Bridget, one of the guys from earlier sided up to the bar. "This guy givin' you trouble, Bee?"

I wanted to slide off that barstool and rear up for a fight.

How dare that jackass insinuate that, just because Maddie had an issue with me, I was automatically the one at fault.

Bridget brushed her hair over her shoulder and shook her head, "Cool it, Detective Brannan. He's fine."

I raised an eyebrow and turned toward the guy. "You're a cop?"

He gave me a nod but didn't show that he'd entertain a handshake, so I didn't offer one. "Chase Brannan."

"Luca DeRossi."

"Yeah, I got that much from Maddie."

I racked my brain for any morsel of information that I had stored away. In Los Angeles, Maddie mentioned that two of her friends were cops, and one of them was her neighbor.

"You Maddie's neighbor or the other one?"

"The other one. Steve and Heather—" he paused, grief washing over him at the realization that only one of them was still here "—Steve's her neighbor."

I looked at the glass of whiskey I'd been nursing for the better part of two hours and nodded. "I, uh, I'm sorry for your loss."

"No, you're not. But thanks anyway."

That made me crack a smile. "What? I'm just here trying

to practice some southern hospitality. When in Rome, right?"

"If you wanted to do as the Romans, you'd be eating boiled peanuts and drinking something on tap. Not the overpriced top-shelf liquor you got there."

I turned to the seat that Maddie had abandoned and looked at the dance floor. She had returned to dancing like an absolute moron. An adorable, heart-stopping, beautiful moron.

I straightened up and took a sip of the room temperature whiskey. "Just pacing myself. Figured Maddie would need a ride home."

Chase stiffened up and pressed his hands against the oak bar. "And you think any of us are gonna let her get in a car with you?"

"Doesn't matter what you think, now does it? She's a grown woman."

"And you're a dick. You even think about leaving any way other than alone, and I'll turn you into chum and sprinkle you in the ocean."

"Chase," Bridget soothed. She reached over the bar and put her hand on his, and he visibly relaxed. She offered me a kind smile and a set of keys. "These are Maddie's. Make sure she gets home safe."

I chuckled and took the set of keys from her. Chase clearly wasn't a fan of the idea, but I didn't give two shits about what he thought of it.

"How'd you get your hands on Maddie's keys?" I had been watching her for most of the day and never saw her hand them over to anyone.

Bridget laughed, tossing her head back, and I snuck a glance at Chase. He was all puppy-dog-eyed and dreamy, staring at her. The man looked like a lovesick kid.

"We all take turns being the designated pickpocket. She lives on the bay. You can just follow Steve home whenever he heads out."

I looked across the bar until I saw the man I assumed to be Steve.

He had made himself at home at a high-top table and had a glass of something strong in his hands. A short girl with dark skin and a bright smile was across from him.

Weird. Maddie had just been with her.

I scanned the bar again until my eyes landed on Maddie, who was—*aw, hell.*

Maddie was at the other end of the U-shaped bar and was climbing up onto it. I had to give it to her—either she was a very competent drunk or she had done this a time or two. I was leaning toward the latter.

She hoisted a beer bottle in the air, blonde hair flying around her as she screamed, "Turn it up!"

Someone punched a song into the old school jukebox and the bar went wild.

I had no earthly clue what the hell was going on, but apparently everyone else did.

Tables were shoved to the wall as Bridget and the other bartender came out from behind the bar.

Either I had missed the line dancing memo, having grown up in Brooklyn, or I had walked straight into some kind of backwoods cult.

*What the hell was happening?*

I looked up and watched Maddie's hips sway as she grapevined across the bar top to the country crooner squalling about moonshine, his granddaddy, and some place called Copperhead Road.

The song picked up. She slapped her heels and scooted across the two-and-a-half-feet of oak like she wasn't three sheets to the wind. She let out a whoop, and the crowd cheered her on.

Maddie looked down from her stage and shot me a grin. The song ended, and Bridget hurried back behind the bar as the crowd lined up for refills.

I reached up and offered Maddie my hand. "You ready to head home?"

"Why Luca Deeeeeee Rossi," she squealed. "You plan on takin' me home?" Maddie swayed into my chest, and I wrapped my arm around her waist to hold her up.

I didn't know how much longer she'd last on her feet. If she got her hands on another drink, I'd be carrying her out of here. *Not that I was opposed to Maddie being ass-up over my shoulder.*

"C'mon, Footloose," I groaned as I shifted her into my other arm and reached for my wallet. "I've got your keys."

I spotted Steve heading for the door and knew I only had a short amount of time to get Maddie's tab settled before he peeled out. I didn't want to have to depend on someone who was five minutes away from passing out to guide me around the winding back roads.

I slid Bridget my credit card and told her I'd be covering Maddie's tab and the one drink I'd barely touched. She handed me a receipt, and I shoved it in my pocket.

I led Maddie toward the door. Just before we stepped out into the night air, I glanced back and gave Chase a nod.

Maddie stumbled across the gravel and, for the first time, I caught a glance at the vanity license plate on the front of her Jeep.

*HER-RICANE.*

If there was ever an accurate description of Madeline Dorsey, that was it.

Steve's Challenger roared to life beside us as I reached

across her body and clicked the seatbelt across her lap. I hopped behind the wheel, and she propped up those long legs of hers on the dash.

"Where we going?" she pouted. Passing headlights illuminated her face every few seconds as I pulled out onto the road. "I was havin' fun." Her head lolled across the back of the seat, and she looked at me. "You didn't look like you were havin' fun. Why weren't you havin' fun, Luca DeRossi?"

I stifled my laugh, not wanting to spoil the quiet of the night. "I had fun watching you have fun."

"You likeeeee me!" she sing-songed.

"'Course I like you, Mad," I said with a grin. "I just can't figure out why you don't like me."

Like the old saying went: the only honest people were little kids and drunks.

Maybe she'd spill whatever it was she was holding on to, and we could clear the air. I hoped we could, at least.

I wasn't a choir boy—I'd had my fair share of fuck-ups. But for some strange reason, whatever happened that made Maddie hate me was one fuck-up I wanted to un-fuck-up.

Maddie huffed like a three year old and closed her eyes. "I can't decide."

"Can't decide what."

"If I still hate you or not."

"Tell me why you think you hate me then."

"Mel says I'm loyal to a fault, and maybe you're okay."

*What the fuck did that mean?*

Before I could ask her to elaborate, she added, "I talk shit about you allllll the time. I wanna tell everyone what a dick you are, but you're makin' it hard now 'cause you're real nice, and you're a lotta fun, and you're a *real good* kisser."

*Okay. Progress. I could work with that.*

Maddie's comment about me being a good kisser made my dick stand up proudly like it was accepting a fucking award.

*Down, boy.*

I cleared my throat and shifted in the driver's seat. "I know. I follow you."

Maddie's mouth gaped open, and she shrieked so loud I thought the windows were going to shatter. "Oh my God!"

"What?"

She pulled her phone out of her back pocket, and her drunken thumbs flew over the screen in a frenzy. "I have to tell everyyyyyyybodyyyy!"

"Tell them what?"

She looked at me dumbfounded. "That *Luca DeRossi* follows me!"

I chuckled and slowed when I saw Steve's brake lights flash in front of me. I turned off the road and guided Maddie's Jeep down a long driveway. A house came into sight and Steve slowed to a stop.

"Mad?"

"Hm?"

"Where's your house?" I asked, hopeful for a coherent response.

She said that Steve was her neighbor, right? That's what everyone else said, too. But the driveway ended, and there was no other house in sight.

Maddie's arm flopped toward the left, where the headlights glinted off the water. "Over there."

I cracked a smile. "So you *are* a mermaid."

"No, silly." She giggled. "My houseboat." Her laugh turned into a pout as she said, "She doesn't like it when I get tipsy 'cause they're 'fraid I'm gonna fall off the side and drown."

"Who's *she*? Do you have a roommate?"

Maddie shook her head. "My mom."

"Does your mom live here with you?"

"No, but she worries when she remembers me."

*Well, that was cryptic as fuck.*

I reached over the center console and unhooked her seatbelt. "Come on, let's get you in your... *houseboat.*"

I helped her down and locked the doors behind me. Maddie stumbled across the dock before a streak of sobriety hit her and she leaped like a ballerina onto the deck of her houseboat.

That was where her gracefulness ended.

She giggled as she held onto the doorframe and wobbled inside. Curious about what houseboat living was like, I followed her in.

She flipped the lights on, and everything came into view. The deck was big. She had a charcoal grill and patio furniture. String lights were mixed with the vines from the plants she had everywhere.

Inside, a tiny kitchen barely big enough for the two of us to stand in opened to a dining room table that could seat four, and a sitting area covered in even more plants.

I followed her down the narrow hall, passing two doors that I assumed to be a bathroom and closet. The hall ended at a bedroom that was surprisingly spacious.

I didn't know what to expect. I'd never been on a houseboat before, but her place was nicer than most apartments.

Maddie stumbled through the bedroom door and flopped face-down on the bed like a dead fish.

I thought she had fallen asleep and was prepared to call an Uber and make my escape when she rolled onto her back and smiled. "Luca?"

"Yeah?"

"You came to the funeral today."

"Yeah, I did."

"Why?"

I sighed and scrubbed my palm over the beard on my face. I needed to shave before I looked like a werewolf in a few hours. "I, uh, I dunno. Wish I did."

"You're in my house."

"Yeah. I brought you home from that bar."

"Why?"

I chuckled, "Because you had some fun, and I wanted to make sure you made it home in one piece."

Maddie smiled lazily. "You're making it hard to hate you." She let out an exhausted huff and added on, "You're wearing me down, Luca."

"That's the plan."

Maddie grabbed the hem of her tank top but, in her drunken state, it got twisted and stuck around her head. Her full tits and lacy black bra were on full display.

I swallowed hard, but couldn't be a gentleman and look away.

She whimpered, and that's when I realized she actually needed help.

I crossed the room and rested one knee on top of her bed. The mattress sank under my weight, and Maddie rolled toward me.

"Stay still," I muttered as I tried to free her from the twisted shirt.

Maddie was a mess.

*How was she so organized and rigid at work, but so reckless off the clock?*

If someone had told me that the drop-dead gorgeous blonde I met in the gym, the severely focused chef competing in *Pastry Throwdown,* and the girl who danced on top of bars was the same person, I'd say they were bat-shit crazy.

I pulled her shirt off her head and tossed it to the side.

Maddie looked up at me with those big gray eyes of hers, and I fucking melted. I hooked my fingers in the belt loops of her denim shorts and pulled them down her legs.

Her matching black thong came into view, and I knew I either had to cover it up or take it off. *Preferably by dragging it down her tanned thighs with my teeth.* There was no in between, and my self-control was waning.

"Are you gonna sleep with me, Luca DeRossi?" she yawned. Goosebumps flooded her skin, and all I wanted to do was massage them away.

I shook my head and pulled the covers back so she could get under them. "Not tonight." I tucked her in and added on, "But only because when I fuck you, you're not gonna be three seconds from falling asleep and it's gonna be damn memorable."

Maddie smiled listlessly. "Can't wait."

*Neither could I.*

Before I could say anything else, I heard the steady rhythm of her sleep-induced breathing.

I pawed around her kitchen and filled up a glass of water.

I was a little surprised that her kitchen was sparse. Takeout containers filled her fridge, and she had very few dishes and utensils. My apartment in New York and my condo in LA both had commercial-grade kitchens. Granted, I rarely used them, but still—they were there.

I carried the water back to her bedroom, stopping in the bathroom to grab some ibuprofen.

I was shocked to find a clawfoot tub squeezed in the small bathroom. Moonlight streamed in from a window above, and I could make out the many plants that made it look more like a jungle than a bathroom.

I left her provisions on the bedside table, plugged her phone into the charger, and locked the door behind me on the way out. Luckily, the ride I ordered was already waiting outside for me.

I needed to leave. I had barely been able to control myself. Another minute around Maddie and I would have been a goner.

## 13

### MADELINE

The pounding in my head had nothing to do with one of my bakers making croissants and everything to do with the massive hangover that made me waver between wanting to throw up and wanting to turn all the lights off.

Those two desires had nothing on the memory of Luca undressing me and saying that *when* he fucked me, it would be memorable.

Yesterday I drank more than I had in a long, long time. But even the fifty gallons of liquor and beer I downed hadn't erased the feeling of Luca's hands pulling my shorts off and tucking me into bed.

I yanked open the door to the walk-in freezer and stepped inside. The sub-zero air was a welcomed reprieve from all the thoughts that made me need to change my panties.

Luca hadn't shown his face at Revanche all day, and part of me wondered if he was avoiding me on purpose.

Maybe I had misremembered how last night went down.

I was trashed, but I was still pretty lucid—or at least I thought I was.

Having my new boss cart me home after a night of drinking should have embarrassed me. But honestly? It didn't even come close to some of the more humiliating things I had done.

It didn't even crack the top ten.

Maybe I should have tried a little harder to act like a professional in front of him, but how I acted off the clock wasn't his problem.

Work hard, play hard.

Besides—I already tried to quit once. If he wanted to keep me around, he'd just have to learn to deal with me.

Take me as I am or watch me as I go.

My team was gearing up for a slammed weekend of weddings and, of course, my sous chef, Rae, had a nasty stomach bug. My head baker was covering for her, getting our wholesale pastry orders baked and sorted. Still, it meant that I'd be handling wedding cakes and overseeing dessert production for dinner service all by myself.

I grabbed what I needed and hurried back into the kitchen, freezing in place when I got back to my work table. A red sports drink was sitting beside the turntable I was using to frost tiers of wedding cake.

My staff had become mind readers over the years, and they knew what the confusion on my face meant.

Javier gave me a grin and tipped his head toward the stairs. "Boss brought it down just a minute ago."

"Chef Christensen?"

Javier shook his head. "New owner—Chef DeRossi."

"Oh..." I raised my eyebrows and looked at the security cameras mounted in the corner.

Luca must have been keeping an eye on things from his

office. *Could something be both charming and incredibly creepy?* I didn't have a minute to spare, so I simply looked at the security camera and raised the bottle toward it in a grateful toast.

Hours passed and then more. Dinner service flew by, and I sang the praises of each one of my pastry cooks.

Perfectly crafted desserts flew out faster than I could blink without a single complaint. The centrifuge whirred happily as my chili-caramel cotton candy made its debut on the summer menu.

Things slowed as the dinner crowd thinned, but the dull ache in my lower back was a constant reminder of how much more I still had to do.

My team cleaned and scrubbed the kitchen to glistening perfection. When the dining room closed for the night, I sent them all upstairs to eat.

The clock was the deciding factor. I hated missing the family meal, but with my right hand at home, throwing up her guts, I couldn't waste any time.

I popped in my headphones, turned on a true crime podcast, took a swig of Gatorade, and kept working.

I lost track of how many times the hands on the clock on the wall went around in a circle.

My feet sang as I steadied myself on the stepladder and grabbed my hammer. Two hard taps and the central dowel rod in the wedding cake would be secure. That cake could get flipped on its side, and it wouldn't budge. *Not that Hannah Jane would ever let that happen.*

She ruled her weddings with an iron fist and a sweet as sugar smile.

Panicking brides? Handled.

Bitchy mothers? No big deal.

Drunken groomsmen who run into the cake table and

almost knock my masterpiece to the floor? Not on her watch.

I double-checked the work orders pinned to the cork board on the wall.

Three of the wedding cakes I was currently working on would be for events she was overseeing at the Taylor Creek Inn.

At least there was an upside.

Sure, I'd work myself to the bone, but Hannah Jane would send me home with a takeout box of catering from each wedding. At least I wouldn't have to cook at home for a few days.

Something touched my back, and I shrieked, flying into a full-blown conniption. I flailed and dropped the hammer on the table, falling backward off of the step stool.

Two strong hands grabbed my waist. Arms wrapped around and caught me as I flew toward the ground.

"What the fuck?!"

"Geez, sorry," Luca grunted as he caught me and held me against his body until I found my footing. "Didn't mean to scare you."

I clutched my chest and closed my eyes.

I probably needed Mel to run some tests to make sure Luca hadn't given me a heart attack, but I didn't have time for that.

I looked down to the spot I had accidentally dropped the hammer, and cursed when I saw a sugarpaste flower smashed to smithereens.

*At least I always made extra.*

I looked at the clock before turning around and facing Luca. He was in dress pants and a button-up. From the way his tie was loosened and his sleeves were mussed, I guessed he had been behind the line in his suit for the dinner rush.

"What are you doing here?"

"I think the better question is, what are *you* still doing here?" he said as he lifted a bag with the Revanche logo on it. "You missed the family meal. I wanted to make sure you ate."

I pointed at the four-tiered cake that was stacked and ready to be decorated. "Still working. Two weddings are going out tomorrow. Three more for Saturday. One on Sunday."

Luca raised his eyebrows, "On top of—"

"On top of restaurant service and wholesale."

"And Rae's still out sick?"

"Yeah, I told her that even if she was feeling up to it, I wanted her to stay out 'til Monday. I'd rather have one person out a few days than have the entire team get sick."

He looked around. "And everyone else is gone?"

"Rae and I are the only ones who make the wedding cakes. Javier helps bake the layers and make the butter-cream, but that's it."

Luca thought for a moment. He rolled the sleeves to his button up and cuffed them just above his elbows.

I allowed myself the pleasure of admiring the tattoos that covered his corded forearms. *Hello, arm porn.*

Walking over to the hooks on the wall, he grabbed a clean apron and put it on. "Alright, Chef Dorsey. Tell me what to do."

"No."

He looked at my production list. "You're not gonna go home until you're done, are you?"

"That's right."

"Then I'm at your disposal."

I sighed, resting my arm on my workspace and cocking

my hip. "And you won't leave me alone until I put you to work?"

"That's right," he said with a stupidly adorable lopsided grin.

*Hell yes,* my lady parts cheered.

I huffed and pointed to the industrial stand mixer that was perched in the corner of the kitchen. "Put the champagne buttercream that's in there into a Cambro, and wash the mixing bowl and paddle."

If Luca was put off by the menial task, he didn't show it. He grabbed a spatula off the tool shelf and went to work.

I kept an eye on him as I finished placing the sugar flowers on the cake and piped little buttercream details on each tier. When I finished, I slid my arms up under the thick board that supported the cake and carried it to the walk-in fridge.

Luca was already three steps ahead of me, opening the door and clearing space on the shelf.

"So, champagne buttercream—what do you pair it with?"

"Vanilla sponge, a champagne reduction, and some macerated strawberries I get from a local grower. It's one of our more popular flavors for weddings, and it's what we keep on hand for when guests have birthdays here. You know—the free little cake we do."

Luca set the tub of buttercream on my table. He reached into the bin of tasting spoons and took a small bite. "Italian buttercream?"

"Yep."

"I like it."

I swatted his hand away before he double dipped. "So do our guests. Leave some for them, will ya?"

Luca chuckled and tossed the plastic spoon in the trash.

For the next two hours, he took direction remarkably well. He got whatever I needed out of the walk-ins, dammed and filled cake layers, and did an acceptable job crumb coating a few cakes.

"What else, boss?" he asked when I rolled the a cart carrying a five-tiered giant into the walk-in refrigerator.

I followed him out of the fridge, wiping my hands on my apron before handing him a rag and a spray bottle of sanitizer. "If you have time to lean, you have time to clean," I quipped as I grabbed my clipboard off my work station. "I'm just gonna double-check my production list for tomorrow and then I'll be outta here."

His chest pressed against my back as he pinned me between his body and the table. His voice dropped to a husky whisper that made flashes of lightning zip down my spine.

"You're enjoying this aren't you?" he murmured in a tone that was filled with gravel and sex. "Being in control?"

My lips parted, and I let out a little sigh as I felt his twelve-hour beard scrape against the nape of my neck. "Something like that."

Luca leaned down and let his lips graze against the soft skin behind my ear. "Don't get used to it," he warned.

I closed my eyes as a shiver worked its way down into my toes. "What do you mean?"

His hands grabbed the edge of the table, arms closing in around me and caging me in. "This is your turf and I respect that. But when you're on my turf, I'm in charge."

My grip on the clipboard that carried my to-do list neared deadly. "Where's your turf?"

I couldn't see it, but I knew he was smiling. "My bed."

LUCA DISAPPEARED up the stairs while I did my walkthrough of the pastry kitchen. I made sure that everything was in its place for my morning bakers. It was late, and they would be here to work in just a few hours.

Finally, I trudged up the stairs. My knees throbbed in protest, my back ached, and my hands were sore after the long day.

I kicked off my clogs and shoved them in my locker outside the main kitchen, trading them for my sandals. I hung up my chef's coat, slammed the locker shut, and grabbed my bag.

I had just put my hand on the doorknob when I heard, "Hold up."

I looked over my shoulder and saw Luca with his suit jacket slung over his arm, locking up his office.

"Something else you need, Chef DeRossi?"

He chuckled. "Nah, I just don't want you walking out to your car by yourself."

"That's... Oddly nice," I admitted. "Thank you."

"Come on," he urged.

We walked out into the warm night—*morning*—air, and I waited under the dim exterior light for him to lock the door. Luca put his hand on my back and walked me to my Jeep.

I tossed my things in, but lingered in the moonlight rather than climbing in. "Thanks for giving me a hand."

"Anytime. It's what I'm here for."

I cocked my head. "The owner doesn't usually double as my gopher when my sous chef calls out. Especially when that owner is also the head of our new umbrella hospitality group *and* a hotshot celebrity chef."

Luca chuckled and shifted between his feet. "I should've said that I did it because I'm here for *you*."

A faint blush crept up my cheeks and I chewed on my lip, fighting off a smile. "I still don't like you."

Luca's smirk curved up into a half-baked grin. "I know. I'm working on that." He shifted closer. "Wanna give me a hint on how I'm doing?"

I just shook my head and slid into the driver's seat. Luca shut the door behind me, and I rolled down the window.

"Goodnight, Luca DeRossi."

He rested his muscled, tattooed forearms on the lowered window and leaned in. For a second, I thought he was going to kiss me.

But he didn't.

Luca's voice was soft. "Goodnight, Madeline Dorsey."

# 14

## LUCA

"I have you scheduled for a club opening next Friday in Vegas. You'll be staying in a suite at the Venetian that night, with a flight to New York the next morning. A few A-listers that have reservations at your restaurants over the weekend. It would be good PR for you to be there to schmooze them during their meals. You know, the works."

Astrid rattled off the schedule she had created for me, but her words blurred together as I stared blankly at the itinerary in front of me.

*I didn't want to do any of that.*

The club opening was a *quid pro quo* thing, so that I'd have a favor to cash in for the future if I needed to.

As for New York, I really hated kissing ass when famous guests dined at my restaurants, but it was always something Astrid insisted on. It had worked well for the last ten years, so I had never argued before.

"You know, I, uh, I think I'm just gonna hang out here," I said as I tapped my pen against the itinerary page and slid it back across the desk to her. "Make sure things are good."

Astrid huffed and snapped the paper off the desk, giving it a harsh glare. "You need to hire a GM so you can leave this town and go back to making money. Your investors—"

"My investors are happy that I bought Revanche. Because unlike most restaurants, this place isn't running on razor-thin margins and paying the employees shit. Everyone here makes a living wage. I just wanna make sure things don't get fucked up with the transition. Besides, the way things are looking, Scott and Maddie could get nominated for a James Beard Award this year, which would go a long way with making this place more of a destination than it already is."

"The draw is *you*, Luca," Astrid advised. "You need to keep being *you* in order to maintain interest in your restaurants." She handed me another sheet of paper.

"What's this?"

"A list of vetted candidates."

"For what?"

"For you to go on dates with."

I laughed in disbelief. "What are you? Match.com? I told you—I'm not going on random dates anymore. If I want to go out with a woman, I'm perfectly capable of finding someone willing," I said as I tossed the paper in the trash.

Her red lips turned into a thin line. She produced a file folder and handed it over. "I'm well aware."

I raised a curious eyebrow and opened it up. Out spilled photos of my date with Maddie in Los Angeles. I probably should have been more pissed than I was, but then I saw a photo of the two of us dancing under the string lights.

Maddie's eyes were light, and her smile was wide. Her head was thrown back as she laughed while I dipped her backward.

I steeled my expression, turning into the asshole judge I was well-versed in playing. "You had me followed?"

"No," she snapped. "I paid off the tabloids that were going to run the photos on the front page of every grocery store magazine in the country." Her pen stabbed the photo with a harsh snap. "This is t-r-o-u-b-l-e, Luca. Do not get involved with this girl."

"Why is it trouble?" I asked. "Maddie's a talented chef."

"She's your *employee*."

I leaned back in my chair and crossed my arms. "Who I date or do not date is not your concern." It may have been a little taboo, but Maddie and I could keep things professional. *If I could get her to stop hating me.*

"It is my concern when it impacts your public image, and thus, your bottom line."

"I'm the one who signs your checks, and I just told you it's not your concern," I said, sliding the folder of photos into my desk drawer. "End of discussion."

Astrid raised her chin and squared her shoulders. "How's the rental property working out?"

"Just fine. How long do I have in it?"

She huffed impatiently like she had better things to be doing. *She didn't.* "Another week. I expected you to turn this place over to management much faster than seems to be the case." Her tone told me she wasn't happy with that decision either.

I thought about the Taylor Creek Inn next door to the restaurant. The oceanfront house on Atlantic Beach that Astrid booked for me wasn't far, but the thought of being closer to Revanche and Maddie was appealing.

"See if you can extend the rental. If not, I'll make my own accommodations."

Her bright red nails clicked against her phone as she

made a note about the house. For a split second, her pointed fingernails looked like the talons of a vulture. *Fitting.*

Astrid looked back up, but before she could get the words out, Maddie stormed in.

"Are you a dumbass?" she shouted as she dropped an open container of what looked like buttercream on my desk. Bits of frosting flew out of the bucket and splattered all over my computer screen and Astrid's phone.

Astrid's face was painted in disgust and horror.

"Mad—"

She plucked a tasting spoon out of the pocket of her chef whites and threw it at me. "Eat it."

I shrugged and obliged her insanity, dipping the spoon into the smooth icing and sticking it into my mouth.

Good texture—light and silky, sweet with notes of champagne and—*oh, God.*

I yanked the small trash can out from under the desk and spat into it before I dry heaved.

I ripped open the door to the mini fridge that Rob Mullon had put in the office and grabbed a bottle of water. I twisted the top off and guzzled half of it down.

"*The fuck was that?!*" I gasped, thankful that the putrid taste was finally out of my mouth.

Maddie spun the bucket so that the label on the front that clearly read *PICKLED JALAPEÑOS ONLY* faced me. "Can you read, DeRossi?" she yelled. "You fucked up a whole fucking batch of *very expensive* champagne buttercream because you didn't read the fucking label on the bucket before you put the fucking buttercream in it last night!"

*Oh shit.*

It was my fault.

If a bin was used to store something aromatic like

peppers, onions, and garlic, it always had a label so that nothing else went in it. Anything else would pick up the latent flavor.

*Something like a very delicate champagne buttercream.*

Maddie was still ripping into me, calling me every name in the book for making such an amateur mistake, but it was all in one ear and out the other.

I looked over at Astrid, who sat pencil-straight in the chair across from me. She had her jet black hair cut in a severe bob that made her face sharp and pointed. She was put together in every way. Calculated and curated.

Then there was Maddie. *She was insane.*

Her mile-long pearl blonde hair piled on top of her head in a wild bun. Astrid was a waif, but Maddie had curves and long legs—muscles mixed with soft edges.

Astrid was cold. Maddie was sunshine.

She was warm and life-giving, but would burn you in a heartbeat if the opportunity arose. *And right now, she was roasting me with a fiery vengeance.*

"Maddie, I'm sorry. I should've checked the bin before I pulled it off the rack."

That response was enough to shock both ladies equally. For once, I felt good. I enjoyed being the nice guy. *Outside of the bedroom, at least.*

My public image was that of the unapologetic hard-ass who had a bone to pick with everyone.

I stood up from my desk chair and rolled up my sleeves, revealing my tattoos. "If you'll pull out the recipe, I'll go down and make another batch."

Maddie looked at me, dumbfounded. It shocked her that I could show remorse.

I was game for whatever would get me in her good graces. If it was apologies, I'd beg and grovel. Hell, I'd eat the whole damn bucket of that nasty ass icing if it meant she'd finally tell me what the problem between us was.

"It's been a while since I've made Italian buttercream, but I have made it before."

"Um... Javier's already working on a new batch," she stuttered.

"Well then," I said as I rounded the desk, picking up the bin of horrifying pickled jalapeño buttercream off my desk. "I'll go apologize to Javier for making his day harder." I gave Astrid a passing glance as I put my hand on the small of Maddie's back and led her out of the office. "Astrid, pleasure as always. Let me know about the house."

As soon as we were out of the office, Maddie caught my arm and pulled me into the storeroom.

Ducking behind a shelf of dry goods, she hissed, "What the hell are you doing?"

"Going to apologize like I said," I whispered back. "Why are we whispering?"

"No, I meant why are you putting your hands on me in the middle of a fucking workday with everybody around?"

"I'm sor—"

"Don't fucking apologize like you're gonna use it to get in my pants."

"That wasn't why I was apologizing, but I like that that's where you thought this was going."

"Not happening, Luca."

I may not have been the asshole she thought I was, but I sure as hell wasn't a doormat. "*Chef DeRossi,*" I countered. "Because if we're gonna do the professional boundaries thing, it goes both ways, Chef Dorsey."

I could see the conflict written across her face like a neon billboard. She wanted to hate me, but she didn't. She wanted to have professional boundaries, but she liked it when I flirted with her. The way her lips were just an inch away from mine and her breath was coming in quick beats told me she had just as good of a poker face as I did, but she was tired of wearing it.

My eyelids lowered to half-mast, and I stared at her pretty pink lips, preparing for the kiss. "So, what's it gonna be?" I asked quietly, sending tendrils of breath dancing across her cheek. "Luca or Chef DeRossi?"

Her tongue darted across her lower lip, making it shimmer. I could feel the electricity prickling at the back of my neck like the kind of buzz that lingers in the air during a summer thunderstorm.

I wanted to push her up against the industrial shelf, between the bins of dry goods and spices, and kiss her until her lips were swollen. But I waited. She was going to have to pick what she wanted. As much as I wanted to push my luck, I couldn't decide for her.

"Mad? You in here?" Scott's voice echoed through the storeroom and I silently cursed my luck. "Maddie, you alright?"

My grip on the bucket of frosting tightened, but I didn't move away from her. If Scott wanted to walk in on this, let him.

But the spell was already broken. Maddie grabbed the bucket out of my hand and pushed past me. "I'm good, I just had to have a few words with—"

I waited to hear what she would call me.

"I just had to talk to the boss about something." She didn't even look back.

## 15

# MADELINE

"How's she doing today?" I asked Linda as I signed in on the clipboard that was perched on the ledge of the reception desk.

Linda beamed behind her cat-eye glasses. The beehive hairdo that had seen better days bobbled back and forth as she reached forward to take the clipboard from me. "She's in good spirits today. Might be a positive visit for you this time."

That would be a one-eighty from the last time I visited my mother. I had stopped by when I got back from California to tell her I won *Pastry Throwdown,* but she didn't even know who I was.

It didn't matter. Mondays were the only day I regularly took off work. Regardless of good days or bad, I came to Harlowe Bay Assisted Living for a visit.

I pulled out the little paper bag from Queen's Coffee and handed it to Linda. "That's for you," I said with a chipper smile.

Linda peeked inside and then looked around to make sure no one else saw. "Madeline Dorsey, you keep bringing me these little bags of sin and I'll have to get one of those standin' desks." She eyed the chocolate croissant again and pulled off a little bite, popping it in her mouth. "Mmm—heaven in a pastry. You sure outdo yourself with these. When are you gonna open your own shop, hm?"

"Maybe someday." I said cheerily, giving Linda a little wave as I headed down the hall.

Everyone always asked me that. Truth be told, I had no interest in owning a business. All the stress of payroll and taxes and marketing? *Nope*. I just wanted to do what I loved and not worry about the overhead.

*And maybe I didn't actually hate being around Luca every day.*

I had avoided Luca like the plague the rest of the weekend. Whenever he imposed his presence in my kitchen, I caught his attention by saying, "hey", rather than using his name or Chef DeRossi.

When I confronted him in the storeroom, I hadn't expected him to turn the tables on me. I had wanted to kiss him so badly. I wanted to press my body against his and moan his name as he erased every reason I had to hate him from my memory.

*Luca.*

I pushed those thoughts aside and walked into my mom's room.

"Maddie Lee!" She smiled as she looked up from her knitting.

Her memory had faded to nearly nothing over the last year, but she still remembered how to knit. Scarves, hats, blankets—you name it.

On her good days, she would tell me she was sorry she didn't remember me the last time, and that she still made me something because eventually she'd remember me again and wanted to be ready.

Those times were getting fewer and farther between as the ugliness of dementia took her away from me, piece by piece.

"Hi, Momma," I said as I sat down beside her recliner and leaned over, giving her a tight hug.

"Sweet girl." She beamed through her frailty. "Come, sit a spell."

I pulled out another little takeout box and handed it over. "Brought you something."

With shaking hands, she took the box and opened it up. "You remembered."

"Of course—I'd never forget your favorite cookies."

It was one of the first things I'd learned to bake in pastry school—almond tuiles. I had brought a box of them home during my first Christmas break and mom had declared them to be her favorite cookies ever.

She loved the thin, crisp crunch and the mellow flavor of the toasted nuts. I didn't make them often enough, but I whipped up a batch late Sunday night instead of sitting down for the family meal with the rest of the staff.

And maybe it was so I could avoid Luca in the process.

Mom crunched on a cookie before closing the top and setting it on the little table where her basket of yarn was perched. "Tell me, Maddie Lee—have you gone to California yet?"

There it was. The painful reminder that she wasn't the same strong woman I'd grown up wanting to be.

She didn't know that I had already had this conversation with her.

With a smile plastered on, I untangled a skein of yarn. "Yeah, I did. I won the competition."

"Good girl! I knew you could do it, Maddie Lee. Now, tell me about the restaurant. Are you busy with the summer-timers yet?"

*Knit one, purl two. Knit one, purl two.*

Mom's knitting needles worked their way through the yarn as I unraveled it for her. We chatted casually for a while, talking about new desserts I was dreaming up for the fall menu, all the changes around town, and all the big names that would show up for the Big Rock Blue Marlin Tournament this season. Word had it that a couple retired professional basketball players were putting together a boat crew to compete this year.

"Now what about you, dear?" she asked. "Is there a fella in your heart yet?"

I giggled. "No, Momma. I'm not seeing anyone."

"Is anyone seeing you?" she countered.

"I just told you I'm not seeing anyone."

Momma shook her head the way she used to when I was too hyperactive to pay attention. "Just because you're not seeing him doesn't mean he's not seeing you. Keep your eyes open, dear." Before I could say anything else, she asked, "Say, how are Steve and Heather Pelham doing? Have they started trying to have kids yet? Those two in love like that—no reason to wait."

I stared down at the yarn in my hands. "Heather's, um—They're, um...." I blinked back the tears. "They're real good, Momma." The lie stung.

Mom smiled pleasantly, "That's good. That's good." She laid down her knitting needles and patted my hand. "Your time will come, Maddie Lee."

I shouldered my bag and waited for Linda to get back to her seat at reception.

Nurse Ratched—*though her name was actually Jackie—*

walked through the lobby with her nose so high she could probably get a cable signal. She gave my short denim shorts a haughty assessment and a humph of snooty disapproval.

Her attitude was the last thing I needed.

The last hour of my visit had been painful. Mom's good day slowly faded, and I watched her slip back into being a stranger.

Luckily, Linda plopped down in her chair before Jackie could give me her unwanted two cents.

She lifted the glasses that hung from a chain around her neck and tapped at her keyboard. "Alright, Miss Maddie. What can I do for you?"

"I just wanted to make sure that the payment I made for Mom's care went through."

Linda typed away on the computer keys. "You'd have to talk to someone from billing, but I don't see any flags on your mom's account, so I'd say you're good to go. Just keep an eye out—if there's an issue we'll give you a call."

"Yes, ma'am. Thanks, Ms. Linda." I hurried out before the grief could crash into me again. The warm sea breeze was a welcomed reprieve from the sterile smell of the memory care facility.

I had a few hours before poker night started. I contemplated heading into the restaurant, but Luca was there and I didn't want to face him.

Not yet, anyway.

If I saw him, I knew exactly what would happen. I'd say his name and there would be no going back.

His name would leave my lips and I'd let him strip me down and take me up against the wall of his office. Bent over the top of his desk. On top of the stainless-steel work tables in my kitchen. I'd kneel in front of him and suck him off while his hands yanked and pulled my hair, demanding everything I had to give.

*Luca.*

I hopped in my Jeep and navigated through Morehead City, heading over the bridge to Radio Island, then over one more to Beaufort.

I curved through Front Street, passing Queen's Coffee and the general store that also doubled as a laundromat.

The Taylor Creek Inn came into view and I spotted Hannah Jane outside, directing the staff from multiple rental companies as they picked up chairs, tents, and tables from the weekend of weddings.

I honked the horn and waved, almost giving into the urge to stop by Revanche to grab lunch, but Luca's sleek black BMW was parked in the lot.

Never mind.

That man never *not* worked, and it was infuriating.

That was *my* thing. I practically lived at the restaurant. Hell, my home kitchen was bare bones. I wasn't actually sure that owned a whisk.

I ate most of my meals at work. If there was room to set up a cot in the pastry kitchen, I'd probably sleep there too.

Now there he was—taking over my turf.

Luca said his turf was the bedroom, and the notion had adrenaline pumping through my veins.

I rounded the block, heading inland. Glancing down at my phone, I thought about calling my friend from my New York days, but what was I supposed to say? *Hey girl, sorry you got fired by this asshat after he bought out the restaurant you worked at, but he's super hot and ridiculously fuckable.*

Maybe I *was* loyal to a fault.

Gravel crunched under my tires as I pulled into the parking lot at Jokers. My stomach was growling, and if I didn't get some food in it in the next ten minutes, I'd go from irritable to unbearable.

"Hey, Mad," Bridget said as I plopped down onto a barstool. "Lunch?"

"Surprise me."

"Drink?"

"Better pace myself. Make it a Cuba Libre. Hold the rum."

Bridget snorted and slid me a glass of Coke. "Don't think you have to worry about pacing yourself with those."

I shrugged and ripped the paper off the straw and stuck it in the glass. "Eh, it's poker night. Weather's nice, the current's not crazy. We'll probably float the bar." I smiled sheepishly, "You know how I get."

She tossed her head back and laughed. "Oh, I know. Bummer I'm gonna miss it."

"What? Why?"

"Kyle's taking me out tonight. Said he got a reservation at this place in New Bern."

I wrinkled my nose. Sure, I was happy for Bridget, but poker nights were sacred.

The door flew open and Chase strolled in. "Well, well, well. If it isn't my two favorite ladies," he said, shooting a wink at Bridget.

She rested her arms on the bar top and leaned over, "What can I do for you, Detective Brannan?"

"Just water, darlin'."

I rolled my eyes. Anyone with a pulse could see that Chase was crazy for Bridget. Well, everyone except Bridget.

"You know, Chase. They have these things called bottles. You can store all kinds of things in them. Some people even put water in them so they don't have to stop at a *bar* in the middle of the day when they're thirsty."

Chase flipped me the bird and took the glass from Bridget. "Last time I checked, you were a professional chef who has access to not one but *three* kitchens, and yet you eat here. Wanna talk about that?"

My stomach growled just as Bridget slid my plate across the bar to me before disappearing to check on a few more customers.

I took a big bite of the chicken salad sandwich and mumbled, "I'm avoiding Luca."

"Seemed like you two were pretty cozy in here the other night."

I picked at the sandwich, pulling the raw tomato off and setting it aside. "I need some space."

"From him?"

"Yeah."

Chase flagged down Bridget and asked for two pieces of bread and some mayonnaise.

"Need me to have a word with him?" he asked when Bridget disappeared into the kitchen.

When she returned and handed Chase the bread and a bottle of Duke's, he slapped the mayonnaise on the bread, stole the tomato off my plate, and made himself a sandwich.

"I can pick up Steve on the way. He'd probably enjoy scaring the shit outta DeRossi."

I shook my head. "No. I just need some space from him. From the restaurant. He's never *not* there."

"Probably because he knows that's where you're gonna be."

"Probably because he just sank a big chunk of money into it and wants to make sure it's not gonna crash and burn now that Rob's gone."

"How much?"

"More zeros than you and I will ever see, that's for damn sure."

Chase just shrugged and busied himself with his tomato sandwich.

I dragged a French fry through some ketchup and popped it in my mouth.

Was Luca actually hanging around to oversee the restaurant?

When a hospitality group acquired a restaurant, it was pretty much unheard of for the CEO to be running the day-to-day of one little establishment. Luca owned restaurants ten times the size of Revanche in destination cities—not a sleepy fishing town in North Carolina.

So why was he still here?

My phone interrupted my thoughts. The number on the screen was from the main line at the restaurant. "Hello?"

"Mad, it's me," Luca began. "Sorry to bug you on your day off."

I nearly choked on the fry and frantically pawed for my Coke to wash it down. "Lu—um, hey."

His gruff chuckle sent a shiver down to my toes. Could the man make me orgasm with just his voice?

"You know, at some point we're gonna have to talk about this, Madeline."

*For the love of God, Luca. Stop talking before I have to change my panties.*

"What can I do for you, boss?"

"Looks like there's some time clock discrepancies with some of your bakers. I just need you to take a look and sign off on the time sheets before it goes to payroll this week."

Oh. He really did just call about work. *Why was I so disappointed?*

"Yeah, um... Yeah, I'll look at it first thing tomorrow."

"Thanks. I'll leave it on my desk and let you get back to your day."

"Okay."

"Oh, and Maddie?"

"Yeah?" I asked with bated breath.

"You sound really pretty today."

And then he hung up.

Damn him and his smooth talking, underwear incinerating, swoony voice. I was going to need a thorough tryst with my vibrator before I went into work tomorrow.

And he wasn't even dirty talking—he just said I *sounded* pretty. How the hell did a thirty second phone call have me teetering on the edge of shattering into a million little pieces?

"You okay, Mad?" Bridget asked. She and Chase were staring at me like I sprouted wings and a unicorn horn.

I looked back down at my phone. "Yeah, I'm good. Just fine."

Chase raised an eyebrow. "You sure?"

"Yeah."

"Need me to have words with DeRossi?"

I shook my head and balled up my napkin, tossing it on the empty plate. "Nah. I can handle it."

# 16

## LUCA

I dropped the phone receiver back into the cradle and tapped my pen on the stack of spreadsheets in front of me.

I couldn't wipe the stupid smile off my face even if I wanted to.

Maddie wouldn't be able to keep this up much longer. I heard it in the way she almost said my name, but stopped herself. The way her breath caught in her throat confirmed it.

*She wanted this just as badly as I did.*

Her willpower would eventually wear thin, and she'd let me in again. *I hoped.*

Something about Maddie had knocked me on my ass when she waltzed into that gym in Los Angeles, and I was still trying to find my footing.

She was a wrecking ball wrapped in a hurricane with a hefty side of kick-assery.

My phone buzzed on my desk and my heart leaped like a fucking child thinking that maybe it was Maddie. *Nope. Astrid.*

Fuck.

I pressed the phone to my ear and offered a gruff, "Yes?"

"Good news," she said, seemingly unperturbed by my tone. She was used to my no-nonsense approach.

The woman was colder than Brooklyn in January, but she was efficient. That went a long way in my book. I didn't need nice little platitudes and hand-holding. I needed someone who got shit done. Astrid fit the bill.

"You have the house for the rest of the summer."

My eyebrows shot up. That was a surprise. I figured the rental company would've had bookings stacked up all season long. It was a prime property. "Thanks for taking care of that."

"Don't thank me until you see the bill."

"That's a non-issue."

"I know. That's why I didn't run it by you first."

"Anything else?"

"That baking show you judged airs in two weeks. You're expected to promote it on your social media."

"Fucking hate those corny network captions," I grumbled.

"I'll send you the information. Just be the jackass America knows and loves to hate."

"Yes, ma'am."

"Uh—" Astrid paused.

*Shit. I'd been in North Carolina too long.*

"Yeah, I'm going to go now. This is weird. Enjoy the house." She hung up without another word.

I opened a drawer and pulled out the file folder that Astrid had waved in my face a few days ago.

Before I knew it, I had spread the photos out on the desk and was unzipping my pants.

*This had to be the last time.*

It was getting ridiculous how much I'd jacked off to the thought of Maddie.

*And then Astrid had given me photos of the two of us on our date.*

Those damn near microscopic shorts she wore. The tank top that gave me a glimpse of that lacy little bra that held up her luscious tits.

Thinking about the way she smiled—how she smelled a little bit like sugar and vanilla.

The way her perfect lips tasted. The quick breaths she sucked in when she was nervous—not that she let anyone notice.

I gripped my shaft like a vise and worked it up and down in a frenzy.

Her long legs appeared in my mind. *Those tan thighs that led up, up, up, to who knows what.* I worked my dick faster and faster. I remembered feeling her pussy nestled up against my cock while she straddled my waist when we made out.

*Fuck yes.*

I kicked the trash can under my desk, moving in front of me as I imagined her dancing on the bar top at that hole in the wall place after the funeral.

Watching her hips sway, thinking about what it would feel like to have those hips in my hands with nothing between us.

What it would feel like to have her waking up next to me, her ass pushed up against my cock. Reaching around to cup her breast. Pinning her down on the bed and spreading her knees wide, tasting her inside and out. Hauling her to the shower afterwards and getting dirty again before we got clean.

"Fuck, *Maddie*—" I grunted as long spurts of my release coated the trashcan.

For a moment I just sat there with my dick in my hand, staring at the photos of the two of us together.

The restaurant bustled just outside my door, and the noise brought me back to reality. I grabbed a handful of tissues and cleaned myself off before zipping my trousers back up.

I tied the trash bag shut and opened a new one to hide the evidence of my lack of self-control.

Fuck it.

I needed to figure out why the hell Maddie was intent on hating me, and I needed to do it fast.

Searching her social media occurred to me, but that would be like looking for a needle in a very hateful haystack.

To my surprise, after I made sure she got home safe from the bar, the mean comments stopped.

She still avoided me like the plague, but I could work with that. Maddie couldn't hide in her kitchen dungeon forever.

I'd give her a day off and then push a little harder.

Truth be told, I didn't need to call her about the time sheets. I could have just as well waited until tomorrow when she was here, but I wasn't going to give her a day without at least making her think about me.

About us.

Something clicked in my very horny brain. I pulled up my email and scrolled through my overflowing inbox until I saw the unread message from the general manager of my flagship restaurant in New York with Maddie's employment history attached.

My eyes scanned the page until I found the section that said "Reason for leaving."

*Bingo.* I grabbed my phone and fired off a text.

LUCA

Let's talk about New York.

Minutes that felt like days passed before Maddie ever responded. When she did, my heart sank.

MADDIE

Let's not.

LUCA

Why not? That's why you hate me, right?
Why you hate the idea of being with me.

MADDIE

Today's my day off. Unless the restaurant is burning to the ground, leave me alone.

LUCA

The restaurant is burning to the ground.

MADDIE

Call the fire department.

The woman was infuriating.

I was ready to torch the place if it meant she'd talk to me.

Maddie and I needed to clear the air before I ran out of liners for the damn trash can. Since I was apparently out of options, I pulled up the website for one of my favorite equipment suppliers and add-to-carted my way back into Maddie's good graces.

# 17

# MADELINE

I stared at the plume of flowers that sat on my kitchen counter.

"So, are you gonna put them in water?" Hannah Jane asked as she loaded my fridge with drinks that she brought over for poker night. "Or are you just gonna stare at them until they die a slow, painful death?"

"Is that what you're supposed to do when a man sends you flowers?" I deadpanned. "I usually just rip the blooms off and stab them into cakes. I've never been given flowers that weren't supposed to be decapitated before."

"Hardy-har-har." Hannah rolled her eyes and plucked the vase off the counter and set it in the sink. "You know, you're also supposed to call the sender and say thank you."

"I don't know who sent them," I lied. "Maybe I have a secret admirer who wants to stay secret. Very, *very* secret."

Hannah grabbed the card out of the pick and read it. "Is secret admirer spelled L-u-c-a? Because it says here that he's thinking about you, *Madeline*." She wiggled her eyebrows and pinned the card to my fridge.

"Here's something to think about." I smirked as I showed her my middle finger.

She snickered and topped off the vase with water before setting the flowers in the windowsill. "Babe. Luca's hot, he's rich, he understands the chef life, and he's totally into you! For the love of God, please explain to me why you're not doing the no pants dance with that gorgeous hunk of a man!"

"You don't know that he's gorgeous. He could be perfectly average for all you know."

"Mad, I'm not blind," she snorted. "I saw that photo he sent in the group text. Those are abs made for licking, honey."

Gravel crunched outside as a car pulled down Steve's driveway.

"You mind flagging the pizza guy down?" I asked Hannah, walking to my bedroom. "I just need to grab some cash for a tip. Tell him to wait a minute and I'll be out."

Getting deliveries to a houseboat could be tricky to say the least. If Steve wasn't home to direct them to the dock, someone had to stand outside and wave them down like a car dealership blow-up doll so they wouldn't turn around and leave.

I counted out a few bills and folded them over as I walked back down the hall.

When I made it back into the kitchen, Hannah was standing there holding grocery bags. "I thought you said you ordered pizza for tonight?"

"I did," I said, hearing the delivery car pull away.

Hannah hefted up the paper bags and set them on the kitchen counter. "Did you drunk order groceries again? You know, you're probably the only person who gets more responsible when you're tipsy."

"Bee can back me up. I haven't had anything more than a Coke at Jokers since the other night after the funeral."

"Then what's all this?"

"You know I'm not that fancy." I pointed to the store label on the bags.

The delivery wasn't from the Piggly Wiggly. They were from an organic grocery store in Morehead that I fawned over. It had been open for a few years, but I never went inside. I knew that if I did, I'd spend every last dime in my checking account on good wine, cheese, and chocolate.

I pawed through the bags until I found the order receipt. *Of fucking course.*

DELIVER TO: *Madeline Dorsey*

    **Message:** *Hope you liked the flowers. Your pantry looked like it was due for some reinforcements. -L*

DAMN THAT MAN. He could send me all the flowers in the world, and I wouldn't feel a thing, but food? Food was the way to my heart.

"Oh my God." Hannah squealed as she hovered over my shoulder and read the note. "He sent you groceries! That's so romantic!"

"That's not romantic! That's creepy as fuck! He went through my cabinets when I was passed out on my bed."

"*He bought you groceries!*" Hannah repeated as she unpacked the bags. "I'm telling you, Mad, this guy—he's the one."

I rolled my eyes and took the wedge of—*oh, sweet baby Jesus*—fontina cheese and popped it in the fridge.

Hannah handed me a few containers of salad mix that

would die a slow death, rotting away in the bottom of my crisper drawer, followed by some fresh cut fruit and a bottle of awfully expensive wine.

I held the bottle in my hands and let out a slow, shaky breath. Sure, we had a curated wine list at the restaurant that was way above my pay grade, but the bottle in my hand was at least two payments on my Jeep.

*Too bad I didn't have any wine glasses.*

I eyed the red plastic cups that were hanging out on top of my fridge and contemplated if putting expensive wine in a plastic cup was sacrilegious.

"Knock, knock." Chase strolled in before I could uncork the bottle. "Where's Bee?"

"New Bern," I said, setting the bottle on the counter. "She's out on a date with Kyle Kingsley."

"Oh," Chase muttered, looking just a little deflated by the news. He perked up when Steve and Melissa walked in.

Mel looked around. "Where's Kris?"

"She's running late," Hannah Jane chimed in. "Had to run home after work and fix dinner for everybody before she could come."

Steve wandered through the kitchen, snooping through the grocery bags. "Since when do you have actual food here that didn't come from the restaurant?"

"Since her boyfriend sent her flowers and groceries." Hannah giggled as she waved Luca's note from the grocery delivery.

"Really, Han?" I flipped her the bird again.

"The fuck is she talking about, Mad?" Steve asked as he stomped his way over to the counter and snatched the note out of Hannah's hand.

Mel placed her hand on Steve's arm. "Steve, it's Maddie we're talking about. She can handle it."

"Don't fucking like it," Chase seethed as he shook his head.

The pizza guy finally drove up. *Thank God.*

I needed a break from everyone else's opinions about my life. I grabbed the cash I had pulled out for the tip and went outside. I hopped up onto the dock and waved the delivery car down the driveway.

Pizzas in hand, I walked back down onto the deck and yelled, "Come and get it!"

The girls barreled on to the deck and grabbed the boxes out of my hand.

"Steve, do you mind putting the bar in the water?" I asked

He grunted something that kind of sounded agreeable as he picked up my swim-up tiki bar and lowered it into the water. It was more like a floating table with an umbrella, but it was still fun.

Melissa plugged in the string lights and lit up the deck while Hannah Jane unfolded the card table and circled up all the chairs.

I grabbed my phone and checked my messages.

"Waiting for a certain someone to call?" Steve asked as he righted himself and wiped his hands on his cargo shorts.

"No," I snapped. "I was just seeing if Kris was on her way."

"Sure you were," he mocked, securing the tethers that kept the bar from floating away.

"Fuck off, Pelham," I said, rolling my eyes.

Okay, so maybe I was checking to see if Luca had texted me.

Mondays weren't that busy at the restaurant, and I was more than a little curious what he was up to.

Still, I wasn't going to admit that to Steve. He was like a

brother to me. We had known each other for most of our lives. Maybe that's why Steve and I never had any sparks after knowing each other after all this time. I rarely talked about my fling of the week with him and, if I did, it was in the past tense.

"You into him?" he asked flatly.

"No."

"Bullshit," he said, studying my face. For the first time in a long time, Steve cracked a wry smile. "Looks like you're gonna lose tonight with that shitty poker face."

————

AND I DID. That's how I found myself standing on the roof of my houseboat while the rest of the crew was down below, screaming for me to jump.

"Do it, Mad!" Kristin yelled from the deck.

"Don't make me come up there and push you off," Chase shouted.

*As if.*

I'd jump on my own damn terms. Although, bringing Chase down with me would be fun.

"Don't threaten me with a good time!" I shouted back.

Melissa yawned, "Hurry up! It's late and I gotta work in the morning. You gonna stand up there all night? You know the drill! Loser jumps!"

"Yeah, yeah," I muttered. I stripped off my *Let's Go Girls* tank top and tossed it down to my adoring public. Headlights flashed down the driveway as I peeled off my shorts and threw them down.

I took a running start and cannonballed fifteen feet down into the bay. Everyone whooped and cheered as I surfaced and swam over to the ladder.

Hannah Jane offered me a hand and pulled me up. I adjusted my black bikini top and held my arms out enthusiastically. "Who wants a hug?"

The girls backed away, but Steve charged toward me, threw me over his shoulder, and tossed me back into the water.

Despite flailing and screaming like a banshee, I still managed to grab onto his shirt and pull him in with me. At least I had the sense to put on a swimsuit. Steve, on the other hand, was soaked.

When we climbed back up onto the deck, he peeled off his shirt and wrung it out.

"Damn," I said, noticing his lean stomach. Even with our completely platonic relationship, I could admit that Steve had always been attractive. The muscles were a return to form.

The resurgence of cancer treatments for Heather meant that he had put himself—and working out—on the back burner so that he could give her all of his time and attention.

"So that's what you've been doing in your garage at midnight when I get back from work."

Steve shrugged and slung his shirt over his shoulder. "Mel, you need a ride home?"

Melissa giggled. "That'd be much appreciated, Detective Pelham. I may have had a *little* too much to drink."

"I can see that. Give me a sec to change," Steve said as he headed back toward his house.

"Han, you riding with me?" Chase asked, fumbling around for his keys. He and Hannah Jane lived close to each other, so they alternated being each other's designated driver.

"Kris, you wanna stick around and play another hand?" I asked.

She yawned and shook her head. "I gotta get going. I probably shouldn't have stayed out this late anyway."

Steve jogged back down the dock in dry clothes and stood at the edge of the deck of my houseboat. "Kris, you want me to take you home too? It's not too far from Mel's place."

Mel glanced down at her feet and awkwardly shifted back and forth.

Kristin shook her head, "Nah, it's okay. I've got my car and I barely had one drink."

"You sure?"

Kristin nodded, "I'm good. Thanks, though."

Melissa seemed to lighten up with that. Steve reached out and took Mel's hand, helping her up onto the dock. "See y'all around."

"Bye, guys," Mel called out as they walked to his Challenger.

Everyone else helped clean up before loading into cars and heading their separate ways.

Everything was quiet.

Crickets chirped and frogs sang a lullaby. The air was warm and soothing, and the breeze that blew off the Sound was calming.

I padded through my house, flipping off lights and making sure the place was tidy.

Usually after poker nights, I was beat. I had an early morning but, for some reason, I was wired.

I pawed through my fridge to take a closer look at what Luca had presumptuously ordered for me.

With a bottle of wine, a corkscrew, and white truffle

popcorn in hand, I walked outside to the deck, plopped down in a deck chair, and began scrolling through Netflix for a new episode of something serial killer related to wind down with.

I stabbed the corkscrew into the cork, gave it a sharp twist, and yanked it out.

"Tell me you weren't about to drink that straight from the bottle."

I whipped my head around to find Luca walking down the dock. He was dressed in gym shorts that hugged his very fine ass, a t-shirt, and his Yankees snapback.

"Well, well, well," I finally said after giving myself plenty of time for my silence to have a dramatic effect.

*So, I was a little petty. Sue me.*

"If it isn't *Hot Guy from the Gym in LA*," I said as I rolled my eyes and stared at the wine bottle that was inches away from my lips.

Yes, I was going to drink it straight from the bottle because I, a professional chef and grown adult, didn't own a set of wine glasses.

"I'm begging you, Mad—please don't desecrate that beautiful vintage."

"What are you doing here?" I asked, ignoring his comment.

"Rae told me you're the one who hosted your, uh, poker nights. Figured since I couldn't get these put on the grocery order that I'd bring them by myself," he said, standing on the edge of the dock and holding up a paper bag.

I raised an eyebrow, but didn't say anything.

"Permission to come aboard?"

"And if I say no?"

Luca cracked a grin. "Then I'll just sit on the dock and talk at you until your neighbor kicks me off his property."

"Steve isn't your biggest fan. You're lucky he's not here at the moment." I waved him over. "Might as well show me what's in the bag."

Luca hopped over the lip of the pontoon and landed on the deck with ease. "Trust me, you'll like it." He set the bag down and pulled out three objects wrapped in packing paper. One by one, he unwrapped the glasses—setting them on the little table that was squished between my deck chair and loveseat.

My lips tightened as I tried my best to hide a smile. "Wine glasses and a decanter."

He grinned and sat down in the loveseat. "Looks like I was just in time too."

"I almost poured it in a plastic cup."

He gave me a dramatic grimace and held his hand out for the bottle.

"Fine." I huffed sarcastically and reluctantly handed it over.

While he poured the wine into the decanter, I picked up one of the empty glasses and inspected it.

Clean lines. A beautiful stem. A deep bowl that narrowed into an angled lip. Modern and elegant.

Not only would the glass add to the experience, reducing the bitterness and creating a smoother flavor, it was aesthetically pleasing.

"Nice choice," I admitted.

Luca set the decanter aside and took the other glass in his hand. "You know, most people just see a glass."

"Not us."

He smiled. "Not us."

"It's forks for me," I confessed. "Whenever I go out somewhere other than Revanche, I get really excited about a nice fork. Good weight, clean lines. Prongs that are spaced, but not too much."

Luca stared at me for a moment without saying anything.

"What?"

He shrugged. "I think that's the first time since California that you've let me see you."

"You see me all the time."

Luca shook his head. "Not like this." He took the decanter and expertly poured a glass, handing it to me before pouring one for himself.

I took a sip, letting the flavor linger on my tongue. "Wow," I said after the first sip. "That's a really good bottle."

"It should be," he quipped. His chuckle was low and raspy. It sent shivers across my skin, and I realized that I was still in my bikini.

I set my glass aside and stood up, "I'll be right back."

"Don't tell me that having a glass of wine with me is making you wanna jump off the roof again."

A deep blush painted my cheeks. "You saw that?"

He shrugged, "I came from the restaurant. Your friends were still here. Didn't wanna interrupt."

I stalled for a minute, but finally gathered my wits and pointed to the screen door that led deeper into my house. "I'm just gonna throw on some dry clothes..."

He nodded and I hurried into my bedroom, slamming the door behind me. I leaned against the door and let out a shaky breath.

It wasn't happening. I couldn't let it happen.

Just being in his presence had me teetering on the brink of either climbing him like a tree or choking the life out of him.

I stripped off my soggy swimsuit and threw on some dry clothes. Sensible underwear and a sports bra with a hole that I should have retired many years ago.

I was going for a look that did not scream, "Please fuck me until I see stars."

I jumped into a pair of yoga pants and a shirt from a Chris Stapleton concert that I'd turned into a crop top.

I contemplated locking the door and hiding until he got bored and left, but that would make me a coward.

That was something that I sure as hell was not.

Steeling myself, I made my way back outside and glanced at Steve's house. He still wasn't back from Melissa's.

"If you're gonna make a run for it, you might want a pair of shoes."

"Just seeing if Steve was back," I said, turning my attention back to Luca. He was stretched out on my loveseat and looked relaxed.

"How's he doing?" he asked.

"What?"

Luca set his half-empty glass on the table and leaned forward, resting his elbows on his knees. "He lost his wife."

I let out a shaky breath. "Yeah."

"And you lost a friend."

I nodded.

*God, what was it about him that had me falling apart all the damn time?*

I wasn't like this around anyone else—not even my girlfriends.

"Yeah," I croaked.

Luca patted the empty spot on the loveseat, and I hesitated.

His playboy smirk faded into a kind smile. "I'm not here to push you, Maddie."

"Then why are you here? The flowers... the groceries... the wine..."

He leaned back against the loveseat and draped his arms

across the length of it. "If I wanted to seduce you, trust me—you'd know it."

"This isn't you seducing me?"

"No."

*Why did I hate that answer so much?*

I waved my hand toward the wine. "Then what is all this?"

"This is me getting to know you."

"But not seducing me?" I clarified.

He held his hands up defensively. "I come in peace."

I grabbed my wine glass and, against my better judgment, sat down beside him. "I don't know how much I believe you."

"What if I told you that I do have plans to seduce you, but this is not part of it and you can just relax. For now."

That did ease a little of the tension in my shoulders. I took a small sip of wine and felt the stress begin to melt away.

*Luca.* I had said his name so many times before, but this time I knew it would be different.

He had given me the choice: *Luca* or *Chef DeRossi.*

I wanted to argue, but even I knew there would never be an in between.

"Maddie, we need to talk about New York."

That was a conversation for tequila and I was fresh out. "It doesn't matter anymore," I said while I stared at my reflection in the wine.

"It does matter," he argued. "Because I plan on making you fall for me, and it'll be a hell of a lot easier if you don't hate me."

I sighed and sulked back into the corner of the loveseat, pulling my feet up underneath me. A gust of wind blew off the water and it made me shiver. Luca instinctively reached to wrap an arm around me, but he recoiled at the last minute.

"The show will be airing soon," I muttered into my wine. "Next week?"

Luca nodded. "Yeah." There was something sad about his smile. "I've gotta turn on the asshole thing for a couple days and do a little press."

"You don't seem happy about that."

Luca draped his arm across the back of the loveseat and let his fingers graze the top of my shoulder. "I know I was hard on you, but it's because I think you're exceptional." He took a sip of wine and added, "Seeing you here at the restaurant—you're more talented than even that competition let on."

I never took compliments well, so I just finished off my glass, letting the slow, creeping comfort of the alcohol dull my senses.

"How's it feel to know you won?"

"Relieved," I admitted all too quickly. I cursed the wine and immediately regretted letting my guard down.

"Why?"

I shrugged, "Fifty thousand goes a long way."

Luca was quiet. For him, that was chump change. For me, it was everything.

He looked up at the string lights on the houseboat, "You, uh, thinking of upgrading? Maybe moving somewhere that has a foundation?"

I pointed a finger back at him, "Don't hate. She's a great little house."

"She?"

"Boats are always named after women."

"So, what's her name?"

"The *Martha Ann.*"

"Why'd you name her that?"

I reached for the decanter and poured another glass of wine. "After my mom."

"Are you two close?" he asked. "I remember in California you told me your dad isn't around anymore."

I shrugged. "We used to be."

"But not anymore?" he prodded.

I just sipped my wine until Luca finally realized that we had reached the end of the conversation.

He looked at me intently. His brows furrowed together, creating a deep crease above his nose. "Maddie, why are you here?"

# 18

## LUCA

"Maddie, why are you here?"

None of it made sense.

Why was she working in a nowhere coastal town when she could have been earning Michelin stars and industry awards left and right?

Sure, Revanche was a great little restaurant, but she was cut out for bigger things.

"What happened that made you leave New York?"

She was quiet and it made me wonder if I had pushed too far.

"My mom was diagnosed with early-onset dementia," she said with an unnatural softness.

*Shit.* "I'm sorry. I didn't know."

She shook her head, dismissing it. "It's fine."

"So, you came back to be with her?"

Maddie nodded and let out a trembling breath.

She looked so fucking cute in her sweatpants and ratty, faded t-shirt. I liked how casual she looked with her hair tied up in a massive bun.

It made me want to drag her into my arms and hold her until the pain went away.

"It wasn't so bad at the beginning, but it's gotten worse over the years. I left New York and moved back so I could live with her and take care of her. With me working all the time and her condition getting worse, I had to make the decision for her to live in a facility that could care for her around the clock. So, I sold her house, moved onto a houseboat, and used the money to cover her care."

I couldn't imagine doing that alone. Sure, my sisters could be overbearing, loud, and obnoxious, but I wouldn't trade them for the world.

I trailed my fingers along the back of her shoulder, rubbing gentle circles. "Do you ever think about leaving Revanche?"

"I used to," she confessed. "I used to think I'd go back to New York or Vegas or Los Angeles. Maybe do a year or two in France."

"Not anymore?"

She shook her head. "My life is here, and I'm fine with that. I missed it when I was gone."

I half believed her. She ran the shit out of the restaurant and had a pack of friends that stuck together.

Whether I wanted to admit it or not, the Carolina coast was growing on me. It had its own kind of charm, and I could see the appeal of living here full time.

Still, I couldn't help but feel like there was something else.

"Did we ever meet? You know—when you worked at my restaurant."

Maddie giggled, and I watched the light return to her eyes. "You know that makes you sound like such a dick, right?"

"I'm just trying to figure out what happened between us."

"Who said it has anything to do with us?"

"Doesn't it?"

Maddie shook her head. "No, we never met."

Deciding to take a chance, I set my nearly empty glass down and reached over, covering her hand with mine. "Then just tell me what the hell I did so that I can make it right."

She chewed on her lip, pulling that plump lower pout between her teeth like she was nervous to bring it up.

"Madeline," I soothed. "I can take it. I can take you hating me as long as I know what I did to deserve it."

She fingered the ends of her hair, twisting them nervously. "Your first acquisition was a restaurant in Brooklyn. Three months later, you brought in a GM who fired the chefs, kept all the line cooks, and brought in new executive chefs and pastry chefs to run everything. So many of my friends lost their jobs because of you. Because you couldn't leave well enough alone. You came in and turned a neighborhood joint into a high dollar restaurant when the market for that kind of thing just wasn't there yet. You pulled the rug out from under everyone. Six months after everyone lost their jobs, the restaurant went bankrupt. It would have been fine without you."

*Damn. That stung.*

The corner of her lip trembled and she took a deep breath to keep it in check. "I don't know if I'm just biding my time here. I feel like I'm just waiting for the other shoe to drop, and it'll be me who's out of a job and out of a home."

"Mad, even if something happened, you'd never lose your—"

She shook her head. "I don't mean my houseboat and

you know it. I'd lose my home. Revanche is my home. The staff is my family. I don't want to work anywhere else."

"Maddie, you realize that you could work anywhere you want to, right?" I asked, tabling Brooklyn restaurant issue for the time being. "Do you know how many emails I've gotten from other restaurateurs asking if you'd do dessert pop-ups all across the country? Hell, you could work anywhere in the world."

"I can't do this," she whispered as she got up from the loveseat.

I shot up to my feet and grabbed her arms. "Madeline, listen to me. You can go anywhere in the world and yet you're here and I have to know why."

"I can't do this. Not with you."

"Why not?"

"Because I look at you and know that you could crush me!" she shouted. "You hold everything that's important to me in the palm of your hand and I can't trust you to not take it all away!"

I slid my hands from her arms to her waist, anchoring her to the deck. "Why does it sound like you're not just talking about the restaurant?"

Maddie looked like she was going to say I was wrong—that she didn't have feelings for me.

To my surprise, she just looked up at the sky and shook her head. "Because I'm not just talking about the restaurant." She turned toward me, with her gray eyes locked on mine, and I felt the force of a hurricane behind them. "Because you have a good poker face and I don't know which side of you to trust—Luke, the guy I met in LA, or Chef DeRossi, my boss."

"I'm sorry about Brooklyn. About your friends," I said. "I made a bad call. I put the wrong person in charge. There were other financial issues with the restaurant that I wasn't aware of before we bought it. I regret what happened, and trust me—I fucking learned from it. Why do you think I'm sticking around here for so long?"

Maddie looked down at her bare feet. "But eventually you'll leave."

"That's how this works."

She nodded and backed away from me. And, like an idiot, I let her.

"Of course you will," she said placidly. "Everybody does." Maddie picked up the empty wine glasses and decanter and walked to the door that led deeper into the houseboat. "I'll see you at work."

———

THE RESTAURANT WAS in a frenzy and, for once, it wasn't because of a slammed dinner service.

I made the call to close early and host a watch party when *Pastry Throwdown* aired. After I showed up at her house last week, Maddie went from having a chilly disposition to avoiding me altogether. Still, when I sent her an email—because that's the only damn way I got her to talk to me—about inviting her friends to join the staff for the party, she was surprisingly agreeable.

Scott and the front line had whipped up a family meal fit for James Beard himself, and Maddie's bakers had recreated her competition desserts for everyone to try.

"Alright, alright," I said as I stood up in front of the crowd while Carol set up the projector. I held up my glass of whiskey and began my toast. "We all know why we're here tonight—to celebrate Chef Dorsey and her badass skills. But

I just wanted to say a few words to all of you before the show starts."

I cleared my throat. "It's been a great month with you all. I know it's been a bit of a shift in management now that the restaurant is under DeRossi Hospitality. But I can't help but be thankful that Mr. Mullon created such a fine establishment. I'm especially grateful for your executive chefs, Scott and Maddie."

I made a point to look straight at her. She couldn't escape me—not tonight.

Someone had given Maddie a sparkly tiara and a sash that read *World's Best Pastry Chef*. And damn if it didn't make her look fucking adorable.

She threw her arms up and wiggled in her chair as her adoring public applauded her.

"So, let's raise a glass to Maddie and get ready to watch her kick some ass on national television."

Maddie sipped her champagne with a humble quietness while everyone got up to clear their dishes.

Javier and Rae began passing out bowls of popcorn as someone jumped up and dimmed the lights.

Everyone cheered when Maddie appeared on screen. She was all dressed up in crisp competition chef whites with her arms crossed, mean mugging the camera in the cutest way.

Her long hair was wavy and ethereal. She was an angel and a mermaid and a unicorn, with a little sprinkling of Satan in there too.

Madeline Dorsey was one of a kind.

She stood straight as a statue in line of competitors as the annoying-ass host introduced the judges. The camera panned from Jenna Lachlan on the far right, then to Winston Nacey on the left.

Finally, it zoomed in on me in the middle. I was scowling, looking as unpleasant as possible.

Astrid would be thrilled.

I peered out of the corner of my eye at Maddie. She looked uncomfortable as she watched herself on screen. Everyone else was enraptured with the competition, but she just stared into her champagne, not even bothering to drink it.

The show went on. When she stood for judging after the first round, I laid into her.

*You took the easy way out.*

*It was just fine, Madeline.*

*I expected more from you.*

The staff booed and threw popcorn at the screen every time I was an ass.

*There was a lot of popcorn to clean up.*

The first round ended with Charissa Miles being sent home.

Maddie took an easy ingredient and used it in complex and versatile ways, but Charissa really did take the easy way out. She did the bare minimum, relying on flawlessly execution, rather than using even an ounce of ingenuity.

For round two, Maddie, Jeff, and Patty had been given a speed challenge: craft a dish in just thirty minutes that reminded them of someone special.

I watched as Maddie moved at a lightning speed, darting around the kitchen to get it done.

The show cut to a shot of her sitting behind a branded backdrop.

"My round two dish is inspired by my mom. One of the first times I drove home to visit her after I started pastry school, I brought her almond tuiles that I made in a lab class. To this day, they're still her favorite cookie. I chose to pair it with hazelnut gelato and a warm pear compote. Growing up, we had a pear tree in our front yard. It reminds me of simpler times."

The lump in my throat threatened to choke me when she talked about her mom. The chef on the screen was poised and professional. The woman I'd had wine with last week was vulnerable and raw.

She wanted to give me hell for my poker face, but I wondered just how much her friends really knew her— really knew what she was capable of. I wondered if they saw just how amazing she was.

The competition moved into round three, and it was down to Maddie and Patty. The old lady was a damn good baker. I'd give her that. Unfortunately, her competition was Maddie and that meant she didn't stand a chance.

I remember the third round more than anything else because I got to enter her universe and watch her create pure magic.

I watched myself linger at her station, asking her about her interpretation of the challenge concept of opposites.

Maddie's mouth curved up in a subtle smile when she said, "Heaven and hell."

I baited her a little more, trying—for my own curiosity's sake—to see if I could rattle her. But nothing did. She had nerves of steel and the confidence of a runway model.

The final product was nothing short of immaculate. Four tiers of luscious angel food and devil's food cake were composed in alternating layers with white chocolate ganache and blackberry gelée sandwiched between the sponge.

Midnight black mirror glaze coated one side of the cake, while the other was stark white. Everything was executed with the precision of an architect.

I had heard Maddie complain enough over the last month to know that square cakes were ten times harder to ice and construct than rounds.

Maddie's corners and edges were tight and flawless. Her buttercream work was spotless—not a seam or crevice in sight.

*Compete what you practice.* In my early days, it's what my mentors had drilled into me.

Sure, I wasn't competing on television like Maddie, but when the dinner rush started, it was an Olympic marathon.

At twenty-nine, Maddie had the finesse of a much older chef. Even my thirty-six years made me feel inadequate compared to her.

I stole a glance at Maddie as she watched the screen. It cut to the final judging session, and her attention was glued to the show.

I realized that Maddie didn't know what was said between the judges during deliberation while she was off set.

"Madeline Dorsey. Hands down," I watched myself say.

Winston leaned back in his chair and crossed one thick arm over the other, "She's talented, yes, but Patty did much more than Madeline did."

Jenna came to Maddie's defense. "In every other round, Madeline came up with fresh ideas and perfect plating. I had no complaints with any of her dishes the entire time. Patty is great, but she lacks the level of polish and expertise that Maddie has."

I rolled my eyes and waved off Winston dismissively. "Her technique far surpasses anything Patty could put out even on her best day. There's only one competitor here that I would ever work for, and to me, that's the mark of a true chef," I barked.

As I watched myself fight for Maddie's victory just as hard as she had competed, I remembered how hard it had been to keep myself from being biased.

I looked over and saw Maddie watching the drama unfold with her lip trapped between her teeth.

The host brought the two competitors back out, and Maddie was crowned the winner.

The dining room was pure pandemonium. Every person in the restaurant went bananas. Confetti popped, popcorn flew in the air, and Maddie was practically crowd surfing on her friend Chase's shoulders as everyone celebrated her victory.

"Mad, you're coming to Jokers for the afterparty, right?" Hannah Jane asked.

Maddie gave her a quick hug and waved off a few of their friends. "Maybe for a minute. I've got an early morning and I need to wrap up a few things here before I go."

The staff stuck around to clean up the mess and reset the dining room for tomorrow's lunch service. As employees began to filter out, Maddie slipped into the main kitchen and then down the stairs.

When the last person left, I shut the lights off one by one. Staring at her on screen for the last two hours had me on edge. It made me remember what had happened between us just hours before the competition started.

*Dancing with her under the lights. Her straddling my hips as I tasted her lips and devoured her whole. Knowing just how good it felt to have her in my hands.*

Now, I had seen her in action—running the pastry kitchen with ruthless efficiency, demanding excellence from herself and everyone around her.

There was something so irresistible about her talent. It was mind blowing and sexy.

No matter how much I tried to get her out of my system, I couldn't shake her.

I didn't want to.

I crept down the stairs and found her bent over a stainless steel worktable, double checking the next day's truck order.

She rested on her forearms with the clipboard in front of her. Maddie's back was arched and her ass was pushed out.

She had let her hair down. It draped around her like angels' wings. Her breasts hung heavy, just above the surface of the table. I could see them down the collar of her jacket.

I gripped the handrail, using the last vestiges of self control I had not to launch myself at her.

Clearing my throat so as not to startle her, I managed to choke out, "Congratulations, Madeline."

She looked up from her spreadsheets, her mouth forming a perfect "O". Her eyebrows raised and she sucked in a sharp breath.

For a moment, all was quiet. Neither of us moved. Electricity buzzed in the air like a brewing storm. My eyes tracked the rise and fall of her chest.

Her lips parted, and she let out a weighty breath, carrying my name on the exhale. "*Luca.*"

# 19

# MADELINE

"L*uca*—"

It was barely audible, but it was enough.

He rushed in, swiped his arm over the table, shoving my clipboard to the ground with a clatter. He grabbed my hips and turned me with enough force that it made my head spin. My ass pressed against the edge. Luca pinned me against the work table and his lips crashed onto mine.

This was nothing like our kisses in Los Angeles.

This was needy and dark. It was cruel and punishing. Luca was taking control, and I had never felt so alive.

It was better than the rush I got from jumping off my roof into the water below. It was better than the feeling when I was three sheets to the wind, dancing my heart out at Jokers. He tasted like top shelf whiskey and bad decisions.

Good thing I was a glutton for punishment.

"Madeline," Luca growled.

His hands skated up my sides to cradle my face. Touching my body was a momentary distraction; he quickly redirected his attention to my mouth.

Luca held my head in place with his big hands. He kept my body still with his hips pressed against mine. The hard length of his massive erection rocked between us. He moaned with every movement.

His tongue pushed against my lips and finally slid up against mine.

*I missed this.*

We moved with such synchronicity and ease. The rich musk of his cologne had me begging for more.

I slid my hands up his suit jacket and fisted the crisp dress shirt he wore underneath. *Wrinkles be damned.*

I pulled away and began undoing his tie. "Luca," I whined, pleading his name.

I wanted this. I wanted him more than I had ever wanted anyone.

His brown eyes turned black. Luca clenched his hands into fists and pounded them against the steel table. It echoed like a gunshot, and I froze.

"Do you want me?" he barked.

"Yes."

He softened. "Are you sure, Madeline?"

I nodded, my eyes never leaving his.

Luca shook his head. He raised his hand and trapped my chin between his thumb and index finger. "Say it."

"Yes. I—I want you."

"Say it," he growled again, caging me against the table.

My breasts were pressed against his chest as he towered over me. He was intimidating and domineering.

*And I loved it.*

"I want you, *Luca.*"

Whatever self-restraint he had been holding onto snapped.

One hand snaked up my back and grabbed my hair,

yanking my head back. The other started undoing the buttons on my chef's coat with surprising ease.

Luca's mouth began working a path from my lips to my jaw. His heavy stubble scraped against my skin, sending shockwaves straight to my core. He pushed my chef whites off, letting them drop to the floor, before grabbing the bottom of my AC/DC t-shirt and yanking it over my head.

"Fucking hell, Mad—"

He groaned as he stared at my breasts like a kid in a damn candy store.

"You're a fucking angel, beautiful." With a surprising gentleness, he unhooked my bra and let it fall away. "Shoes off," he commanded.

I kicked off my work clogs and he grabbed the waistband of my black pants, shoving them down. I worked them off my ankles while Luca kissed the valley of my breasts, down the line of my abs, to my hip bone. He bent down in front of me, wrapped his arms around my thighs, and lifted me to sit on the table.

"I can't tell you how many things I want to do to this perfect body of yours," he rasped as he slid his hands up my legs. "But this is where I'm gonna start."

I didn't even have time to comprehend what the hell he was saying before his hands were spreading my thighs.

"Oh God, Luca," I whimpered as he dragged the thin strip of fabric in the middle of my panties aside. Cool air rushed up against my skin and I shivered.

With one hand, he twisted my hair around his fist and tugged my head back. He leaned close to my ear—close enough that his rough jaw brushed my lobe with every dirty promise he made.

"What am I gonna find when I shove my fingers into your tight little pussy, Madeline?" he murmured.

Luca's gravely timbre damn near took my breath away.

"Are you wet for me?"

I could feel the curl of his wicked smirk on my ear. I whimpered in response, but it wasn't good enough for him.

He gave my hair a warning tug. "Answer me," he demanded.

"Yes," I whispered through labored breaths.

Luca teased my slit with a feather-light touch. "Dirty girl."

He chuckled before planting a searing kiss on my lips.

Luca was warm and good, but dangerous in the same. He was safe, but vicious.

One finger slid into my slick core, then two.

I gasped and threw my head back.

He withdrew his fingers before driving them back in again. "Remember what I told you, Madeline?"

"W-what?"

How the hell was he expecting me to play twenty questions when he was doing unspeakable things to my body?

I felt him curl his fingers as he stroked my G-spot, and I cried out in ecstasy.

Usually I had to draw the guy a fucking map. Not Luca.

"Remember that I said I'd respect you on your turf?" he asked.

I probably responded, but it wouldn't have been admissible in court.

Something about duress and not being coherent enough to speak when the man was intent on giving me a fifteen minute orgasm.

Not when he used his other hand to palm my breast and roll my nipple between his fingers.

"I told you that when you're on my turf, *I'm in charge.*"

It was a reminder laced with a threat, triple dipped in dark promises.

"This is my turf, Madeline," he grunted, surging his fingers deeper and deeper in a steady rhythm. "Mine."

I nearly buckled over when he leaned down and captured one pert nipple in his mouth, sucking and nipping until I had tunnel vision. He wrapped a strong arm around me and held me up. Held me close.

"Luca—" I mewled, "I-I'm gonna—"

And then the earth shattered. The stars rained down, and the sky fell.

"Oh my God," I whispered as I collapsed in his arms.

With a practiced efficiency, Luca pulled a condom out of his wallet and tore the foil open with his teeth.

He unzipped his trousers and freed the erection that was as big as a fucking rolling pin and rolled the condom on.

I'd been with well-endowed men before, but nothing—and I mean *nothing*—could have prepared me for Luca DeRossi.

The table was too high for me to sit on, and the fact that we were two grown ass adults meant we couldn't lay down on it.

Luca grabbed the side of my panties and ripped them in two. He gripped the other side and did the same thing.

Before I could protest or finish working out the mechanics of exactly how this was going to go down, he lifted me up and threw me over his shoulder like a sack of flour.

"Luca!" I squealed.

I wasn't arguing, though—the man had a great ass and I was staring straight at it.

I gave his butt cheek a frisky pinch and he retaliated with a harsh spank on my bare ass.

The shocking sting melted into pleasure. My heart raced with a cocktail of excitement, anticipation, and nerves.

The room flipped as he slid me down his chest, still holding me in his arms. My back bit into the cold metal siding of the walk-in freezer.

My feet hit the floor, and I realized that I was completely naked while Luca was still in his suit and tie.

Well, except for his giant cock hanging out of his fly.

I hated vulnerability and I *never* let a man dominate me —a few had tried, but they didn't get that far.

It wasn't that I was opposed to it, but no one had ever been as convincing—as resolute in that role. Luca wasn't playing pretend. Every touch. Every kiss. Every dirty thing he said was a reminder that he was in charge.

"One foot on the ground, one around my hips, Maddie," he commanded.

I lifted my leg, but when I wasn't fast enough, he grabbed my thigh and positioned me himself.

There was no warning. No lead-up. He didn't prime me. *He didn't need to.*

Luca shoved his cock into my pussy, and I nearly choked on my tongue.

My vision went sparkly, and I pressed the back of my head against the cool metal panel behind me to keep from overheating.

"That's not all of it, beautiful," he soothed with a satisfied smirk. He worked my hips to angle with his. "Relax for me."

I let out a slow breath as he slid all the way in.

"Luca," I whimpered.

One hand left my hips, and he cradled my jaw, "I'm with you, beautiful. Keep my name on your lips. I've got you."

Slowly, he began to pump in and out. My muscles flexed

and released with his in a mirrored tempo. When I got comfortable, he bent his knees and drove in hard and fast.

"*Luca!*" I screamed. "Yes—"

"You. With me. Madeline?" he grunted out between thrusts.

"Yes. *Yes,*" I pleaded in return.

He surged harder and my toes began to curl. My grip on his shoulders turned rigid as heat built faster and faster in my center.

I was a volcano about to erupt.

Luca's eyebrows dipped into a deep crevice above his nose. His features tightened, and I felt his steady rhythm take a dive toward spastic.

"Come with me."

I nodded listlessly, because an audible response was out of the question. The first wave of his release jerked inside me, detonating my own orgasm.

Luca pressed into me and rested his forehead on mine. Sweat dotted our skin, but neither of us cared.

"How do you feel?" he asked between heavy breaths.

"Glittery," I said with a giddy smile.

He drew me in to a slow kiss while he was still inside of me. "I'll take that as a good thing?"

I closed my eyes, trapping my lower lip between my teeth to keep from smiling like the Cheshire cat, and nodded. "Yeah."

Luca nodded in agreement. "Me too." He gave me another chaste kiss before murmuring, "Give me a sec, okay?"

He lowered both of my feet safely to the ground and made sure I was steady before walking away to deal with the condom.

I quickly gathered up my clothes and threw them back

on—*sans underwear*—and grabbed a bottle of sanitizer to scrub down every inch of the kitchen that we'd touched.

A few minutes later, Luca came back into the pastry kitchen looking completely unscathed.

*What I wouldn't give to see him wake up with morning breath and bedhead.*

Just the thought of waking up to Luca sent nervous butterflies fluttering around in my stomach.

He crossed the room and immediately took me in his arms, pulling me in for a long, lingering kiss. It was slow and sultry, but carried the heat that still raged between us.

"How does a grilled cheese sound?" he asked when he finally pulled away.

I laughed, because no one in the history of my sexual escapades had ever offered me a grilled cheese after sex.

"Sounds amazing. That was quite the workout, Chef DeRossi."

He dipped his hand into my bra and gave my nipple a sharp pinch. "I thought we agreed on *Luca,* remember?"

"Outside of work I'll call you Luca."

"Why?"

"Because I work hard, and I don't want people thinking that I'm getting to where I'm going because I'm sleeping with my boss."

Luca seemed perturbed, but didn't push the topic any further. "Fine. Meet me on the roof. I'll be up in a minute."

"With grilled cheeses?"

He smiled. "With grilled cheeses."

Apparently when Luca promised something, he went all in. Luca didn't just slap a slice of suspiciously processed cheese on some Wonder Bread and call it a day.

He used a beautifully crusty sourdough my bakers made, layering the thick-cut slices of bread with crispy pancetta, muenster cheese, and thinly sliced pears. He slathered both sides of the sourdough with Duke's mayonnaise and seared it to a perfectly tangy, toasty crisp.

"Oh my God," I moaned as I took another bite. "This is the best grilled cheese I've ever had."

Luca grinned and tore off a piece, dropping it into his mouth. "So, the worst chef on the planet must be able to do something right."

"What?"

"I follow you online, Maddie."

*I, Madeline Lee Dorsey, was going to need a shovel.*

*A big one.*

*I was going to have to figure out some way to dig my own grave, hop in, kill myself, and then bury my own body.*

*On second thought, maybe a backhoe would be easier.*

*Could I rent a backhoe this late at night?*

"In my own defense, I thought you were Satan in chef whites."

His low chuckle had my body revving up for round three. "Have I, uh, done anything to change that thought? Even a little?"

I pointed a finger at him. "The orgasms definitely help your cause."

He winked. "More where that came from, Madeline."

I picked at the crumbs on my empty plate. "No one uses my full name, you know."

"They should," he countered. "Just like you, it's beautiful."

I snorted. "That was such a line, DeRossi."

He leaned over the table and pecked my lips. "It's the truth, *Madeline*."

"Have you ever seen the horses?" I asked.

He shook his head.

We got up from the table, and I took his hand, liking how natural it felt. I led him to the edge of the rooftop dining area that looked out over the Sound to the barrier islands that separated us from the ocean.

It was dark, but there were just enough lights that I could point out the wild horses. "Look. See there?"

"The horses live on that little island?"

I nodded. "Spanish mustangs. They've been here for centuries."

Luca's chest pressed against my back. His muscular arms wrapped around my waist, keeping me close. "Come home with me."

"I have to be here early in the morning."

He leaned down and nibbled on my ear, mumbling, "Rae can handle it. Play hooky—just for the morning."

I closed my eyes and leaned back into his arms. "I shouldn't. And you're my *boss*. You shouldn't be telling me to call out just so I can wake up in your bed."

"Will the guarantee of more orgasms help sell it?"

"Mmm, sorry. I'm more Rae's type than you are." I clicked my tongue against my teeth and grinned. "I doubt she'll be swayed with your offer of a few orgasms."

He dropped one hand and smacked my ass. I let out a little yelp and he chuckled.

"Smart ass. Besides, I didn't say just a *few* orgasms."

I turned in his arms and draped mine around his neck. "I should be heading home."

"I'll take you. I'll pick you up in the morning."

"It sounds like you're fishing for an invitation to stay over at my place."

"Maybe I am. Maybe I just want to make sure you get home safe."

"You seem to forget that my neighbor is a cop. I'll be fine. Try again."

Luca's cocky grin faded into a wistful smile. "I just want to make sure this is what I think it is."

"And what do you think this is?"

"You and me." He pecked my lips, punctuating his point. "The way we should have been." He kissed the tip of my nose. "After California." He pressed a long kiss to my forehead. "I feel like the minute I let you go, you're gonna disappear on me again."

"I feel like I should be the one who's worried."

His thick brows furrowed. "What do you mean?"

"I follow you too, Luca—I've seen your dating history. Am I just another girl who's temporarily on your arm in a long string of conquests?"

"Never. Like I said—I'm with you."

"People say a lot of things during sex."

Luca cradled my jaw in his hands and gently stroked my cheek with his thumb. "Not me. I say what I mean."

"Did you actually mean what you whispered to me the day that I won the competition? What you said when you shook my hand?"

"Yes." Luca looked me in the eye as he repeated the words he murmured in my ear when the confetti fell. "I think you're spectacular. You have the kind of spark that sets the world on fire and I find myself constantly wonderstruck by you."

# LUCA

I was home alone, but not before following Maddie back to her house and kissing her goodnight on the dock.

And at her door.

And again at her bedroom door.

And stretched out on top of her on her bed where I took my time getting to know every little part of her.

Driving back to a big, quiet beach house with a raging hard-on had been a begrudging act of discipline.

I wanted her to be here with me. In my bed at night. In my kitchen drinking coffee in the morning. Stretched out on the couch. Curled up in a hammock on the deck.

It had been a long time since I'd had sex that made me feel that alive.

She wasn't just another notch in my metaphorical headboard.

Maddie was wild and fierce. She was untamed like the mustangs that roamed the island between the sound and the ocean. What made those horses so powerful was their rawness. They were meant to stay unbroken.

You either ran with them or let them go.

The tumbler of bourbon in my hand was nearly gone when my phone rang. I smirked at the screen.

*Right on time.*

"Well, well, well. I had you pegged as the *wait two days to talk to him again just to make him sweat* type," I teased.

"You asshole!" Maddie shouted over the phone. "You stole my vibrator!"

I looked over at the kitchen island where the device sat, tucked away in its velvet bag. She had it sitting on her night-stand, and the opportunity was just a little too good to pass up.

"Figured after that goodnight kiss you might go for some solo action. Didn't want that happening if I wasn't around to watch."

I heard her breath hitch and there was a long pause before she spoke again.

"Well," she began, trying to regain her composure. "Good thing I have a perfectly capable shower head. So screw you."

"How 'bout you keep your hands and your fucking shower head away from where my hands should be, and I'll cook you dinner the day after tomorrow."

"But I—"

"You have an early out that morning, and Rae's running dinner service. I already checked the schedule."

"Yeah, but—"

"No buts."

"Fine. But only so I can get my vibrator back."

I chuckled. "Goodnight, beautiful."

"Night, asshole."

I laughed and shoved my phone into the pocket of my trousers. I loosened my tie and unbuttoned my dress shirt.

*What a fucking night.*

I was tired as hell, but there was no way I could go to sleep. Not with the adrenaline still coursing through my system after finally having Maddie.

The beach house had a pool, and doing a couple laps to work off the excitement sounded like just the right thing.

I padded into the bedroom and stripped down to my boxers, before pawing around my suitcases for a pair of swim trunks.

I'd been in Beaufort for just over a month and still hadn't unpacked.

I knew it wasn't home. It was all temporary.

Still, the thought of Maddie staying the night at the rental house made me want to put my jeans in the dresser drawers and hang my shirts in the closet.

The front door opened and closed.

For a minute, I wondered if maybe Maddie had driven out here. Without bothering to put pants on, I ducked into the hallway only to find Astrid letting herself in.

"Dammit," I groaned as I dove back into the bedroom for a pair of pants.

"Don't be a prude," Astrid said, rolling her eyes as she waltzed through the living room in a tight pencil skirt and blouse that made her look as uptight and unapproachable as her personality. "Nothing I haven't seen before."

*And I sure as hell wouldn't be making that mistake again.*

One lonely night after a restaurant opening in Seattle, Astrid had dumped my tipsy ass into a car and driven me back to my hotel room. I vaguely remember inviting her in for a nightcap. One drink became four and the clothes started flying.

Astrid was a professional and never brought it up. She

didn't even stay the night, slipping off to her own room after the deed was done.

Our working relationship had never been affected, so there wasn't any reason to replace her.

I pulled on a pair of sweatpants, still forgoing a shirt. It was my fucking house after all.

"I need to know who you're taking to the James Beard Award Gala in September so I can make arrangements. The list I gave you with vetted companions—"

"Astrid, I'm thirty-six years old. I can get my own date for a damn gala," I said bluntly. It came out much harsher than I intended, but I wasn't going to entertain the idea that I'd go with anyone other than Maddie.

She huffed and crossed one slim arm over the other. "The right date will boost your image and provide great PR for both of you. I really don't understand why you're fighting me on this. Look, I'll take care of everything like I usually do. You just have to show up and look pretty."

I gritted my teeth. "I'm not going with one of your vetted air-headed bimbos who'll just pick at their plate the whole time."

Astrid raised an eyebrow, her clinically perfected lips turning into a thin line. "You're seeing someone, aren't you?"

"Ast—"

She held her hand up, and I heeled like a damn dog. "Who is she?"

"That's none of your business."

"Who is she and how long has it been going on?" she asked again while she pulled out her phone and began tapping away at it like a woodpecker.

I pressed my hands to the kitchen island to keep from strangling her. It wouldn't take much effort—she'd snap like a twig.

"Not your concern," I repeated.

"It is very much my concern when it affects your image. Why you're being so hostile about this one is beyond me."

I sighed and looked up from the speckled marble. "Madeline Dorsey. And it's new. *Very* new. So, I'd appreciate it if you kept a lid on it until I say so. Got it?"

She laughed sarcastically. "Please tell me you did not sleep with that girl."

When it sank in that I was serious, her eyes bugged out of her head.

"Even you can't possibly be so boneheaded that you would screw an empl—"

"That's enough," I snapped. Usually, I was fine with Astrid's pointedness, but not when it came to Maddie. "I'm telling you like it is. This thing between me and Maddie is new, and I expect you to do your job and keep it away from the court of public opinion."

"And if it gets out?"

"Spin it like we're the food industry's new power couple or something like that. I don't give a shit. But you do not put out anything without my approval. Clear?"

"Crystal," she said without looking up from her phone.

"Anything else?"

"Use a condom," she sneered. "You don't want anything tying you to this town."

"I own a restaurant here," I countered.

"You know what I mean," she said, strutting to the door and adding, "I'll check back in next month with an updated list of *vetted* dates for you."

She was out the door before I could grab a knife, fillet her, and feed her to the fish.

I was so fucking wound up, but as soon as my phone

flashed with Maddie's name, I felt the knot in my gut begin to loosen.

MADDIE

You still awake?

LUCA

Yeah, beautiful. Everything okay?

My phone rang the minute I responded to her text. "Hello?"

"Hey," Maddie said.

Her voice was quiet and timid. I wasn't sure if she was just sleepy or if there was something on her mind.

After watching her around her friends and the staff at Revanche, I knew she was a damn good actress. She could put up a front with the best of them. But with me, she had only let her guard down a few times.

Sitting outside her hotel room in California.

On the deck of her houseboat.

Watching her come apart in my arms as I drove her to orgasm.

"You alright, *Tesoro*?" I asked.

"Um, what?"

I chuckled quietly as I stretched out on the couch and crossed one ankle over the other. "It, uh, it means "treasure" in Italian, but it's more like a term of endearment. Our version of 'darling.'"

"I like that." Maddie's voice was soft.

I imagined her curled up in that big bed of hers, smiling in the dark. I wondered what kind of pajamas she wore. Were they big and cozy or thin and easily torn? Did she sleep naked? The thought had me reaching to tame my dick.

Her quiet whisper was like a dream. "So, DeRossi isn't

just a fancy stage name? I didn't know if you were actually Italian or not."

"My grandparents immigrated from Livorno when my mom was in elementary school. My dad was born in Brooklyn, but his parents were immigrants too."

"I remember you telling me about your sisters. You said they're both married with kids?"

I closed my eyes and stretched an arm behind my head. "Yeah, shit—Daniella has three and, uh, Anna-Marie has three now too. She just had a baby girl last month. Hold on, I'll send you a picture." I pulled my phone away from my ear and scrolled through my photos until I found the one I wanted, and texted it to Maddie.

"Wow," she said quietly.

"That's the whole crew at the hospital when Valentina was born."

*Crew* was an understatement. My whole family still lived in Brooklyn, so everything was a big affair. My parents, Daniella and her family and in-laws, my mom's parents, and Anna-Marie's family and in-laws had all crammed into the hospital room to meet the newest addition.

"You, um, you have a big family."

"Big and loud. Nonna says we yell because we love each other."

Maddie giggled. "I'd like to see that. It sounds entertaining."

*Damn, she was going to wreck me.*

She muttered something unintelligible before quickly adding on, "I—I didn't mean it like that. Luca, I swear—"

"It'd be okay if you meant it like that, you know." I grinned. "Look, I'm glad you called because there's something I wanted to talk to you about."

"Oh? What's that?"

"The James Beard Awards."

"What about it?"

"I want you to go with me."

Her tone picked up in excitement. "Did Revanche get nominated?"

"Not to work, Mad. I want you to go as my date. Or I can go as *your* date. I don't have a problem being Mr. Chef Madeline Dorsey for the evening."

She groaned. "Why are you doing that?"

Her exasperation had me full-on belly laughing. "What do you mean, *Tesoro*?"

"Why are you making me fall for you so hard this fast?"

"I could say the same thing about you," I teased.

There was a comfortable silence between us. A confidence knowing that we were finally on the same page.

"So, about the awards—It's, uh, it's in September. It'll be after Labor Day, so things should slow down enough for both of us to be able to get away. What do you think? Spend a few days in the city with me? Go with me to visit my family in Brooklyn?"

"You plan on being here until after Labor Day?" she asked, completely circumventing the whole *wanna meet my family* thing.

There was a surprise in her voice that cut me deep. That little reminder that she still didn't trust me.

Did I plan on being here after Labor Day?

I'd have to have Astrid find a new place for me to stay. But in the off-season, that shouldn't be a problem. I checked in with my other restaurants on a regular basis. They were all self-sustaining and profitable.

I had a condo in L.A. and an apartment in New York City that were sitting empty. Sure, I'd have them ready for whenever I had to go there for appearances, but neither of them actually felt like home. *And I owned those outright.*

The beach house was a temporary rental, but it felt like home.

Did I really have a good enough reason to leave? I sure as hell had a damn good reason to stay.

"To be honest, I haven't really figured it out yet, Mad."

"Oh."

"Tell me something."

"Hm?"

"Do you want me to stay?"

I was going for it. I was pushing her, and I knew it. This thing between us—whatever it was—was new, and yet I felt like I'd been chasing Maddie for a lifetime.

Maddie was quiet for a long time and I assumed she had fallen asleep. "Luca?"

"Yeah, beautiful?" I mumbled through a daze of exhaustion.

"I don't hate you being here."

I groaned as I turned and flopped onto my side like a breaching whale. There was a perfectly good king-size bed just down the hall, but talking to Maddie on the phone, stretched out on a lumpy couch, was a comfort in itself.

"Is that the same as you wanting me to stay?"

"Why'd you pick up when I called?" she asked, ignoring my question.

"Why'd you call?" I countered.

"Because I knew you'd pick up." Her voice was slow and quiet; probably laced with a sleepy smile.

I wished I could have seen it for myself.

## 21

---

## MADELINE

It was the weirdest workday in the history of workdays.

Two days had passed since Luca and I had christened the pastry kitchen. I immediately scrubbed every single surface after we put our clothes back on. I did it again when I showed up the next day—long before the rest of my staff—to give it an extra thorough clean.

Today I showed up ready to kick some pastry ass, and was greeted by boxes.

*A lot of boxes.*

*And a very sexy Luca in a crisp navy suit and burgundy tie, holding a boxcutter.*

"What's all this?" I asked as I surveyed the room. It looked more like a mail distribution center than a commercial kitchen.

Javier and Delores, a baker in training, piled up behind me when they came down the stairs.

Luca's mouth curved up in a devious smirk. "New tools and utensils. A new stand mixer. There's a new cart that needs to be built, too. It folds up flat. Figured it'd be useful when you and Rae deliver wedding cakes."

My jaw hung open and I didn't do a damn thing to close it. "Chef DeRossi..."

Luca smiled sheepishly before steeling his expression to one of indifference.

He cleared his throat and nodded to the stairs. "Chef Dorsey, a moment in my office if you don't mind?"

He passed the boxcutter off to Javier and put his hand on my lower back to lead me upstairs.

When we got into his office, Luca closed the door, captured my face in his hands, and kissed me like I had never been kissed before.

His lips were warm and still tasted like the half-eaten cinnamon roll that was sitting on his desk. The shadow of scruff on his jaw scraped my cheeks like sandpaper. I wrapped my arms around his neck, and he slid his hands down my waist to my hips, pulling me closer and closer.

"Morning, beautiful," he mumbled when we finally broke away for air.

I clasped my hands behind his neck and blushed. "Morning, you."

He tucked an unruly strand of hair behind my ear and rested his palm on my cheek. I instinctively leaned into it, reveling in the safety and peace I felt at his touch.

Luca stroked my cheek with his thumb and smiled down at me. "It's been too long since I've kissed you."

"It's barely been forty-eight hours," I teased.

He shook his head as he leaned down and pecked my lips one last time. "Too long."

"But you get me all to yourself tonight."

"That I do, *Tesoro*. You, uh, you sure you can't skip out early?"

"I have work to do, and so do you," I reminded him, poking my finger at his lapel.

Luca groaned and tossed his head back in disappointment. "How 'bout I just close up the restaurant? Then we can both go home and I can have you all to myself."

"I'm getting off early in the middle of the summer—you should feel so honored."

"When I do I get you all to myself? Say, for an actual weekend?"

"Hurricane season," I quipped.

Hurricane season technically stretched from the beginning of June to the end of November, but our storms tended to hit in the fall. Good thing business slowed down after Labor Day anyway.

He spun me around, put his wide hands on my shoulders, and began to work at the tense knots that never seemed to go away.

The more he massaged my shoulders, the more I relaxed into him.

"Have you given any more thought to New York?"

"I've thought about New York, yes."

"So, is that a *yes,* you'll go with me?"

I forced myself to pull away from Luca's touch or I knew I would get sucked into it all day and not get a single thing done.

"Can we talk about it tonight?" I asked, turning back to face him.

"Of course."

"Luca, about the new equipment—"

He shook his head and crossed his arms over his chest. "Scott got the same haul for his staff. But yes—it was for you. I want to make your life easier."

*Not the answer I was expecting.*

"You bought me bowls and whisks?"

Luca chuckled. "Don't pretend like you didn't like it. I've

seen you eye the supply catalog. You look at kitchen equipment the way other girls look at shoes."

"You're lucky. I'm cheap." I smirked.

He grinned. "One day you're going to have to let me spoil you."

I glanced at the clock and sighed. "I have to get back down there. Was calling me up here just a ploy to kiss me, or did you actually need to see me?"

He anchored his hands to my hips and pulled me close again. "Did I need to see you? Yes. Did I need to see you about work? No."

I eased up on my tip toes and initiated the kiss. It was a fleeting peck, but no less effective. "I'll see you tonight, Luca. Text me your address?"

He nodded and gave my ass a mischievous pinch. "Tonight, beautiful."

When I got back down to the pastry kitchen, Hannah Jane was standing at my work table with an almond croissant and a cup of coffee from Queen's in hand.

"Well, I was beginning to think you were dead, but the pastry order kept showing up to the inn on time, so I figured you were just camped out here."

"Busy season. You know how it is." I shrugged as I tied my hair up in a bun and grabbed my clipboard.

Hannah raised an arched eyebrow and sipped her coffee. "I got worried when you bailed on drinks at the bar, and then I heard from Steve that you didn't come home from the watch party until really late. He also mentioned that a certain someone showed up with you and stayed for a few minutes."

"Steve's worse than a damn grandma."

"So, is it true?"

"Is what true?"

"That you're seeing him?" Hannah asked as she popped another bite of her croissant in her mouth. "Or at least finally sleeping with him?"

"Geez." I grabbed her arm and yanked her out the back door that led outside to the dumpster pad. The last thing I needed was my staff overhearing the gossip. "Between you and Luca I'm never gonna get any work done."

Hannah grinned and tucked her short, chocolate brown hair behind her ears. "So, that's a definite yes. Spill."

I glanced back at the door to make sure no one was listening. There was no way in hell I wanted all of this to get back to the staff, but Luca wasn't exactly being subtle.

"We may or may not have hooked up after the watch party."

She threw her croissant and coffee filled hands in the air and squealed. "I knew it! The whole time the competition was airing he looked like he was three seconds away from throwing you over his shoulder and hauling you into his office to fuck you over his desk."

"That's more or less what happened."

Hannah's eyes widened. "So, give me the more or less— why are you being so cagey about this? You're totally into casual flings."

"Wow, way to make me sound like a whore, Han."

She shook her head. "I didn't mean it like that. You've just always been more confident in that department. You can separate sex from dating, unlike perpetually single me."

"You'll find your person."

"And given how hush-hush you're being, I'm gonna go out on a limb and say that you might have found yours."

I looked down at my sensible black work clogs and kicked at a stray piece of gravel. "I'm going to his place for dinner tonight."

Hannah's eyebrows shot up. "You're taking off work during high season to have your boyfriend cook for you? Damn girl, this must be serious for you to do that."

I crossed my arms. "It's not like that. He knows my schedule. Rae's running dinner service."

"You make your own schedule, and since when do you let Rae run dinner service?"

"Since I fucking decided to schedule her that way!" I shouted. "It's not a big deal!"

"It is!" Hannah argued. "Mad, you haven't actually *dated* anyone since I started working at the inn, and how long has that been?"

"Fine. Point made," I grumbled. It had been a while.

Hannah finished off her croissant and wiped the powdered sugar off her fingers. "This is a good thing, Mad. You deserve some happiness."

"I'm perfectly happy, thank you very much."

"Stop pretending like you don't know exactly what I mean. If sexy ass DeRossi makes you happy, then go for it."

Her words were like arrows, hitting their mark. Maybe she had the smallest of points.

Hannah glanced at the sophisticated gold watch on her wrist and sighed. "I gotta go. Bridezilla incoming in T-minus fifteen minutes."

I grimaced.

Hannah Jane and I often shared wedding clients, and I knew exactly just how bitchy brides could be.

The two of us swore that we'd never let each other act that entitled when our time to walk down the aisle came.

"Just the bride or is a mom-zilla making an appearance too?"

Hannah snorted. "God, I hope not. But if Steve and

Chase show up and haul me away in handcuffs—the woman got what was coming to her."

I cackled as Hannah started off toward the inn next door, and I turned to walk back inside.

———

THE HOURS FLEW BY. Wholesale pastries were crafted, and cakes were baked. Mousses, gelées, sorbets, gelatos, and custards were made. Individual batards were shaped and lined up like soldiers to rise, ready for the oven before they would be put in bread baskets for dinner service.

I loved working in the mornings.

It was a flurry of organized chaos. Tasks were timed down to the minute, and my staff always showed up ready to slay.

It was going to be a great weekend.

"Chef Dorsey?"

"Yes?" I looked up from my worktable and spotted the server standing at the stairs.

"There's a table who wants to send their compliments to the chef for their dessert."

"Thanks. I'll be up in a sec." I quickly finished plating an example of the dessert I wanted Rae to replicate for dinner tonight.

"Table fifteen. On the roof by the fireplace. Two gentlemen."

"Got it." I hung my apron on the hook by the stairs and uncuffed the sleeves of my chef coat.

Hurrying up the stairs, I cut through the kitchen and gave Scott a quick salute as I headed up to the rooftop dining area. I scanned the area for the table I was supposed to greet and—

*Of fucking course.*

I laughed and rolled my eyes when I saw Steve and Chase finishing up a late lunch at a table by the fireplace.

"So, this is how my tax dollars are going to good use, huh? Protecting and serving the patrons of my restaurant?"

Chase wiped his mouth and set the cloth napkin aside. "We're off duty."

I raised an eyebrow. "Is that why you're wearing your gun and badge? Something going on around here that I need to be aware of?"

Steve shook his head and leaned back in his chair. "Nah, just keeping an eye on the town."

"Keeping an eye on the town or on me?" I pursed my lips and closed my eyes to keep from killing two of my best friends. "Let me guess—Hannah Jane texted you and told you about my plans tonight."

"We work with confidential informants all the time. We're good at protecting their identities," Steve said.

I pinched the bridge of my nose. "My phone's in my locker. How bad is it?"

"Hannah put it in the group text," Chase admitted.

"Good fucking heavens. Next time I'll just put it on a billboard out on Highway 70 so the whole fucking state can see," I exclaimed a little louder than I should have.

Patrons popped their heads up from their meals like gophers.

I gave them a placid smile and turned my attention to Steve and Chase.

"So that's why you came for lunch? To harass me about having a date?"

"Not you," Steve said. "Him."

"*Excuse me?*" I growled as I leaned down and pressed my

hands against the crisp linen tablecloth. "Tell me you did not talk to Chef DeRossi."

Chase's mouth turned up into a smirk. His devious eyes sparkled. "Is that, uh, is that something you do? Get off on calling him *chef*?"

"Fucking perv," I muttered just loud enough for him to hear. "And no, I call him Chef DeRossi because *I am at work right now and he is my boss*," I hissed.

Steve gave Chase a look of warning. "Chill, Maddie— we're just looking out for you."

"I am almost thirty years old."

"And he's an ass that you've hated for years," Steve countered. "Give us a break for being a little worried that you're suddenly head over heels for the guy."

"You need to back off," I warned.

Chased raised his palms in surrender and dropped a few bills on the table to tip the server. "I just hope you know what you're doing, Mad."

I was still from my run in with Steve and Chase as I stomped toward the back of the building and knocked on the door to Luca's office. \

"Come in," he called out.

"Hey." I poked my head in and smiled pathetically. "Got a minute?"

Luca was standing behind his desk with his palms pressed to the top as he studied a stack of charts and graphs.

His suit jacket hung on a coat stand, and his sleeves were rolled up to his elbows.

I wanted to study those strong, tattoo-covered forearms.

He shot me that irresistible, panty-melting grin, and shuffled the papers into a stack. "For you, always. Everything alright, *Tesoro*?"

My heart fluttered.

Hearing him call me *Tesoro* was even better in person than half-asleep over the phone. "Yeah. I, um, I was just curious if Steve Pelham and Chase Brannan stopped in and talked to you."

Luca chuckled quietly and circled around his desk, half-sitting on the front of it. "They did a little bit ago, yes."

I groaned and pressed my fingers to my temples in frustration. "How much do I need to kill them? I swear, I didn't put them up to anything—I didn't even tell them. Hannah Jane Hayes from the Taylor Creek Inn came by this morning, and I mentioned it to her and she told them. I swear I didn't—"

"Mad, it's okay," Luca said, smiling reassuringly. He took my hand in his and lifted it to his lips. "I can handle your boys being a little protective. If they weren't, I'd worry about what kind of men they are."

The nerves that had my stomach twisted in knots began to unfurl. "You mean that?"

Luca nodded. "They just wanted to make sure I was gonna treat you right." His hand found my hip and he gave it a little squeeze. "And I plan on treating you right, beautiful."

"Just tell me they didn't say anything embarrassing. I've known Steve for a long time. He was there for my awkward middle school years."

His grin turned devilish and he shook his head, "Now, that I can't say. Can't break bro-code."

"I'm gonna kill them."

Luca eased up and pecked my lips. "Wait until after tonight. I don't wanna have to bail you out until I've had you in my bed."

I raised my eyebrows, "Is that what you think is happening tonight? Because I remember you promising me dinner."

"Dinner and dessert."

I wrapped my arms around his neck and he slid his big hands up under my chef's coat, branding my skin.

"How 'bout I bring dessert?" I offered.

Luca circled his fingers over the small of my back, tracing abstract shapes on my hips. "Mmm. I think that sounds fair."

He removed his hands from my skin much sooner than I would have liked. I whined when he reached over and grabbed his blazer from the coat rack.

"I'm about to head out. You clocking out soon? I saw Rae come in a while ago."

"Yeah, I just have a few things to finish up. I'm gonna grab a quick shower at my place and then I'll head over. Is seven alright?"

"Perfect," he said, grabbing his keys off the desk before shutting off his computer. Luca lifted my chin and kissed me again. "See you in a bit, *Tesoro*."

———

I WAS FLOATING on cloud nine the rest of my shift.

Of course, my bubble of giddiness immediately burst when I saw two cars parked outside Steve's place.

I knew damn well they weren't there for him.

*Well, Bridget wasn't there for him. Melissa was another story.*

"What the hell," I said to Melissa and Bridget as soon as I got out of my Jeep.

"Hear us out," Bridget began as she stood on the dock beside Melissa. "You need help."

"It's just dinner. We're not even going out anywhere. Just hanging out at his house."

"Just dinner my ass," Melissa sniped as she grabbed my arm and hauled me over the lip of the dock onto the deck of my houseboat.

I had a solid eight inches on her, but Mel was strong.

Her five-foot-nothing height didn't hold her back in the slightest. She did CrossFit, had a membership to a rock-climbing gym, and would rather run through sand, than on a treadmill.

Maybe she was the one who had gotten Steve to start working out like a mad man.

"What were you gonna wear?" she asked.

"Jean shorts, a tank top, and either my sandals or cowboy boots. What else would I wear?" I scoffed.

Bridget and Mel shared a concerned look.

"Yeah, you need help," Bridget declared.

While Bridget shoved me into the shower with the order to shave everything, and tossed a towel in after me, Mel raided my closet.

That was fine. There was literally nothing interesting for them to find in there—like my vibrator.

*Friggin' Luca.*

I was glowing when I stepped out of the shower, thanks to the steam and a coconut exfoliating scrub I'd splurged on during a day-off browse-a-thon.

I walked into my bedroom and found Bridget and Melissa grinning like two devious closet elves.

There was no use prolonging the inevitable. When Mel and Bridget got an idea in their heads, there was no convincing them out of it. Then again, they would say the same about me.

There wasn't a question in my mind as to why we were friends. Peas in a pod.

"Alright—hit me with it."

Bridget held up the hanger. "We stole it from Hannah's closet with her blessing."

I fingered the hem of the soft black fabric. The dress would hit above my knees, but the neckline was an inch shy of a turtleneck.

"It's a little...matronly."

She spun it around to show me the back—or lack thereof.

"Okay, fine." I grabbed at the dress, but Bridget jerked it away.

"Not so fast," Mel cut in. She pointed to the bed to a set of lingerie I'd bought on an online shopping binge.

I never even took the tags off.

"You're wearing *this* underneath," Mel said.

"I think it's a bit much. I'll compromise on matching underwear. I just did laundry."

"You were the one who just complained that the dress was too conservative," Bridget said. "Put the damn lingerie on. You'll look sexy as hell in it."

"He's a man. Men like this stuff," Mel said. "Why'd you buy it if you don't want to wear it?"

"Because sometimes I want to feel sexy just for me."

"Oh, stop with the clichés and put the lingerie on," Bridget huffed. "You're running out of time and you still have hair and makeup to do."

"He's seen me at work without makeup and my hair in a bun. It doesn't matter."

"*It's Luca DeRossi,*" Mel exclaimed. "Look me in the eye and tell me you don't wanna knock the designer socks off that fine ass man. We're trying to help you."

I had a feeling they weren't going to let me leave until I agreed. The longer I prolonged the inevitable, the longer it would be until I got dinner.

"Fine."

# 22

# LUCA

The doorbell rang just as I pulled the roasted vegetables out of the oven.

Most people would think it was weird for me to cook in a three-piece suit, but I was just as comfortable in that as I was in sweatpants and a t-shirt.

Besides, Maddie had looked at me like I was a fucking dessert when she stopped in my office earlier.

I wiped my hands on the dish towel and walked to the door. My heartbeat ramped up like a race car the moment I opened it.

Maddie was a fucking knockout. The little black dress she was in came up high on her neck, completely covering her collarbone and shoulders. The sleeves were angled like wings, and stopped at her elbows.

My eyes trailed down where the fabric stuck to her ass and legs like a second skin, stopping just above mid-thigh, showcasing her mile-long legs.

We were eye level since she had traded her work shoes for a pair of black leather heels that were strappy and sexy as fuck.

"Damn, baby—you look fucking gorgeous." I grinned, leaning in for a kiss before opening the door wider and inviting her inside.

She passed by me, revealing the back of her dress.

*There was no back to her dress.* The high neckline of the front dropped off into a deep V, baring her tan back all the way down to her waist. The rest of the fabric crisscrossed at her hips and clung to her like a skirt. She'd pulled her long hair into a wild ponytail, showing off the backless dress.

Yep. I was dead, and this was heaven.

As much as I wanted to stare at her all damn night, I wanted the thing off her even more.

Maddie breezed into the house like a goddess, carrying two bags from the restaurant in her hands. "I brought dessert," she said, lifting the bags. "Is the fridge okay?"

"Yeah—uh, yeah," I stammered. "Just make room if you need to."

She smiled and rummaged around for a minute before they both fit. I knew I still had steaks to sear and a demi-glace to finish, but I couldn't peel my eyes off her. *Or my hands.*

It was like she had put her hair up in that ponytail just for me to pull when I pushed her face-down on my bed, straddled her ass, and bent low to whisper *exactly* what I was planning on doing to her.

Maddie closed the refrigerator. The second it shut, I pushed her back against the stainless steel door and caged her in. She smiled against my mouth, tipping her chin up.

"We meet again," she teased.

A low growl ripped through my throat as I slid one hand behind her neck, digging my fingers into the skin at the base of her skull just hard enough to make my intentions clear.

"Madeline…"

Her long lashes fluttered, and she looked up at me with doe eyes. "Dessert before dinner?" She smiled like a seductress and it nearly brought me to my knees.

*But that's not how things were going to go.*

"Not a chance, *Tesoro*." I smirked. "You're wearing that dress like you're doing it a favor. It'd be a shame if I had to rip it off of you so early on in the night."

She sucked in a sharp breath, and her eyes widened.

Had anyone ever talked to her like that? Had she ever been dominated? The idea of being the first to take her that way made my pride swell. *And made my cock strain against my pants.*

I backed away. Her eyes immediately dropped to my belt, and I let her get a good look at the bulge in my trouser. It was a silent preview of what was to come.

"Come. Sit."

I settled my hand on her waist and led her to the barstool across the island where I was preparing dinner. I pulled the stool out for Maddie, before circling around, pouring a glass of cabernet, and sliding it across the marble countertop to her.

I dropped the cracked pepper crusted steaks in the searing hot skillet. The hiss was music to my ears.

I washed my hands and turned back to Maddie. "How was the rest of your day?"

"Good," she said, nodding as she sipped her wine. "Nothing too crazy. It feels weird to be off before midnight."

"So goes the life of a chef."

"Only for the insane and the passionate."

"You definitely have to be a little of both to make it," I said.

And she was. Maddie was a lot of both.

I glanced over my shoulder to make sure the steaks were

alright. "So, tell me," I began, taking the conversation toward something more serious. "How the hell are you still single? I mean, come on—you're a fucking blast to be around, you kick ass in the kitchen, and on a scale of one to ten, you're at least a thirty."

Maddie smiled humbly and trailed her fingertip around the rim of the wide wine glass. "I could say the same about you. What would your answer be?"

"I work too much, I don't stay in one place for long, and I haven't met the right one."

She picked up her glass and toasted me. "Minus the whole *moving around* thing, ditto." Maddie took a staying sip and added on, "But contrary to popular belief, I'm not lonely."

"No, I don't imagine you are." I chuckled as I gave the steaks a flip and added a pat of butter so I could baste them as they finished up.

I poured in a finger of whiskey and tipped the skillet into the flame on the gas range to flambé the steaks. Fire licked up and filled the skillet as the alcohol burned off.

"Not with friends like yours anyways. You, uh, you've got a big circle."

She laughed quietly.

This version of Maddie was much more demure, but no less alluring. It was fascinating to peel back the layers and see a different side of her.

"What about you?" she asked. "Who's in your circle?"

That was a loaded question. "I keep my circle small."

"I assume so it's easier when you pack up and move?"

*Damn. Girl went right for the jugular.*

"Yes," I replied. "Not to sound like a prick, but my, uh, public image means I have to keep my circle small and trustworthy."

I heard the quiet clink of her setting her glass down as I pulled the steaks out of the skillet and let them rest as I plated up our dinner.

"Is that your lead-in to having me sign an NDA or something?"

"What? No—hell no. Maddie, I would never ask you to do that."

"Look, if it makes you feel more comfortable with this... situation... I'm fine with it. Really—I understand."

Okay, so maybe it had been a while since I actually had to put in work to win over a woman. And maybe I was a little out of practice. Crow did not taste good.

"Mad, I didn't mean it like that," I said as I busied myself with building our plates. "Have I had women sign NDAs in the past? Yes, but that was because those were a mutually beneficial business arrangements. This is not that."

"What is this then?"

My hands stilled after I swiped a streak of demi-glace on the plate.

I was thirty-six. I was far too old to be calling a woman my girlfriend. On the other hand, I didn't want Maddie getting the notion that I wasn't serious about her.

"New. This is new."

"I concur." She smirked. "But that's not an answer, Luca."

"How about this," I said as I cleaned the rims of the plates with my side towel and washed my hands. "I want you in my bed tonight. I want you there when I wake up in the morning. I'm going to kiss you every day, and it may or may not be in front of the staff. I'm going to win over your friends, even if it takes a while because I know they don't like me. You're going to be in my *very* small circle, because I trust you without there having to be paperwork involved."

"I'll agree to that on the condition that we keep this separate from the restaurant. I don't want my team thinking that I'm not on their side. Scott and I work well together, and I can't say that for every executive chef I've ever worked with. I don't want to fuck that up."

"I can agree to that *for now*," I said.

Damn. The next time I needed something negotiated, I'd send Maddie instead of Astrid. The woman was a shark.

"But come September, I plan on showing you off in New York and it won't stay quiet."

She let out a little sigh. "I guess I'll have between now and then to figure out a way to make it work at the restaurant."

"So, you'll come to the gala with me in September?"

"Yes," she mumbled into her wine.

I chuckled and picked up our plates. Maddie followed me out to the balcony where I had meticulously laid out two place settings. "Don't sound too excited about it."

"I just... I don't know what to expect. I'll have to find something to wear."

With the plates on the table, I took her hand in mine and made her slowly turn so that I could take in all her beauty.

"Madeline, listen to me. You could wear a paper bag and you'd still be the most stunning woman there. But, if it helps, I can get Astrid to have a few dresses sent to you."

"Astrid, your assistant?"

"Astrid, my jack—er—*Jane* of all trades."

"I'll figure it out," she said dismissively.

I pulled her chair out and helped her get seated. After a quick trip back inside, I brought out our wine glasses and the rest of the bottle and found Maddie admiring the place settings.

"I'm impressed. It looks better than what our front of the house does at the restaurant."

I grinned proudly as I sat down across from her, and motioned for her to dig in.

"My first job was working as a busboy. I was thirteen, so they paid me under the table. Eventually the waitstaff started letting me flip tables during service and put out the place settings. I earned a cut of the tips and a great appreciation for a well-set table. I can press a linen like nobody's business."

Maddie laughed, and it sounded like wind chimes.

I swore to myself then and there that I'd do anything to hear that sound as much as possible before I went to my grave.

It wasn't long before wine was gone, and our plates were cleaned off. This was the fastest dinner I'd ever eaten, and not just because I wanted to get to the aforementioned dessert.

It was refreshing to be in the company of a woman who enjoyed food. I'd had just about enough of taking socialites out on fake dates only to have them pick at a sorry excuse for a salad or tell me that they were on a juice cleanse.

Food meant something to me. It was family. It was heritage. It was passion. If I was being really fucking honest, it was how I showed love.

Finding someone who appreciated it the way I felt a little bit like a miracle.

Seeing Maddie eat was foreplay. I had watched her knife cut through the steak like it was butter. She speared it on her fork and brought it up, opening her mouth and wrapping her lips around it, slowly dragging the prongs between her teeth. The woman was making love to each bite, and it had my blood simmering.

I loaded the dishes into the dishwasher and swiped a towel across the countertops. There wasn't much left to clean since I tidied as I went.

Maddie was out on the balcony nursing her second glass of wine. I pulled out the bags that Maddie had stuffed in the fridge and stole a peek at what she brought over for dessert.

*Dirty girl,* I thought to myself, smiling as I put one of the bags back in the refrigerator.

Maddie walked inside and set her half-empty glass on the marble island. "This house is stunning. Usually, beach rentals are super kitschy."

I lifted the bottle to give her a refill, but she waved it away.

"That was all Astrid. She sets up my accommodations for me. I only have the rental for a little while longer, but I'm looking at buying a property out here."

Her eyebrows raised. "Really? Here?"

I shrugged and pulled a tumbler from the cabinet and poured myself two fingers of bourbon. "I like it here. Revanche is here. Makes sense to get a property. If I acquire any more restaurants in the southeast, this can be my home-base."

Maddie's lips quirked in a stifled sort of smile. "Ah, yes. *Luke* who oversees *business acquisitions*. I forgot about him," she teased.

I set my bourbon down and caught her around the waist, trapping her between the unforgiving kitchen island and my arms. "You're one to talk, *Maddie who likes to bake*."

Maddie pushed back against the island like she was trying to escape. Her long ponytail swished back and forth, teasing me. Taunting me.

"I want to be clear about something, Madeline," I said, lowering my voice to a husky whisper meant to intimidate. I pressed closer, skating my hand up her thigh. "You are with me, and you will not be sleeping with anyone else. Are we on the same page?"

Maddie's breath disappeared. Her eyes closed as my mouth lingered at her cheek.

I slid my hand up the curve of her ass, to the small of her back. I pulled her closer, pressing her hips to mine and grinding my erection against her.

"Do you trust me?" I asked.

Maddie gave me a timid nod.

I rested my other hand on the crook of her neck, letting my thumb graze over her throat and up the line of her jaw.

"Do you trust me to make you feel good?" I murmured.

She nodded.

I tightened my grip and held her head firmly in its place. "Answer me."

"Yes," she whispered.

The sun was on its way down, and the colors seeping in through the windows painted her in flaming oranges and reds. Dark shadows cast through the curtains, shrouding me in black.

"If you want me to stop—you tell me, and I will. Do you understand?"

Her knees quaked and I wrapped my arm around her waist to hold her up.

"Do you understand me?"

Gray eyes darkened to slate as a haze of lust clouded her vision. "Yes."

## 23

# MADELINE

Luca leaned down and pressed a kiss to my throat. "Walk down the hallway and go in the last room on the left. Stand at the foot of the bed and wait for me."

My brain was telling my feet to move, but part of me wanted to know what would happen if I didn't.

"Madeline," he warned as his grip tightened. "*Tesoro, fai come dico.*"

I didn't want to walk away from him. I wanted him to keep whispering sexy things in Italian in my ear all night long.

My breath caught in my throat. "What? I don't..."

"Do as I say, *Tesoro,*" he said in a low timbre that made heat quickly pool between my thighs.

I pinched my legs together for a little relief, but it never came.

"Last door on the left. Go on." Luca stepped back and nodded toward the hallway. "I'll be right behind you," he soothed as if he knew I was just a little nervous.

I peeled myself off the kitchen island and headed down the hallway.

"Last one on the left," I whispered to myself when I arrived at the door to the main bedroom.

I flipped the light switch, but nothing happened. The sun hadn't completely set yet, but the only thing I could make out were the shadowy outlines of the furniture.

I felt around the lamp on the bedside table for the switch. The dial clicked, but the light didn't turn on.

"Um, Luca?"

"I told you to wait for me at the foot of the bed, *Tesoro*." His growl came out of nowhere and I jumped at the sound. A nervous squeak escaped my mouth.

"Oh God—you really are a serial killer, aren't you?" I tried to make it sound like a joke, but there was a tremor in my voice that was a dead giveaway.

I heard the rustle of Luca moving around the room, then a soft glow when he turned on the light in the bathroom and cracked the door.

It wasn't much, but it was enough to let me see the sharp outline of his face.

I let out a little sigh of relief. I had been curious about what sex like this would be like, but I didn't trust easily. Certainly not enough to completely relinquish control.

But in a weird way, I did trust Luca.

"*Tesoro, fai come dico.*"

This time when he told me to follow his order, I did.

"Face the bed," he said from somewhere behind me.

I heard the quiet rustle of a paper bag and assumed that he found the dessert I brought.

He set it aside before moving to stand directly behind me.

Luca brushed my ponytail off to my right shoulder and trailed his knuckles down my bare spine. "*Sei bello.*"

I shuddered at his touch and wobbled in the high heels.

He steadied me with a strong hand on my waist, pressing a gentle kiss to the nape of my neck.

I hummed in satisfaction.

Luca was a walking, talking contradiction. *Soft and strong. Smooth and rough. Suave and raw.*

He pushed one side of my dress off my shoulder, then the other. The fabric pooled where it clung to my hips. Luca tucked his fingers into my dress and pushed it the rest of the way down. It fell to my feet and he stood in front of me and took my hands, helping me step out of the tangle of fabric.

I stood perfectly still in my lingerie and heels as Luca circled me like a hawk.

His arms were crossed, and a fist was tucked beneath his chin as he assessed me.

Sparks skittered across my skin at his obvious appraisal.

The backless corset covered in black lace made my tits look fantastic. Crisscrossing straps connected the bustier to my matching thong. The lingerie paired with the heels made me feel like a warrior.

Whatever nerves I had at the beginning melted away into the confidence of a femme fatale.

I lifted my chin and enjoyed the feeling of his gaze on my body.

Luca knelt in front of me and helped me out of my heels —a small act of trust.

When he rose, he pressed his hand to the small of my back and urged me onto the mattress. "Go on."

I scooted back against the mountain of pillows and watched.

Luca toed off one leather loafer and then the other. He

took off his suit jacket, opening the closet and taking his time as he hung it up.

The anticipation was killing me, but he wasn't done.

Luca unbuttoned the sleeves of his dress shirt and rolled them up to his elbows. First the left and then the right.

He looked me dead in the eye when he unbuttoned the top three buttons of his shirt, loosened his tie, and slid it out of his collar.

He made getting undressed better foreplay than a drawer full of toys.

*I was going to die if I didn't have an orgasm STAT.*

Luca prowled toward me, crawling across the bed on his hands and knees. He was at me with his tie in hand before I could even blink. He grabbed my hips and yanked hard, pulling me to the middle of the bed.

He straddled my waist, grabbed my wrists, and pinned them above my head. The silk tie was soft when he bound my wrists together. He tested the snugness by looping his finger between the tie and my wrists.

I could get out if I wanted to, but I didn't want to.

He was unnervingly quiet as he tied the loose tails to the metal rungs of the headboard and surveyed his work.

I wanted to squirm—to get some relief from the mounting pressure in my core—but he sat firm.

"Here are the rules, Madeline," Luca began. "You don't get to orgasm until I say so."

"Uh—okay?" I chewed on my lower lip and laid there—a helpless bundle of anticipation.

Luca leaned down and gripped the sweetheart neckline of the corset top in his hands. "I just want to say, you look sexy as hell in this little number and I'm truly sorry to see it go."

And then he ripped it right in two like it was nothing.

He grabbed the black straps that were tethered to my panties and pulled them apart, repeating exactly what he had done the first time we'd had sex at the restaurant.

History was making an encore appearance. Here I was—completely naked—and Luca was still fully clothed.

Hopefully this time I'd get a better peek at what was underneath all those designer suits.

"That's twice now that you've completely ruined my underwear." I blamed the adrenaline rush on what came out of my mouth.

Without warning, he spread my legs and trapped them open with his knees. Luca let his fingers tease my folds, spreading my wetness around.

"Is it?" he mused, feigning ignorance.

His hand left my pussy for a split second before a harsh smack lit up my clit.

I writhed beneath him, gasping and struggling against the restraint. The startling pain turned to overwhelming pleasure when his fingers returned and soothed me with a gentle touch.

He left my body for a moment and climbed off the bed, returning with the bag from Revanche.

"What do we have here?" he mused as he unloaded all the containers onto the nightstand. "Chocolate ganache. Whipped Cream. Berries." He pulled out a container and frowned when he couldn't immediately identify it. "What's this?"

"Saffron-honey mousse," I croaked

A wicked smile crossed his face. "The same kind you made for the competition?"

"Yes," I replied breathlessly.

The plastic cracked as he pulled off the lid and crawled back on the bed.

"You know, I fantasized about licking this off your body." He chuckled to himself. "Now I get to."

The cold mousse against my skin made me shiver the moment he smeared a line of it on my breast.

He pressed his finger against my lips, and I swirled my tongue around, licking the remnants of the creamy mousse off of it.

Satisfied, Luca leaned down and captured my nipple with his teeth, nipping and pulling at it until I was squirming beneath him. He released it, licked the mousse off the swell of my breast, and kissed me hard.

The sensation was magic.

The sweetness of the honey and the savory saffron— tasting it on Luca's mouth was other-worldly.

He painted the valley of my breasts with dark chocolate ganache, burying his face there before bringing the taste back to my lips.

Every touch—every taste—was something new. The near-blackness of the room meant that everything was a surprise.

*Pleasure.*

*Pain.*

*Sweet.*

*Tangy.*

*Cold.*

*Warm.*

Luca had me gasping and aching at every touch.

Staving off an orgasm was going to be harder than I thought, and he didn't seem to be in any hurry to make it happen.

"Luca," I whimpered against his mouth as he worked my clit with his thumb, and slowly stroked my G-spot with two thick fingers. "Please."

"What do you need, *Tesoro*?" He brought me to the edge over and over again, but never let me fall.

"To finish," I whimpered as I squirmed on the sheets, desperate to ride his hand just a little harder.

Luca's chest rumbled with amusement as he pecked my lips. The lingering taste of the raspberry he had eaten clung to his tongue.

"Patience."

*He was going to make me die of desperation with just his hand, and that wasn't how I wanted to go out. If I was going to die because of an orgasm, Luca's cock had to be involved.*

My shoulders ached from being tethered to the headboard. My pussy throbbed with need, and he began to slow his movements. The orgasm waned again.

"Luca!" I yelled in frustration, pulling at the tie.

"Trust me," he coaxed quietly in my ear. "Breathe."

I closed my eyes and forced myself to relax. My lips parted ever so slightly as I sucked in a shallow breath.

Luca's fingers surged deeper, filling and stretching me.

I cried out in ecstasy, straining against the tie that bound my wrists. My back arched and I tried hard to pull my knees together, but Luca kept me positioned just how he wanted me.

My body was chasing an orgasm that it knew it couldn't have, and the torture was exhilarating.

Luca pressed his thumb against the tight rosette of muscle hidden between my cheeks, and I gasped.

"Relax. Breathe," he soothed as he tested it with a teasing pressure. "Let me play with your body. It's what I've been dreaming about."

All too soon, Luca removed his hand from my pussy, held my thighs wide with a punishing grip, lowered his head, and swirled his tongue around my aching clit.

"Oh—oh God, Luca!" I begged. "Please!"

One hand left my thigh, and he used it to drive his fingers hard into my pussy, working the inside of my sensitive body while he devoured me on the outside.

My legs trembled and my arms were exhausted. Every scrape of his stubbled jaw against the soft skin of my thighs had me begging for relief. For release.

"You're the best fucking thing I've ever tasted," he growled as he licked up my slit and sucked hard on my clit.

I was ready to take my chances and kamikaze toward my own end.

The second I made the decision to risk whatever delicious sort of punishment he had in the back of his mind, Luca bit down on my clit, making me squeal.

"Don't you dare, Madeline," he warned, reading my mind as he rose back on his haunches and left me teetering on the brink of storming off and finding wherever the hell he hid my vibrator.

Luca quickly popped open the buttons of his dress shirt and stripped it off. He grabbed the back of his undershirt and pulled it over his head.

His muscles rippled with every motion. I was on the edge of coming apart just looking at him. His sleeves of tattoos made him look dangerous, but the tenderness in his eyes made me feel safe.

He stood on the edge of the bed and stripped off his pants and boxers. His erection sprung free and, for the first time, I saw Luca in all his brutally masculine glory.

"Oh my God," I whispered, swallowing my nerves.

He was *all man*.

Wide shoulders, a grid of abs that shouldn't have been humanly possible, and a dark trail of hair that led down from his navel all the way to his hard manhood.

A pearl of wetness dotted the tip, and I reveled in the satisfaction of making him ache for me just as much as I wanted him.

Luca straddled my hips and untied my wrists. I whimpered when the strain against my arms and shoulders released, groaning quietly as I pulled them down to my sides.

He reached over and pulled a condom out of the nightstand, tearing it open and rolling it on his thick shaft.

"Hands and knees, beautiful." Luca grabbed my waist and flipped me to my stomach without warning.

He manhandled me so easily and, in some weird, twisted way, I loved it.

Kneeling behind me, he jerked my hips higher until I was ass up and face down.

I heard the spank before I felt the sting—the sharp smack followed by a blinding heat and burn. He massaged the place where his handprint marked my cheek and worked away the bite of pain.

Luca reached between my legs and flicked my clit at a staccato rhythm as he positioned himself at my entrance.

"Deep breath. Don't come until I say so."

I didn't even have time to think, much less breathe, before he surged inside of me.

"Luca!" I screamed.

He plastered his palm on my chest and lifted me up so that I could grab onto the rungs of the headboard.

His fingers wrapped mine around the cool metal rungs of the headboard and held them there as he pistoned deep inside.

He set a grueling pace and, with every snap of his hips, pushed me further and further to the point of no return.

He squeezed my hand around the headboard then grunted, "Hold on tight."

With swift motions, he grabbed my ponytail and jerked my head back. His other hand left mine and snaked around my hips. He began to roll my nipple between his fingers, and I cried out in elation.

"I—I can't," I mumbled. "I'm—gonna—"

"No," he growled in my ear.

He released my pebbled nipple and smacked my ass.

There was no soothing massage this time. Two more spanks and I was teetering on the edge.

Every time we would sink into a comfortable rhythm, he would change his ministrations—the angle, the position. Luca drew out my orgasm until it was excruciating.

"Luca," I moaned.

"Say it, *Tesoro*," he snarled.

"*Luca—*"

He plastered his chest to my back and powered hard inside of me, leveraging with his knees and thighs to hit my G-spot with every stroke of his cock.

Being wrapped in his arms, being filled by him—it was the best feeling in the world. It was safe and terrifying and comforting and thrilling.

It was freeing.

Luca dropped one arm and toyed with my pulsating clit.

I nearly crashed over the edge. "Please," I begged in a whisper. "Please."

He pushed in hard once, then twice, and a third time. Luca used the arm around me to give my nipple a sharp twist. The other hand flicked at my clit in perfect synchronicity to his thrusts.

"Let go, beautiful. Let me see it."

Every sensation, every touch was piling on top of each other.

I went rigid as my inner muscles clenched and squeezed around his heavy shaft, and cried out in ecstasy.

Luca's hips jerked once, then twice, as he unloaded into the condom.

As the last tremors of my orgasm ripped through my body, I fell forward toward the pile of pillows, unable to hold myself up.

Luca caught me in his arms and pulled me into him, murmuring sweet nothings against my skin.

## 24

## MADELINE

L uca held me longer than anyone ever had. He kissed my shoulders, my neck, and the sensitive spot behind my ear.

When he finally pulled out, I felt empty.

He disposed of the condom in a little trash can by the bed, and sat against the enormous pile of pillows—all the while showering me in an endless string of praises.

"How are you?" he asked, as he pulled me into his lap and gently tugged my hair out of the ponytail and massaged my scalp.

I melted into his touch and closed my eyes. "Good."

"Just good?"

I laughed nervously. "I think that was the best orgasm I've ever had."

And it was. I felt tingly and light. I was exhausted in the best way.

I had never been used and manipulated in quite that way, and I wanted more of it.

He wrapped his arms around my waist and pulled me into his chest. I closed my eyes and relaxed in his embrace as he dropped a kiss on top of my head. The simplicity of it made me smile.

Angry red lines streaked around my wrists from his tie. Luca reached down and lifted my hand to his lips, pressing a kiss to the center of my palm before lavishing the red marks with tender pecks.

He repeated the process on the other wrist. "Are you okay? I didn't hurt you did I?"

"No—No, I'm fine. I'm good."

"You sure, *Tesoro*?"

I craned my head up and kissed him. "Promise."

I did my best to put the worries I had of our evolving *situation* out of my mind.

So, I was sleeping with my boss and my sworn enemy— there had to be worse things people did.

After all, I still wasn't as bad as the jackasses who left grocery carts strewn in the middle of the parking lot.

I always returned my buggy, come hell or high water.

I peeled my hair away from my chest and laughed softly. "I'm a little sticky."

"Don't go anywhere," he said as he hopped up from the bed.

Not even a second later, I heard the shower squeak on, then he was back. Luca stood at the bedside table, reached into the lampshade, and twisted the lightbulb back in.

*Sneaky.*

Light filled the room, and he offered his hand and a kind smile.

I let him lead me to the bathroom where steam was billowing out of the walk-in shower.

He helped me into the spray of water and slid the glass door behind us. Luca turned me so that I was facing the shower head and he was at my back.

The stickiness left from the ganache, mousse, and whipped cream were quickly washed away. His big hands started on my shoulders, gently massaging away the soreness from being tied up. In silence, he worked his way down to my biceps, leaning down to kiss the side of my neck and across my shoulder.

I had never been with a man who took his time. Who took it upon himself to make me feel—well—*everything*.

Being with Luca was like riding a rollercoaster I never wanted to end.

Everything he did was done with the sole purpose of making *me* feel good.

Maybe it was a little selfish, but part of me loved relinquishing that control and trusting someone else with my pleasure.

*Maybe I wouldn't need my vibrator back after all.*

The only reason I had gotten the damn thing in the first place was because I was sick and tired of being jackhammered for a minute flat during a hookup. I had a penchant for picking dumbfucks who were more concerned with a one and done, than making sure my needs were taken care of too.

*Not Luca.*

He had soaped up a washcloth and was in the process of washing away the sweat and sugar. I stood still as he knelt in front of me and washed between my thighs with a gentle touch. When he looked up with an adorable grin, I placed my hands on either side of his jaw. My happiness mirrored his.

Luca stepped out of the shower first and offered me his hand. He wrapped a towel around my shoulders, then gave my arms a gentle squeeze before wrapping one low around his waist.

I watched him walk out of the bathroom, sneaking a peek at those two dimples on either side of his spine, just above his fine, *fine* ass.

When Luca returned to the room with the other bag I'd brought from the restaurant, he found me sliding back into my dress.

The lingerie was unsalvageable, so I didn't even bother.

"Nuh-uh. Take it off," he ordered.

I laughed. "If Steve or Chase arrest me for driving home naked, I'll never live it down."

"Get back in bed, Madeline."

"Luca, I have to work tomorrow."

"And? So do I."

I raised my eyebrows and cocked my hip. "Are you forgetting about the conversation we had where you agreed to keep whatever this is out of the restaurant? Showing up to work wearing last night's dress isn't exactly subtle. I didn't bring clothes to change into and—*what are you doing?*"

Luca had pulled the covers back on the bed and was flinging decorative throw pillows left and right. "Doing this right."

"What are you talking about?"

"Get in the bed, Maddie."

"Not until you tell me what the hell is going on."

Luca whirled around and pinned me up against the wall. "Don't make me rip this dress too."

"Don't you dare. It's Hannah's and she'll never forgive me."

"Then you better do as I say, *Tesoro.*"

"Tell me what's going to happen if I do."

Luca's touch turned gentle as he tucked his fingers into my hair and massaged my scalp again.

*God, the things this man could do with his hands.*

"We're going to eat the crème brûlée you brought while snuggled up in this big ass bed, because I love cuddling and crème brûlée. Tomorrow, I'll wake you up early enough so you can go home and change before work." He worked his way down to my shoulders, taking his time with the knots that plagued me incessantly. "And because I know that you stop at Queen's Coffee every morning, I'll swing by and get you your usual so that you don't have to worry about it."

"How do you know what my usual is?"

"Because the other morning when I kissed you in my office, you still tasted like coffee and cinnamon. I'm thinking you get a vanilla latte with an extra shot and a sprinkle of cinnamon."

"Dirty chai, but you were close," I said. I bit down on my lip. "And if I want to go home?"

He stopped massaging my body and pinched my chin, drawing my lips to his and kissing me softly. "Do what you want,. But just know that the second I see you at Revanche, I'll kiss you. And I don't care who sees."

My lips curved up in a smile. "You play dirty."

He grinned and lowered his eyelids, kissing me again. "I'm just getting started."

---

THE SUN WAS BARELY PEEKING over the horizon when I pulled up to my houseboat. Getting out of Luca's bed was an act of sheer will I never wanted to have to face again.

Waking up in his arms was the best feeling in the world, and I kind of hated myself for liking it so much.

*The orgasm he woke me up with added a point in his favor.*

Part of me knew that I should have packed an overnight bag, but I didn't want to be presumptuous. I sure as hell didn't want to give him the satisfaction of thinking I was already his.

"Look what the cat dragged in," Steve grunted as he hooked the claw of his hammer into a nail and pulled until it broke free from the splintered board. "If you're still tipsy, watch your step. I don't want to have to pull you out of the water."

"What the hell are you doing to my dock?"

"*My* dock," he corrected. "Fixing some of the loose boards before the summer storms roll in and rip it up." He gave me a once over. "Looks like you had a good night."

"Bite me," I hissed as I stepped over the gaping hole in the dock and walked to my door.

My complete lack of bra and panties was hidden by wearing one of Luca's t-shirts over my dress, tied off at the waist.

It worked in a boyfriend-chic sort of way, but Steve knew me too well to know that it wasn't how I left my house yesterday.

"You stayed over at his place last night?" Steve hollered from the dock.

I left the door open so I could hear him while I got ready for work. "So what if I did?"

"Not like you, Mad."

"Um, have you met me? Besides, you didn't get this bitchy when I had that sleepover that turned into a week-long situationship before California. I don't see why this is any different."

Steve popped his head in just as I pulled my t-shirt over my bra. "You eat your summertime hookups for lunch. You're not yourself when you're around DeRossi."

"And how do you know that?"

Steve shrugged. "Be careful, Mad. A zebra can't change

its stripes. You've always been good at reading people and you pegged him as a jackass from day one."

I pulled on my last clean chef's coat and cursed the fact that I needed to do laundry again.

"Look, as chivalrous as the big brother act is, it's getting real old."

He stomped back out to the dock that didn't really need repairing as I slipped on my clogs and grabbed my keys, phone, and wallet.

I walked back out to my Jeep and paused.

"Steve," I called out.

He looked up with deep circles around his eyes.

I softened my tone. "I miss her too. Don't worry about taking care of me. I'm a handful. Take care of yourself."

Steve offered a sad kind of smile and looked down at his tools. "You let me know if he needs his ass kicked."

I opened the driver's side door and grinned. "If he needs an ass kicking, I get first dibs. But you'll be next in line."

My good mood was short-lived.

By the time I made the last turn onto Front Street, I'd gotten two calls and a text about problems that were already popping up in the pastry kitchen.

Exhausted and under-caffeinated, I cursed the fact that I was depending on Luca to remember to pick up my coffee.

I felt a little guilty about doubting him when I opened my locker and found a coffee cup sporting a brown Queen's sleeve. It was waiting for me on top of a box that was tied with a pink satin ribbon.

Looking left and right to make sure no one was watching, I untied the bow and popped the top off the box.

I pulled back the tissue paper and fingered the luxurious nightie.

The dark blue silk looked almost liquid, and I couldn't

wait to try it on. There was a matching lace bra and panty set hidden underneath that was just as lavish.

The small, handwritten card had me stifling a smile as I closed the box and spun the lock on the metal door for safe-keeping.

*I will never take more from you than I give.*

*-L*

## 25

## LUCA

It took two weeks to convince Maddie to let me have a seat at poker night.

Two weeks of her playing hard to get.

Two weeks of her teasing the hell out of me.

Two weeks of dirty texts and late-night phone calls.

The woman had a mouth on her that made my head spin. She was a temptress of the workaholic variety, which was an infuriating combination.

The restaurant kept us busy. Well, it kept *her* busy.

Scott, Maddie, and Carol ran a tight ship, which didn't leave a lot for me to do. I was basically using Rob's old office at Revanche as a base to oversee all of my establishments.

Sure, I could have been doing that from my *actual* office in Brooklyn, but this was better.

Did I miss having nightlife options that were open past nine PM? Sure.

Was seeing Maddie everyday worth it? Bar none.

I didn't mind the change of pace. Something about the slower lifestyle made my brain kick into overdrive.

For the first time in a long time, I had been able to make

clear decisions about new investments and acquisitions that usually would have stressed me out.

I had stepped back from being *Luca DeRossi,* and it was a breath of fresh air.

No late night clubbing, no public appearances. Hell, I hadn't even been on social media since the baking competition aired.

I had put up a "Congratulations, Maddie" post on my Instagram and hyped up the restaurant now that it was under the DeRossi Hospitality Group.

After that? Nothing.

Apparently, my absence from the public eye was creating a problem—a public relations hellscape. Or so Astrid said.

Frankly, I didn't give a damn. That was her problem to deal with. I wasn't in my early twenties anymore. Or late twenties.

Or early thirties.

Forty was looking closer than I liked to admit, and the appealing shine of the party boy lifestyle had begun to dull.

My sisters were constantly on my case about when I was going to settle down.

Even after agreeing to go to the James Beard Awards with me, Maddie still seemed skittish about the New York trip.

I wasn't sure if it was the idea of making a public appearance with me, or if there was something else going on.

Beaufort, North Carolina was a popular little tourist spot. We weren't cut off from the rest of the country, but it felt like we'd been living in our own little world.

After the night that I cooked her dinner and she stayed over, Maddie hadn't been back to my place.

Hell—the two of us hadn't been alone since then. Part of me wondered if she was avoiding me on purpose.

She had even avoided talking to me in person.

Maddie would text me if she had a break in her day, or late at night when she got home. But rarely would she stop in my office. If I went down to the pastry kitchen, she was always busy.

I started to wonder just how much of her packed schedule was self-inflicted.

I was taking a chance when I threw a toothbrush and a change of clothes in a bag and tossed it in the back of my BMW.

The drive from my rental on Atlantic Beach to her houseboat on Davis Bay wasn't long, but I managed to hit every damn stop light coming through Morehead City.

I thought back to the house listings I'd looked at.

I liked living on the beach, but part of me wondered if a little place inland would be just as relaxing. It would definitely be more secluded.

I let out a nervous breath as I pulled up beside Maddie's Jeep. Steve Pelham had his garage door open and was in the process of putting down some rubber flooring for the barbells and weight plates he had stacked up on the side.

I offered a quick wave and stepped over the lip of the dock to Maddie's houseboat.

"Knock, knock," I called out as I let myself in. "Mad? You here?"

I heard a panicked squeal and a hard thud come from her bedroom.

"Maddie? You alright?"

"I'm fine! I'm fine! I'm good—don't come in!"

*Not a chance.*

I cracked the door open to make sure she was okay. A laugh ripped out of me before I could control it.

Maddie was on the floor with her foot caught in a pair of shorts.

"Damn pockets," she groaned.

I knelt beside her and helped her pull her foot out of the giant hole on the front where half of her shorts should have been. The threads were snagged on her sandals. The more she tried to get out, the more tangled it became.

"Looks like we only have one option, Mad."

She glowered. "I swear if you tear up another piece of my clothing, I'll kill you."

I chuckled. "I was talking about your sandals. Take your shoe off."

I supported her ankle while she pulled the leather strap out of the buckle and wiggled her foot out. Maddie let out an adorable sigh of relief when she was able to slide the shorts off and untangle her shoe.

"You can't wear those tonight, you know."

"Excuse me?"

Her indignant southern drawl made me smile.

"You wear those little things around me all night, and I'll be hiding a hard-on the whole time your friends are here."

Maddie pursed her lips to stifle a laugh. "So, what do you suggest I wear then?"

"You got like... sweatpants that are three sizes too big? A big sweatshirt?"

She rolled her eyes. "It's over ninety degrees outside. That sounds like a *you* problem and not a *me* problem. You're just gonna have to think about something that'll keep your dick in check."

My eyes trailed up her long, tan legs to where a skimpy pair of familiar lacy blue panties were peeking out from under her *I Ain't Here for a Long Time, I'm Here for a Good Time* tank top.

I slid my hand up her leg and dug my fingers into her ass cheek. "Every time I see you, you look like a fucking wet dream."

I scooped her up in my arms and threw her down onto the bed. She let out a giggle as I crawled over her legs until I straddled her waist.

She writhed underneath me, trying her best to escape.

"One night together and you've been avoiding me for weeks," I said as I grabbed her wrists and shackled them above her head with one hand. "Wanna tell me what the fuck that's about?"

She smirked. "I don't know what you're talking about."

I leaned down and nibbled the curve of her ear. "You're a tease."

Maddie sucked in a short breath and moaned as she arched her back and ground her hips into mine.

"I haven't kissed you in fourteen fucking days, Madeline. I'm going out of my mind."

She tilted her chin up, inviting me in. "Maybe you should put us both out of our misery and kiss me."

I let go of her wrists and cradled her face in my hands like the priceless treasure that she was.

Maddie tasted like the summer. Her lips were warm and soft. They were citrusy like lime, but still sweet. She smelled like vanilla. It was one of the first things I'd noticed about her when we met at the gym in Los Angeles.

At first, I just thought she liked that kind of perfume. Now I knew it was because she was always covered in buttercream and surrounded by desserts.

"I missed you," she whispered as she grabbed the hem of

my shirt and pulled it up. Her fingertips ran over the ridges of my abs.

I thrusted my hips against the thin strip of lace between her legs and ground my erection into her core. She let out a little whimper and pushed up against me to get a little relief.

"Why have you been missing me when you could've just had me?" I grunted.

"Just busy."

"Bullshit."

Maddie wrapped her legs around my waist and pulled me in closer. As much as I wanted to rip her fucking clothes off like a caveman, I knew I needed to cool things off before they got hot and heavy. If I didn't, her friends were going to show up hear me fucking her stupid.

Reluctantly, I sat up.

"Luca," she whined.

"So, it's Luca now, is it?" I teased. The rare times I cornered her at work, she called me boss or Chef DeRossi.

*Like I hadn't been the one to tie her to my bed and fuck her six ways from Sunday.*

"You're in my bed, aren't you?" she teased as she tugged on my shirt, trying to pull me back down.

I reached down, grabbed her shorts off the floor, and tossed them to her. "Talk to me, Mad."

She shrugged and pulled them on. The denim covered the blue lace panties, but not by much.

Her perfectly round ass cheeks still peeked out the frayed bottom. I resisted the urge to bend her over this bed and punish her for being so hot and cold.

Maddie hopped up and grabbed her sandals, sliding them back on. "I've been busy. You know that."

"Just busy or busy avoiding me?"

"Just busy," she said as she walked down the hall into

her little kitchen. I followed her and leaned against the counter as she talked. "I told you—I want to keep things separate." She motioned between us. "Whatever this is needs to stay out of the restaurant, and since I basically live there, it means you're gonna have to take what you can get."

"Let's talk about the restaurant."

"It's my day off. How about not."

"Fine. I'll see you in my office first thing tomorrow morning."

Maddie rolled her eyes. "Whatever. Just make it quick. Your work talk is cutting into my drinking time."

"You're overworked and overqualified," I said, ripping the proverbial Band-Aid off. "You need to hire more staff for your team and fucking *delegate.* There's no reason for you to be carrying the whole pastry program on your shoulders when it's more than in the budget to expand. You're doing tasks that interns could be doing."

Maddie frowned and slammed the fridge door. Bottles of beer clinked against each other as she huffed. "So?"

"So, you look like a raccoon with those bags under your eyes because you barely sleep. You work all fuckin' day and then you go blow off steam. You need some balance."

"Work hard, play hard," she countered.

I pushed away from the counter and caught her around her waist before she could storm away. Her muscles were tense, and her gray eyes were drilling a hole into the floor.

"Maddie, the hardest part about being in charge is trusting your employees to do the jobs you hired them to do."

She relaxed in my arms and looked up at me. "I'd rather just do everything myself."

I knew she was only half kidding. If Maddie could get

caffeine in an IV drip and drag it around with her every-where, the woman would never sleep.

"Hire a full timer and a part timer, and schedule yourself to have one more day off every week. And no more closing down the kitchen. If you're working dinner service, you're out as soon as the dining room closes."

She smirked. "Or what?"

Her long white-blonde hair was hanging down in those long mermaid waves I loved so much. I grabbed a fistful and tugged her head back to expose her neck. I leaned down and kissed under her jaw where her rapid pulse thrummed.

"Or else."

Maddie melted against me, her delicate eyelids flut-tering closed as I kissed my way down her neck.

"I did miss you," she admitted. "A lot."

"Give me four nights a week."

"Two."

"Two nights and a whole day whenever you have a day off."

Maddie shook her head. "I can't do that."

"Why not?" I frowned.

She pushed away from me. "Because I have shit to do on my day off!"

"Like what? What did you have to do today that precludes you from seeing me?"

Maddie's mouth opened and closed like a fish. "You know, this pushiness is really unattractive, DeRossi," she finally spat out.

"Mad," I groaned in frustration. "Talk to me."

"I see my mom on Mondays, okay?" she clipped. "And sometimes I'm just not in the mood to talk to anyone afterwards."

Maddie's eyes welled up with tears as her neighbor, Steve, walked in.

She blinked her eyes to hold back her emotions, muttering, "Be right back," before power walking to the bathroom and slamming the door.

Steve's eyes narrowed in on me. He was a big guy, but we were about the same height. Sizing him up, I guessed I had more muscle on me.

He glanced at the bathroom door, then back at me. "Did you make her fucking cry?" he growled.

"What? No, I—"

Another man walked in, and I vaguely remembered Maddie calling him 'Chase'. He and I stood eye to eye, but the dude was *built*.

If things went south, there was no way in hell I could take them both.

*And they thought I upset Maddie.*

Chase looked at Steve, then at me. He crossed his arms and stood shoulder to shoulder with Steve. "What's going on?"

"Fucker made Maddie cry."

Chase's face turned lethal. His fists clenched and his nostrils flared with anger. "Three seconds to explain yourself."

"Look, it's not—"

"Three."

"Seriously, I didn't—"

"Two."

I held my palms out to show I wasn't a threat. "Man, I would never—"

"Back off, Chase," Maddie snapped as she breezed through the houseboat. "He didn't make me cry."

*Thank fuck.*

I splayed my palm across Maddie's stomach, stopping her in her tracks. I lowered my lips to her ear as I murmured, "*Stai bene, Tesoro?*"

Her eyes flicked to meet mine and I saw the slight red rims that she had tried to hide under a little makeup.

"Are you okay?" I repeated in a tone that was just barely audible. She gave me a little nod, and I dropped my hand from her body as she passed me by.

"Hey, party people," a breezy blonde shouted as she boarded the houseboat.

Maddie cleared her throat as three more girls crowded into the kitchen. "Luca, you remember everyone, right?"

She went down the line, reminding me of who was who and introducing me.

I remembered Bridget, the breezy blonde bartender from Jokers. She was the one who pickpocketed Maddie's keys to make sure I got her home safe.

Melissa was next. She barely reached my hip—probably under five feet tall if I had to guess. What she lacked in height, she made up for in muscle and a laugh like a firecracker. Her dark skin made her bright smile shine like a diamond.

I'd met Hannah Jane a few times. She tucked her short, brown hair behind her ear and gave me a polite hello. Usually when I saw her, she was in her professional attire—pencil skirts and blouses that said she was all business.

Seeing her standing in front of me in shorts and flip flops, I realized that the photo on Maddie's phone that I had seen at the gym in LA was of the two of them on the beach.

Kristin was last. I couldn't remember meeting her before, so I shook her hand and offered a friendly smile. She was younger than the rest of Maddie's crew—maybe not even old enough to drink the beer that was in her hand. I wondered how she fit in with the rest of them.

"Nice to meet you, Kristin," I said with a red-carpet grin.

Kristin squealed and fanned herself. "Oh my God!" she said in a stage-whisper.

Maddie rolled her eyes. "Please, he's not that great."

"I beg to differ," I chuckled. "I'm a fucking blast."

The girls giggled, and I reveled in the praise. Maddie, Chase, and Steve looked like they wanted to barbecue me.

"Kris has your ab photo as the background on her phone," Hannah spilled.

"Do not!" Kristin gasped.

Something that looked a lot like jealousy flashed in Maddie's eyes, and I decided that I really needed to see that look again.

Crossing the room, I wrapped my arm around her shoulders, nearly engulfing her. Kristin had to be more than a decade younger than me. I didn't have younger siblings. I was the baby of my family. But this—this felt like family, too.

I tugged my phone out of my pocket and snapped a selfie with her. Lowering my phone, I let her watch as I made the photo my background.

"There." I winked. "Now we're even."

"You're like... The hottest person I've ever seen." Kristin swooned and then immediately cupped a hand over her mouth. Her face turned beet red at the confession.

I looked up to find murder in Maddie's eyes. It only stoked the mischief in mine. If she wanted to play hard to get, then I was gonna do everything in my power to annoy her into being with me.

"Take him upstairs," Maddie hissed.

Chase and Steve moved toward me on her command. I

rooted my feet to the floor and raised my eyebrows. "Wait—what?"

"Don't fight it, bro," Chase said, grinning. He grabbed my bicep and Steve grabbed the other, dragging me toward a spiral metal staircase.

Steve was less cordial. "You're getting off easy," he complained. "If it was up to me, you'd be in a body bag."

*I believed him.*

They marched me up the staircase, to what I could only assume was going to be a human sacrifice. Chase pushed against what looked like an attic panel, then slid it away. Sunlight poured in.

"Up you go, pretty boy," Steve clipped.

I climbed out onto the roof, followed by Steve and Chase. One by one, the girls came up behind us.

Maddie pulled up the rear. She stood in front of me and held out her hand. "Empty your pockets."

"So, *you* are gonna kill me." I smirked. "You know, I never expected that the plot twist would be that *you* were the serial killer."

Chase took a step toward me, and I decided it was in my best interest to heed her instructions. I pulled my keys, phone, and wallet out of the pocket of my gym shorts and dropped them into her hands.

Maddie's looked down to my sneakers. "Shoes off."

I shrugged and toed off one shoe, then the other, and then stuffed my socks inside. Maddie grabbed me by my shirt and marched me to the edge of the roof.

Kristin, Melissa, Bridget, and Hannah Jane started chanting, "*Take it off! Take it off! Take it off! Take it off!*"

I looked back at her crowd of friends and made a show of stripping my shirt off like I was in *Magic Mike*.

They let out a deafening cheer and I thrust my pelvis

and rolled my hips like a high dollar stripper. I tossed my shirt over to Bridget and gave Maddie a big flex as I clapped my hands and bounced on my toes in anticipation of the jump.

Maddie had a wild gleam in her eye that was partially feral and wholly intoxicating. She pointed to the water that was a good fifteen feet below us.

"Any last words, DeRossi?" she yelled over the girls' chanting.

"No words," I grinned as I grabbed the back of her neck and yanked her in. Her friends went ballistic as I planted a hard kiss on her mouth on the edge of the rooftop. I dipped her backward and dug my fingers into the back of her thigh as I held on.

Without warning, hands came out of nowhere and shoved the two of us off the roof. Maddie flailed and shrieked. I roared as we began to fall, somehow keeping hold of her hand as we crashed into the water.

The saltwater stung as I opened my eyes under the surface and swam to her. We both broke through the surface and took big gulps of fresh air.

I grabbed Maddie by the waist and pulled her against my body.

She wrapped her legs around my waist. I used one arm to hold her against me and the other to wipe damp strands of hair out of her face.

Cradling her cheek, I slid my fingers behind her neck— gently this time—and kissed her long and deep.

She tasted salty like the sea. I was drunk on her. Those dimpled cheeks that made me weak were in full display. The wide smile on her face told me that my antics had been forgiven.

"Initiation?" I asked.

Maddie nodded. "Welcome to the club."

**26**

## MADELINE

I instantly regretted giving Luca a seat at poker night.

Not because I didn't want him around or because my friends didn't like him. They did.

Well, except Steve. But truth be told, Steve didn't like anybody these days. I barely made the cut.

No. We regretted it because the man had an unbeatable poker face.

Hand after hand, he raked in the winnings.

We never played for much. Whoever won was supposed to use the money to buy drinks and dinner for the next poker night. It kept things fun and no one ever lost too much.

From the look of it, I was going to have to let Luca come back next week to bring the pizza and beer.

"So... he's kind of great," Bridget said as she helped me stuff the empty pizza boxes into the trashcan and collect the empty beer bottles. "Tell me he's amazing in bed. He just *looks* like he'd be amazing in bed. He's got that big dick energy."

I laughed and snapped a pizza box in half. "I don't kiss and tell."

"Bullshit!"

"Okay, okay—we've only hooked up twice and it's been..." I sighed wistfully. "It's been great. Like, best sex of my life."

Bridget wiggled her shoulders in some kind of dorky celebratory dance. "Good for you, babe!"

I smiled sheepishly and tied the trash bag off. "I've kind of been avoiding him."

"And why would you do a dumbass thing like that? He's crazy about you."

"Because I don't know... It's been a long time since I've felt like this about someone, and it scares me how much the universe seems to be throwing us together. I mean, first we meet at a random gym on the other side of the country, then he just so happens to be a judge for the competition I was in, and then he buys the restaurant I work at."

Bridget paused. "Do you think he's, like, a stalker or something?"

I shook my head. "No. I talked to Rob Mullon. The restaurant buyout was in the works way before Luca and I met in LA. Rob just kept it quiet. He didn't want the staff thinking they'd lose their jobs and everybody leaving when it changed hands."

Bridget tied up another trash bag. "Well, it sounds like *maybe* you're supposed to be together. Did you ever think about that? Don't look the gift horse in the mouth—*especially* when the gift horse gave you that beautiful specimen."

"What about you? How are things with Kyle Kingsley?"

She had a dreamy little smile on her lips. "It's good. He's great. I mean, he takes me out all the time and comes by the bar to see me when I'm at work. He wanted to go out tonight, but I told him that poker night with you guys was sacred. And since I already missed one night because he took me to New Bern, I wasn't going to miss it again."

"Sounds like you guys are getting serious."

She shrugged. "My lease is up in a couple months and he's already talked about me moving in with him rather than renewing it for another year. I mean, it just makes sense."

"Yeah, but doesn't he live in Havelock?"

"I'll still work at the bar. You'll see me all the time."

"*Come posso aiutarti*?" Luca said as he stuck his head into the kitchen.

He was showing off by speaking in Italian, but I kind of loved it.

Luca took the trash bag out of my hand and gave me a peck on the cheek. "How can I help?"

I pointed to the trash bag in his hand. "You can take that over to Steve's house. The trash cans are around the back."

"Sure thing, *Tesoro*." He took the bag out of my hand and one out of Bridget's. "Let me get that for you, sweetheart."

Bridget lifted her eyebrows and guffawed in disbelief as Luca headed to Steve's house. "*Tesoro*? What does that mean?"

I blushed and busied myself with wiping down the counters. "It means treasure, but apparently it's just the Italian version of calling someone *darling*."

"Stop it," she gushed. "Darlin' is my favorite nickname. That's adorable." Bridget threw her head back and whirled around like a Disney princess. "Marry that man and have his babies. It's the only reasonable course of action."

I just laughed and shook my head as Chase walked in and looked at Bridget. "Me and Hannah are heading out. You want me to take you home, Bee?"

Bridget shook her head and looked at the time on her phone. "No, Kyle's picking me up. He'll be here in a minute."

There was a flare of something uncharacteristically negative that flashed across Chase's face, but I couldn't quite put my finger on it.

It wasn't jealousy, and it definitely wasn't his usual lovesick puppy face.

Chase nodded and shoved his hands in his pockets. "I'll uh, I'll see you around then."

Her voice got soft. "See you, Chase."

I waved him off and caught a glimpse of headlights coming down the drive.

"That's probably Kyle," Bridget said. "Tell Luca he's welcome at the bar anytime. I know it's kind of a locals-only place, but I'll still serve him."

"Later, babe."

She grabbed her keys and hurried out to Kyle's waiting car.

Kristin walked in with Luca behind her. He went to the sink to wash his hands while Kristin grabbed her keys off the counter.

"I'm out. Gotta get home. Thanks for the break, Mad."

"Oh, hold on a sec—" I said as I ripped open my fridge and pulled out a big bag from the restaurant. "Scott sent me home with a bunch of leftovers from the restaurant. I can't eat all of this by myself. You wanna take it home?"

Kristin's eyebrows raised. "Are—are you sure?"

"Yeah, of course. I mean, I eat there all the time. The food gets old after a while."

She took the bag and gave me a humble smile. "Thanks." Kristin gave Luca a nervous wave. "Nice to meet you."

Luca's eyes creased at the corners as he gave her a kind smile. "You good to drive?"

"I'm good. See y'all."

He came around and pressed his hands on the kitchen counter, caging me in his arms. It was my favorite place to be.

"What was that about?" he asked as he lowered his forehead to mine.

"What was what about?"

"You weren't at work today, and I know damn well Scott didn't have that many leftovers."

I raised an eyebrow. "You gonna rat me out if I tell you?"

Luca smirked. "I'm your boss—who would I rat you out to?"

"Kristin's having a tough time right now, but she's stubborn and doesn't like accepting help, much less a handout."

"So you..."

"So, I ordered some takeout from the restaurant and had Scott put it in leftover containers so that Kris wouldn't think it was charity."

Luca leaned back and crossed his arms. "What's going on with her? She works at the Taylor Creek Inn, right?"

I sighed and ran my hand back through my almost-dry hair. "Yeah, she's one of the housekeepers. A few years ago her parents got busted for selling drugs, so Kris dropped out of college, moved back home, and got a job here so she could get custody of her younger siblings. She went from being a college senior to a single parent of four kids overnight. Steve and Chase were the ones to make the arrest. They felt a little bit responsible for her getting screwed over because of her parents' shitty life choices, so they started looking after her and made sure she had what she needed. We started inviting her to poker night so that she could blow off a little steam and feel normal once in a while."

Luca exhaled sharply and shook his head. "Damn."

"You spill any of that and you'll be dead to me. Heard?"

"Heard," he affirmed. Easing forward, he placed his hands on my arms, and gave my biceps a gentle squeeze. "What can I help you with?"

I looked around the kitchen. Everyone always pitched in to clean up, so there wasn't much left. "Grab me a beer out of the fridge?"

Luca grabbed two. I took his hand and led him back up the spiral staircase to the roof.

Unlike some of the other houseboat owners, I didn't keep anything on the roof. The weather on the coast was unpredictable, and harsh winds coming off the ocean tended to fling furniture off the deck or the roof.

There was nothing worse than having to swim out to retrieve a lawn chair that was stranded in the middle of the Sound.

"You know, that jump was pretty fun." Luca chuckled as he sat down on the edge of the roof and let his feet dangle off the edge.

I dropped down beside him and cracked open my beer. "You're not as stuffy as I thought you'd be."

Luca's grin was blinding.

His thick lashes, his dark stubble, the way his complexion glowed—I could have stared at him all day.

Luca still hadn't put his shirt back on, even after we dried off from jumping into the Sound.

I didn't mind in the slightest.

He was so guarded when he was *Luca DeRossi*—when he was the curt restaurateur who was never seen in anything other than a four-figure custom-tailored suit.

The person sitting beside me now was Luke—the man I met in California who took me out for carnitas and Coronas.

He was wearing athletic shorts and no shirt, just like the day we ran together at the gym.

I loved seeing his tattoos, and I cursed the fact that I hadn't spent every spare minute of my time memorizing each stroke and curve of the ink that wrapped around his muscles.

More than anything, I loved seeing his tattoos. Probably because I knew that no one else got to see them.

As much as he was active in the public eye and on social media, he did manage to keep his personal life *personal*.

What I originally thought was a man without scruples, was actually someone who valued his personal life so much that he had learned how to play the game. He'd distract the public enough with his grumpy asshole act so that he could go about his business in peace.

I leaned my head on his shoulder, and he wrapped an arm around me as we sat in comfortable silence and finished off our beers.

It was such a simple moment, but I couldn't think of anything that made me feel more safe.

Luca wiggled back and threw his leg over to the other side of me so that I was sitting between them. He wrapped both arms around me and rested his chin on top of my head.

I loved his gentleness. His kindness.

I loved how focused he was in the restaurant and how commanding he was in the bedroom.

I loved the way Luca smelled. His warm musk was masculine and luxurious.

I closed my eyes and leaned back against his chest. "Luca?"

He craned his head down and kissed my shoulder. "Hmm?"

"Will you stay?" I felt the corner of his mouth twitch against the shell of my ear.

"I thought you'd never ask."

I was about to ask how long he was going to stay after the summer ended, but voices carried through the air. I turned my head and peered over his shoulder to see who it was.

The light in Steve's garage was on and the door was open. Steve was sitting on a weight bench, talking to someone who looked a lot like Melissa.

"They a thing?" Luca asked as he followed my line of sight.

I shook my head. "Nah, they've just known each other for a long time. Mel brings him dinner sometimes. She's been helping him out since Heather passed."

I watched a little longer. When it looked like Melissa was about to leave, Steve wrapped his arms around her tiny frame in a lingering hug.

It definitely wasn't the kind of hug he gave me, but I didn't say that out loud.

Steve had been grieving long before Heather actually died. A little more-than-platonic companionship would do him good.

"What about us?" Luca asked as he pressed a kiss to my shoulder. "Are we a thing?"

I tipped my head backward and looked up at him. "Are you asking me or *asking* asking me?"

Luca held both of my hands and laced our fingers together. "I'm asking you if I can stay tonight. I'm asking if you'll come home with me tomorrow. I'm asking if I can take you out on proper dates and show you off. I thought I could ask for just one night, Mad, but I can't. I'm asking for all of them."

I bit down on my lip to keep from giggling. "Then ask."

"Madeline." Luca smiled against my neck. "Be my girl?"

I sighed dramatically and smiled. "Fine."

A hearty laugh ripped out of his chest as he laid back on the roof and pulled me on top of him. "You're trouble, you know that?"

"You quoting Travis Tritt just to make me fall for you?"

Luca's brows knitted together. "Who's Travis Tritt?"

I groaned and rolled away, but he pulled me back.

"I'm gonna kiss you tomorrow," he warned.

"Why not tonight?"

"I'll kiss you tonight," he said, cupping my jaw in his hand as he brushed the pad of his thumb over my lips. "But I'm gonna do so much more to you tonight. And tomorrow when I come into the restaurant, I'm gonna go downstairs and kiss you just to make sure that there isn't a doubt in anyone's mind that you're mine."

———

I LOOKED at the clock as the short hand ticked closer and closer to eleven.

Luca was usually in by ten in the morning. He left my place at the same time I did, but needed to drive back to his beach house before coming in.

Part of me was thankful that, as of yet, he hadn't stuck his tongue down my throat in front of the staff.

The other part of me was sorely disappointed.

I sighed and went back to work.

The hand ticked around the clock once more before I heard footsteps on the stairs. Luca's voice echoed as he got closer. My blood simmered, and I quickly brushed away the bits of flour I had on my hands and snuck a glimpse at my reflection in the side of a stainless-steel bowl.

I'd put a little more effort into my appearance today. Something about being Luca's girl made me just a little bit insane, so I dabbed on a little foundation and some mascara.

And then some powder and a little blush.

And then some eyeshadow.

And then liner.

And then a natural lipstick and some gloss.

I felt a little silly going all out for him like I was back in middle school, trying to impress my first crush. So when I stopped at Queen's for my coffee, I didn't bother reapplying the lipstick that printed on my cup.

"And this is our pastry kitchen," I heard him say as he rounded the landing and began to walk down the last few stairs.

*He's giving a tour*. Okay, so it made a little more sense why he hadn't come down as soon as he got here. I pushed my bruised ego aside and looked at the door.

Luca emerged in a grayish-green suit that, on anyone else, would have looked completely douchey.

My gaze roamed up the the shiny black loafers to the trim pants that stopped just above his ankles. His white shirt was unbuttoned a little lower than what would usually be appropriate, and the trim sage jacket with a perfectly creased pocket square had him looking like an Italian supermodel.

The woman he was with carried the same sense of confidence.

Her blonde hair was twisted back in a sleek chignon. She wore a cream-colored blouse that was practically see-through, but had a spaghetti strap camisole underneath.

Her coal pencil skirt started at the middle of her tiny waist and ended at the middle of her calves.

The red soles of her black pumps screamed *money*.

Her complexion was flawless. All she added to it was simple mascara and a bold red lip. She was elegance and grace in a perfectly poised package.

Luca put his hand on the small of her back, just above her lack of an ass and led her through the hustle and bustle. "Celeste, this is Chef Madeline Dorsey, the executive pastry chef here at Revanche."

My cheeks burned with jealousy, but I put on my game face and extended my hand. "Pleasure to meet you, ma'am."

"Celeste Montgomery." She smiled as she returned my handshake and looked around. "You run quite the operation here, Chef Dorsey. Luca has been telling me all about how you and Chef Christensen have redefined southern cuisine into a fine dining experience."

*Oh, so I'm Chef Dorsey, but he's Luca to her?*

Warning sirens blared behind my polite smile.

I looked up and saw Luca wearing the best poker face I'd ever seen. He quickly ushered her away without a word to me, and showed her around the kitchen.

As he led her back to the stairs, Luca put his hand on her back and motioned for her to go up.

Celeste reached over and gave his bicep a squeeze as she said, "I hope I don't sound too eager, but I'm dying to get to that lunch you promised me."

*And I reached nuclear meltdown.*

# 27

# LUCA

This afternoon was never going to end.

I had never been so miserable in my life, and that was including the time that my sisters made me watch *Sleepless in Seattle* and *Sense and Sensibility* in exchange for their silence to our parents regarding a few dirty magazines that the two of them had found in my room.

Celeste was fine, but all I could think about was Maddie and waking up beside her this morning.

Her houseboat was surprisingly comfortable. Not my usual choice of accommodations, but the water was smooth as glass and the gentle rocking was soothing. Having Maddie wake up in my arms was the icing on the cake.

*And so was the quickie in her shower before she left for work.*

I had promised to kiss her as soon as I got in. I knew that it was going to embarrass the hell out of her, but she seemed excited to get things out in the open.

I had learned her tells. *The way she'd bite her lower lip and then roll it out when she realized she had done it. How she'd look up at me all wide-eyed and innocent and then look down.*

The woman was a spitfire, but she had a way of wrapping me around her finger until she had all the power.

*I didn't mind one damn bit.*

"So, as I was saying—the article discusses the relationship between food, fashion, and sex." Celeste raised her glass of chardonnay, subtly tipping it toward me. "You embody all three."

I grinned and leaned back in the chair as I sipped on my bourbon. "If all the journalists who wanted interviews flattered that way, I'd probably be more willing to sit down with them. It would save my assistant a lot of headache."

Celeste smiled coyly and sipped her wine. "Ms. Bancroft may have implied that you would be less than cordial about this being put on your schedule so last minute, but I couldn't give up the chance to interview one of the hottest men in the country. I mean, you were number two in *Sexiest Men Alive last year*."

I chuckled.

"Thank you for your hospitality. The tour, the food—it's been absolutely incredible. You're fascinating, and I can't wait to get started on this editorial piece. I wish we had more time to chat. I'm sure with your career, you'd have some sordid stories to tell."

I glanced over and saw Maddie walking out of the main kitchen with our server as he brought over dessert. "I think the best is yet to come."

Celeste smiled and reached over, placing her hand over mine. "It certainly is, isn't it? You know, Ms. Bancroft did mention that you might be interested in continuing this conversation at the James Beard Awards in September. I'm based out of New York, so if the offer still stands, I'd love to attend with you."

I opened my mouth to cut her off, but she kept going.

"You know, for someone who has no problem being in the public eye, you're quite protective of your personal life. I'd love to get to know you more so I'm able to write more accurately about the man behind the name."

I didn't have time to jerk my hand away before Maddie was at the table.

I couldn't cause a scene, so I slid my hand out from under Celeste's, picked up my drink, and cleared my throat. "Chef Dorsey."

Maddie stood slightly to the left of the server as he placed two perfectly plated desserts in front of us. She kept her eyes low and her jaw set as she calmly explained the dish and urged us to enjoy it.

Flames of hurt and anger burned in her eyes. Maddie didn't like being perceived as anything other than a professional, so I didn't make a move to talk to her while Celeste was still sitting across from me with her phone on the table, recording the conversation.

I made a point to keep my hands clasped together for the rest of the interview. But on more than one occasion, Celeste's high heeled foot made its way over to my side of the table.

I wondered what exactly Astrid had said that would gave her the impression that I wanted take her to the James Beard Awards as my date.

I certainly hadn't told Astrid that I was available. In fact, I had told her rather explicitly to make arrangements for Maddie to go with me.

The lunch with Celeste wrapped up, and I didn't even stop at my office before jogging down the stairs to find Maddie.

I spotted Rae getting ready for the transition between lunch and dinner service, but no Maddie.

"Rae, where's Chef Dorsey?"

"She went over to the inn for an event walk-through with a bride and Miss Hannah."

"Thanks." I darted out the back door that led out to the dumpster pad. I could cut across to the inn, but I didn't want to interrupt her if she was with a client, so I decided to text her instead.

LUCA

Can we talk? That wasn't what it looked like.

I sent the text and turned around to go back inside, but stopped when I heard the chime of an incoming text.

I pulled my phone out but there was no new message. *Huh.*

I typed out another text and hit send.

LUCA

Maddie, I need to see you.

The sound chimed again.

"Maddie?" I called out as I crossed the pavement to where some line cooks had overturned crates to serve as seating for their smoke breaks.

I rounded the corner of the dumpster and found Maddie sitting alone. *Shit.*

"Mad, that wasn't what it looked like."

She shook her head and dabbed the rims of her eyes with her fingertips. "It's whatever. I need to get back to work."

*Damn, she looked pretty today, and I'd made her fucking cry for real this time.*

"It was a last-minute interview that Astrid sprung on me.

I didn't even know she was coming when I left your house this morning."

"I don't fucking care about some stupid interview, Luca."

"*Ascolti, Tesoro*—listen to me, it was just business. You're the one who didn't want anyone to know about us. What was I supposed to do?"

Maddie swallowed hard and nodded. "You're right. You had no reason to tell her you already had a date. You had no reason to tell her to back the hell off and act like a damn professional."

I knew she was being sarcastic, and I deserved every ounce of it. Still, I couldn't help but feel just a little bit of satisfaction. "Are you jealous, Maddie?"

"Yes, I'm jealous, you idiot!" she shouted, throwing her hands in the air. "Because fucking *gorgeous* women like her throw themselves at you every damn day! What the hell am I supposed to do with that? I hate being jealous! I'm not that kind of girl!"

"Good!" I shouted back. "Because it's about damn time you admitted that you want me as fucking bad as I want you! You know how much it's sucked chasing you around just to get bits and pieces of you, but not the whole damn thing? *I want you, Maddie!*"

Maddie shook her head. Tears filled her eyes as she stammered. "You don't! You think you do, but you don't, Luca."

She wiped the rivulets of tears away and tried to put on a brave face. I reached for her but she jumped back.

"I'm not the girl that guys settle down with. I'm the girl they have a good time with before they find what they really want. Half of the women in this town owe me a fucking fruit basket for turning their boys into men and sending them off to their forever homes—committed, loyal, and responsible like I'm a damn animal shelter or some shit."

I ached to touch her as she gasped for air through the tears.

Maddie shook her head. "I can't do it with you. It'll hurt too bad when it's over. You'll move on to be with a woman like that. But me? I won't survive you, Luca. You're going to leave, and I'm going to be here."

"*Tesoro*," I soothed as I put my hands on her waist.

She was trembling. I wanted nothing more than to pull her into my arms.

"It was just a misunderstanding. This doesn't change anything. Last night—you and me—we decided that this is what we want. *You* are what I want."

Her lip trembled and she grimaced as she shook her head. "You don't know that for sure."

"You're right," I began. "I don't. I don't have a crystal ball that's gonna tell me what's going to happen in the future, but I know that one thing is for sure—I haven't stopped thinking about you since the moment I saw you walk into the gym in California. Not one minute, Madeline. Not when I watched you kick ass at the competition. Not when you stormed out of here telling me you quit. Not then. Not now. And if I have my way—I'll never stop thinking about you again."

Maddie turned to pull away. "I can't do this."

"No." I raised my voice and grabbed her arm.

y now I was sure that every single staff member was watching from the corner of the rooftop dining space, but I didn't care.

"You're not the only one here with something to lose, Mad."

"Luca, please," she said as she swiped at a tear that was

running down her cheek. Her voice turned to a solemn whisper as she begged. "This is embarrassing. Let me go do my job."

"No."

"Luca—"

The door to the pastry kitchen opened as I grabbed a fistful of the front of her chef's coat and pulled her in.

I held the back of her head steady and kissed her hard.

For a moment, she was stunned.

Maddie let out a little whimper when my tongue pressed against the seam of her lips, but I swallowed it down.

The door slammed shut. I looked up to see Scott and Rae, but I didn't pay them much attention. Maddie had tears in her eyes, and I wasn't about to let them see her like that.

"I want you," I snapped. "And I'm pretty fucking used to getting what I want. So if you back out now, just know that eventually, this—*us*—is going to happen."

"How are you so sure?" she cried.

Maddie let her forehead rest against my chest, and I felt her walls begin to crumble.

I held her, letting her hide in my arms before she raised her head to look at me.

"*Tesoro,* if you don't think I have anything to lose here, then I haven't done a good job of showing you just how much I want you."

"I get jealous. I don't like feeling inferior or like I don't belong with you." Maddie's professional tone had a heavier dose of her southern drawl. Her cute little twang came out when she was either tipsy or pissed.

And she wasn't tipsy.

I scraped my thumbnail over my lower lip and shook my head in confusion. "Why would you feel like you don't belong with me? Especially here."

"I'm not talking about here. New York? The awards?" She lowered her voice. "Someone like Celeste is who you're *supposed* to be seen with."

I winced. I had hoped that she hadn't been close enough to hear Celeste's proposition, but that just reminded me that I had an assistant to kill.

"You heard that part?"

Maddie nodded. "Luca, we both have careers to think about. I need to be able to do my job without everyone thinking that I'm sleeping with the boss, and you need someone on your arm who can help you maintain your image. I get that. Look, last night—"

"Last night was not a mistake," I said, effectively cutting her off. "Neither was dinner at my place or being with you the night of the watch party. This is not a mistake. You're scared."

"And you're not?" she exclaimed.

I grinned and placed a soft kiss on her lips. She let out a little sigh and I felt some of the tension melt away from her shoulders.

"Of course I am. You scare the hell outta me, Mad."

I watched the sunshine return to her eyes. She tucked her forehead into the crook of my neck and rested there. I pressed a kiss into her hair and stroked my fingers along the back of her neck.

"Everyone's watching, aren't they?" she asked.

"Yep."

She tilted her chin up so that her forehead was pressed against my lips. I gave her a little kiss with a smile.

Maddie closed her eyes. They crinkled at the corners just like they always did when she was happy. "So much for keeping it quiet. People are gonna talk, you know."

"I know. Let 'em talk."

Maddie turned her head and looked over her shoulder to where the entire staff stood, watching. They craned over the railing from the rooftop dining area, spilled out the back door of the pastry kitchen and main kitchen, and peered out the windows of the dining room. No one was getting any work done and, for once, I didn't care.

There was something I still needed to do. In all the last minute mayhem caused by Celeste showing up, I never went to the pastry kitchen to kiss Maddie.

"Madeline?"

"Yeah?"

"I'm gonna kiss you now."

She didn't say anything—just lifted her chin and let her lower lip graze mine as her mouth parted and she sucked in a quiet breath.

I kissed her soft and slow.

She let me cradle her cheeks in my hands, stroking her soft skin. I slid my hands down her neck to her waist and rested them on her hips, pulling her closer.

Maddie snaked her arms around my neck and kissed me back.

Whoops and cheers carried through the warm air as Maddie broke away from me, laughing.

I grinned, wrapping her up in my arms. "We should probably get back to work."

"Probably," she laughed.

I picked up her hand and kissed the back of it before lacing our fingers together and turning back toward the building.

"You two lovebirds done making out behind the dumpsters?" Scott asked. He was leaned up against the brick wall with his arms crossed.

Maddie turned a deep scarlet, but we both knew Scott wasn't mad.

"Back to work, everybody." I barked.

Scott pushed away from the building and started our way. "Not so fast. Weather report says that the hurricane that's out in the Atlantic is turning and coming our way."

"How many days until it hits?" Maddie asked

Scott shrugged. "Right now we've got forty-eight hours, but you never know. She's stalling as a Category 3 right now and getting stronger, so it could get real bad. Carol's got her staff already starting on weatherizing."

I look down at her. "Fill the outsider in. What's happening?"

Maddie gave my hand a squeeze before letting go. "We have a hell of a lot of work to do."

# 28

# MADELINE

I loved hurricanes. I loved the buzz of energy in the air before a big storm. There was really nothing like it. It got my blood pumping and my senses heightened like nothing else. I loved the rush of going head-to-head with Mother Nature.

My team and I worked non-stop getting the restaurant ready to take a beating. We doubled up on our wholesale orders and delivered extras to all the businesses that carried our pastries. If we were shut down, they would still have plenty of product to sell.

Everything that could be stored in the freezer was moved over so that it was packed as tightly as possible. Everything would stay much colder with it being full. If we happened to lose power, we wouldn't lose ingredients while we waited for the generators to kick in.

The storm was six hours from making landfall. I did the final checks of the restaurant before locking up and praying for the best.

It wasn't uncommon for me to be the last one at Revanche before a storm. Scott and Carol both had families, so I always volunteered to do the final walk-through while everyone else made their way home.

I made a quick stop at Harlowe Bay Assisted Living to see my mom, just in case I couldn't make it on Monday. But by the time I ran out of the building and through the parking lot, the rain had picked up and was letting loose in a torrential downpour.

My phone rang the second I slammed the door to my Jeep. I swiped across the screen as soon as I saw Luca's name. "Hello?"

There was a pause, and I could barely hear him over the battering rain on the roof. "Tell me you're not still out in this mess."

"I'm about to head home."

"Where are you?"

"Morehead City. I came out here to see my mom before the storm came in."

"Stay where you are and send me the address. I'm coming to get you."

"Luca, you don't have to do that. I'll be fine. I'm heading home right now."

I heard the faint sounds of a door slamming before he growled. "To a fucking houseboat."

"Not my first hurricane, DeRossi."

"Send me the damn address, Mad."

I huffed and fired off a text. Luca's beach house was closer than driving back to my place. My Jeep really needed new tires, and it would save Steve from having to put up with me.

I usually stayed in the guest room at his house if I didn't feel safe on the water. Staying at Luca's sounded nice, especially after the hectic days leading up to the storm making landfall.

I felt stupid for losing my cool over Celeste Montgomery throwing herself at Luca. I was rarely threatened by other women, but something about being with Luca made me insecure as hell.

Every time I looked at my phone, I was reminded just how different we were.

*Maddie who?*

*OMG, she's so normal.*

*She's got tits and an ass. No wonder he's tapping that.*

*That's his rebound from Amalia? Yikes.*

Last night we took a picture together. Luca came home with me and sat on my roof to share a late, *late* dinner before calling it a night.

He snapped the photo when I fell asleep on his chest. Only half of my face was visible since I was using him as a pillow. My eyes were closed, and I was serene.

The selfie had Luca craning his neck down and kissing the top of my head. He posted it to his social media with the caption, *La mia tesoro*—my treasure.

As the kids say, the internet was shook.

Still, every time I looked at Instagram and saw the picture of us snuggled up, I smiled.

And then when I saw comments about his ex-girlfriend, Amalia, I was constantly reminded just how insignificant I was.

*Luca had dated a fucking supermodel, and I was just... me.*

Headlights cut through the parking lot as Luca guiding his BMW through the deep puddles.

Luca got out and hurried to my door with an umbrella. "Is your Jeep gonna be okay staying here?"

I nodded as he guided me to the passenger's side of his car. "Yeah, it's fine, but I don't have clothes or anything with me."

Luca chuckled as he shut my door. He ran to the other side and slid in behind the wheel as he shot me a devilish grin. "Well then. I guess you'll just have to wear what I let you wear while we're stuck at my place."

————

To my surprise, Luca actually had clothes for me to wear.

Kind of.

He took my hand and led me straight to the bedroom after he pulled his car into the garage.

"I had Astrid pick up some stuff for you in the event that you decided to stay with me more than a night at a time. I, uh, I hope it's alright."

It was mostly pajamas and loungewear, but it was more than any other boyfriend had ever done. *Even if it was done by the assistant who had made it clear that she did not approve of me.*

I found them already folded and tucked into a drawer in Luca's room. It was a little surprising since this it was just a rental house, but the effort wasn't lost on me.

"*Hai trovato quello che cercavi, Tesoro?*" Luca came up behind me and wrapped his arms around my middle as I held the drawer open.

I leaned my head back on his shoulder and kissed his neck. "You know I love when you ramble in Italian, but you either have to teach me or translate."

He craned his head around and kissed my cheek. "Find what you were looking for?" His husky murmurs vibrated against my skin. Fire zipped down my spine, and I curled my toes against the hardwood floors.

I nodded, unable to form even the simplest of words. Not when he was kissing down my neck. Not when his hands slid under my drenched shirt and massaged my hips. Not when his bulge was pressed against the crease of my ass.

His stubble roughed up my skin, leaving it raw and red as he turned me and peppered my throat with kisses.

My chest heaved and he pushed his hips into mine until I was trapped between him and the dresser.

Luca peeled the wet top off my torso and tossed it aside. He grabbed my hands and laced our fingers together before bringing them to his lips and kissing across my knuckles.

Outside, the rain battered against the windows and the wind howled as the storm got closer and closer. It was barely after five in the evening, but the sky was pitch black.

Lucky for us, it had lost power and was coming in as a Category 2. Watching the raw, untamed power of Mother Nature left me riding a high better than anything else.

Luca tilted his head and nipped at the soft skin under my ear. "Cook with me?" he asked in a gravelly timbre.

I nodded in agreement as Luca's hands moved to my waist, unbuttoned my damp shorts, and dragged the zipper down. He pushed them down to my feet and hooked his fingers in the waist of my simple cotton panties.

"Are these wet too?" he asked as one finger slid down the crease between my thigh and my throbbing pussy.

I gave a listless nod as my eyes closed. I sucked in a breath and waited for the delicious pressure of him shoving two of those exceptionally talented fingers deep into my core.

It never came.

"Good." He slid his hand into my panties and cupped my sex. I let out a quick gasp, but Luca didn't give me any relief. "That's how I want you, Madeline."

I whimpered at being toyed with when he pulled his

hand away. My nipples were diamond pointed, and my pussy ached for relief.

"Cook with me. That way we can eat, and then I can have you for dessert."

*Hot damn.*

The culinary gods had smiled upon me. At this point, I'd sell my soul to a sea witch if I could have Luca taste every inch of my body at his leisure.

I made a move for a pair of pajama pants, but he shook his head.

"Trust me. You won't be needing those." Luca slowly unbuttoned the light blue dress shirt he was wearing, pulled it off, and handed it to me. It still had traces of his cologne. I wanted to bury my nose in it.

I slid my arms in and noticed the monogrammed initials on the sleeve. *Because of course it was custom embroidered.*

I was southern and had an appreciation for a good monogram. My Jeep had a curly, vinyl cutout of my initials on the back window.

This was rich person monogramming.

This was *don't lose my expensive as hell dry cleaning* monogramming.

I pushed that thought to the back of my mind and fastened two buttons just below my breasts. My ass hung out the bottom, but there wasn't much I could do about that.

Luca had already walked back to the kitchen and was checking on something in the oven when I tiptoed in.

He gave me a smile as he set the oven mitts aside. "You're much different when you're here. You know that?"

"What do you mean?"

I leaned across the island and watched his knife fly through the vegetables. It was mesmerizing.

For someone who wasn't in the kitchen everyday

anymore, his knife skills were still impeccable. He had done a julienne that would make chef instructors everywhere weep from the uniformity and precision.

He shrugged. "You're quiet here. Not, uh, not shot-gunning beers and having dance parties on top of bars."

"Must be the company."

"Am I really that boring?" He chuckled. "I know I've got a few years on you, but I thought I still had some game left."

I slinked toward him and stood to his left. I peered around his shoulder and watched as he finished slicing and dicing.

"You're not boring," I quickly clarified. "I dunno. I just think I'm comfortable around you."

Luca hummed and nodded. "I like that."

"Is that an issue for you? The age difference?" I asked.

Seven years wasn't a lot, but it wasn't nothing either.

He shook his head and pointed for me to check on the sauce he had simmering on the range. I gave it a little stir and grabbed a spoon to taste it.

Not bad.

I poured some salt in my hand and took a pinch, sprinkling it over the surface before stirring it in. Luca brushed by to get to the fridge, trailing his hand across the small of my back with a kitchen warning of, "Behind."

That's how we made dinner. The two of us were quiet as we danced around the kitchen—stealing glances and touches here and there.

His hand on my hip as he leaned over me. Me squeezing his ass when I spun around to grab a tray off the island.

It was a waltz.

We moved around each other with ease. Reading each other's mind and predicting what to do next. It was a comfort I hadn't felt in a long time.

Luca left me to plate the pasta while he got the fireplace roaring. Sure, it was a balmy eighty degrees outside, but with the storm raging, it felt right.

The flames crackled as we sat at the dining room table and ate. The raviolo al' uovo was divine. The pasta was perfectly tender and the runny yolk in the center blended with the sage butter sauce and blistered tomatoes.

"Luca, this is divine."

He dabbed his mouth with his napkin and smiled. "Should be. I've been making it since I was a kid. Family recipe."

"You cooked a lot as a kid?"

Luca nodded. "My Nonna taught all of us as soon as we were big enough to stand on a chair and watch."

I smiled into my wine and sipped, enjoying the medley of flavors on my tongue. "So you just kept cooking? Did you always know you wanted to be a chef?"

He chuckled. "Are you interviewing me?"

"Just trying to get to know you," I admitted as I swirled my fork through the last streaks of sauce on my empty plate. "I don't really know a lot about you."

"You didn't know me, but you decided that you didn't like me?"

"Something like that." I sighed. "Have I apologized for that yet?"

Luca cleared our dishes and loaded them into the dishwasher, kicking it closed with his foot. "You haven't," he began. "But I'm glad you didn't like me."

"Until I thought you were just a guy named Luke who hit on me at the gym."

He dimmed the kitchen lights and walked into the living room, taking a seat on the couch. I followed him, eager to snuggle up and get warm since I was still in his shirt and a pair of thin panties.

Luca tucked me into his side. "Remember when you asked how I was so sure that I wanted you?"

I nodded.

"It's because of that. Because you were so convinced that you didn't like me. I knew that if I could make you want me as much as I wanted you, that this would be real."

My heart pounded against my ribcage. I had been fighting him hard—or so I thought.

I tried everything to keep from falling for him. Hell, I even tried to quit my job.

Somehow, Luca stuck to me like a tick on a deer. And the more I was around him the harder I fell.

There was no escaping it. He blew into my life like a hurricane—whirling in and turning everything on its head. He wrecked every obstacle that I put in his way.

There was no stopping him. No hiding from him.

"Luca," I panted, full of trepidation. Electricity blazed through me; the current shaking me down to my bones.

"Yeah, *Tesoro*?" His brown eyes were dark and fraught with lust.

My chest rose and fell with weighted breaths. By the time I looked up at him, he was already working at the buttons that fastened the shirt I wore.

"I want you."

Luca's patience drained. He jerked the sides of the shirt away and pulled it off my arms. He grabbed my panties and yanked them away, leaving me naked and desperate for him.

The windows shook and the storm waged war with the coast, but in here—here with him—I was safe.

Luca grabbed the neck of his undershirt and pulled it

over his head. He loosened his belt buckle and unbuttoned his jeans, but left them on.

"You like storms, Madeline?" he growled as he pulled me to my feet.

"Love them."

"Is there anyone on the beach during one?"

I shook my head no.

"Good," he rasped as he twisted my arms behind my back, cuffing my wrists with his hand as he marched me to the side of the A-frame house that faced the beach.

It was all windows and had a stunning view of the Atlantic. But tonight, it was black.

Luca pressed me, naked, up against the cool glass and my nipples perked in response. He wedged his foot in between my ankles and kicked them a shoulder's width apart.

I gasped when he lowered his lips to my ear and slowly raised one of my hands, then the other, pressing them against the glass so that I was spread wide. He had me completely exposed and bared.

Luca's teeth grazed the curve of my ear. He bit down on my lobe before gruffly whispering, "You know what someone would see if they happened to be on the beach right now?"

He punctuated his question with a firm bite on my neck. "They'd see you completely naked. They'd see your perfect tits smashed against the window."

He trailed his knuckles down my ribs to the dip at my waist. "They'd see your flawless curves."

Luca bent low and knelt behind me. He ran a finger from my ankle, up the side of my calf, to the back of my knee. He trailed it up my thigh, stopping just shy of where I craved him most.

"They'd see your legs—legs like a damn dream, Madeline." He kissed the back of my thighs—first the right, then the left.

He rose to his feet and gathered my hair together, twisting it three times around his hand and forcefully jerking it to the side so that my neck and back were open to him.

"The world deserves to see how beautiful you are. Open your eyes."

It was a feat of strength to peel my eyelids apart. When I did, I saw the storm surge.

The wind whipped the palm trees back and forth. Rain pounded the windows.

*And I was staring it down. He was Poseidon and I was his goddess. Luca made me feel powerful.*

My body trembled as he caged me in, bracketing my spread feet with his. He placed his hands over mine and pressed his cock against the curve of my ass. Luca dropped a kiss on the crook of my neck and said, "Are you ready for this, *Tesoro*?"

Somehow, I knew he wasn't just talking about sex. I didn't know if there was really any way to be ready for what being with Luca might bring.

But in that moment, I swore I was invincible.

"Yes," I said as my breath fogged the glass.

Luca slid his hand between my legs and dipped his fingers into my hot core. I whimpered as he tested me, circling one finger around inside of my pussy.

It was just enough to make me cry out when he didn't immediately give me more. He grazed my G-spot, and I pounded my fist against the glass in frustration.

I heard the zipper on his jeans lower. The tear of the foil. The muffled roll of the latex over his shaft, and felt the warm head of his hard cock when it pressed against me. Luca bent his knees and drove in once, then twice.

"Luca—" I begged.

"Patience, *Tesoro*. I don't wanna hurt you."

*Damn him and that big dick of his. It really was unfair to the rest of the men on earth. There was no contest.*

Luca drove in a third time, giving me all of himself. I nearly choked at the fullness. He brushed my hair aside and peppered my shoulder with kisses as I relaxed around him.

He wrapped his arms around my chest and palmed both of my breasts in his hands. He rolled my nipples between his fingers as he began to thrust. My forehead dropped onto the window when I let out a cry of ecstasy and anticipation.

"Yes—*oh, oh!*" I groaned as my senses heightened.

Luca dropped one hand and gave my clit rhythmic flicks as he took me against the window.

"Luca!" I screamed as the mounting pressure building inside of me became unbearable. "Please—"

"*Tu sei tutto per me,*" he whispered again as he quickened his pace. I felt the tremble in his body and knew that he wasn't far behind. "Come for me, beautiful," he commanded.

I shattered and cried out as every muscle in my body poured into my climax.

Luca threw his head back and smacked his hand against the window when his release overtook him. He closed an arm around me and held me close as the hurricane around us kept roaring.

"*Tu sei tutto per me,*" he mumbled into the top of my head.

"What's that mean?" I panted as I came down from my high.

He placed a soft kiss into my hair, his gruff timbre sending aftershocks rippling through my body.

"You're everything to me."

# 29

# LUCA

"**Y**ou okay?" I asked quietly as I held Maddie against the window.

The power flickered as the storm billowed and waged war around us.

Maddie nodded, leaning her forehead on the glass as she caught her breath. Our bodies were slick with sweat. She wrapped her arms around her waist, and I kept her close. Eventually, though, I had to let her go so I could deal with the condom.

When I came back after changing into a pair of gray sweatpants, she was curled up on the couch. She had slipped my button-up back over her shoulders and was holding it closed with a tight grip. Her eyes were closed and her breathing was steady.

Maddie stirred as I settled on the couch. "Hm? Whatimezit?"

I chuckled and nudged her so I could get my thighs underneath her head. She let out a soft exhale and laid her head in my lap.

Gently, I pulled her hair out from under her and

smoothed it down. Her delicate eyelids closed again, and she let out a contented sigh.

For hours we stayed like that. Sometimes one or both of us would doze off. Sometimes we'd talk about nothing important, simply enjoying the quiet company and companionship. Around Maddie I didn't have to be *Luca DeRossi*. I didn't want to be him.

Around me, she was calm.

When we were together, we didn't have the pressure of living up to what everyone else expected us to be.

I couldn't imagine living in the same place I grew up like Maddie.

Staying where I was raised would have made it impossible to leave the younger me behind and grow into who I wanted to be.

For me, I had the pressure of living up to my name, keeping tons of people employed, and leveraging my celebrity to keep my star rising.

They say it's lonely at the top, but no one ever warned me about how shitty that feels.

I didn't need someone who "got it". I needed someone who didn't want to get it. Someone who didn't care if I was a celebrity chef or just a cook. I'd had my fill of women using me for my name. I was done with that.

Maddie snuggled closer as the clock rounded two in the morning. I scooped her up in my arms and kissed her forehead as I carried her back to my bed.

---

"Mornin', sexy." Maddie grinned as I stumbled into the kitchen. Her little southern accent was on full display this morning. "How do you like your eggs?"

I rubbed the sleep from my eyes and walked up behind her while she pulled the eggs from the fridge.

"How long have you been up?" I mumbled as I stood at her back and wrapped my arms around her waist. I kissed her cheek and then her neck.

"Since five."

I looked at the clock. It was a quarter after nine. "Shoulda slept in." I nuzzled the scruff on my jaw against the crook of her neck. "I woulda made you breakfast in bed."

She closed the door to the refrigerator. "Internal alarm clock. Too many years of waking up before the sun. I can't sleep past five unless I'm hungover. Besides, you cooked last night. Only fair I tackle breakfast. Eggs?"

"Soft scrambled."

"With butter?"

I chuckled. "Is there any other way?"

She cracked a couple eggs in a bowl with a practiced efficiency.

"Coffee?" I asked.

Maddie pointed to the coffee maker that was still steaming and the empty mug that sat beside it. "I didn't know how you took it, so I figured I'd wait."

I filled the *OBX* mug to the brim and took a cautious sip. "Just black," I said as I leaned back against the counter and watched her whisk the eggs in the skillet over a low flame.

"I'll remember that for next time."

I liked the sound of that—that she would be here again. Not because I asked, but because she wanted to be here.

The relentless downpour from the hurricane making landfall had turned to a miserable drizzle. It was daylight, but the ocean was still a bleak, angry gray as the last of the storm churned up the coast.

Maddie slid a plate and a fork across the counter to me and dropped the skillet in the sink.

"How's your mom handle all this?" I asked as I shoveled in the first bite. *Breakfast heaven.*

I couldn't remember the last time someone had cooked for me outside of a restaurant.

My ex sure hadn't. Then again, she didn't eat much of anything. It was always *juice cleanse* this and *lose five before Milan* that.

I swore after I broke things off with Amalia that I'd never go back to someone like that.

At its best, our relationship was cordial. At its worst it was her breathing down my neck or whining to trying and get me to go out to clubs and red carpet events.

Maddie was content closing down her favorite hole-in-the-wall bar or spending her nights in with her friends. Not once had she ever been looking at her phone when we were together.

Maddie shrugged and sipped on her sand-colored coffee. "Fine. Most of the time she doesn't even know what's going on nowadays."

"It's just you and her, right? I mean, you don't have any siblings?"

She wagged her finger at me and shook her head. "Don't start that, Luca. This isn't a pity party. It is what it is, and I've learned to live with it."

"Just trying to get to know my girlfriend."

Her eyebrows raised. "Your what?"

"You heard me."

"I know I heard you. I was just giving you a chance to take it back."

"Why the hell would I do that? We're sleeping together — *exclusively*, I might add. I've met your friends and you're gonna meet mine. When we're in New York I'm gonna take you home and you're gonna meet the whole motley DeRossi crew. And when you're comfortable with it, I'm gonna go with you one of these Mondays and meet your mom."

Maddie blew out a nervous breath, "Oh, you—you're saying a lot of things, DeRossi."

"I'm not saying anything that I don't mean."

"Luca..."

"I'm all in, Maddie."

She turned away and dropped her mug in the sink. I pushed off of the kitchen counter and grabbed her arm. "Talk to me, Mad."

"I just... This is... It's moving really fast, Luca."

"I've been chasing you for months—you're just finally catching up, *Tesoro*." I said, sliding my hand down her arm and clasping her hand, leading her to the couch.

I sat on one end, but when she moved a throw pillow and sat down at the other, I dragged her across to lay with me.

"New York," she began.

"What about it?"

"I just... I don't know what to pack or plan for. You need to give me dates so I can book my plane ticket."

I knew she was changing the subject, but I decided to go with it for now.

I laughed and bent down to give her a peck. "Maddie, I'm not letting you buy your own plane ticket."

She frowned and began to sit up, "I'm more than capable of paying for my own ticket, thank you very much."

"Are you always this stubborn?"

"Yup."

I shook my head. "Mad, it's not up for discussion. Look, I'll give you the dates, but only so you can make the schedule and have the rest your team cover the days that you're gone."

She laid her head back in the corner of my chest and closed her eyes. "Tell me what we're gonna be doing so I know what to pack."

"Well," I began. "We'll get there on Friday and stay at my place in the city. There are a couple events I wanna take you to over the weekend. The awards are on Monday, and, uh, after that I figured we'd spend a day in Brooklyn with my folks before flying back."

I could see her doing the math in her head and freaking out inside.

"Hey," I soothed. "It's gonna be great."

Maddie nodded and closed her eyes, drifting off as the rain pelted the windows.

Just as she settled into a comfortable sleep, her phone rang. I looked over my shoulder and saw it lit up on the kitchen counter.

Carefully, I slid out from under her, and walked over to pick it up before the shrill ringing woke her. I saw Steve's name on the screen and swiped to answer.

"Hello?"

There was a pregnant pause. "Oh. It's you."

I rolled my eyes. "Yeah. Uh, Maddie's asleep. Want me to take a message?"

"Isn't that what voicemail's for? Why the fuck are you answering her phone?" he grunted.

I pressed my fist against the cool countertops to keep from saying something that would make her friends hate me. *Or kill me.* "Like I said, she's asleep."

Steve was quiet again for a moment before he finally said, "No message. I was just checkin' on her."

"She's good."

"Alright. Make sure it stays that way. I don't wanna have to come break your face."

"Understood." Just as I hung up her phone, Maddie wandered in.

"Who was that?" she asked as I set her phone down. She rubbed her eyes and let out a little yawn as she stretched her arms.

"Steve. Just making sure you were okay."

Maddie nodded and took my hand, leading me back to the bedroom without another word about the fact that I had answered her phone.

There was a screened in-deck off the side of the main bedroom. She pushed back the heavy sliding door and stepped out.

The air was heavy and humid. A little cooler than usual, but that just meant it didn't feel like I was living in a boiling pot of soup.

I didn't spend a ton of time in the south—usually bouncing between Los Angeles, Las Vegas, Chicago, and New York City. I was not prepared for the humidity.

The first day I had gotten settled at the rental house, I put on my sneakers to go for a run on the beach—one of my favorite things to do in California.

I didn't even make it a mile before I was drenched in sweat and felt like I was choking on a soggy sock.

Maddie laid her palms on my shoulders and pushed me down onto the wicker loveseat. The canvas covered cushions sank as she straddled my hips, facing me and wrapping her arms around my neck.

The rain had turned to a gentle pitter patter. I put my hands on her hips to help steady her.

Instead of the pajamas I kept here for her, Maddie was in a pair of my boxers and one of my undershirts. The hem was tied off in a little knot, showing a strip of her tan stomach.

"Are you gonna break my heart, Luca DeRossi?" she asked with a toss of her hair.

It was so out of the blue. I didn't even know how to respond.

Instead, I just responded with a question of my own. "Are you gonna break mine?"

A little smile toyed at the corner of her mouth. I didn't know where her head was at. There was something going on behind those gray eyes that was as tumultuous as the sea.

She'd told me a little about her mom's dementia. Still, she kept her cards close to the vest.

Maddie prided herself on being the strong one—always being the one to be there for everyone else. I saw it in the way she worried about her staff, taking the brunt of the workload. I saw it in the way she cared for her friends— giving her friend, Kristin, meals that were already made so that she didn't have to stress about cooking.

She would call Steve to have him come over and fix things on her houseboat. At first that annoyed the hell out of me. I wanted to do those things for her. Then I realized that she was just giving him something to do.

"Tell me about you dad," I said, shifting her so that she was sitting in my lap.

Maddie let out a non-committal hum and just shook her head. "You don't wanna hear about my daddy issues."

"Don't say it like that, *Tesoro*."

"Like what?"

"Like whatever he did is your fault. It isn't."

She let out a sarcastic laugh. "Don't start with this, Luca."

"Maddie, listen to me. Saying *daddy issues* like it's some

kind of self-deprecating insult is fucked up. It's not on you that your dad wasn't the man he should've been. His failure to be a fucking parent is on him and him alone."

She blinked and looked up at the ceiling as if she were praying to be whisked away. "Never underestimate the power of silence."

"What do you mean?"

She cleared her throat. "When I was in fourth grade, he kissed me on the head and saw me off to the bus before school. When I got home, he was gone. Never came back."

There was a weight to the silence that followed, and it broke my heart for her. I tightened my grip around her.

"Have you heard from him since?"

She tucked her head between my neck and shoulder and quietly sniffed back tears. "He, um... he left my mom a note. Said that living here, being tied down to a wife and a daughter—it wasn't enough for him. He always wanted to be a country singer. He did pretty good playing bars around here and thought he'd take his act to Nashville. Make it big, you know? Every time he'd move or get a different place, Mom would send him pictures and letters, telling him how I was. He never wrote back. I never tried to get in touch with him."

"When'd they divorce?"

"They didn't." Maddie dabbed at her eyes and toyed with a loose string on the hem of the boxers she was wearing. "It wasn't that he didn't want me or mom, or even that he didn't love us. We just weren't enough for him. Somehow, I think that made it hurt worse." She sniffed. "If he didn't love me, I could get over that. Being hurt by someone who loves you? That kind of pain hurts the deepest."

Maddie took a deep breath as I rubbed idle circles on her thigh, just to let her know that I was there.

"Mom kept holding on to the hope that maybe he'd get his fill and come back to us. Even back then I knew that he wouldn't. I wanted them to get divorced. It would've been easier. I wanted her to remarry someone good who would take care of her and give her a good life. She just kept holding out hope before the dementia got bad."

With one hand, I brushed her long tangles of hair out of her face and cradled her head against my chest. With the other, I took her hand in mine and pressed a kiss to the back of her hand, then into her palm.

Quietly, I asked, "Is it too soon for me to tell you that I love you?"

Maddie looked up at me with eyes wide. She stammered and stuttered for a moment, pushing away from me and beelining to the other side of the little deck.

She crossed her arms over her waist and shook her head. "Luca, I—I can't... I just... I'm not ready. I—"

Slowly, I got up and walked toward her.

Maddie looked shaken. I wasn't sure if it was from the *I love you* or talking about her dad. Either way, I wasn't running.

I stood in front of her, toe to toe, and held her pink cheeks in my hands. I cradled her jaw and took in the symmetry of her heart-shaped face.

Her flawless skin with its beautiful, sun-kissed glow.

The way her silver eyes widened.

Her pink lips that were so good at kissing.

There wasn't a damn question in my mind whether or not I loved that girl.

I leaned down and placed a gentle kiss on her lips and then rested my forehead on hers. "That's okay, *Tesoro*. I have enough love for the both of us. You just use it until you're ready."

# 30

## MADELINE

HOT GUY FROM THE GYM IN LA

Have a great day, beautiful. I love you.

I smiled at the text from Luca before pocketing my phone into my chef whites. The damage from the hurricane wasn't severe, so two days after the storm passed, it was back to business as usual.

Luca had some business to attend to in Los Angeles. He begged for me to come with him. Since I was already leaving the kitchen for our New York trip, I passed.

Every morning he was gone, Luca set his alarm so that he would wake up when I got to work. And every morning like clockwork, he texted me that he loved me. It terrified and utterly disarmed me.

"Madeline Lee Dorsey," Hannah Jane said as she traipsed into the pastry kitchen, her heels clicking across the floor.

She was the perfect image of a modern southern belle. Her leopard print pencil skirt hit just below her knees. She had a breezy blouse tucked in at the waist and a pearl necklace around her throat.

"Where the hell have you been?"

I looked around the busy kitchen. "Um... working?"

"Not what I meant!" she hissed. "You always ride out hurricanes at Steve's house! You had us worried sick!"

I went back to piping delicate tiny beads around each tier of the wedding cake that was sitting on my turntable.

"I was at Luca's," I mumbled.

Her eyes widened, and she let out a restrained squeal. "*Please* tell me you two are finally done dancing around each other. I heard about the kiss behind the restaurant. Me and Kris pulled up the security camera footage from outside the inn. Watched the whole damn thing."

I huffed and set my piping bag down. "We're about as official as you can get," I admitted. I looked left and right before lowering my voice. "He said *I love you.*"

Hannah Jane bounced up and down so hard I thought she was going to snap a heel. "Ohmygodohmygodohmygod!"

"Will you shut up?" I hissed in a stage-whisper.

"That's it. I'm going. I need to get started planning your wedding. I'm clearing my whole calendar for next summer. We're gonna have to plan a trip to Raleigh to go dress shopping. Don't worry about the cake! I have a girl for that. You're not making your own cake."

Before she could ramble anymore, or shove me in the damn white dress herself, I slid off my stool, grabbed her wrist, and pulled her into the walk-in fridge.

Hannah Jane shivered and rubbed her arms. "It's cold in here."

I shrugged. "You get used to it."

"Why are we in the fridge?"

"Because this is where I come to scream when I'm pissed off, and the staff knows not to come in."

Hannah's face bleached. "Oh God. You're gonna kill me, aren't you?"

I rolled my eyes. "No, I just don't want more rumors about me and Luca getting started."

"Because you made out with him in front of the entire restaurant," she pointed out. Hannah's voice softened and she smiled. "Mad, you're crazy about him. Stop pretending like he's still the asshat you thought he was. I think we all know he's one of the good ones."

"He wants me to meet his family when we're in New York."

"So? That's how these things go, Mad."

I pulled my hair out of the bun it was in and rubbed the sore spots on my head. "I don't know what I'm doing," I groaned. "He's just so sure of himself all the time. He says he wants this and that he loves me and all these sweet things that I should be really happy about, but I'm not!"

"You know what you need? G.N.O.—you, me, Kris, Bee, and Mel. We're going out tonight, we're getting good and wasted, and we'll call the boys to get us home."

"Luca gets home from California tonight. He's coming to my place as soon as he gets in."

"Great! He can be your designated driver. Have him pick you up at the bar. Problem solved."

"Han—"

It was too late. Her thumbs were already flying across her phone as she rallied the troops. "Eight-thirty at Jokers. Be there. Look hot." She pushed the door to the walk-in fridge open. "I gotta go convince a bride that no matter how much bourbon she buries, an outdoor reception without a rain plan is a recipe for disaster."

I PULLED on my favorite pair of cowboy boots and wiggled my toes to make sure they were just right.

We didn't joke around about girls' night. It was a revered tradition of drinking, dancing, and shameless flirting. Usually we would go to a bar in Morehead City or drive down to Emerald Isle to get away from Beaufort, but Bridget had to work. So, Jokers it was.

"You ready, Mad?" Melissa called out as she let herself into the houseboat. "Steve's driving us."

I tucked the hem of my tank top into the front of my denim cut-offs and let the back hang loose.

"I thought we were meeting at the bar? What are you doing here?" I slipped a hair tie on my wrist, knowing I'd need it when we got good and rowdy.

Mel shrugged and leaned against the wall of my bedroom. "I had leftovers. Dropped them off with Steve so he'd have something on hand if he didn't want to cook."

"Kind of how I always happen to have stuff from the restaurant for Kris?" I gave her a knowing look. "You've been spending a lot of time over there lately."

She pointed her finger at me and waved it in my face. "Don't you start with me. We take care of our friends."

"Come on, Mel. Admit it—you've always had a little bit of a crush on him."

She grimaced. "Is it that obvious?"

I waved her off dismissively and grabbed my bag. "Nah, he's a man. They're not exactly great at picking up on subtle hints."

She let out a sigh of relief and picked up the picture frame I had by my bed. "When was this?"

I glanced over and couldn't be bothered to hide my

smile. "California. The night Luca and I went out. You know —before I knew who he was."

It was a great photo, even if it had come from some slimy paparazzi. Luca told me about how Astrid had gotten her hands on the images to keep them from being released to the tabloids.

For once, I was actually thankful for her. I had no interest in being the headline of some trashy grocery store checkout magazine.

Still, when I found the frame in my locker at work the morning he left for his business trip to California, my heart did that stupid pitter-pat thing that made me feel like a damn cartoon princess.

All I needed were some singing mice and a couple of blue jays to help me get dressed, and I'd be set.

The little Post-it note he stuck to the front of the glass only made the uncontrollable swooning worse.

*The night that changed everything. -L*

That photo was the first thing I saw in the morning and the last thing I saw before I fell asleep.

The strings of market lights painted us in a magical glow. We were dancing, and Luca was whispering something dirty in my ear that made me giggle.

My eyes were crinkled shut, and my smile was wide and full of laughter. His hands were on my ass, and my arms were wrapped around his neck.

We didn't have a care in the world. The realization that I trusted Luke, the stranger, more than I was trusting Luca hit me like a ton of bricks.

Maybe it was because I thought Luke and I would have one spectacular night and then never see each other again.

The thought of an indefinite thing with him scared me, and I hated that.

People left. They always would, and there was nothing I could do about it except not need them.

"Y'all are so freaking cute," Mel said with a giggle.

There was a rough knock at the door.

"Y'all comin' or what?" Steve bellowed.

"We're coming, we're coming," I shouted. One last check in the mirror, and we were off.

Jokers was unusually packed for a weeknight, but that didn't stop us from taking over.

Steve and Chase decided to stick around and shoot some pool, most likely just to keep an eye on us. There were a few catcalls from some old-timers as Melissa and I strutted in. There wasn't a doubt in my mind that it was because my shorts were three inches shorter than indecent. I was just showing off my ass so they could kiss it.

Bridget smiled from the long line of taps as she poured a beer and slid it across the bar to a customer.

"Well, well, well. Hey, stranger. Nice of you to show your face around here," she teased.

I rolled my eyes as I plopped down on a stool and drummed my knuckles on the bar. "Fireball and fast, babe."

Bridget let out a sharp whistle, and Kristin and Hannah Jane crowded in. She lined up the glasses and poured out five shots. We each picked one up and clinked them together before knocking them back.

Kristin groaned and wiped the taste off her mouth. "Yep," she hissed. "Still hate that."

I laughed and slung my arm around her tiny shoulders. "Don't worry, peaches—we'll have you corrupted in no time."

Someone cranked up the jukebox, and Trace Adkins started blaring over the speakers.

Bridget poured another round of shots and, faster than we could blink, four of us were running to the dance floor while she danced around behind the bar.

Peanut shells and stray pretzels crunched underfoot as we boot-scooted to our hearts' content. Three or four or ten songs later, we were out of breath, a little more than tipsy, and starving.

Chase mother-henned us into a booth and shouted orders into the kitchen for fried everything.

"Ugh—Han, you were right," I mumbled as I took a big bite of a mozzarella stick. "This is *exactly* what I needed." I waved my hand in the air. "Everything changed after California. I'm ready for it to get back to normal."

"What if it doesn't?" Hannah Jane asked as she snagged a fried pickle and dragged it through the cup of ranch.

Bridget slid into the booth and muttered something about being on a fifteen minute break.

Hannah finished her bite and took a big gulp of water. "I'm just saying—change isn't a bad thing, Mad. You're dating Luca. Bee's with Kyle Kingsley." She shrugged. "We're growing up and it's about damn time. If I'm not next, I swear I'm gonna become a cat lady."

"You hate cats," Kristin pointed out.

"Exactly," Hannah said. "I'm thirty, Mad's turning thirty this year, Bridge and Mel aren't far behind. Kris, you still have time, but the rest of us aren't fresh out of college anymore."

I rolled my eyes. "You make it sound like we're gonna turn into pumpkins at midnight if we don't marry off and have the required two and a half kids."

She glanced over her shoulder, checking to make sure

Steve and Chase were out of earshot. "I mean, Steve is our age, and he was married for almost a decade before... *You know.*"

A moment of silence blanketed the table as we remembered Heather.

Finally, Melissa broke the silence. "You're just saying that because you spend all your days surrounded by happy brides and weddings. Your biological clock is *fine.*"

Hannah shook her head. "My point stands. Mad, Bridge —lock 'em down, ladies. The rest of us need to go man hunting."

I shook my head. "Enough of this. This is girls' night out, and we're doing way too much talking about boys and not nearly enough drinking."

"I still have ten minutes on my break," Bridget whined. "Please just give me ten minutes, and then I'll get margaritas all around."

The opening fiddle notes of Shania Twain's "Any Man of Mine" played through the speakers and we cleared the booth faster than bulls out of a stall at the rodeo.

Chase abandoned Steve at their pool table and made a beeline for me. "C'mon, Mad Dog—you and me."

He took my hand and spun me three times under his arm. Most nights when we drank at the bar, Chase and I would end up dancing together. Tipsy or sober, we were actually fairly good.

Country swing was fun and one hell of a workout. He grabbed my waist, and I jumped. Our hands connected as he swung me through his legs, and I twisted back up to my feet. I laughed and whooped as he pulled me back in, and we floated across the dance floor.

A shadow loomed over my shoulder, and a familiar voice said, "Mind if I cut in?"

Chase chuckled and let go of my waist, "Good to see you, man." He offered Luca a handshake that turned into a bro hug. Chase left us to find Bridget and drag her out from behind the bar for a dance.

"Hey, beautiful." Luca grinned as he cupped my jaw and gave me a toe curling kiss. "Missed you. Sorry for crashing your girls' night."

I wrapped my arms around his neck. "If you're gonna crash, you owe me at least a dance."

The song switched, and Sam Hunt started crooning over the jukebox. I leaned into his arms and he held me close as we swayed. "You know, we haven't danced together since California?"

I sighed happily. "Damn shame."

Luca leaned down and buried his nose in my hair. It was the little things like that that made me fall head over boots for him.

"You know, I got real jealous when I saw you dancing with another man."

I laughed. "It was just Chase."

"I know." He grinned. "I like that you have them. I felt kinda bad coming straight here instead of waiting for you to call, but I had to see you."

"You were only gone a few days."

"Like I said. I missed you." Luca laced his fingers into mine and kept his other hand securely on my lower back. "But next time, you'll be traveling with me."

I blew out a nervous breath. "I think I'm gonna see if some of the girls will go to shopping with me so I can find a dress for the awards."

He chuckled and tucked my hair behind my ear. "How much would you kill me if I said I had it taken care of?"

I reared my head back and looked at him quizzically. "You... Got me a dress?"

Luca nodded.

"Like... For real?"

"For real." He laughed. "Unless you don't like it or don't want it... I mean, the designer who made my suit wanted to make sure we were both wearing his label, so..."

I laughed in disbelief because there was nothing else I could do.

I was dating a man who not only bought me a custom designer dress, but had communicated with the designer himself.

My plan had been to drive to a mall inland and hit up every department store until I found something that didn't look too much like a prom dress.

"Luca, I—"

"*The fuck is this*?!" an angry voice yelled.

Our heads snapped to see a very pissed off Kyle Kingsley on a warpath over to where Chase and Bridget were dancing.

I grabbed Luca's hand and pulled him with me as Chase let go of Bridget and scooted her behind him. Chase stood between her and Kyle.

"Chill out, man. We were just havin' a dance." Chase jerked his thumb toward me. "I was dancing with Maddie before Bee, and you don't see her man gettin' up in arms about it."

"I don't fuckin' care what you do with bitches like that. She's probably under a new man every night," he sneered toward me.

"Hey, now," Luca growled as he and Steve moved in to stand shoulder to shoulder with Chase. "You don't talk about a lady that way. *Especially* not mine. And you better straighten out your tone before you even think about speaking to Bridget."

Kyle had to get up on his toes to be in Luca's face, but Luca didn't even blink.

"I don't know who the fuck you think you are, but you best be gettin' the hell outta here," Kyle snarled, craning his head around to get a look at Bridget. "You told me you were workin' tonight. I came all the way out here to make sure you got home alright, and I find you dancin' with this son of a bitch."

Before Bridget could respond, Steve stepped forward and put his hand on Kyle's chest, forcing him to take a step back. "You need to go outside and cool off, Kingsley. Bridget will be here when you're good and ready to talk to her like a gentleman."

When Kyle didn't move, Steve guided him out the door.

Chase turned around to Bridget, "I'm sorry, Bee—"

She shook her head and waved it off. "It's fine. I should probably get back to work." She gave him a sad sort of smile and squeezed his hand as she headed back to the bar. "Thanks for the dance. It was fun."

Chase nodded at Luca. "Thanks for the backup, DeRossi."

"Anytime."

Mel, Kristin, and Hannah Jane swarmed Bridget as soon as she got back behind the scratched up oak bar.

Luca put his hand on my cheek. "You alright, *Tesoro*?"

I let out a furious breath. "Other than wanting to kick the shit out of Kyle, I'm fine."

Luca's brow knitted together with worry. He pressed a kiss to my forehead. "He was outta line with Bridget *and* you."

I dropped my shoulders and looked down at the toe of

my boots. "My relationship history isn't exactly a secret around here. I don't exactly have a record of stellar life choices."

"Who the fuck cares, Mad? I don't. And a piece of shit like that certainly doesn't get a say." He grinned. "Besides, the way things are going, I plan on keeping the past in the past. You and me from here on out."

Out of the corner of my eye, I saw Kyle calmly walk back in and sit down at the bar. Bridget hurried over and rested her elbows on the bar as they talked.

"Looks like all's good with your girl," Luca said.

Steve walked in after Kyle and sauntered over to us.

"You get him to calm down?" I asked.

Steve shoved his hands in his pockets. "Just needed a little de-escalating. Had a bad day at work. Wanted to go out with Bee tonight, but she said she was working—which is true. It was just a misunderstanding." He looked at Luca, but instead of his usual frown, his mouth was simply in a pursed line. "DeRossi."

"Pelham."

"Wow, you two are a talkative bunch," I muttered.

Luca stifled a grin, and Steve just shook his head as he wandered back to where Chase was stewing and watching Bridget like a hawk.

Something inside swelled when I thought about Luca standing up for me. He came back from his trip to California and came back to me.

As much as I wanted to shove my foot so far up Kyle Kingsley's ass that he could taste the leather of my size ten cowboy boots, I liked the feeling of Luca stepping up for me even more.

What was that? That feeling when you could rely on someone. When you knew that they were going to be there no matter what? What was that mix of safety and comfort? The sweet cocktail of knowing that you could stand up for yourself, but craving the feeling of someone else doing it for you?

Luca was all those things.

I couldn't quite wrap my head around it. All I knew was that I was in a reckless free fall.

# 31

## LUCA

July and August quickly passed. Maddie and I fell into a comfortable routine. By the middle of September, we were both wondering why we thought that being together would be such a problem.

On workdays, I'd stay over at her place so that her drive to the restaurant wasn't so long. On weekends, she would drive over the bridge and stay at my rental on Atlantic Beach.

The only downside was that Astrid was constantly on my case about hiring a general manager for Revanche.

She absolutely hated the slower pace of the North Carolina coast—preferring to spend the time that I didn't need her in New York City.

I hadn't bothered with headhunting a general manager yet because I wanted it to be an internal hire. That would have all been fine and dandy if I had actually been looking at the staff to see who would be a suitable candidate.

Truthfully, I was just sticking around to be close to Maddie. The restaurant could run itself. Most of the time I spent in the office at Revanche was used to oversee other business interests.

Apparently, our trip to New York for the James Beard Awards was the most time Maddie had taken off in years.

*Fucking years.*

After her confession, I immediately fired off an email to all the employees telling them to use their damn PTO.

No one got brownie points for working themselves to death.

I made her take an extra day on the front end of the trip so that we could drive inland and stay the night in Raleigh before we flew out.

Of course, that meant she doubled down on her workload in the weeks before we left so Rae wouldn't feel like she was drowning.

Maddie wanted to make a stop to see her mom before we hopped on Highway 70 and headed for the capital. When we got to the assisted living facility, I got out to go inside with her, but she dug her heels in and told me to wait in the car.

We finally compromised, and she let me sit in the lobby while she went back to her mom's room.

After a while, I got tired of mindlessly scrolling through social media and looking through the emails that Astrid would answer.

I posted a photo of Maddie and me on one of my pages and lingered on it while the likes and comments came flooding in.

With a little help and scheming from Rae and Scott, I dragged Maddie out of work early one night and the two of us went to the beach.

Just as the sun painted the sky in bright pinks and

oranges, I set my phone on a timer, dragged her out to the edge of the water and planted a kiss on her mouth.

Of course, a big ass wave came in, swept us both off our feet, and knocked us on our asses. The camera snapped us in mid-air as we flailed before hitting the water.

*Still falling for you. -L*

Maybe the caption was cheesy. I didn't care.

I wasn't trying to be sentimental, but Maddie had twisted my heart in ways I didn't know was possible.

Not once since I showed up at Revanche had I missed my condo in Los Angeles.

In fact, I had let my buddy, Isaac, crash there when he was in town on business. The man had my net worth a hundred times over, but he was still cheap as shit.

All I could think about was when I would close on my house here.

I had found a great piece of property right off the Sound. With the right renovations, it would be perfect.

I hadn't told Maddie about it yet. I hired a builder from two counties over to remodel the place just so she wouldn't hear about it through the grapevine.

It was gonna be one hell of a surprise when we got home from New York.

I shoved my phone in my pocket and sat back. The vinyl waiting room chair squeaked under my weight.

The lady behind the front desk looked over at me. "You need anything, honey?"

I gave her a polite smile and shook my head. "No, ma'am."

She adjusted her cat-eye glasses and craned her head to get a better look. "Are you that fella who finally took our Maddie off the market?"

"Yes, ma'am." I chuckled. "Guilty."

"Well. We heard you were a city boy, but you don't look so bad. I don't care so much for that Yankees hat on your head. But if Maddie thinks you're alright, then you're okay by me."

I chuckled and gave her a nod. "Thank you, ma'am."

She just waved me off. "You can call me Ms. Linda."

I sat in silence for a little while, but my boredom got the best of me. "Ms. Linda," I said as I wandered over to the front desk. "How, uh, how much does it cost for a resident to live here?"

She tapped her long, red fingernails against her desk and sighed. "Well, it depends a lot on the level of care that they need."

"What about Maddie's mom? How much does Maddie pay?"

Ms. Linda gave me a kind smile. "I can't give out that kind of information, sweetheart."

"What can you tell me?" I pressed, giving her my best smolder to get the information I wanted.

She grabbed a worn novel and fanned herself with it.

I recognized the cover. It was one of the old bodice rippers my mother liked to read—had Fabio on the front and everything.

"You know, if you were twenty years older I bet I could teach you a few things in the bed, sweet cheeks."

I winked. "I bet you could. But what are you talking about twenty years? You can't be a day over forty-five."

*She looked like she was at least seventy, but flattery gets you a lot of places.*

Ms. Linda blushed and scribbled a number on a scrap of paper. "I won't tell if you won't," she said. "But just know that if it gets out that I gave that to you, it's gonna be a damn shame that I'll have to wreck your pretty face."

I inspected the high four digit figure she put down on the scrap of paper before shoving it in my pocket. "That's every month?"

Ms. Linda nodded. "Yep. Don't know how Maddie does it. Insurance helps a little, but that girl works her itty-bitty tail off. She's never missed a payment."

Suddenly, I wondered if Maddie's workaholic nature was because she loved her job or because she actually needed the overtime.

She had told me that she sold her mom's house and moved onto the houseboat to cover the cost of the care, and that her winnings from *Pastry Throwdown* went to it too.

I knew what Maddie made at the restaurant and did the math. There certainly wasn't any wiggle room in her finances for emergencies.

"If I wanted to talk to someone who handles billing, is there a number I could have my assistant call?"

She plucked a business card out of a drawer and slid it over the counter to me. "Rhonda's in the office nine to five, Monday through Friday."

I tapped the card on the counter. "Thank you, ma'am."

Just as I spun to return to my seat, Maddie came walking into the lobby and gave me a tired smile. "Hey. Ready to go?"

I nodded and gave Linda a wave goodbye before walking Maddie out to the car.

———

TRAFFIC BLARED around us as I put my hand on Maddie's back and guided her up the front steps of my building, giving the doorman a nod. I punched the button in the elevator to take us up and let out a breath as the doors closed.

I was a little nervous. It had been a long time since I'd brought a girl home, and I wasn't just talking about my apartment in the city.

As much as I liked Beaufort, I loved New York. It was my home.

I wanted Maddie here with me for the awards and to meet my family, but I had the habit of thinking ten steps ahead.

What if she didn't like New York? I mean, I knew she'd spent some time working here early in her career, but that was a long time ago.

After our conversation at my beach rental, Maddie began spilling more bits and pieces about her childhood.

How she vowed to not marry young like her parents did. How she promised herself that she would make a life that she was proud of *in Beaufort* as a quiet middle finger to her dad after he left to chase bigger and better.

I didn't quite know how to wrap my head around that last one.

Beaufort was a nice stop, but I loved it mainly because I loved Maddie. It was her home, but it wasn't mine.

New York was my home. I had to keep reminding myself that Beaufort wasn't permanent.

Being back in the hustle and bustle had me buzzing with energy.

When I twisted my key and let Maddie walk into my apartment ahead of me, I could barely stand still.

"Wow," Maddie said as she strolled through the living room. "Nice place."

I dropped my keys on the coffee table and looked around. It had been months since I'd been here. Before Beaufort, I had been in California. Before California, I was in Vegas.

"Good to be home," I said on an exhale.

Maddie immediately went over to the window that overlooked my view of the Upper West Side.

I stood at her back and wrapped my arms around her. "I like you being here."

Maddie tipped her head back and gave me a soft smile. "It's been a long time since I've been in New York."

"How does it feel to be back?"

"Like deja vu. I never thought I'd come back."

"Not even if Revanche got nominated for a James Beard Award?"

She jerked around and looked at me as her eyebrows raised. "The restaurant got a nomination?"

She deflated just a little when I shook my head.

I took her hands in mine. "No, *Tesoro*. The restaurant didn't get nominated. *We did.*"

Maddie stared at me, dumbfounded, before blinking once, then twice. "I don't follow."

I chuckled. "Mad, you're up for Outstanding Pastry Chef, and I'm up for Outstanding Restaurateur. *We* are nominated."

She shook her head. "I... I don't understand. I looked at the list of nominees myself when you sent it out in the managers' email."

"Yeah, I know. I was hoping I tricked you. I took our names off of it on purpose. I wanted to surprise you."

Maddie's face went through a full range of emotions. It was like scrolling through emojis on my phone.

"Oh my God," she whispered. "You asshole! What would you have done if I just kept on hating you?"

I grinned and kissed her, knowing she wasn't mad. She was just processing. "Plan A was to make you mine. Plan B was to hogtie you and toss you in the trunk."

Maddie broke out into a fit of raucous laughter. "I was fucking nominated for a James Beard Award and you didn't tell me for *months*?!"

"Scale of one to ten. How angry are you?"

"Angry? I'm fucking pissed at you, but I lo—" Maddie stopped herself. "Thank you. For bringing me here—for getting me nominated."

I shook my head, just a little disappointed that she didn't say the L-word. "Maddie, I didn't get you nominated. You earned that on your own well before I bought Revanche." I cracked a brief smile. "But I sure as hell voted for you when the ballots were sent out. Do you remember in California when I told you that I knew who you were?"

Maddie nodded.

"I wasn't kidding. You aren't nobody, beautiful. It's time you figured that out."

She let out a shaky breath, and her gaze darted to the garment rack that was set up in the living room. "Is that my dress?"

"Mhmm."

"God, I really hope it fits now," she groaned.

Because she spent a few years working in New York, I didn't feel the need to show her the sights—I wanted to show *her* off. Maddie threw on a little cocktail dress and I put on a suit for a late dinner.

I slid my watch onto my wrist to cover the part of my sleeve of tattoos that peeked out from under my blazer.

I went casual tonight. Well, as casual as *Luca DeRossi* could be.

Going out around town in shorts and a t-shirt was something I had gotten comfortable doing in Beaufort. Everyone knew who I was, but nobody cared.

I wasn't shy about my celebrity. Hell, getting out of the

kitchen and leveraging that had propelled me to be in the position I was now.

I wasn't a sellout. I created jobs for my employees and memories for my guests. I'd use every bit of social capital that I had to keep doing just that. Outside of Beaufort, I had an image to uphold.

Maddie stepped out of the bathroom with her head bent to the side as she fastened her earrings.

"How do I look?" she asked as she straightened up.

"Holy shit," I stammered.

She looked down at the brassy brown dress that clung to her like a damn dream. It had long sleeves, but that was the most skin that was covered. The neck dropped in a deep V all the way down until it stopped just before her navel. The hem barely covered her ass. Her long legs were golden from the sun and completely bare except for a matching pair of heels.

I crossed the room and put my hands on her waist. "I'm going to make a fool outta myself because you look like a fucking goddess."

From her pearl white hair to her golden skin, those silver eyes, and that bronze dress—she looked like she should be worshiped in a temple. The woman was my idol.

Her long hair was in a big bun with a few loose curls spilling out, framing her perfect face.

Maddie fiddled with the hem, tugging it down as far as she could. "Astrid said this would be okay..."

I chuckled quietly. "You look perfect, *Tesoro*. You ready to go?"

Maddie peeked out the window, down to the sidewalk where paparazzi crowded around the entrance to my building. "You sure you don't wanna order in? Stay in and wear sweatpants? Netflix and chill?"

I stood behind her and put my hands on her shoulders. "It's okay to be nervous."

"I'm not nervous."

"Your poker face is shit."

She turned away from the window and into my arms. "I like when we're just Maddie and Luke."

That's what I was afraid of.

I wanted someone who had no interest in my lifestyle, but being in the public eye was an unfortunate and necessary evil for me and would be for my partner. I needed someone who was tough as nails and could handle it.

"I love you," I said as I wrapped her up against my chest.

Every minute of every day, I wanted to push her up against a wall and fuck her to kingdom come. Now, I just wanted to hold her and make her feel safe.

I wasn't swayed by the fact that she hadn't reciprocated those three little words. She'd say it when she was ready.

"Mad, whether you're with me or not, people should know who you are. Take up the space that you deserve."

She looked at me with trust in her stormy eyes. "Hold my hand?"

I unfolded her fingers and pressed a kiss into the center of her palm before lacing our hands together and leading her to the elevator. When we got into the lobby, I gave her hand a reassuring squeeze before letting go so that I could put my hand on her back.

"Walk straight to the car. I've got you."

Cameras flashed and I kept my expression unbothered.

It was the longest five feet of my life.

Every gut instinct I had told me to throw Maddie over my shoulder and get her away from those people, but I didn't.

Whatever nerves she had about going out on my arm

disappeared. She put on her sunshine smile and gave the photographers a coy wave as I led her to the car. My driver had the back door open, and I ushered her in first to make sure she was safe before sliding in beside her.

"How'd I do?" she asked when we were finally alone.

I tucked a crooked finger under her chin and drew her in for a kiss.

The windows were tinted, though I didn't care if the paparazzi got a shot of us like this. I wouldn't care if they plastered it in the middle of Times Square.

I wiped the pad of my thumb across her lower lip and chuckled. "Like you were made for this."

# 32

# MADELINE

New York with Luca was a whirlwind. Everywhere we went, people wanted a piece of him and, by association, me.

Every step of the way, he was at my side, guiding me through social events and helping me navigate the press. At every turn I was reminded just how comfortable he was with this life, and what a fish out of water I was.

My phone vibrated on the bathroom vanity as I took my time fixing my hair and putting on my makeup.

Astrid was appalled that I would even thought about doing a DIY hair and makeup job, and insisted on bringing in a professional team.

I said no.

Then she turned to pestering me to death about getting a manicure for my "ogre hands." I was going back to work as soon as we landed in North Carolina. My nails would have to stay clean and unpolished.

Finally, Luca got her to back off after I told him that I would feel more like me if I did my own hair and makeup. That was that.

Astrid was a royal pain in my ass, but she had been hanging around the apartment for the better part of the day and had been mildly pleasant. Honestly, I wasn't mad about it. It was nice to have another woman around for a big event like this.

Usually if I had to get gussied up for something, I'd go to Hannah Jane's house and we'd watch our favorite rom coms while we helped each other get ready. I didn't have my girls in New York with me, but they were there in spirit and text message.

HANNAH JANE

OMG! I just checked out at the grocery store and you and Luca were on the cover of a magazine! Girl, you looked HOT!

MELISSA

I need a copy! Tell me you bought more than one.

HANNAH JANE

Of course I did! Bought out the whole rack. We have to save these so we can show their kids one day!

MADDIE

Y'all better cut it out. You know Luca's in this group text now, right?

LUCA

You better stop texting and quit hogging the bathroom.

CHASE

Still too much estrogen in this group text.

KRISTIN

Ooooh! I need a copy too! We should put them out in the lobby of the inn!

MADDIE

Hell-fucking-no.

BRIDGET

Send us pictures, you two! Good luck,
Mad Dog!

I laughed and shook my head. My friends were slightly insane and sometimes insufferable, but I loved them. They were the family I was supposed to have.

I didn't know what kind of dress hid under that garment bag, so I kept my look clean and demure.

My hair was in beach waves. One side was pulled back behind my ear with two gold hair pins. My face was clean— just a dab of foundation and concealer and a light brush of powder. My cheeks were rosy, and my eyes were simple with just a few swipes of mascara.

I eyed the tube of red lipstick, then the more subtle shade I usually wore.

"Fuck it," I muttered under my breath as I grabbed the red and carefully filled in my lips.

There was a knock at the door. "Ready for your dress?" Astrid called out.

I twisted the doorknob and let her in. "I guess."

If Astrid had any opinions on my lack of enthusiasm, she didn't make them known. She hooked the hanger on the back of the door and unzipped the bag.

"Holy shit," I whispered.

"Let's get you dressed," she said without further ado.

I was speechless from the moment she opened the garment bag to when I was zipped into it.

The dress was a black matte satin that made me feel badass. Two thin spaghetti straps held it up. The sweetheart neckline dipped dramatically in the middle, showing off a thin strip of skin between my cleavage.

Off the tiny straps, gold studs and beads created a cap on top of my shoulders that reminded me of little wings. The dress hugged every inch of my body until it flared out to a dramatic train.

It was gorgeous and kick-ass, but somehow still me.

Astrid helped me into a pair of heels and adjusted the train so that I could walk.

Luca was in his tux, waiting in the living room. His jet black hair was styled to handsome perfection, and he had shaved his thick stubble into a debonair five o' clock shadow.

He was scrolling through his phone and sipping on a glass of bourbon when I walked in. The moment he looked up, Luca left his glass and phone behind and was on his feet, crossing the room in purposeful strides.

"Lipstick," I warned him. "Don't mess it up."

Luca had a fleeting moment of irritation at my admonition, but it quickly passed. He took my hand. "Turn for me, beautiful. Let me see my girl."

Slowly, I spun and gave him a full view of the dress.

"Dammit, Madeline—you take my breath away." His chest was heaving and his voice was raspy. For once, I believed him.

Luca looked absolutely delicious in his tux.

I let out a nervous breath and squeezed his hand. "This is it."

Never in a million years did I think that I'd ever be going to the James Beard Awards, much less as a nominee.

And certainly not with Luca DeRossi as my boyfriend.

He kissed my forehead and reached inside his tuxedo

jacket, pulling out a small box. "I, uh, I got something for you."

There was no mistaking the teal box or the iconic white ribbon that went around it. "Luca—"

"Just open it."

I untied the ribbon carefully. *Obviously, I was going to save it.*

I pulled the top off and gently traced my finger around the gold bracelet. The metal had been twisted and tied into a knot in the middle.

A little charm with the letter *L* was hooked on the knot. I looked up at him with wide eyes.

"Luca, this is too much. The—the trip, the dress, all of it."

He just chuckled and shook his head like he always did. "One time I was in Tokyo, and the owner of the restaurant I was eating at came and talked to me and my buddy, Isaac, for a minute. He showed me a picture of his wife and told me how they met. The two of them kept trying to run from each other, but life had a way of throwing them back together. He told me about this myth about a man who lives on the moon and comes out at night to search the Earth and unite two people who are meant to be together. When he finds them, he ties them together with a thread so that they will eventually find their path to each other. Some peoples' strings are short, and some are long. Some find their person right away and for others it takes a long time."

Luca took the bracelet out of the cushioned box and slipped it around my wrist. "I like to think that my string is tied to you."

*Oh no. Oh God.*

*Oh, no, no, no.*

Luca was making my heart race like a hummingbird

who drank an energy drink. I swallowed the lump in my throat and gingerly touched the bracelet with my finger.

Finally mustered the courage to look at him. "Thank you."

Luca took my hand and led me to the door. "You ready for this?"

---

"REMEMBER what I did to you last night?" Luca whispered as we stood on the red carpet and posed for the cameras. My cheeks flushed with heat.

*Did I ever.*

Luca's friend, Isaac, flew into the city for business. Since they hadn't seen each other in forever, he joined us for dinner and drinks at Luca's flagship restaurant.

When Isaac left with a woman he met at the bar, we stumbled back to Luca's apartment.

He shredded the outfit I was in, laid me out on his kitchen island, and devoured me like he was a starving man.

"I don't think this is the best place for that conversation," I mumbled, trying my best not to move my lips too much.

"I'm just teasing you, *Tesoro,*" he grinned as he shifted his weight and turned slightly, giving the photographers a different angle. "I like seeing you get nervous."

I let out a shaky breath and turned in toward him. "You don't have to tease me to get me nervous. I'm three seconds from beelining for the bar."

"You have nothing to be nervous about. You look stunning, Maddie."

It wasn't often that Luca actually called me Maddie.

Usually it was *Tesoro,* beautiful, or Madeline. Not that I

minded any of those, but hearing him call me Maddie put me a little more at ease with the whole situation.

The red carpet moved at a snail's pace. When I started to get antsy, Luca turned to me, put his finger under my chin, and tilted it up just enough to give me a modest kiss.

The photographers went ballistic.

He slid his hand down to my lower back and led me off the carpet and into the theater.

Lincoln Center was packed out. Everywhere I turned, I was starstruck.

I was actually breathing the same air as chefs I had idolized for decades.

A baldheaded man in a dark burgundy suit strutted toward us with a grin on his face.

"DeRossi, it's about time you popped out from wherever it is you've been hiding." His accent was thick. If I had to guess, I'd peg him as Australian or maybe South African.

"Aiden, my man." Luca grinned as he shook his hand. "What's it been? A year since we saw each other?"

*Holy shit. Luca was talking to Aiden Crawford.* His eyes landed on me and I felt sweat prick at the back of my neck.

Aiden Crawford was as influential as they came. He was a food critic with a penchant for making or breaking careers.

Usually I hated anyone who called themselves a critic, but Aiden was a successful chef and restaurateur as well. He knew his stuff in and out.

"And who is this lovely lady?"

Luca smiled down at me and said, "This is Chef Madeline Dorsey. She was kind enough to let me be her date tonight."

"Ah, yes—I've heard wonderful things about you, Chef Dorsey. Revanche, right?"

"Um, yes. I'm the pastry chef," I stammered.

Aiden gave me a broad smile and let out a bellowing laugh. "I know. I'm planning a trip down south so I can see whether or not the hype is true."

My eyes nearly bugged out of my head. But, miraculously, I kept my wits about me. "It's a pleasure to meet you, Mr. Crawford."

He disappeared into the crowd, but when I turned back to Luca, he was nowhere to be found. Before I could even think to panic, a tall woman in a sleek gray dress slinked up to me.

"Chef Dorsey, good to see you again," she said with a smile. "Celeste Montgomery—we met a few months ago when I came to Revanche to interview Luca DeRossi."

"Oh, yes. Nice to see you again." I eyed the slim tape recorder in her hand and pursed my lips.

Celeste followed my line of sight and let out a quiet laugh. "Don't worry, it's not on. This is off the record."

"Oh." I smiled as I let out a sigh of relief.

"You must be excited. Up for Outstanding Pastry Chef and Luca is up for Outstanding Restaurateur. It's practically unheard of for the same establishment to have more than one nomination."

I almost apologized or downplayed the significance of the nominations, but Luca's words echoed in my mind.

*Take up the space you deserve.*

"I've worked hard to build the pastry program at Revanche. It's an honor to have that recognized."

Celeste smiled. "Well said." She looked around. "Who is Luca here with tonight?"

I pursed my lips to keep from saying something incredibly stupid like, *back the hell off, bitch.*

"He's actually—"

Before I could finish, Luca appeared at my side. He slid his arm around my waist and gave me a peck on the cheek. "There you are, *Tesoro*. Sorry, I got pulled away."

Celeste nodded knowingly. "Luca, I was just talking to Chef Dorsey about your respective nominations. Congratulations. That's an impressive accomplishment."

Luca pulled me into his side. "Awards are great, but finally convincing this lovely woman to give me a shot is a thousand times better."

Celeste bowed out gracefully and Luca took my hand and led me to our seats.

"Laying it on a little thick there, DeRossi," I said when we were settled in the front of the theater. "Next time I'll wear a sign that says *I'm with Luca* just to make it easier."

Luca draped his arm across the back of my seat and leaned down. "One day you will realize just how extraordinary you are, and you'll understand that being your man is a privilege that I don't take for granted."

*Swoon.*

The awards ceremony began. One by one, the winners of each category were called out.

Luca won Outstanding Restaurateur, and I couldn't help but smile. He looked at me from the stage when he was awarded his medal and gave his acceptance speech.

When he walked off the stage and back to his seat, he leaned in and gave me a kiss before sitting down.

Was it actually possible that the man I once thought was Satan incarnate was actually a pixie dust covered unicorn of a man? He was magic, and being with him made me feel magical too.

The ceremony began to wind down. When the only awards left were Outstanding Chef and Pastry Chef, I started to get nervous.

Luca gave my hand a squeeze and brought it to his lips, giving me a kiss on the back of my hand for good luck.

"And the winner of the James Beard Award for Outstanding Pastry Chef is—"

I held my breath and squeezed his hand.

"*Chef Madeline Dorsey of Revanche in Beaufort, North Carolina.*"

"Oh my God." I sat anchored in my seat.

Luca jumped to his feet with the rest of the theater and applauded. He reached down and took my hand, helping me up.

I threw my arms around him and whispered into his ear. "I did it."

Luca laughed and squeezed me tight. "You fucking did it, Mad."

I didn't remember walking to the stage to accept the award. I didn't remember a damn thing I said into the microphone, but Luca said it was great. I just remember walking back to my seat with the medal around my neck, beaming from ear to ear.

"I'm so damn proud of you," he said with a grin when I finally sat back down.

At that moment, the crowd around us didn't matter. It was just me and Luca.

He slid his hand around the side of my neck and stroked the base of my head, tangling his fingers in my hair. "I love you, Madeline."

I leaned my cheek into his hand and closed my eyes. I was shaking with excitement, and he was the only thing keeping me grounded.

These were the moments in life that I wished things were different.

I wished that my mom was here.

I wished my dad wasn't the man he was.

I wished I had a sister or a brother to tell me congratulations—that they were proud of me.

I wished that I would never have to sleep alone again.

I wished for someone to share the burden of caring for my mom.

For someone to share the stress of making Revanche a success.

I wanted someone who would stick it out. Someone who I could trust to leave and actually come back.

I opened my eyes and saw that person staring back at me, beaming from ear to ear.

"I'm proud of *us*," I said.

Luca wrapped his arm around my shoulder and rested his other hand on top of mine as he held me close.

As the award ceremony wrapped up, Luca and I got pulled in different directions. People I didn't even know were handing me business cards and giving me job offers. It was absolute madness.

*Work here in NYC.*

*Come to San Antonio.*

*We're opening a restaurant in San Diego. We want you.*

*How do you feel about St. Louis?*

*Call me.*

*Send me an email with your salary requirements.*

*Let's have lunch in Miami. Let me know when works best for you.*

By the time I found Luca again, my head was spinning, and my clutch was full of cards with phone numbers and email addresses.

Luca guided me through the crowd to the waiting car. I pulled the train of my dress in behind me so that Luca could sit down. When he closed the door, I let out an exasperated breath.

The second the car pulled away from the curb, Luca ruined my lipstick.

His lips were on mine, slow and steady. His tongue breached my mouth and invaded every sense with long, languid strokes. His big hands cradled my jaw as he soaked in the taste of me.

When we finally broke apart, he kept an arm around me and tucked me safely into his side, gently stroking my arm with his thumb. We were quiet on our walk inside. He opened the door for me and flipped on the lights before loosening his tie. His hand never left my body.

Luca guided me into the bedroom and stood in front of me as he slowly lowered the zipper on the side of my dress.

I felt the bodice open and fall away. Luca took my hands and helped me step out of the gown. His gaze skated down my body, from my bare breasts to my black thong edged in lace.

Luca reached up and pulled the two gold pins out of my hair and gently worked his fingers through my waves to loosen them. I let out a little moan of delight.

His hands felt like magic as he made the stress melt away.

He shed his jacket and slid his belt out of the loops.

With every button of his shirt that he undid, Luca took a step forward, backing me up against the bed.

He pulled his dress shirt off and tossed it on the floor. I laid back on the mattress. His tattoos rippled as he braced his arms on either side of my head.

The restrained power was intense. I could see the desire building behind his eyes like a volcano about to explode. He was a predator, and I was his prey.

I needed it.

I needed him to ravage me, ruin me, and wreck me.

I needed to feel used.

Luca loved too hard. It was too much for me, and I wouldn't survive it.

I needed him to dominate my body for his pleasure.

That's what had kept me grounded all these months. I needed his aggression in the bedroom to balance his tender words.

"Luca," I whimpered as I reached up and trailed my fingertips down his sleeves of tattoos. "Take me."

I liked that he kept them hidden. I liked that it was this little secret that separated the Luca that the world got to see and the Luca who loved me.

He straddled my hips and bent in half, giving me a sultry kiss.

It was soft and intentional and I felt a tear prick at the back of my eyelid.

I needed it hard and fast. I needed him to be a selfish bastard. I needed to hold on to a little bit of hate because I knew that as soon as I let it go, I'd be his.

Completely and utterly his.

"Not tonight," he said in a gruff murmur. "Tonight, I'm gonna worship you, *Tesoro*."

*No. No, no, no.* I couldn't take it.

"Please, Luc—"

"That's right," he mumbled as he kissed a path from my jaw to the crook of my neck. "Just you and me, beautiful. Just Luke and Maddie."

**M**addie was quiet on the trip to Brooklyn. She had been ever since we got home from the awards last night. She was especially quiet after I gave her a handful of orgasms, then pulled her close and held her afterward.

I tried not to let it get to me, but as she said a long time ago, never underestimate the power of silence.

I wondered if this was too much, too fast.

It was a good thing she didn't know I was going to be moving into a house in Beaufort when we got back.

Part of me was beginning to think that maybe that was a mistake.

I couldn't get enough of Maddie yesterday. Every time I'd get pulled away for an interview or to talk to an acquaintance, I found myself looking around for her, missing the feel of her beside me.

Never in my life had I been like that with a woman.

I had to touch her constantly, like she was the only thing holding me on to this earth. I stretched my arm across the back of the passenger's seat and gently played with the loose braid she had her hair in.

Maddie looked fucking adorable. When we got back to North Carolina, it would still be blistering hot, but late September in New York meant that fall had arrived. She put on a loose sweater, some ripped up jeans, and a pair of light brown ankle boots that put her at my height.

I fingered the soft knit fabric and gave her a reassuring smile. "Don't be nervous. They're gonna love you."

Maddie leaned her head on my arm, "I'm tired of being nervous, but that doesn't make it go away. It's been... a lot."

I glanced at her and then forced my eyes back to the road. "A lot *good* or a lot *bad*?"

"Just a lot."

That was the worst possible answer she could have given me.

I pulled my arm away and scraped my thumbnail over my lip, shifting my hands on the steering wheel. "Mad, if you're not in this with me, just fucking tell me."

She pressed her head against the back of the seat and closed her eyes. "I'm just trying to keep up."

"Listen to me," I snapped. "I don't know how to convince you that I'm not like the shitheads you've been with in the past. All I can do is show you how fucking crazy I am about you. I know that this is a lot, and I know it's moving fast. But I'm not interested in wasting my time when I know what I want. And what I want is you."

Her eyebrows knitted together, and she grimaced in a way that made me think she was in actual pain.

The woman sitting next to me was not the quick-tempered, sassy-mouthed Madeline Dorsey I knew.

My parents' house came into view, and I pulled off onto the curb and put the car in park.

"I want you, and it scares me," she admitted.

"I know it does."

"I want you, and I need you. And that scares me." Her voice quieted. "I don't like needing people."

The corner of my mouth twitched with a sly smile. "I know that too."

"I haven't met a guy's family since high school."

"I've never brought a girl home."

Her eyebrows raised and she finally made eye contact with me. "Really?"

"Cross my heart."

She bit her lip and looked down at my hand as it rested on the gearshift.

"I'm not ready to say it," she blurted out in an anxious mess.

Her wide eyes looked up and met mine, and I couldn't help but feel a little gutted.

"I'm just..."

I shook my head. "Like I said—I love you enough for the both of us. I'll keep loving you until you're ready."

She looked out the window at my parents' house, then back at me. "Hold my hand?"

"*Sempre, Tesoro,*" I promised. "Always."

Maddie stepped out and looked at the house. "This is where you grew up?"

"The very place."

It had been months since I'd seen everybody, but there was never a doubt in my mind that this was home. We made our way up the cracked concrete path that led up to the front door.

Before we even made it to the stoop, the screen door flew open. A kid with jet black hair and a cocky grin came strutting with all the swagger that a thirteen-year-old could possibly muster.

"What's up, Tris?" I asked.

"'Sup, Uncle Luc," my nephew, Tristan, replied, nodding his head like the little punk he pretended to be. He was wearing a Yankees hat, just like the one I had on.

My oldest sister, Daniella, always said Tristan was my mini-me. When I promised that I'd take him for his first tattoo when he got old enough, she nearly beat me over the head with a dinner plate.

I leaned down and muttered in Maddie's ear, "Told you they call me *Luc*."

She rolled her eyes, but couldn't conceal the smile toying at the corner of her mouth.

I laced our fingers together and led her inside. "Ma! We're here."

*Big mistake.*

I should have kept my mouth shut. The minute the door slammed behind us, all hell broke loose.

"Brace yourself," I groaned.

We stood in the narrow entryway that was covered with the same beige and maroon wallpaper that had been there since I was in diapers.

Maddie looked up at me with panic in her eyes. "For what?"

"My family."

On cue, the DeRossi herd stampeded from the kitchen to the foyer.

"*Bino*! You get your ass over here this instant!" My mother led the charge and flung her arms around me. Flour sprayed off her apron and onto my henley, but I didn't care.

"*Mi sei mancata*, Ma," I croaked out while she strangled me like an anaconda.

"Oh my GOD!" my sister, Anna-Marie, shouted. "Dani! She's actually real! Come here!"

I wiggled out of my mom's grasp to save Maddie from the inquisition. I wrapped my arm around her waist and pulled her into my side.

"She's real, so don't scare her off. Got it?" I looked down at Maddie and grinned. "I like this one."

My mom and sisters nearly crashed into the wall, pretending to faint. The crowd parted as Nonna came marching out of the kitchen.

She stood toe-to-toe with Maddie, barely reaching her waist. "Nonna, *questa è la mia ragazza*, Madeline," I said, introducing Maddie to my grandmother.

"You can just call me Maddie," she said, smiling politely. "Luca's told me all about y'all."

"Oh my God, your accent is adorable!" Daniella squealed. "*Luca's told me all about y'all*," she mimicked, sounding more like she was from *The Beverly Hillbillies* than North Carolina.

Nonna looked up at Maddie. "I hear you are a cook too?"

"She's a pastry chef, Nonna."

Nonna just tut-tutted me and took Maddie's hand. "Come. You'll help me make the pasta. But first, we drink wine."

Maddie grinned at me as Nonna dragged her toward the kitchen, mouthing, "I like her."

"*Bino*—it took you finding the love of your life to come and visit. What's the matter with you?" Ma scolded me when Maddie was barely out of earshot.

It'd been a long time since I'd heard her call me *Bino*, and I missed it.

The way I toyed with my public image made me look

like I was a playboy. But, contrary to popular belief, I was always monogamous.

Being an active part of my family meant a hell of a lot to me. When my head would get big, I could always count on them to keep me grounded.

Nothing good could come of my girlfriend was drinking wine with my ninety year old grandma. Absolutely no one in the DeRossi family had a filter.

I chuckled and stuffed my hands in my pockets. "Ma, she's just my girlfriend. Don't go scaring her off, 'aight? It's only been a couple'a months."

*Geez—five minutes in Brooklyn and my New York accent was back.*

"*Just your girlfriend?!*" Ma shrieked as she swatted my stomach. "Don't tell me lies, Luc. You come in here making those eyes at that girl, and I half expected there to be a ring on her hand! I see what I see!"

"*Tesoro,* give the boy a break," my dad chimed in as he shuffled toward us.

For as long as I could remember, my dad had called my mother *Tesoro.* Almost sixty years of marriage later, he still looked at her the same way he did in their wedding photos when they said *I do* at eighteen.

Never once had I called a girlfriend *Tesoro.*

To me, that was what you called your true love.

My parents painted an intimidating picture of a successful marriage. They fought with each other hard and loud, but they loved even harder.

Living up to that example was scary as shit. The first time I had called Maddie *Tesoro*—my darling, my treasure— I didn't even think about it until after the words were out.

It just felt right.

"Dad," I said as my father pulled me into a back-slapping bear hug.

He looked me in the eye. "Is she as pretty as the girls are saying?"

I cracked a smile. "Even more beautiful."

Anna-Marie grabbed my arm and dragged me into the living room. "Luc, Come meet your newest niece."

I followed her until the hallway split into the open concept living room and kitchen.

My two brothers-in-law were on the couch watching *Sports Center*.

Anna-Marie walked over to her husband, Danny, and scooped up their baby girl. "Valentina," she cooed, "Meet your Uncle Luc."

"Hey there, pretty girl," I soothed as I took her from Anna-Marie and bounced her in my arms.

Like the rest of the women in my family, she had olive skin and tufts of inky black hair.

Valentina opened her eyes and let out a gurgling laugh.

I looked over my shoulder at Maddie, who was staring back at me over the rim of her wine glass.

She had a coy smile on her lips as Nonna kept talking her ear off.

Apparently, Valentina didn't like sharing the attention. She let out a high-pitched squeal to make her displeasure known.

With their wine glasses empty, Nonna grabbed the ball of pasta dough that had been resting, and instructed Maddie on just how to do things.

Maddie had probably made pasta a million times over, but Nonna would insist on teaching her *the right way*. Arguing was futile.

I cradled Valentina in my arms and walked over to the kitchen island to watch.

Maddie dusted the countertop with a pinch of semolina and rolled out the dough according to Nonna's orders.

I had learned early that it didn't matter how good I was at being a professional chef. In Nonna's kitchen, *she* was the boss.

"Very good, *passerotta*," Nonna smiled, patting Maddie's wrist. "You have good hands. Not like *polpetto* there," she said, pointing a crooked finger at me. "My Luca has fingers like sausages. Such a shame he has clumsy hands."

Maddie giggled. I passed behind her and whispered that Nonna had called her *little sparrow*, and called me a meatball.

"Luca made raviolo al' uovo for me a while ago," she told Nonna. "He said it was a family recipe?"

Maddie's comment simultaneously redeemed me from the curse of apparently having clumsy hands and impressed Nonna.

Maddie worked meticulously as my grandmother went on and on about the holy terror I was when I was a child.

I was a little nervous about leaving her alone, but she seemed comfortable in the kitchen.

"She fits," Daniella said when I joined her on the deck. The crisp autumn breeze felt like a breath of fresh air.

Daniella was the oldest out of the three of us DeRossi siblings. I had no doubt that the flecks of silver in her dark hair were the result of her nearly-feral kids, Tristan, Marco, and Guilia.

"Nonna certainly likes her."

"I love her," I admitted.

Daniella didn't look surprised. "She's the first one you've let us meet. I figured it was serious. It's about time."

My family erred on the side of young marriages.

My grandparents married when my Nonna was sixteen and my Nonno was seventeen. My parents were both eighteen. Daniella was twenty-one when she and Enzo said their vows. Anna-Marie and Danny were the oldest, getting married at twenty-four and twenty-seven.

At thirty-six years old, I was the odd one out.

"You gonna put a ring on it?"

"Working on it. Took a lot of convincing to get her to go out with me in the first place. I, uh, I doubt she'll make forever easy on me."

"Good. You need someone to knock you down a peg or two since you're never around here."

"Gee. And y'all wonder why I'm always gone," I joked.

Daniella laughed long and loud, "You did *not* just say y'all. Oh my God, Luc—"

"I bought a house in North Carolina," I said just to shut her up. "Don't say anything to Mad."

My sister's smile softened. "Good for you. Happy looks good on you."

"Pshh—I always look good."

"There he is," Daniella said with a laugh. "For a second I thought she'd totally tamed you and I was going to have to have her teach me her ways so I can keep Tris in check." She caught my gaze as I peered back through the sliding glass door, keeping an eye on Maddie. "Have you met her family yet?"

I shook my head and looked back at the yard. "Nah, it's, uh, it's just her. Kind of. I mean, she's an only child. Her dad left when she was a kid and her ma's in a home—she's got dementia."

"Shit."

"Yeah."

"Have you met her ma at least?"

"No. Maddie—she's a little cagey about it."

Daniella looked over her shoulder toward the kitchen where our mom had joined Maddie and Nonna. "Must be a big change for her—going from being alone to being, well, here with all of us."

I hadn't thought of that.

On the drive over, Maddie looked like she wanted to crawl in a hole and die. It felt like she was pulling away from me, and that was terrifying.

I never considered that maybe the idea of family scared her.

"Yeah," I mumbled. "Maybe."

## 34

---

## MADELINE

Dinner with the DeRossis was a riot. Nonna was my favorite person on earth, and my new drinking buddy.

We were sipping on our second—or third—glasses of wine when Luca's dad wandered over and tapped my shoulder.

"Come with me."

I glanced over to where Luca was in deep conversation with his mom before following his dad to a small sitting room right off the front of the house.

Mr. DeRossi pulled out a cloth-covered scrapbook and sat down on the yellow upholstered loveseat. He patted the spot beside him, and I sat down dutifully. I shifted uncomfortably as he opened the photo album.

"That's Luca, right?" I asked, trying to fight my smile at the messy-haired boy with mischief in his eyes.

"When he was seven. Got himself stuck up a tree. I wouldn't help him down." He snickered. "Luca figured out how to get up; he could figure out how to get down. My *Tesoro* took a picture, though."

"Wait, you call Luca's mom—" I began, taken aback.

The way he referred to his wife with that name carried a weight that wasn't lost on me.

"You call her *Tesoro*?"

He nodded as he turned the page to a photo where Luca and his two older sisters were all crammed in a bath full of bubbles.

"Since the day we met." He gave me a sheepish smile. "The only time we call each other by our names is when we fight. She's my greatest treasure. Even more than my Daniella, Anna-Marie, and Luca—and I would die for them."

A knot clogged my throat. "That's really beautiful."

For a long time, we sat and flipped through photo album after photo album.

Sometimes he would tell me the stories behind the photos, other times we just looked in silence. Occasionally I would ask him questions and he would tell me about Luca growing up.

I was nervous about being around Luca's dad simply because my track record with dads wasn't the greatest.

The whole way to Brooklyn, my blood had burned with jealousy. It was a stupid reaction to meeting my boyfriend's family, but not once had I ever claimed to be reasonable.

I had always craved everything that Luca had.

I wanted to be a part of a big, loud family. I wanted the hoards of kids running around and the good-natured shouting matches between siblings. But all I ever got was quiet. The silence was always deafening.

My mother worked her ass off to provide for the two of us after my dad skipped town. She did the best she could. Her example gave me a work ethic that put most everyone else to shame. She taught me the value of stretching a dollar and budgeting. She made sure that I surrounded myself with good friends.

Still, when it came time for me to go on my first date, I didn't have a dad around to scare the hell out of that unlucky boy by sitting on the front porch with a shotgun.

While my friends were at daddy-daughter dances, I faked having the flu.

YouTube taught me how to change a tire and check my oil and tire pressure.

On parents' weekend when I was at culinary school, I told my roommates that my folks couldn't make it because they couldn't get off work. That, at least, was partially true. Mom could rarely take a day off, and I imagined that my dad was setting up for a show at some dive bar somewhere.

There were hugs all around as Luca and I said our goodbyes.

Luca's sisters put their numbers in my phone so we could keep in touch, and Nonna made me promise to come back and cook with her. Luca's dad gave me a bear hug that forced me to choke back tears.

We walked hand in hand back to the car. I waited as Luca opened my door and helped me in.

The trip back to the Upper West Side was silent. When we pulled up to his building, he opened my door while the valet took the wheel.

"You hungry?" he asked as we walked inside.

I sighed contentedly. "I don't think I'll be able to eat for days. I'm so stuffed."

He grinned, giving my hand a squeeze as we took the elevator up to his floor. "That's what happens when you eat with my family. No one ever goes hungry. Nonna won't allow it."

"I really like them," I said as we walked down the hallway.

"Oh yeah?"

"They're exactly what I thought they'd be like."

Luca laughed. "I don't know if that's a good thing."

"It's a good thing," I promised as I flipped the lights on and kicked my shoes off.

It was our last night in New York. We would catch the first flight back to North Carolina in the morning. I couldn't wait to get back to work. To routine. To normalcy.

With our bags mostly packed, I went through the motions of getting ready for bed, but I couldn't shake the unsettling feeling that was nesting deep inside.

The jealousy I had felt on the way to Brooklyn had shattered into something more.

It turned into desire.

I wasn't jealous of Luca. I wanted Luca. I wanted him more than I had wanted anything.

Luca walked into the bedroom after making sure that the lights in the rest of the apartment were off. He found me standing at the foot of the bed, still in my jeans and sweater, waiting for him just like he had asked me to the first time I went to his beach house for dinner.

"Maddie?" His voice was a low rumble.

I looked up at him. My lips parted and I sucked in a nervous breath. "I—"

Either he was a mind reader or he had recalled the same memory I did. Luca stood in front of me and ghosted his fingers over the side of my sweater. His other hand came up and stroked my cheek.

"Tell me what you want, *Tesoro.*"

I leaned into his touch, resting in the comfort that I felt there. "Luca..."

"Tell me what you need."

His eyes were dark like melted chocolate. Warm. Comforting. Sensual.

My tongue peeked out, and I wetted my lips. Luca tracked the movement like a hawk.

I placed my hands on his broad chest and held his gaze. "I need you to make love to me."

Luca's face flickered with surprise. I didn't blame him.

Our sexual preferences edged on the dark and dirty. It was always hard and brutal, and God—I loved every minute.

But that's not what I needed tonight. I needed to feel him love me. I needed to let myself feel it.

I needed to show Luca how much I loved him. Maybe I wasn't ready to say it, but actions spoke louder than words.

"Maddie—"

My chest heaved as nervous breath after nervous breath pumped in and out of my lungs. "Please," I begged in a whisper.

Luca tucked a strand of hair behind my ears and cupped my jaw in his hands.

Slowly, he lowered his mouth to mine and drank in my lips.

The kiss stretched out for an inordinate amount of time. He wasn't in a hurry, and I wasn't in a rush. We were memorizing each other—taking our time to brand one another.

"*Ti amo, Tesoro.*" he murmured against my swollen lips. "I love you."

Luca bent his knees and scooped me into his arms, cradling me as he walked over to the side of the bed and laid me down.

He took a step back and slowly stripped down as I watched. First, his shirt hit the floor. Then, his pants. Luca shoved his boxers down and his thick erection sprang free.

Still, he didn't make any sudden moves toward me. He reached over and flipped off the bedside lamp, bathing the room in darkness.

"Close your eyes, *Tesoro*," he urged. "Just feel."

I heard the scrape of a drawer opening and the slight crinkle of foil when he set the wrapped condom on the bedside table.

"Luca—"

"Yeah, beautiful?"

"I'm... I'm good... I'm on birth control. And I've never—"

"I haven't either."

"Really?"

"Really," he said as he slipped his hands under the hem of my sweater and lifted it over my head. "Never felt right before."

"Before what?" I asked as he pulled the button of my jeans free and tugged them off my legs.

Luca crawled over my scantily clad body. His beard grazed my cheek as he kissed a path of fire up my neck. "Before you."

Instead of pinning my wrists above my head, he sat back on his haunches and took my hand in his, massaging my fingers and my wrist. I let out an involuntary moan.

My hands hurt all the time from piping designs on wedding cakes.

Luca laughed the first time, but had gotten used to my very unsexy routine of wearing wrist braces on both hands while I slept.

Carpal tunnel was a real bitch.

His thumbs worked at the tension in my hands and arms. When he was finished, he pressed a kiss into my palms and one on each wrist.

He lowered himself and bit down on the side of my pink

lace panties before dragging them down my legs with his teeth.

Goosebumps skittered across my skin as he started with my ankles and kissed his way up to my knees.

With a painful slowness, he separated my thighs and peppered the soft skin between my legs with feathery kisses.

I groaned in delight when he dipped his fingers into my pussy and nibbled at my swollen clit. The ache in my core was unbearable. Every muscle clenched around the emptiness inside.

"Luca—" I choked out.

The head of his cock pressed against my entrance as he kissed his way up my stomach and nuzzled his head between my breasts.

"I think I've loved you since the day we met." His coarse whisper sent shockwaves down my spine.

I tangled my fingers in his hair and pulled him up to my lips. I could still taste the bourbon from the nightcap lingering on his tongue. It mingled with my minty breath as I wrapped my arms around his neck and hooked my leg around his waist.

Luca's hands snaked around my back and unfastened my bra. He laid me back down and pulled it off my body. He palmed each breast in his hands and kissed my nipples—first the left and then the right.

"So damn beautiful, Mad." Luca's dick prodded at my pussy, and I bucked my hips in impatience.

He put a firm hand on my hip and kept me still against the mattress.

"Luca," I begged again. "I need you."

"Not yet."

"Luc—"

He shut me up with two fingers plunging deep into my

center. I gasped and arched my back, pressing closer and closer to him, fisting the sheets as he stroked my walls.

My body trembled, and my eyes threatened to roll back in my head.

"Let go, *Tesoro*. Trust me—I've got you."

"I—" The pressure that built inside unfurled, and my body shook as the orgasm crashed over me. My head dropped back onto the pillow. My eyes met his in the shadows. "I love you, Luca."

"Say it again," he said as he dove down and gave me a hard kiss. "Say it."

I snaked my arms around his neck and kept him close, whispering in his ear. "I love you."

"Again." His fingers were back inside my pussy, spreading my wetness around.

I wrapped my hand around his shaft and pumped in quick succession. He grunted and dug his hand into the pillow behind my head, bracing as I worked him into a frenzy.

"I love you, Luca," I confessed again. "I love you so fucking much."

Luca twisted his hips, leaning down and kissing me. "Are you ready for this?"

I was ready for everything. "Hell yeah."

He eased his cock inside me at a snail's pace—taking his time to savor the feeling of being bare and deeply connected.

A tear escaped the corner of my eye, and I swiped it away as he thrust hard.

*I was not going to be the girl who cried during sex.*

Luca rested his forearms on either side of my head as he snapped his hips into mine.

He pressed his lips to my temple where my tears had left a glistening path. "I've got you," he promised.

It wasn't long before we both crashed over the edge. Luca wrapped me up in his arms and held me snug against his chest.

Something passed between us that was deeper than anything I'd ever experienced in my twenty-nine years.

It connected us in every way possible.

His heartbeat kept time with mine as our panted breathing slowed. He pressed his lips against my temple, and I closed my eyes.

# 35

# LUCA

I held Maddie's hand the entire way back to North Carolina. There was no way I was letting her go. Not for a second.

When we left Beaufort to go to New York City, I knew things wouldn't be the same when we came back. Before the trip, I felt like Maddie was barely mine. Now, she was all in.

I eased back in the driver's seat and draped my arm over Maddie's shoulders. "What's going on in your head?"

She leaned back against my arm. Her smile was sunshine and fucking glitter. "Just happy."

I gave her shoulder a little squeeze as I pulled into the parking lot at Harlowe Bay Assisted Living. "Alright, big shot. Go brag. I'll be here when you're done."

Honestly, I wanted to go in and see her mom's reaction when she told her about her win at the James Beard Awards, but I had pushed her enough over the last few days. That would have to happen on her terms.

Maddie's hand hovered over her seatbelt, and she looked at the building.

"You alright? You said you wanted to stop by as soon as we got back in town."

Her lips parted and shut again.

I reached over the center console and gave her thigh a gentle squeeze. "Mad?"

"You, um... You wanna come in?"

"Yeah, I can wait inside."

She shook her head. "No, like... Come in and meet her..."

I raised my eyebrows. "You sure?"

Maddie nodded. "Yeah. I want you to meet her. It's just... She has good days and bad days, and I never really know which one I'm gonna get. The mom who remembers everything about me or the mom who doesn't even know where she is."

"Hey," I said as I twisted the key and cut the car off. "I'm all in, *Tesoro*. I'm in this with you."

The dimples in her cheeks creased as she smiled. "I know."

Maddie led me into the lobby and made a pit stop to sign in at the front desk.

Linda gave me a sly smile and a wink when Maddie wasn't looking.

Astrid had taken care of the headache of making sure Maddie's mom's care was covered financially until I could lock Maddie down for good. *Not that I mentioned the last part to Astrid.*

Still, she'd have to be stupid to not see that I was making moves for the future. Astrid wasn't a dumbass. She was a professional and kept her opinions to herself—most of the time.

Maddie quietly knocked on the door before poking her head in.

The room was clean and simple, but still comfortable. The curtains were drawn back, and natural light flooded in from the picture window.

Her mom sat in a recliner with a ball of yarn on her lap. Her knitting needles worked away at whatever she was making. *The Price Is Right* was on the television, but it was muted.

I looked over to the right and saw that the bed was neatly made, and a vase of fresh flowers sat on the nightstand.

"Maddie Lee." Her mom smiled. "Come, sit a spell. Tell me, sweetheart—have you been baking?"

Maddie sat down in the chair beside her mom's recliner and tipped her head to the edge of the bed.

I sat down, catty-cornered to the ladies.

Maddie took the yarn out of her mom's lap and began to untangle it. It seemed like the kind of thing they had done a million times before. There was comfort in routine.

"I just got back from New York, so I didn't have time to make you any cookies this time, but I'll bring you a whole bunch next time." She looked over at me and then back at her mom. "But I brought someone I wanted you to meet." She reached over and laid her hand on my knee. "This is my boyfriend, Luca."

"It's nice to meet you, Mrs. Dorsey."

She gave me a quick glance up and down and then turned to Maddie. "He's quite a looker!"

Maddie giggled. "I think so."

Mrs. Dorsey gave me a slight nod and looked back down at her knitting.

For a while, the two of them made small talk. Maddie told her mom about New York and winning Outstanding Pastry Chef at the James Beard Awards. They chatted about the weather, what had been on TV, and how big the winning marlin was at the Big Rock Tournament a few months ago.

After a while, Maddie's mom stopped talking altogether.

Maddie chirped on for a few more minutes, but I could feel the shift in the mood.

Mrs. Dorsey kept looking between Maddie and me. She was quiet, but clearly agitated. Her thin lips pursed into a frown as she gathered her knitting and tucked it away into a basket.

"I don't like it when you people think you can just come in all willy nilly and touch my belongings. Don't like it one bit," she said, glaring at Maddie as she grabbed the yarn out of Maddie's hands. "I don't like it."

"I'm sorry," Maddie stammered, but kept her composure. "We'll be out of your hair in just a minute."

"Get out of here," she snapped.

Maddie stood up and grabbed her purse, the corner of her lip quivering. She leaned in and gave her mom a gentle, one-sided hug. "I love you, Momma."

"I don't know who you think you are—putting your hands on me. Get out of my room before I call the police."

Maddie's voice broke as she whispered goodbye.

I put my hand on her back and walked her out. The door shut behind us, and Maddie crumbled into my chest. She sobbed, her body trembling against mine.

I pressed a kiss into her hair and fought against the knot forming in my throat.

There wasn't a word or promise I could utter that would cure that kind of hurt. I cradled her head against my chest and stood with her while she grieved.

Maddie eventually took a step back and wiped her red-rimmed eyes.

"I'm sorry for getting all weepy." She shrugged and

forced a smile. "It's not the first time that's happened, but I..." Her voice caught. She cleared her throat and looked down at her feet, shaking her head. "I never get used to it."

I took her by the hand. "You're not alone in this, *Tesoro.*"

She looked up at me with sadness lingering in her eyes. "I love you."

"I love you," I said, gently squeezing her hand. I couldn't help but smile—I loved hearing her say that. "Ready to go?"

She moved closer and pecked my lips. "Yeah."

We left the care facility and drove across the bridge to Beaufort. There was a hair tie and a pile of bobby pins in my cup holder. Maddie's chef whites were neatly folded in the back seat, and a ticket stub from a movie we saw a few weeks ago was still on the dash.

Slowly but surely, she was leaving her mark everywhere.

I had grown comfortable with the rental car that Astrid had arranged for me, so instead of having one of mine brought to North Carolina, I simply bought it from the rental company.

Roots felt good.

Instead of turning left to go to Front Street and head to the restaurant, I turned right.

Maddie's eyebrows knitted together. "Where are you going?"

I grinned. "Taking my girl out for lunch."

"I have to work."

"Not today. I had Rae cover for you one more day."

"Luca!" she shrieked. "You can't fuck with my schedule like that!"

"I can and I did." I smirked as I pulled into the parking lot at Jokers. The lunch rush was in full swing, but the bar wasn't overly crowded. I held the door open for Maddie and waved at Bridget.

Bridget squealed and ran out from behind the bar. "Oh my goodness gracious! I can't believe it! You won a freaking James Beard Award! I'm so proud of you, babe!"

Maddie nearly toppled over when Bridget threw her arms around her. "Can't... Breathe."

"Whoa. Are you choking? Bee, that's not how you do the Heimlich." Chase chuckled as he slid off his bar stool and walked over

Maddie shook her head. "I'm good. I'm good."

Chase scooped her up in a bear hug and spun her around. "Way to kick ass, Mad Dog." He put her back down on her feet and extended his hand to me. "Same to you, man. Congrats."

"Thanks."

Chase crossed his arms. "When you gonna work out with me and Steve?"

Bridget's eyes widened, and I heard her giggle to Maddie. "Oh my God—it's a three-way bromance now!"

Steve grunted something unintelligible from his spot at the bar and Bridget assumed that it meant *I need a refill.*

Maddie put our orders in with Bridget, and we moved to a table with Chase and Steve.

"I'm still mad at you for messing up my schedule."

"I know." Little did she know, that wasn't the only thing I had up my sleeve today.

"How was poker night?" she asked Steve and Chase.

Steve shrugged as he swallowed a bite of his burger. "Didn't have it. Y'all were outta town. Bee had a date with Kingsley. Mel was on call at the hospital."

Maddie frowned and stole a fry off Steve's plate. "He always takes her out on poker night."

I shrugged and draped my arm across the back of our

side of the booth. "Probably just the night they both have off."

"Fuckin' hate that guy," Chase muttered.

*Aha.* I knew that look. Either Bridget had shot him down, or he'd never told her that he was into her.

Bridget came by and dropped off our plates and topped off Steve and Chase's water glasses.

Chase gave her a half-smile. "Thanks, darlin'."

When Bridget was out of earshot, Maddie leaned across the table. "You know she's only with Kyle because he's the one who asked her out, right?"

Steve hid his laugh in a cough. Apparently, Chase's little crush was common knowledge. I held Maddie's hand under the table while we wolfed down our lunches.

"Y'all been busy?" I asked as I took a sip of tea. Maddie laughed and Steve and Chase looked at me like I'd grown a second head.

I frowned. "What?"

Chase laughed. "You said *y'all.*"

"So?"

Steve chimed in. "It's unnatural. Like seein' a pig in a dress."

Maddie nodded in agreement and gave me a patronizing smile. "Nice try, sweetie."

"What!" I laughed. "I've been around here too long. *Y'all* are rubbing off on me."

Steve and Chase laughed, but Maddie grew quiet.

When the guys got called out for police business, I paid our tab and tipped Bridget.

"When are you leaving?" she asked as soon as we got in the car. The girl didn't hold any punches.

"What do you mean?"

"I mean, I know that at some point you have to go back

to doing your thing with DeRossi Hospitality and that means you can't be here. Even if you want to be."

"I intend to be here as much as I can," I offered.

"The road to hell is paved with good intentions."

I scrubbed my hand down my cheek and sighed. "I'm going to Texas at the end of the week." Maddie nodded, but before she could get another word out, I added on, "But I'll be back in a few days. Nothing too long."

"This time."

"What's that supposed to mean?"

She sighed and leaned back in her seat, watching the fields fly by as we cruised down Highway 101. "It means that at some point you're going to realize that being tied to fucking Beaufort isn't what you want."

"Where's this coming from?"

"You said it yourself. You've been around here too long."

"Maddie, I didn't mean it like that."

"Luca, let's be real. As much as I want this to be forever, I know there's an expiration date on us. I want someone who's going to be *here.* Not LA and New York and everywhere in between."

She was making good points, but that wasn't the part that I heard.

"You want this to be forever?"

Maddie stammered and stuttered. "Well... I mean... I just—" She paused and looked around as the car came to a stop. "Where are we?"

"Home."

Maddie shook her head. "I don't understand... We're on the other side of the bay and this isn't—"

I pointed to the big ass house that sat right on the water. "This is home, *Tesoro.* I bought it. It's only a few miles from your place. Hell, you could probably swim from here across the bay to your houseboat. I didn't want you to feel like I was taking you away from your friends or your mom." I reached over and popped open the glove box, pulling out a key. "And in case you want to move in, I had a key made."

Her eyebrows raised. "You what?"

"I'm not fucking around with us, Mad. Hell—I'll give you all the fucking keys. To the house here. To my apartment in New York. To the condo in LA. All of it."

Maddie's head snapped toward me. "You bought a house here."

"Yeah, I did."

"And you want me to move in with you?"

"Yeah. I do."

"Luca, I—"

"Madeline." I groaned as I ran my hand back through my hair.

This woman was so infuriating. How the hell didn't she see it?

"I don't know how the fuck to say it so that you hear me. I fucking love you."

Maddie put her hand on top of mine and wrapped her fingers around the key. "I hear you."

"And?"

She smiled sheepishly. "And I love you."

"And?"

"And I want to go see your big ass house."

"And?"

"Maybe we'll take the whole moving-in thing kinda slow?"

"And?"

"And I'm sorry for freaking out on you?"

"And?"

Maddie looked confused. "And... I don't know what else."

I chuckled. "I know. I was just seeing how far I could push it."

She smacked my arm and opened her door. "Jackass."

"C'mon, *Tesoro*." I grinned as I rounded the hood of the car and took her hand. "Let me show you around."

# 36

# MADELINE

I had no words. The house was a dream.

The hardwood floors were a beautiful dark brown that reminded me of well-tempered chocolate. Windows covered almost every wall. The kitchen that rivaled the one at the restaurant. Every detail was mind-boggling.

The main floor reminded me of the beach rental—a big A-frame that looked out over the bay. Luca wasn't lying; I could see my houseboat and Steve's house from here.

Two built-in bookshelves that were begging to be stocked full of paperbacks sandwiched a stone fireplace. A leather sectional couch that could hold the entire staff of the restaurant filled out the living room.

It was clean and masculine, but the natural light and near jungle of plants made it soft.

There were four—or maybe it was five—guest bedrooms. I lost count.

Luca made passing comments about converting one to a home office, but leaving the rest tastefully furnished in case his family visited. The basement was a full-on man cave and, honestly, I was a little jealous. That was, until Luca said he had it decked out with poker night in mind.

It reminded me of a prohibition-era speakeasy. He had gone with dark walls that were illuminated with pendant lights. The wet bar and butler's kitchen would make for easy entertaining. He had even instructed the builder to convert a closet into a wine cellar.

If I had any doubts about whether I was in love with him, Luca sealed the deal when he showed me a bottle of the same vintage he had sent me when he surprised me with a grocery order.

"One more thing to show you," he said as he took my hand and dragged me back up the stairs.

We left the man cave and went back into the living room. Luca led me around the massive butcher block island in the kitchen and around another tight corner.

He opened the door that I assumed to be the pantry. Instead, there was a steep staircase that was barely wide enough for Luca to squeeze his broad shoulders through.

I followed him up and my jaw dropped.

It was light and airy.

An oasis.

Maple floors with a light stain covered the massive bedroom. A king-sized bed was pushed up against the wall that was opposite the view of the bay. White linens and pillows were piled high on top of it. Dark wood beams stretched across the apex of the ceiling. Rays of sunshine peeked in from the skylights.

"Oh my God," I whispered as I pushed open the French doors that led out to the widow's walk.

I had always dreamed of a house with a widow's walk...

I could see across the bay to the Sound, and over the barrier islands to the ocean.

Luca came up behind me and wrapped his arms around me like Jack and Rose in *Titanic*. "What do you think?"

It wasn't often that I was speechless, but Luca took every word out of my brain.

He brushed my hair aside and pressed a kiss to the side of my neck and hummed. "You like it?"

"Luca, it's—"

"Ours. Just ours. The rest of the house—my family, your friends—they can all come visit and hang out. But up here is just for us. No one else."

It was our own little world. Just Luke and Maddie.

I let out a slow breath. He had me spinning, and I didn't know what to do with that.

"Mad, you're my girl."

I turned around and wrapped my arms around his neck, gently stroking the buzzed hair at the base of his skull. "How long are you gonna be in Texas again?"

"Too long," he murmured. "I'd rather be here."

———

HOT GUY FROM THE GYM IN LA

Miss you. Call you when I'm out of this meeting. Let me know if you're free to talk.

I HADN'T CHANGED Luca's name in my phone since California. I liked it better this way.

The one-eighty of who I thought he was the day we met in California to who he was to me now was still a little mind-blowing.

He wasn't the hot, cocky playboy who hit on every girl in sight. He wasn't the asshole judge. He wasn't the cruel boss I thought he was going to be.

Behind the harsh, tattooed exterior, he was soft and loving. I couldn't hide the fact that I was head over heels for the man, so I stopped trying.

I had been in a shitty mood ever since he left to go to Texas, and it had everything to do with the fact that I was sleeping alone.

Luca had only been gone for four days, and I was flogging myself for how much I missed him already.

Every day, I'd drive by the house to water all the plants and lock everything up, but I slept at my place. It felt weird to be in that big house without Luca.

The first day he was gone, I dragged Hannah Jane over with me. Of course, she fawned over every square inch of it. I'd given her the grand tour except for the hidden suite upstairs. That was mine and Luca's alone.

Goosebumps cropped up on my arms, and I closed my eyes as I remembered the one night we spent in it.

I had to brace my hands against the headboard to keep Luca from driving my body into the wall with each thrust. Every dark promise, every dirty praise—he drew me further and further under his spell.

My phone buzzed again, but this time it was a selfie of Luca and a cow.

> HOT GUY FROM THE GYM IN LA
>
> This one looks tasty.

The next photo he sent was him and four other men— the Griffith brothers. Luca had gone down to a little town in Texas to see about opening a restaurant on the Griffith Brothers Cattle Ranch.

It was going to be a carnivore's destination eatery.

Grass-fed, dry aged steaks from cattle raised right there on the land. Everything on the menu would be locally sourced. He wanted to model the building after Revanche—exposed brick, indoor and outdoor dining, and a view that couldn't be beaten

I couldn't argue. It was a damn good business plan. Luca seemed confident that he wanted to get in on this project, so when he told me he would have to extend his trip by a few days to work out the partnership agreement, I didn't think anything of it.

I had him more often than not. Who was I to complain?

"Hey, babe," I said as I trapped my phone between my ear and shoulder and emptied my locker for the night. "How's it going down there?"

Luca sounded exhausted. "It, uh, it's good. Negotiations are tough, but I think it's coming together. How was your day?"

"Busy. Slammed service. Lots of weddings this weekend. I had to sit in on a few catering consults with Scott for next year."

"You sound tired."

"I could say the same about you."

"I miss you." He sighed. "Damn. It's been a few days, and I feel like a middle schooler pining over the weekend because he can't see his crush until Monday."

I giggled as I locked the restaurant door behind me and walked to my Jeep. "Well then, maybe you should come home."

"You know, I like the sound of that."

I slid in behind the wheel and shut the door. There was something sad in the sound of his voice worried me.

"But?"

Luca sighed. "But I'm gonna have to head back to New York right after I get things squared away here."

"Oh."

"Yeah." He groaned and muttered something under his breath. "This sucks, Mad."

"How long are you gonna be in New York?"

"Few days. Investor meeting."

"And after that?"

"Then I can come home to you."

I backed out of my parking space and headed toward Jokers. I didn't feel like going to Luca's house or to my houseboat. Frankly, I was tempted to go back inside and keep working.

I switched the phone to my left hand. "I'll be counting down the days."

"You and me both, *Tesoro*. I love you."

"I love you too."

"Hey—" Luca cut in before I hung up.

"Yeah?"

"Call me when you get home, will you? Just so I know you're safe."

Something warm and fluttery broke loose in my chest. No one except my mom had ever said that to me before. *And it had been a long time since my mom had said it.*

"I will."

"Love you."

"Bye." I sighed as I yanked the steering wheel and practically careened into the parking lot at Jokers.

I got out and shivered as the October breeze blew off the coast. I should have put on a jacket, but what was the point when I had whiskey to warm me up?

The yellow of the lights mixed with the blue neon beer signs and cast a friendly glow inside. I took my usual spot at the bar and flagged down Bridget.

I spotted Steve and Mel sitting at a booth. "What's that

about?" I asked Bridget as I nodded my head in Steve's direction.

Bridget shrugged. "Came in about an hour ago and had dinner."

"They came in together?"

She nodded. "What are we drinking tonight?"

"Jack. In a glass. Neat. I don't even care what kind of glass. Just whiskey in some kind of container that's easy to refill. Lord knows I'll probably finish the bottle."

"That bad, huh?"

"I miss him," I grumbled.

Bridget laughed as she grabbed the bottle of Jack Daniels off the shelf and poured me a healthy serving. "Babe, that's a *good* thing."

"Doesn't feel like it."

"Well," she said as she swiped the terrycloth towel across the bar and tossed it in a bucket of sanitizer. "You know what they say about bartenders—we're cheaper than therapists."

I snorted into my glass." Pretty sure that's what alcoholics say."

"Hannah Jane told me the new house is a fucking mansion."

I nodded and sipped on my drink. "He wants to have everyone over for poker night the next time he's in town."

"I'm so down for that." Bridget gave me a hard assessment. "Why don't you seem thrilled that your man actually gets along with your friends? You know that Kyle actually got mad when I invited him to come to poker night a few weeks ago? Said he wouldn't be anywhere that Chase was. And he said that he didn't like me spending so much time with other guys."

"You and Chase have been friends since forever. If something was gonna happen, it would've happened already."

"That's what I told him. He just gets jealous... It's kind of sweet. I guess I like having someone who really wants me. Kind of like you and Luca, you know? It feels good."

I shrugged as I tipped the glass back and finished it off.

"Another round?"

"Yes, ma'am."

As Bridget turned to grab the bottle, my phone lit up on the bar. A number I didn't recognize flashed on the screen.

Maybe it was Luca calling from a different phone.

"Hello?"

"Is this Madeline Dorsey?"

*Not Luca.* Probably just some stupid spammer who was going to tell me I won the lottery, but the deposed king of Nigeria needed the winnings.

"Speaking. Who is this?"

"Chef Dorsey, this is Aiden Crawford—we met at the James Beard Awards last month."

I choked on my whiskey and furiously waved down Bridget and mimed that I was going to take the call outside. She slid my glass behind the bar as I stepped out into the parking lot.

"Of course. What can I do for you, Mr. Crawford?"

He chuckled on the other end of the line, "I, uh, I'm sorry for ambushing you like this. Usually I'd go through your employer, but—"

"But my employer is Chef DeRossi?"

"Mixing business colleagues and personal contacts can be tricky."

I crossed my arms over my chest to ward off the nip in the air. "What exactly is this about, Mr. Crawford."

"Aiden, please."

"Aiden."

He cleared his throat. "I'm calling on behalf of a friend of mine who's opening up a new restaurant in the city. They want you, and I said I'd make a call to see if you were interested."

"The city as in—"

"New York City. You're bound for big things, Chef Dorsey. It's time you started looking outside of that little town of yours."

"Listen," I said with a short laugh of disbelief. "I'm flattered, but I'm not looking for another job right now."

Aiden chuckled. "I figured you'd say that, but I feel the need to mention that François Toussaint is the one headhunting you. He's putting together the pastry team. French cuisine with a modern twist. You'd be his sous chef."

*Holy fucking shitballs.*

François Toussaint was a culinary god. He was a master pastry chef who had put together not one, but three pastry teams that had earned Michelin stars.

"I'll take that silence to mean that you're interested," Aiden said.

"I, uh—I mean..."

*How could I not be interested in the offer of a lifetime?* Luca had an apartment in New York. His head office was there. His family was there.

Would leaving Beaufort really be such a terrible thing?

I felt guilty keeping Luca tied to Beaufort. Sure—he bought a house here, but he had houses everywhere.

"Can I think about it?"

"Of course. I'm just making the call on behalf of Toussaint. I don't have numbers or dates, and I'm sure that's something you'd need before making a big decision like this. I'll have my assistant get you connected with the hiring manager."

"Thank you. That sounds great."

"And Madeline, if I may, it might be easier to stay where you are, but the easy choice might not be the right one."

"Thanks for giving me a call. I really appreciate it. I'll look out for a message."

"Have a good night."

I hung up and blew out a breath as I leaned against the chipped siding of the bar.

I scrolled through my messages, hoping to see one from Luca.

*Nothing.*

I tapped his name and waited patiently for the call to connect, but instead of picking up, Luca immediately sent it to voicemail.

There was a quiet ding as an email from Aiden's assistant popped up on my screen.

She had forwarded an official offer from François Toussaint. The number on my screen nearly knocked me on my ass.

The base salary was way more than what I made killing myself working overtime at Revanche.

It would be enough to finally breathe easy when it came to paying for mom's care. Hell, I could actually start squirreling away part of my paycheck in that retirement account that mocked me every time I looked at the balance.

Even with the cost of living being higher in New York, it wouldn't matter.

*François Toussaint wanted me on his team.*

The door to the bar opened as a few men stumbled out. I caught sight of Bridget, Melissa, and Steve huddled up together, laughing.

*Dammit.*

Was that loss worth the price?

# 37

## LUCA

"This is Maddie! If I didn't pick up, it's probably because I'm working and you should know better than to call! Text me instead!"

I growled as I got Maddie's voicemail again.

It had been three weeks. Three mother fucking weeks.

The delay in Texas backed up to my quarterly investor's meeting. That backed up to a last-minute appearance in San Diego. Then I had to head back to New York to finalize another deal. It had been over three weeks since I'd seen her.

At first it wasn't bad. We talked a few times a day. But after the first week, it dropped to once a day.

Then we started talking every other day.

Then it turned into voicemails back and forth.

Between the scheduled meetings and bits of public image maintenance, I didn't have any free time.

Celeste Montgomery had reached out to see if we could sit down again. She needed a little more for her article since she spent the entirety of our first meeting flirting instead of listening.

Not that she'd ever admit that.

Celeste said the magazine had given her a bigger spread for the article and she had more space, so she wanted to meet at my New York apartment to see me at home.

Of course, Astrid had to open her big mouth and tell her about my recent real estate investment in Beaufort.

Astrid had a key and Maddie wasn't sleeping there while I was away, so I gave Astrid and Celeste permission to have it photographed for the article.

The beep from Maddie's voicemail snapped me back to the present.

"Hey, beautiful. Just calling to let you know I'm on my way. I'm about an hour outside of Raleigh. Be there this evening."

I tossed my phone into the passenger's seat and cursed the fact that I hadn't checked the staff schedule at Revanche to see if she was at work or not. Knowing her, she was.

I set the cruise control, hopped on the bypass, and sunk back in the seat.

Maybe it was good that Maddie and I had some space. It was going to be the norm if this thing between us was going to be a long-term relationship.

*And I wanted it to be.*

That didn't make it any easier, but at least I knew we could handle it.

I finally bit the bullet and hired a business manager for Revanche.

Really, I just needed someone to be my eyes and ears and act as a mediator between Scott, Carol, and Maddie if the need arose. Not that I thought it would.

The three of them ran a well oiled machine, but I didn't want it to look like I was playing favorites with Maddie. A third-party manager was a good safety net.

Maddie didn't seem thrown off by it. Then again, she probably had the poor guy shaking in his boots. Maddie could be downright terrifying when she wanted to be. Underneath all that sunshine and southern hospitality, she was a shark.

I passed through New Bern and Havelock. By the time I rolled into Morehead City, there was a smile on my face for the first time in weeks. Just as I got into town, my phone rang.

"DeRossi."

"Mr. DeRossi, this is Linda from Harlowe Bay Assisted Living."

I shifted my grip on the steering wheel and prepared to yank the car over the median to turn around.

"Yes, ma'am. What can I do for you?"

"Well, you remember that conversation we had a few weeks back when you came to visit with Maddie? You slipped away and asked me if I could give you a call when Mrs. Dorsey was havin' a good day. And I said that I couldn't give you that sort of information because of privacy laws and such?"

"Yes, ma'am—I do."

After the first time Maddie brought me to meet her mom, I had quietly talked to Linda while Maddie used the restroom before we left.

I wanted to visit Maddie's mom and talk to her when she was having a good day, but I didn't exactly want to upset Maddie with the request. Especially after that visit had ended.

"Well, this is me reminding you that I cannot tell you whether someone's havin' a good day or a bad day. But if you wanted to drop by and spend some time with some of our residents, I'm sure they'd appreciate the company."

I eyed the yellow light and floored it, cutting through some backroads that I knew led back to the side of town the assisted living facility was on.

I was proud of myself for learning the layout of the coast in such a brief time. Especially when I was used to being chauffeured by a driver.

I thanked Linda and hung up before I got in a car wreck. I strangled the steering wheel with a relentless grip as I swerved into the parking lot in record time.

Before I signed in at the front desk, I stole away to the men's room to splash some cold water on my face.

I hadn't exactly planned on doing this today, but if it was my only shot, I was going to give it my best.

I knocked on Maddie's mom's door and poked my head in. "Mrs. Dorsey, is it alright if I come in for a few minutes?"

Martha Ann Dorsey peered over her knitting basket and eyed me from across the room. "Well, that depends. Can you unravel my yarn for me?"

I cracked a smile and eased in. "Yes, ma'am." I pointed to the chair beside her recliner where Maddie would sit. "Mind if I sit beside you?"

"Have at it, handsome," she said as she handed me a skein of black yarn. "This one's gonna be for my Maddie Lee. Black's her favorite color, though I don't know why." She tut-tutted quietly and shook her head. "She doesn't like wearing hats in the winter because her darn hair's so big, so I make her toboggans with a hole in the top so she can pull it over her big ol' bun."

I chuckled quietly and worked to unravel the yarn the same way Maddie had. "I think she'll look real nice in it."

Thinking about Maddie all bundled up with a wind-nipped nose kissed in pink had me staving off a hard-on. *She'd look so fucking cute.*

I cleared my throat.

I didn't really know the best way to get at what I needed to talk to her about. I didn't even know if she knew who I was.

"I, uh, I should have introduced myself. My name's Luca—"

"Luca DeRossi. I know who you are. You think I'd let a stranger in here?" Martha's thin lips twisted up in the same amused smile that Maddie's did. "I didn't let you in here on your looks alone, sugar. My Maddie Lee's told me all about you."

She pointed a gnarled, arthritic finger at the nightstand where a picture frame sat. I leaned over and picked it up.

Maddie had printed out a picture of the two of us on the red carpet outside of the James Beard Awards and framed it for her mom.

I didn't realize how long I'd been staring at the photo until Mrs. Dorsey piped up. "Looks like love to me."

I set the photo back on the nightstand and made sure it was at just the right angle for her to see it from the bed.

"I do. I love your daughter. A lot."

Her knitting needles stilled and she patted my arm as I sat back down beside her. "I can tell. She's never brought anyone with her when she comes to visit before."

"You remember me coming to visit?"

A faint sadness washed over her face, like a wave lapping at the shore. It was so brief that if I hadn't been looking at her directly, I would have missed it.

"I don't," she clipped. "But Maddie told me that she brought you by a few weeks ago and that you've been travelin' for work since then."

I nodded. "Yes, ma'am."

Martha waved her hand dismissively and went back to

her knitting. "So, tell me, sugar—what brings you by today? You look like you've got the weight of the world on those strong shoulders of yours. Take a load off, sweetie."

I grinned as I worked at the yarn in my hands. "I came to talk about Maddie, actually."

She hummed. "I thought that much. I don't mind you coming to visit me just to talk about my daughter. You're sure nicer looking than the fellas from the Methodist church that come around to visit all of us. Tell me, what's on your mind?"

"I want to marry her." The words slipped out much easier than I thought they would.

It was the first time I had said them out loud. My palms grew clammy and a trickle of sweat beaded down the back of my neck into my button-up shirt.

Mrs. Dorsey snickered as she worked her way around the half-finished hat. "Sweetheart, let me tell you something. If you've come to ask my permission—you're not getting it. My Maddie Lee doesn't need her momma's permission for anything. If you think you can put up with that girl for the rest of her life, then best of luck to ya. She's a damn handful. You'll need luck and prayers and a genie in a lamp to handle my Maddie."

A deep laugh ripped out of my throat. That certainly wasn't the answer I was expecting.

Truthfully, I wasn't asking for permission. Maddie and I were grown adults, and it was up to us whether we wanted to promise 'til death do us part.

Mrs. Dorsey's response caught me off guard, but it left no doubt in my mind that she and Maddie were kin. It was a miracle Beaufort had survived the two of them raising hell at the same time.

I held the ball of yarn in my hands and stared down at the sterile tile floor. "I just wanted to tell you how much I love her. And that I'll do whatever it takes to give her everything."

There was a little table on the other side of Mrs. Dorsey's recliner. She pulled out a drawer and lifted a small photo album out. She put her knitting needles and the yarn in a basket and set it aside.

"Look here, hon," she said as she opened the photo album.

Pictures filled up every single page. Each one was labeled in Maddie's crisp handwriting, describing who was in the photo, where it was taken, and when.

Most of them were recent. To my surprise, I was in a lot of them. Maddie had even printed screenshots of me judging her work during *Pastry Throwdown*.

The label read, *My boyfriend, Luca DeRossi, judging my desserts for a TV competition. He was an asshole, but I love him.*

Mrs. Dorsey turned the page. There were pictures of the two of us out on a rock jetty right off the coast. Maddie had taken me to see Fort Macon.

After learning all about the history of the fort being built to keep the coast safe from pirates or invaders, we went on a walk down the beach, onto a long jetty that sluiced into the ocean.

"Maddie Lee put it together to help me remember everyone. I look through it every day."

She pointed to the photo where Maddie was taking a selfie with me, but I was looking at her. The corner of Mrs. Dorsey's mouth quivered and she clasped her hands around mine.

"I don't remember much these days, and I probably

won't remember you or Maddie next time you come by, but I do remember what it looks like to be in love." Her wrinkled finger pointed at my face in the photo. She tapped twice to make her point clear. "That's love, sugar. The way you're looking at my Maddie—that's the kinda love that sticks no matter what." She peeled back the plastic cover, took the photo out, and held it in her hand. "On the bad days, when I don't remember much, I still remember what love feels like —how wonderful it is. Even on those days, I still remember to thank the good Lord that my Maddie found it."

I sat there in silence, dumbfounded. Mrs. Dorsey put the picture back in the photo album and closed it up.

I leaned back in the chair and let out a billowing breath. "Thank you."

"Don't thank me yet," she snickered. "Bring me that little box on top of the dresser, will you?"

I did as she told me and brought her what looked to be a jewelry box. I sat back down as she opened it up and pulled out a little velvet case.

"You still have to convince that crazy girl to marry you, but I think I have something that might just help your case." Mrs. Dorsey popped open the square box and handed it to me. "I know a fella like you could buy her a big ol' hunk of a ring if you wanted to, but that one was her grandmama's and, for a minute, mine. Only seems right that it goes on to my Maddie."

I had been planning a trip to a jeweler when I went back to New York, but this ring was perfect. It looked vintage— almost art deco. It had a large oval cut diamond set on a thin, white gold band. Smaller marquise diamonds circled the center stone and jutted out like an exploding firework. It was brilliant.

"She'll love it," I choked out as I closed the box and held it in my hand. "I know she will."

"One more thing, sugar," she said as she pulled a wrinkled envelope out of the box. "Give this to her after you pop the question, will you?"

*Madeline Lee Dorsey* was written in perfect cursive on the back of the envelope. I slid it into the inner pocket of my suit jacket for safekeeping.

My phone buzzed in my pocket, and I pulled it out to check it. Three missed calls from Astrid and four from the general manager of my restaurant in Los Angeles. *Fuck.*

I flicked through the most recent all-caps text message from Astrid and catalogued the highlights. Sexual harassment lawsuit against the executive chef at my LA restaurant. Damage control needed. Chartered flight out of New Bern leaving in an hour.

*Fuck, fuck, fuck.*

New Bern was forty-five minutes away. I glanced at the time and realized there was no way I could see Maddie and make the flight.

I fired off a text, letting Astrid know I was on my way to the airstrip, then promised Mrs. Dorsey I would give Maddie the letter. She smiled when I told her that I'd come back to visit soon. Hopefully, as her future son-in-law.

Rushing toward the exit, I thanked Linda for the courtesy call.

"Next time you eat at Revanche, it's on the house."

Jogging out to my car, I pressed the phone to my ear and prayed that Maddie would answer as I jumped behind the wheel.

*"This is Maddie! If I didn't pick up, it's probably because I'm working and you should know better than to call! Text me instead!"*

"Dammit!" I slammed my phone into the dash. Running a hand through my hair, I breathed out slowly to calm down before texting Maddie.

LUCA

> Wasn't able to make it back. Crisis in LA. Flying out in an hour. Call me when you can. Love you, Tesoro.

## 38

---

## MADELINE

This wasn't happening.

I stared at the text, ready to call Luca back, but I was frozen in place.

*He didn't come back.*

He fucking turned around and left.

Hurt and anger bubbled up in my gut as the lump in my throat expanded.

I looked at the happy couple across the table from me and politely smiled. "If you'll excuse me for just a moment, I'll go and print off that contract with the invoice details, and that will get y'all squared away."

Hurrying toward Luca's office, I prayed that it was empty.

The new business manager—the one I ignored most of the time—had taken it over.

No more stolen kisses when I ran upstairs for something. No more flirtatious advances when we were supposed to be talking about scheduling, payroll, and hiring. No more sneaking off for a quickie while the rest of the staff ate the family meal after dinner service was done.

Luckily, the office was empty.

I closed the door and printed off the paperwork I needed my clients to fill out to book their wedding cake.

The printer whirred to life and, for once, I prayed for a paper jam. Anything to give me a few more minutes of privacy.

Tears welled up in my eyes, but I sniffed them back. I hadn't seen Luca in almost a month, and now he was leaving again without so much as a hello or a kiss on the cheek? Did he even make it back to Beaufort before he left again?

Is that what the future would look like?

The printer spat out an extra page. I went to toss it in the trash when something in the bin caught my eye. I pulled out a thank you card and flipped it open to read the message.

*Luca,*

*Thanks for meeting me so last minute. I love the new house. Hopefully, I can come by again sometime. Can't wait to see you soon.*

*- Celeste*

*No.*

*No, no, no.*

No way this was happening. My heart raced and my pulse cranked up to a drumroll. I dropped the card as if it had burned me. It landed back in the trash.

Luca had barely been at his new house since he bought it. We only spent a handful of nights there before he left for Texas, and—supposedly—he hadn't been back since.

When the hell did he sneak off to meet Celeste Montgomery there?

The reasonable adult in me knew I should call him as soon as my cake tasting was over. But the southern girl in me was fixing to tan his hide.

I went through the motions of booking the couple and sending them on their merry way. I clocked out, emptied my locker, dropped my chef whites in the backseat of my Jeep, and stomped over to the Taylor Creek Inn.

It was an unseasonably warm fall day. The warm sea air felt good as it blew across my bare arms.

The irony of my *I Got a Real Good Feelin' Something Bad's About to Happen* shirt wasn't lost on me. I yanked the hair tie out of my rat's nest of a bun, shook my hair out, and tossed it to one side, pretending that the volume was intentional.

The bar inside the inn looked appealing, but that wasn't where I was headed.

I rounded the front desk and gave Kristin a wave as she cut through the lobby. I yanked hard on the courtyard doors, knowing that's where I'd find Hannah Jane.

"Oh, sweetie," she said as she looked up from her floor plan print-outs.

Tables and chairs were scattered around, and she stood beside a giant stack of folded linens.

"You look like I need to get a body bag." Hannah Jane looked down at her signature stilettos. "Don't worry—I have my work flats in my office. If we're disposing of some poor, unfortunate soul who did you wrong, I'll change in a jiffy."

Hannah Jane was the picture-perfect southern belle. But beneath the pearls and lace, she was full of piss and vinegar. The woman was elegant to a T, but she'd make a body disappear if someone crossed her.

Hannah Jane Hayes took no shit and gave no fucks. Her skin was thicker than an ornery alligator's, and I was pretty sure that's what her high heels were made out of.

I needed her signature no-nonsense take on the situation. That's why I nearly knocked over a planter, cutting through the front lawn of the inn to get here before I did something insanely rash and, most likely, illegal.

"And you're positive he hasn't been back since he bought the house and left for that business trip to Texas?" she questioned after I explained everything.

The missed call. The text message telling me he wasn't coming back. The note from Celeste I found in the office trash can.

"Positive. He hasn't been to the restaurant. I check on the house every day. And, other than Astrid's, my alarm code is the only one that's been used. Besides—It's a small town. If he had been here, I would have known about it just from the gossip."

She tapped her perfectly manicured nails on top of a cocktail table. "Do you actually think he'd cheat? That he's been faking everything between y'all this whole time? I mean, the man's absolutely head over heels for you. The way he looks at you—you can't fake that."

"What other explanation is there?"

"That he *actually* had a work emergency, and he *actually* had to turn around and leave."

"Why are you playing devil's advocate here?" I snapped. "You're supposed to be on my side, Han. If I wanted someone reasonable, I'd go talk to Mel."

"I'm just trying to keep you from flying off the handle and making a mistake. Luca is *it* for you."

I spun and stormed back toward the lobby. Why the ever-loving fuck was she siding with Luca on this?

Hannah Jane's heels clicked on the flat stones that filled out the courtyard, but I didn't turn around.

"Maddie, wait," she snapped in her *I'm the wedding planner and I'm in charge* voice. "I'm not taking his side. I'm just saying that maybe you should assume the best in him before you jump to conclusions. Just call him. Ask him the tough questions, but give him a chance to explain himself."

I slumped against the wall and looked up at the ceiling. "I can't talk to him, Han."

"Well, you probably have a few hours 'till he lands in California. Go get something to eat and take a nap. You make dumb decisions when you're tired and hangry."

I narrowed my eyes and stared at her through a hooded gaze. "Don't use your bride-whisperer voice with me."

"Is it working?"

"Maybe," I grumbled.

"Go see Bee. Get some food and then make your big life decisions."

Bridget wasn't much help either, but at least she had mozzarella sticks waiting when I dragged my feet into Jokers.

Good thing Chase was there. Out of all seven poker clubbers—eight with Luca—Chase was probably the best at girl talk.

"Bee, me and Mad Dog are gonna grab a booth," Chase said as soon as my hands braced against the bar.

Bridget handed him the plate of mozzarella sticks and pointed to an empty booth in the corner. "I'll bring your drinks over in a sec."

"Thanks, darlin'."

"I take it Hannah called you," I said as I followed him and sunk down onto the lumpy leather bench.

"You know how it works," he said as he stabbed a mozzarella stick into the marinara sauce. "You're awfully calm."

I sighed and rested my elbows on the table between us and dropped my head into my hands. "I'm trying this new thing called being reasonable. I hate it."

Chase let out a full-bellied laugh and shook his head. "You're not reasonable. You're *hell hath no fury*."

"That's why I said I was *trying*."

His fun-loving demeanor shifted to something serious. Chase looked less like my good-time guy friend and more like the man with the badge and gun he had on his belt.

"I shouldn't be sayin' this 'cause I'm on duty, but if he actually fucked around with that reporter, I'll beat the shit out of him."

I cracked a wry smile and picked at a groove that cut through the top of the wood table. "Not really sure that's what the Beaufort P.D. classifies as *protecting and serving*."

"I'm serious, Maddie."

"I know." I groaned in frustration and rested my head against the back of the booth. "I was so stupid, getting involved with a guy like him. I knew *exactly* the kind of person he was before I got in bed with him. I was a dumbass to think I could change that or believe he could be someone else."

"Mad, listen to me. It's not your damn fault. Don't saddle yourself with feeling responsible for that motherfucker's shitty choices."

I left the bar feeling slightly better after Chase's profane version of tough love. That was, until I pulled into the driveway at Luca's house and saw Astrid's car in the drive.

"Madeline," she sniffed with her nose so high in the air that it looked like an antenna.

"What are you doing here?" I said as I slammed my Jeep door. "Shouldn't you be in LA doing damage control with Luca?"

She gave me a pitiful smile and sneered. "I wasn't needed in Los Angeles. He's there making sure his restaurant is safe, and the investors are happy. I'm here making sure that his image remains appealing to the masses and the few that *actually* matter."

"And just who actually fucking matters?" I snapped. "If you know something, just come out and say it."

Astrid smoothed her hand over the side of her slicked-back hair. The tight bun made her look even more severe and cold than usual.

"I have no idea what you're talking about." She feigned innocence, but it was all just one big steaming pile of bullshit.

"Celeste Montgomery," I clipped. I was done beating around the bush. I deserved a damn answer.

She gave me a slight smile that was more victory than pity, and opened her car door. "I don't comment on the personal life of Mr. DeRossi unless I'm speaking publicly on his behalf. I'm sure you, of all people, can appreciate my discretion, Miss Dorsey."

"Is he sleeping with her?"

Astrid's smile turned downright wicked as she slid behind the wheel, gave the key a sharp twist in the ignition, and said, "No comment."

Tears streamed down my cheeks, burning my skin as Astrid pulled out of the driveway. I stared up at the house, knowing I needed to go inside and take care of things, but I didn't have the strength to take the first step toward the door.

My phone buzzed in my pocket and, half-heartedly, I hoped it was Luca.

It wasn't.

I took it as a sign from the universe and scrolled through to find his number. I held the phone up to my ear and waited.

And waited.

And waited.

Right before the ring that I knew would send me to voicemail, Luca's voice filled my ear. "Hey."

*Seriously? Hey is all I got?*

I bit my lip and tried my hardest to keep my tone even. "Do you have a minu—"

"Look, I know we haven't talked in a couple days, but now's not a good time."

"Are you kidding me?" I laughed in disbelief. "Luca, I haven't seen you in a month, and now I find out that—"

"I gotta go, Maddie. Talk soon. Love you."

*And then the line went dead.* Tires crunched up the driveway, and I whipped around, hoping that maybe, just maybe, Luca would materialize behind me and everything would be okay.

Instead, I saw Steve's black Challenger idling beside my Jeep. He got out and shoved his hands in the pockets of his faded jeans that had been worn well past their wear.

"Figured you'd be over here," he muttered.

My lip trembled, and I clutched my phone like a lifeline. With each one of Steve's steady strides, I felt myself crumble a little more.

"Don't tell anyone I cried over him," I whispered as Steve wrapped his arms around me and pulled me in close.

"Your secret's safe with me," he muttered. "I owe you. Remember?"

I did. The night that Heather passed away and we sat on the dock—I never uttered a word to anyone about Steve shattering to pieces.

"I don't know how you get up every day," I sniffed, trying my best to keep his soft flannel shirt snot-free.

One of my many flaws was that I was an ugly crier. Snot

bubbles and dry heaving—the whole nine yards. It wasn't attractive in the slightest. But around Steve, I didn't care.

"I can't imagine how it felt for you to lose your soulmate because this hurts like hell."

"Maybe it's supposed to hurt," he finally said after a long silence. "The pain tells us we're still alive and breathing."

I laughed through my tears. "When did you become such a fortune cookie?"

Steve's lips quirked in a sort of dopey, lopsided grin. "Can't take credit for it. Mel says it to me all the time."

"Of course she does," I said. *Because she was totally into him.*

"You're gonna be alright, kid."

"What about you?" I asked. "Are you gonna be alright?"

Steve rested his chin on top of my head and, for the first time, I realized that hugging him now didn't feel like it used to.

Where he had been solidly in the dad-bod, teddy-bear category, his soft sides were gone. Instead, his shirt strained against defined muscles and sharp edges.

He had even gone from being clean-shaven all the time to sporting a scruffy beard.

How had I missed all that? Steve was my neighbor and one of my best friends. Had being with Luca blinded me to what was happening all around me?

He shrugged. "Pain reminds us we're alive, but I think pain is a warning not to get hurt again."

# 39

## LUCA

I grabbed the crystal decanter and poured myself a healthy glass of bourbon.

Instead of stopping at a finger or two, I filled the tumbler to the rim.

Tonight wasn't the night for measuring alcohol by the ounce and drinking like a gentleman. I loosened my tie and made my way to the leather couch that was calling my name.

I felt like shit, and not just because I had to blow off Maddie earlier. I owed her an apology for leaving town before I could make it to Beaufort to see her, but the situation in LA was worse than I thought.

The—*now unemployed*—executive chef of my Los Angeles restaurant was scum of the lowest variety.

Not only had he been preying on young employees, but he'd also done so while promising raises and promotions if they fulfilled his sick desires.

The evidence was damning, and he had admitted to every disgusting thing.

All it took was one employee coming forward and

spilling the details to the third-party human resources firm for an investigation to get started. One employee willing to talk turned into two. Those two turned into six.

*Six women who had been manipulated and coerced by that bastard.*

I was fucking furious.

If the revelation hadn't already ruined the man's life, I would have beaten him into the ground myself.

But that wasn't what my investors wanted to see, and it certainly wasn't what my L.A. employees needed.

They needed me to be a strong, level-headed presence. They needed stability and someone reasonable to get things back on track.

I cared about my employees. Sure, I didn't know all their names. But from my first restaurant to the rest of the acquisitions that came after, I was hell-bent on creating a safe working environment for the people who invested their time there.

This bullshit wasn't tolerated in the slightest.

"You look like hell," Isaac said as he let himself in. He glanced at my glass as he picked up the nearly empty decanter, putting the pieces together. "That bad, huh?"

"You have no fucking idea," I groaned as I sipped the bourbon and relaxed as the warm, smokey burn coated my tongue. "It's a shit show."

"Come out with me. You look like you need a good time to unwind. I met this chick getting coffee this morning. She's a journalist or something—total babe. I'm meeting her at a club downtown. I can have her bring a friend."

I grunted something noncommittal and took another swig from the glass. "You know, for a guy as filthy rich as you are, I can't figure out why the hell you still go inside a coffee shop and get your own coffee."

Isaac grabbed the bottle of cognac I kept on the bar cart and poured a finger into an empty glass. "How else am I supposed to meet women? All the ones I see at work are corporate lizards in power suits."

Isaac was the sole heir to a massive real estate fortune. He was the next generation of the firm his father and grandfather had built, and that meant putting in a hell of a lot of work.

Isaac's motto hadn't changed since his Ivy League days—work hard, play harder.

"Get your assistant to give you a list of women wanting to use you for money and fame," I grumbled with a dry sense of annoyance.

Isaac cracked a grin as he downed his glass of cognac. "Your lizard still trying to get you back with Amalia?"

"Nah—even Astrid knows I'd rather be castrated than get back with her. Now she's got it in her head that she's gonna set me up with Celeste Montgomery."

"Who?"

"Contributing editor for that magazine that's running a story on me. She's been a fucking thorn in my side for months while she's been writing this piece. Astrid's making me play nice, but Celeste can't take a fucking hint."

"Ah." He chuckled. "The woes of the rich and famous. Too bad you're sexy as hell too—that must be a real bitch."

"Takes one to know one, dick head."

"What happened to that little east coast ten you were seeing? I swear, man—my secretary's got a thing for you. I caught her staring at the red carpet photos of you and your—"

"Maddie."

"You and Maddie from some event last month." He

plunked down in the wingback chair across from me and propped his ankle on his knee. "Things serious?"

"I have a ring. Just haven't been able to pop the question yet."

"Damn, DeRossi. I always knew you were a sentimental son of a bitch. You're serious?"

"Dead fucking serious."

"Good for you," he said casually. "Happy for you, man."

"That's it? No argument that I'm giving up my bachelorhood for a ball and chain?"

Isaac grinned. "Why would I argue? It's a numbers game, man. You being off the market means more pussy for me."

I should have laughed, but I couldn't. Not when I remembered how wrecked Maddie sounded during the twenty seconds we talked on the phone.

Still, there was something that I was sure of. "She's it for me." I slid my phone out of my pocket and fired off a text.

LUCA

You busy? Call me if you're free.

She responded almost instantly. I could feel her anger seeping through the screen.

MADDIE

Working.

I was only a few sips into the bourbon I'd poured myself, but I knew if I kept going that I'd inevitably do something stupid.

*Something stupid like getting on a plane and flying across the country to see a girl who had been on my mind every day for six fucking months.*

I walked my tumbler over to the sink and poured seventy-five dollars worth of Blanton's down the sink.

"How the hell am I supposed to make it work with her when she's in North Carolina, and I'm all over the fucking place ten months out of the year?"

"Beats me. That's why I'm going out like my granddad. Bachelor until he was sixty, married a hot, young thing, got her pregnant and kept the family tree going."

I sneered in disgust and shook my head. "You realize you just called your grandma a *hot, young thing*, right?"

"I said what I said."

"You sure did," I muttered under my breath. "So, you're really ready to hit the big four-oh in a few years and still party like you're in a fraternity?"

"Please," he said, looking at the one of a kind watch on his wrist as he made his way to the door. "I'm Isaac-fucking-Lawson. The parties I go to now are *much* more legendary than when I was in college. You look like you need a night out. Come on. My driver's downstairs waiting. Let's go out, get you loose. Just like old times."

Being in a hot, crowded club with migraine-inducing music and whiny drunk girls sounded about as appealing as a doctor telling me to turn my head and cough.

"I'm good. I should get some sleep. Few more days and I'll be outta here. Just need to finish cleaning up the cluster-fuck at the restaurant."

"Good," Isaac said as he made his way to the door. "You're really cramping my style. Can't exactly bring girls back here when your mopey ass is slumming around."

"Last time I checked, this was *my* condo. And you're welcome for me being a saint and letting you crash here when I know damn well you could get your own place."

I had built my restaurant empire from the ground up while Isaac was born with a silver spoon in his mouth. He was the cheapest rich person I knew.

"Hey—I spend my money where it counts."

"Like on nightclub VIP sections and top-shelf bottle service to impress the undergrads you pick up at your coffee shops?"

I knew I was giving him a hard time, but truth be told, Isaac was always the first person I went to when I was thinking about making a risky business move.

He had a head for numbers and, regardless of his party boy antics, he was a shrewd businessman with the irrational confidence of a honey badger. It worked for him, so who was I to judge?

Isaac left to go paint the town, and I turned down the hallway toward my room.

At least he had been crashing in the guest room.

I didn't want to think about what kind of debauchery would have happened on my sheets had he taken up residence in the main bedroom.

No laundry service in the world could get my bedding clean enough for me to sleep on it again.

I wasn't one to leave a mess, but I didn't give a rat's ass when my suit hit the floor and I didn't hang it up to send it to dry cleaning.

I changed into a pair of jeans and a t-shirt, then grabbed my Yankees hat, and threw it on.

I was sick of being *Luca DeRossi*. I was ready to be Luke again.

The taco truck was hopping. The night was still warm, and people milled about.

I grabbed my styrofoam container and dropped a wad of cash into the tip jar.

Wistfulness crept through me like a snaking vine. *Fuck, I missed her.*

It was nearly eleven in California, which meant it was

two in the morning back in Beaufort.

There was a chance that Maddie was still awake if she had closed the restaurant for dinner service. I took a picture of the taco truck and fired it off.

LUCA

Wish you were here. -Luke.

Maybe she was onto something when she told me that all she wanted was Luke and Maddie.

My condo—even with Isaac crashing there—felt empty.

The Blanton's I fancied tasted like tap water.

My stress levels were nearing nuclear, and the only thing that would make it better was her.

My phone buzzed and, like a moron, I had hope.

It wasn't Maddie texting me back. Maybe she had already gone to bed, or maybe she was just ignoring me. I couldn't really blame her for either.

I swiped across the screen and saw that Celeste had tagged me in a post online.

*Of her.*

*In my bedroom in the new house.*

Someone—*a soon to be murdered Astrid*—had taken a photo of Celeste in my bedroom. She was standing on the widow's walk overlooking the bay. The French doors were wide open, and the sheer curtains were billowing in the breeze. Celeste's hands were outstretched on either side of the railing. The silky, black dress she was in looked like fucking lingerie.

*I know the real Luca DeRossi. The question is, do you? Read all about the industry's sexiest chef in "Luca DeRossi: Food, Fashion, and Foreplay." Find it in next month's issue.*

# 40

# MADELINE

HOT GUY FROM THE GYM IN LA

Maddie, please call me back. I need to talk
to you, Tesoro. I love you.

I didn't even have to open my eyes to know that it was
going to be a dreadful day.

I wasn't sure that my phone had ever stopped
ringing throughout the night. When I woke up and actually
looked at the damn thing, it was a million times worse than
I had expected.

It wasn't a dreadful day—it was the *worst* day.

It was the day that my world came crashing down.

Screenshots of the post were in almost every text from
Hannah Jane, Melissa, Kristin, and Bridget.

I had at least a million copies of Celeste Montgomery
and her tousled sex hair standing on the balcony off of the
hidden suite in Luca's house.

The place he said was for us and us only.

I was angry. But more than that, I felt violated—used
and then thrown away.

Luca's name flashed on the screen. It had to be at least his three-hundredth attempt at reaching me.

From the looks of my call history, he had been at it all night long. Without even thinking, I hurled my phone across the room and screamed. Hot tears rolled down my cheeks.

Suspecting my boyfriend of cheating was one thing, but having it rubbed in my face was another thing entirely.

"Mad?" Melissa called out. "You dressed?"

I looked down at the pair of Luca's plaid boxers I had on and the buttercream-splattered t-shirt I had been too lazy to change out of last night.

"Enough," I mumbled.

Footsteps neared, and the door cracked open. "Where is he?" Steve barked as he loomed in the doorway behind Melissa.

"Los Angeles," I mumbled, not even caring that he was going to disembowel Luca when he got the chance.

My feet hit the floor and I moved like a zombie. I pushed through Steve and Melissa to get to the kitchen and punch the button on the coffee maker without feeling much of anything.

Numb.

"Maddie," Melissa said as she followed me. "Is there any chance that this is just a misunderstanding?"

"Probably a snowball's chance, but I haven't been able to stomach the thought of talking to him. The last time we did, he practically bit my head off."

"Maybe you just caught him at a bad time. I mean, he had to go do damage control, right?"

*Why the fuck was everyone defending him?*

I grabbed a mug out of the dish drainer and filled it to the rim. "It doesn't matter now, does it? He made his choice when he let her into our bedroom. I think what happened is pretty clear." The words brought bile up with them as they ran off my tongue. I choked down the lump in my throat. "I'll be fine."

"We all know you'll be fine, Mad. But you're not fine right now."

I thought back to the phone call I had made last night. The one I made as I left Luca's house after running into Astrid.

"I have to pack."

Steve crossed one muscled arm over the other. "Where you goin'?"

"New York."

"For what?"

"A job interview."

Mel and Steve looked like I had told them I was planning on shaving my head and running naked down Front Street.

"Why the hell do you have a job interview in New York?" he shouted.

"I got an offer a few weeks ago and I've been mulling it over."

"Bullshit. You weren't even thinking about taking some other job. You're running away."

"It's like... My dream job. And it's not like I'm running. I worked in New York years ago and really liked it."

That statement was only partially true, but I wasn't about to admit it. I wanted to be anywhere but Beaufort. Everything reminded me of him, and I couldn't take it.

My house, his house, the restaurant, Jokers—there wasn't a single place on the whole damn coast I could go that wouldn't have his mark on it.

I couldn't even risk going to visit my mom and seeing that photo album out on her knitting table.

"And in a city of almost nine million, you think it'll be easier to hide from him than little ol' Beaufort?" Melissa snapped. "Madeline Lee Dorsey—you are not a scaredy cat, so stop acting like one."

Steve hunched over and rested his forearms on my kitchen island. "Tell me about the job."

Mel whipped around, but he held his hand out to stop her from biting his head off.

I drained my coffee and set the mug in the sink, somehow managing to muddle my way through the call from Aiden Crawford.

"I'd be stupid not to go at least interview for it. I might not even get it, but I have to try," I said as I finished my spiel.

"Bullshit," Steve said as he pushed off the island and headed back toward my room. He grabbed something and was back in the kitchen. "You're gonna get the fuckin' job if you go up there and do the interview." He slammed my phone down onto the island and shoved it toward me. "I'll drive you to the fuckin' airport myself, but I'm not doing it unless you call that bastard and get his side so I know what kind of jail time I'm looking at when I end him."

Steve walked Mel out as I threw mostly clean clothes in a suitcase and double-checked my flight status. I grabbed my wallet from where it was perched right beside the photo of me and Luca that I kept on my bedside.

It was ironic, really. He had lied to my face the very first time we met.

He pretended to be someone he wasn't.

Unfortunately, the lie was better than the truth. I had fallen for someone who didn't exist.

Steeling myself for the tears, I yanked the zipper around

my carry-on with a vengeance. I sat on the edge of my bed and hesitated before swiping through my phone and tapping Luca's name.

"Maddie—" he blurted out after the first ring. "Fuck, baby—I've been trying to call you all night." He sounded exhausted and worn. Then again, keeping up with two personas will do that to a person.

Just the sound of his voice had my heart aching and my stomach twisting in knots. Heat flashed around my neck, and I beat down those pesky butterflies that boiled up inside.

"*Tesoro, per favore dì qualcosa. Ho solo bisogno che tu mi parli. So che sei arrabbiato, ma ho bisogno di sentire la tua voce,*" he rambled.

Even if he spoke in English, I wouldn't have been able to understand him with how fast the words rolled off his tongue.

"Maddie, I know you're pissed—and you have every right to be—but it's not what you think. Jesus, I miss you so fucking much. Please, *Tesoro*... Just talk to me. Please."

I laid back on my bed and stared at the ceiling. One tear turned into two that turned into ten.

"I can't do this, Luca," I finally said as I rolled over and silently sobbed into my pillow.

"Just give me a day. *Please,*" he begged. "I'll be back tomorrow. I just—dammit, Maddie—don't do this."

I shoved my phone into my pillow so that it would hide my sobs. I heard Steve's Challenger roar to life and knew that our time was up.

"I have to go," I whispered.

"Fuck going to the restaurant. Have it out with me right fucking now. You want a fight? I'll give you a damn fight. I'll argue with you. Just don't walk away, Maddie. Stay and let's have a fight."

"I'm not going to the restaurant," I said as I grabbed a Kleenex from the almost empty box and dried my eyes. I tossed it in the trash and grabbed the handle of my luggage.

"Where are you going?"

There was no sense in lying. "New York."

"I'll catch a red-eye tonight and be there."

"I'm interviewing for a job with François Toussaint. As my current employer, I'd appreciate it if you *didn't* show up." I tried to be as cold as I could, but there was no way I could hide the hurt in my voice.

Luca stammered and stuttered before his timbre dropped into a low growl. "Stay." Something shattered on his end. "Dammit, Maddie. Just stay."

"You're the one who told me I was meant for something more than Beaufort," I cried.

"I lied."

I looked around at my tiny little houseboat. The life I had built. The promise I had made to myself that I would create a life I loved in Beaufort.

I wanted to light a match and set the whole thing on fire. The wheels of my suitcase clacked as it bumped over the deck and onto the wood-slatted dock to Steve's waiting car.

I chewed on the corner of my lip and took a steadying breath. "Goodbye, Luca."

———

I PUSHED through the freezing rain and sprinted three blocks from the subway entrance to my hotel.

Luca had texted me half a million times, begging me to stay at his apartment. *Not that I answered any of his texts.*

I needed to clear my head. A couple days away in the city would do the trick.

No Luca. No pressure to stick around in Beaufort and be the Maddie my friends expected, the daughter my mom needed, or the pastry chef the restaurant required.

Despite the chilly air and the near-arctic rain that sloshed under my boots, I felt lighter.

The interview had gone perfectly. I wasn't expecting to meet François Toussaint in the flesh. But there he was, sitting across from me in a wrinkled button-up with a mustard stain on the pocket. It was always nice to have a reminder that my heroes were human.

Aiden Crawford had been there too. He was in town for an event and Toussaint invited him along since he made the introduction. I worried that Aiden would bring up Luca. Thankfully, he didn't.

We didn't talk about working hours or negotiate my salary. We chatted over coffee about the restaurant industry and discussed baking methods and techniques like old friends. It was the most relaxed I had been at an interview, well, ever.

I stomped up the front steps of my hotel and shrugged off the rain before heading for the elevator.

"Dammit," I muttered as I dug through my bag in desperate search of my room key.

I felt the smooth plastic under my fingers and pulled it out from under the pile of gum wrappers and old receipts.

"Aha!" I rounded the corner.

Just when I thought I was home free, there was Nonna.

My smile turned to a frown. "If he's here, I don't want to talk to him," I said as politely and firmly as I could.

It would be just like Luca to send his adorable grandma as bait.

Nonna clicked her tongue at me and waved her hand. She dug around in that big bag slung on her shoulder and pulled out a bottle of wine.

"I don't want to see that *culo* either," she spat in her thick Italian accent. "Let's get a move on, *passerotta*."

I wasn't really sure how she got here in the first place. Did she come all the way from Brooklyn by herself?

I shoved my key card in the slot and pushed the door open. Her short stature didn't hinder her surly demeanor. Nonna's wispy white hair was pulled back in a staunch braid, and her mouth was set in a hard line.

She was little, but she was scary.

"You have stories for me, *passerotta*," she said as she pulled a bottle opener out of her bag and yanked the cork out. "Tell me why you look so glum. A girl like you with a bright future should be all smiles. How was the interview?"

I made myself comfortable in a chair by the window and let Nonna do as she pleased. "How did you know about the interview?"

Nonna snickered as she grabbed two coffee mugs from beside the standard hotel coffee maker and filled them with wine.

"Any cup can be a wine glass if you believe in it." She toddled over to me with a mischievous smirk and handed me a mug. "My boneheaded grandson raised hell trying to find out where you were staying. He wanted his sisters to come talk some sense into you. I told them that if they stepped one foot out of Brooklyn that I would haunt them for all eternity."

"Nonna!" I exclaimed.

*Either I had fallen into an alternate dimension or I was drinking wine out of coffee mugs with my ex-boyfriend's ninety year old grandma. Then again, weirder things had happened.*

She waved me off and added, "I had a feeling that a smart girl like you had her reasons. Reasons my Luca probably didn't listen to. He's a man, you know. The men—they tend to think with the wrong head."

*It was definitely thinking with the wrong head that got him into this mess.*

I snorted at Nonna's anecdote while I inhaled a big gulp of wine. It lodged in my throat, and I nearly spat it out when I collapsed into a coughing fit.

I finally composed myself and took another sip to calm my nerves. "He didn't deny that he did it."

Nonna set her mug on the coffee table between us and clasped her hands in her lap. "Do you think he would be that foolish, *passerotta*? Trading sunshine like you for a woman without *seni* and *natiche*?"

The woman was determined to kill me.

I nearly wretched on my wine again when Nonna mentioned my well-endowed tits and ass and Celeste's lack thereof.

*Well okay then—I see we're past the point of ladylike conversation.*

"Enough about my *idiota* grandson. Tell me—are you going to take this new job?"

"I'm thinking about it." I sighed as I looked at my reflection on the dark surface of the wine in my mug.

"You'll be miserable if you do," she clipped as she drank the last drops of her mug and poured herself a little more. "New York is my home. It's not yours. You're a sparrow. Full of hope and meant to be in the sunshine and the air. The piece of your heart that is hurting will not heal here. That wound will only grow and fester if you run away from where you're supposed to be."

Nonna was the second person to tell me I was running away and I hated it.

"I can't go back to him, Nonna," I admitted as I toed off my boots and pulled my knees to my chest. "What he did..."

"Tell me, *passerotta*, what did he do?"

"He slept with another woman." My voice faltered on the last few words.

*Had he, though?*

"Well, if he did—I will make his life miserable. You have my word."

"And if he didn't?" The words were out before I had time to think about what I was saying.

There was a part of me—a rather large part—that thought maybe he didn't do it.

"No one faults you for trying to protect yourself. You know your heart best. My Luca is a sweet boy. Sometimes stupid, but he would never be so careless with the ones he loves.

"Nonna..."

"Do you still care about him, *passerotta*?"

I looked down into my half-empty cup as a tear sprang into the corner of my eye. "I don't know how to stop loving him."

"But?"

"But I'd be stupid to trust him."

"You're not a stupid girl, Maddie. You know deep inside whether you can trust him," she said without a care in the world as she plugged the wine with the cork and put the bottle back in her bag. "I'll see you soon, *passerotta*."

I hoped she was right.

Nonna walked to the door. I got up to let her out and say goodbye, but when I opened it, a tall, blond man stood in the doorway with his fist raised to knock.

He was the complete opposite of Luca. Tall, yes. But where Luca had black hair and eyes the color of bittersweet chocolate, this man's hair was a sunny, golden blond and his eyes were a crisp blue.

The last time I had seen him was over dinner with Luca during our trip to New York for the James Beard Awards.

"Why are you here?" I clipped.

"Isaac Lawson," Nonna exclaimed as she pushed me out of the way. For a little sprite of a woman, she was strong. "What are you doing here, *guastafeste*?"

Isaac leaned down and gave Nonna a kiss on the cheek. "I could ask the same of you, but I have a feeling I know the answer." He looked straight over her at me and flashed a billion-dollar smile. "I'm here to show Maddie a sex tape."

# 41

## LUCA

A strid sat across from me, her back straight as an arrow. She didn't seem nervous, or at least concealed it well.

Three sets of documents were arranged on the desk between us—a lawsuit, a contract termination, and copies of the social media bullshit that she and Celeste broke the internet with.

The moment I got into Beaufort, I ordered her to meet me at Revanche.

I got to the restaurant, politely told the new GM to get lost, and escorted Astrid into the office for her haranguing.

I had already cut off her access to my bank accounts and had someone changing the locks to every door I owned.

I'd give her a ticket to get out of North Carolina, but after that, she was on her own.

I pressed my palms together and rested them on top of the desk before me, covering the copies of the lawsuit my lawyers had filed against her, Celeste, and the magazine.

"Do you want to explain what the fuck possessed you to

do what you did, or should we just get on with it?" I said with as much professionalism as I could muster.

If she wanted to try and explain her way out of the grave she dug for herself, so be it. But the deed had already been done. There was no coming back from this one.

Astrid sniffed indignantly like she still wielded power here. "The social media traction that you've gained from Celeste's posts is worth the blowback. People want the rich, mysterious man who takes lovers. Not whatever this whipped, emasculated thing is that you've been sporting these days. I did my job."

"*Worth the blowback?*" I barked as I rose to my feet and craned over the desk, towering over her.

For the first time, I saw a worry in her eyes.

"Worth the fucking blowback? Are you kidding me, Astrid? You and *Ms. Montgomery* implied that I had an affair with a woman who was supposed to interview me in a professional capacity. You intruded on my personal space when I gave explicit instructions on where I allowed people in my home. You made the love of my life believe that I fucking cheated on her! You tarnished my name to get ahead, and you know damn well that's not how I do things."

"Right, because you're such a choir boy," she retorted. "The next few million you earn will be the result of everything I've done for you, and you know it."

I drove my fist into the solid wood desk and growled. "There is no dollar amount on this earth that would make what you did acceptable. Ever."

"Please. Maddie Dorsey is just another notch in your belt," she said as she folded her hands in her lap like she was about to have tea. The woman was a stone cold bitch. "*When* you realize that she's just a detour in your path to bigger and better, you'll see that I did you a favor and you will *beg* me to come back."

"A detour?" I scoffed, laughing at the ceiling. "You think Maddie is a fucking detour?" I reached in my pocket and pulled out the ring I had carried with me everywhere I went.

Astrid's jaw dropped just a little.

"She's it for me. She's still going to be it for me. What-ever I have to do to fix the mess you created, I'll fucking do it. But let's get one thing crystal clear before I have your signature on the last NDA you'll ever sign. Maddie is fucking priceless, and I'll spend every penny I have to protect her integrity and mine. People like *you* will never understand that because you don't have a decent bone in your body."

I practically threw the contract termination and non-disclosure agreement at her. She scribbled her name at the bottom and, with the last vestiges of her pride, gathered her things and left.

———

ISAAC

Fun fact. Telling a pissed off girl you want to show her a sex tape isn't the best opening line. I might have made it better. I might have fucked it up. Your guess is as good as mine. Good luck, bro.

ISAAC

Also, fuck you. Where the hell did you find a woman like Maddie and why have you been hiding her from me? She's a fucking dime piece. She got any friends? Hook a guy up.

ISAAC

> By the way, your Nonna is still cool as shit.
> You think she'll adopt me as an honorary
> DeRossi?

JUST FUCKING GREAT.

I tried calling Isaac back, but he wasn't answering. *Probably because he knew I'd kill him for whatever he said to Maddie.*

Then again, he couldn't really make things worse. I had already done a bang-up job of that.

I paced the deck of Maddie's houseboat, surprised that I hadn't worn a hole in the wood yet.

Maddie had only been gone for three days, but the mood when I walked into the kitchen at Revanche yesterday after firing Astrid was nothing short of homicidal.

Scott looked like he was ready to dice me up and put me on the dinner menu. Carol seemed like she wanted to gag me with the linens and stab me with a fork.

Everyone knew why Maddie had gone to interview for a job in New York. Everyone had seen the damn picture.

The one that I had filed a lawsuit over.

The one that I fired Astrid over.

The one that I was willing to put every dime I had toward fighting.

I wasn't bullshitting Astrid. I'd go broke if it meant that I did everything in my power to prove to Maddie that I was worth her love.

I wrung my hands and crossed my arms over my chest. Halloween was right around the corner. The frigid air blowing in was fitting for the chill I'd felt ever since Maddie called me to end things.

The moment she hung up the phone, I knew that we were far from over.

I'd fight for her. I'd fight with her. All I knew is that I wasn't done with Madeline Dorsey.

Not since the moment I laid eyes on her ten miles of pearly blonde hair swinging back and forth at the gym. Not since I fucked her hard in the kitchen of the restaurant. Not since I pushed her to take a chance on me.

I had lost track of how long I had been at Maddie's house.

All I knew is that I got a cursory text from Steve telling me she'd be back today. It was the most I had to go on, so I showed up, and I waited.

My mind went back to my conversation with Mrs. Dorsey—when she said the kind of love I felt for Maddie was the love that sticks.

She didn't say it in so many words, but I could tell there was something in her that wanted to ask if I'd stand by Maddie even when the going got tough. Even when someone was ready to walk away.

Hell or high water, I was going to stick.

A car rumbled up the drive, and my heart nearly ripped through my ribcage.

Headlights flashed across the grass and lit up the water. The light inside Steve's sports car turned on, and I saw Maddie sitting in the passenger's seat. They exchanged a few words before he cut the car off, jumped out, and popped the trunk. He pulled her suitcase out and set it outside her door.

"Just give her a minute," he said as he wandered over to the dock. "She'll talk when she's ready."

I nodded and shoved my hands into the pockets of my jacket. With the hood flipped up over my Yankees hat, I looked more like Luke from the first night we met than the Luca she hated.

Truth was, I wanted to be both people. I wanted to be *Luca DeRossi*—who the hell wouldn't? I worked hard for what I had and had earned my station in life. I wasn't about to apologize for being proud of that.

On the other hand, I wanted the ability to be a chameleon when I wanted to.

Beaufort gave me the luxury of anonymity that came with people not giving a flying fuck how many zeroes were at the end of my bank account balance.

If she'd just hear me out, I knew she could handle both sides of me.

She could handle the pressure of the public eye with grace and that sass I loved so much.

Maddie liked the small town life as much as I did. This was her home.

I wanted—no—I needed it to be *our* home.

Still, if she decided to take the job in New York, that wouldn't be a deal breaker for me. I wanted her more than I wanted anything else.

The passenger door clicked as Maddie pushed it open. She stood up and looked at me with dead eyes.

*Great.* Just fucking great.

She came back home, but not back to me.

Maddie took measured strides across the grass at a peaceful pace. Her long silver and gold waves were bright against her leather biker jacket. She wore a pair of light, acid-washed jeans that looked like they'd been painted on.

I stood frozen on the deck of her houseboat as she walked down the dock.

She looked back over her shoulder at Steve's house. The lights were off, but his garage door was open, and I heard the faint sound of weight plates being loaded onto a barbell.

Maddie turned her head to me and looked down at the

inch of water between the dock and the boat. "How'd you know when I'd be home?"

I took a step forward until less than a foot separated us. "Well, I'd like to say it's because I waited here for three days until you came back, but that'd be a lie. Steve texted me this morning and said you were coming back today." Inhaling a deep breath, I added, "Truth is, I wouldn't have waited for you to come back. I would have come after you."

She bit down on the corner of her lip and shuffled her feet back and forth, working her toe against a loose slat on the dock.

"Luca..." Her voice disappeared into the wind. She looked up at the stars and shook her head. "What happened with us?"

"I need to know if I'm losing the love of my life *and* my pastry chef or just my pastry chef."

That got her to look me in the eye. "What?"

"Look." I shrugged. "If working for Toussaint is something you want, then I'm happy for you. But I'm more concerned about whether I'm losing the one person I care about most in this world. It doesn't matter to me if you're on my payroll or not. I just need you—however you'll let me have you. If New York is something you want, I'm there."

"Are you happy?" she asked.

"Not since you walked out of my life."

"Good," Maddie said as she hopped over the lip of her houseboat and closed the distance between us. "Because I'm miserable."

"*Tesoro*," I said in a near growl.

It had been a month since I'd touched her. Held her.

I needed all of her, and I needed it right fucking now.

Static-filled tension hung heavy between us. I wanted to

lay my hands on her as much as I wanted to breathe, but I drew on my last bastions of self-control and gripped the inside of my jacket pockets instead.

"I was scared," she admitted.

"Why? You know how much I love you."

"You can love someone and still leave." Her voice softened to a whisper. "Everybody leaves."

"But you left me this time."

"I thought it would make it better, but it didn't. I thought if I was the one leaving that maybe it wouldn't hurt as bad."

"And?"

"It sucked, Luca," she said with a tremor in her words.

I leaned down and kissed the top of her head. "Hey," I soothed. "I should have come to see you before I left to deal with shit in California."

Her dark eyelashes batted like feathered wings as she slowly wrapped her arms around my neck and looked up at me. "Isaac dropped by for a visit when I was in New York."

"I, uh, I may have heard something about that." A minuscule smirk curved up the corner of my mouth. "I can't be held responsible for whatever the hell he said. He doesn't have a filter."

Maddie's face lightened, and she let out a quiet giggle. Those dimples that I loved so much popped out on either cheek.

"He's somethin' alright." Her fingers gently stroked the back of my neck. I felt her belt rock against the bulge in the front of my jeans teasingly. "He told me everything."

Slowly, I pulled my hands from my pockets and settled them on the dip in her waist. "As much as I want to hear whatever the hell he said, it's been way too long since I've seen you. I can't wait another damn minute," I croaked out as I pulled her flush against me. "God—I missed you so much," I murmured into her hair. "Missed you so fuckin' much, beautiful."

"Nonna came to see me too."

I chuckled.

"Any idea how she found where I was staying?" she asked as she cocked her head to the side and raised a suspicious eyebrow.

I grinned and brushed my lips against hers. "I may have done some digging to find you."

Maddie tipped her chin up and nipped at my bottom lip. "I figured that much, smartass."

"I took a stab in the dark and guessed that Crawford must've made the introduction for Toussaint. They've always been tight, so I called him up. He told me what hotel you had booked."

"And you sent Nonna instead of coming yourself?"

"Mad," I began as I tucked her hair behind her ear and rested my palm on her cheek. "I wanted to be there, but you didn't need me. I will always be your biggest fan. There's no way in hell I would try to screw you over if that job was something you wanted. No matter how much I want you to be here." I drew her in and placed a gentle kiss on her forehead. "And it might be selfish, but I want you here."

She leaned into my caress and closed her eyes. "I missed you."

I couldn't take it anymore. I grabbed the back of Maddie's neck and crashed my lips to hers. My tongue swept through her mouth, and I swallowed down the little whimper that escaped her lips.

Pulling back, I let out an unsteady breath. "Whatever you decide—I don't want to change your mind. But I will not make saying goodbye easy. I'm gonna make you miss me."

Maddie looked up at me. The lights from the deck of her houseboat danced in her eyes the same way that moonbeams glimmered on the water.

"Luca DeRossi, you are the love of my life and the biggest pain in my ass."

"Say you'll stay," I begged in a hoarse whisper.

She looked around, then finally turned back to me. "How could I leave?"

"Maddie—"

"I'm staying."

"Say it again," I murmured as I kissed her hard. A tear streaked down her cheek and I wiped it away with my thumb.

Maddie trembled, and I cradled her against my chest. I rested my chin on top of her head and held her close.

"I'm staying," she whispered again.

"I love you, Mad."

"I love you more."

I cracked a smile and kissed the top of her head. "Doubt it, but I'll let you have the win for now."

I needed all of her, and I needed it right now.

The details could wait.

What she found out from Isaac could wait.

We could talk about her conversation with Nonna later.

I needed Madeline Dorsey more than I'd ever needed anything.

I lowered my lips back to hers and, with a reckless hunger, walked her backward to the front door of the houseboat. I put my hand in the back pocket of her jeans and gave her ass a hard squeeze as I slid her keys out of her pocket and unlocked the door.

We stumbled through the kitchen, grabbing at each other's clothes, sending fabric flying everywhere.

My shirt ended up in the sink. One of her boots was on the threshold of the front door, and the other was by the bathroom.

We ping-ponged through the narrow hallway toward the bedroom. Maddie barely made it onto the bed before I was grabbing at her knees, spreading them wide, and diving between them like a desperate man.

I kissed a path up the supple skin of her inner thighs and let my hot breath linger over the silken entrance that was soaked just for me.

"I need you," she whined.

That was all it took to make me snap.

Madeline Dorsey was a taste I would never get enough of. She was more complex than the finest wines. Sweeter than the best dessert and had a spice that rivaled the hottest peppers. She was the kind of savory that could sustain a man for life with the unexpected notes that would keep things interesting.

Everything about her was a craving that would never be satisfied.

I licked my way up her center with the flat of my tongue. She let out a shocked gasp and fisted the bedspread. I pushed her legs further apart and dove in deeper, sliding two fingers into her core. I curved them up and slowly stroked that magical spot that had her mewling in delight. I bit down on her clit and sucked as I felt her shatter. Maddie's body was wracked with tremors as she reeled from her orgasm.

I wasn't giving her a single second to recover. I grabbed her thighs and flipped her over to lay on her stomach.

"Hands and knees, beautiful."

Maddie scrambled to obey, presenting that gorgeous ass nice and high for me. Her back arched seductively, and I trailed my finger up and down, teasing the cleft of her ass as I lined myself up with her opening.

"Do you want me to get a condom, Mad?"

We'd started going without them. Maddie was on birth control, and both of us were clean. Still, I asked because like it or not, Astrid forced Maddie to doubt my integrity.

"I swear to you, I haven't been with anyone else," I said as I placed an anchoring hand on her hip.

Before she felt forced to make that decision, I decided to back off and grab one. As much as I wanted her to trust me, I knew it would take time to earn that privilege back.

Cool air rushed between us as I went in search of my jeans.

*I think they ended up in the bathtub when I kicked them off.*

"Luca—" Maddie called out.

"Yeah?"

"Come here."

I blindly fumbled around the dark room, desperately looking for my pants. "Just a sec. I just gotta find my—"

"Luca, I swear if you don't get on this bed and fuck me in the next three seconds, I'm gonna grab my vibrator and do it myself."

"Maddie—"

"I trust you, Luca. I wouldn't have been able to come back if I didn't. I'm here. And I need you so bad that I think I might die. So please—" She was begging at this point and damn if it didn't inflate my ego just a little. "God, Luca—I love you and I've been dying without you. I just—"

I tackled her like a linebacker and threw her back down

on the bed. She let out a little squeal as she bounced back up toward me. I pinned her arms to her sides and shut her up with a kiss.

"Say it again."

Maddie's eyes found mine in the dim light. "I love you," she choked out. "I think I always have."

# 42

# MADELINE

"Astrid convinced Celeste to post it as a publicity stunt for the article," Luca said as we filled each other in on the bits and pieces of what the hell happened while we were apart. "I let her photograph the new house, but I didn't know they were gonna... you know."

We were laying under the covers, a tangle of arms and legs in a mess of sheets. The glow of sex was still rampant on our skin.

I had told Luca what I knew. Isaac apparently met Celeste at some nightclub in LA. Some girls recognized her from the infamous photo and asked if she was hooking up with Luca.

Being the devilish playboy he was, Isaac convinced her to go back to a hotel room with him.

He kept feeding her shots until she spilled the whole damn thing. He recorded the entire drunken conversation on his phone and brought it to me as proof. Apparently Celeste wanted to get freaky and make a sex tape to prove she actually hooked up with Isaac Lawson.

He used the brains inside that pretty head of his and turned the tables on her.

At least he didn't actually make me watch the sex tape. Just the confessional.

Astrid came up with the hare-brained scheme to boost Luca's sex appeal—not that it needed boosting.

She wanted me out of the picture since I didn't fit the mold of who she thought was appropriate for Luca to be seen with.

Ladder climbing bitches are sneaky little fuckers. Astrid was worried that Luca's image would go swirling down the toilet if he wasn't with some kind of socialite, and she was willing to do anything to send me running.

*She almost won, too.*

Luca wiggled down under the covers and tucked me into his side. It was a small gesture that I'd come to love.

"How's Nonna?"

I giggled as I traced the lines of his tattoo sleeve with my finger. "She brought me wine."

"Ah, I see. So, she's your favorite now, huh?"

"She also made me promise to come visit for Thanksgiving," I said as Luca reached around and pulled me up so that I was on my knees, straddling his waist.

I felt the solid length of his erection pressing into the apex of my thighs. *The man was never not hard.*

"And I think that if I don't show up, she'll put some ancient curse on me or something," I teased.

It had been a long time since I'd had a family Thanksgiving. With November right around the corner, I was just a little bit giddy to try it out. Usually I spent the day—or at least as long as I could—with my mom, eating hospital-grade turkey and mashed potatoes.

I had always been invited to Steve and Heather's or

invited to join Chase's family, but I hated being the third wheel.

His chest rumbled with a deep chuckle, and it put my heart on a tumble dry setting. "I, uh, I was thinking..."

"Hm?" I murmured as I leaned down and peppered the expanse of his chest with featherlight kisses.

"We should host."

I sat up, smirking as his cock twitched against my ass. "Host?"

Luca propped himself up on his elbows, and I caught a glimpse of that mischievous smile on his mouth.

"Have my family come down here. Have your friends join. Steve will probably need somewhere to eat. You can invite Kristin and her crew. Hell, we've got the room. We can fill all those empty rooms at the house with my batshit crazy family and all their little rugrats and whoever else."

I'd never hosted a holiday before, but the idea of being surrounded by everyone *here* did stupid things to my already reeling heart.

Luca shifted until he was sitting up against the headboard. One hand slid between my legs and teased my pussy. The other brushed my hair off my shoulder and cupped my cheek. "What do you say?"

I dropped my head back and groaned in delight. "You keep doing that, and I'll say yes to anything," I gritted out.

"How 'bout we put that to a test?" he asked with a soothing voice as he coaxed me closer and closer to another climax.

I bit down on my lip to keep from crying out, and he wasn't having that. The blunt head of his cock prodded at my entrance, and I slowly eased down onto his steeled shaft.

He let out a grunted profanity and set a steady pace. "Move in."

I gasped. "What?"

"Move. In. With. Me," he gritted out, punctuating each word with a snap of his hips. "No more taking it slow. This is it. You're it."

"Luca—"

He smirked and drove into me hard and fast. Stars burst into my field of vision and, for a second, I thought that the roof caved in.

I screamed as I hit my peak. Luca's body shuddered as he fell into his release.

"I dare you, *Tesoro*," he grinned against my collarbone as we caught our breath. "I dare you to give me a shot at forever."

*Well, hell.*

I was a lot of things, but chickenshit wasn't one of them.

*I dare you.* They were the exact words he had texted me in California, as he tried to convince me to go out on a date with a total stranger.

*I dare you.*

I needed that push. I needed someone to dare me to take a chance on myself. On someone else.

I needed someone to dare me to love.

———

"Mad, wake up," Luca whispered.

I blinked my eyes a few times as they slowly adjusted to the darkness.

I pawed for my phone, mindlessly feeling around, and looked at the time.

"Babe—it's five in the morning. You have another hour before the turkey needs to go in."

The house was still quiet, but it wouldn't be for long.

The DeRossis were an unruly bunch, and I loved it. Everyone had shown up for Thanksgiving. Air mattresses were sprawled around the living room, and every couch was occupied.

The bedrooms on the second floor were packed. I had never been so thankful for the privacy of our suite.

Family was wonderful and stressful all at the same time. Still, I was grateful.

It was a good thing we were both professional chefs and had Nonna to keep us in line. We needed it since it seemed like we were going to be feeding half of North Carolina.

"Get up and get dressed," he whispered. When I nestled back into my pillow, he yanked the covers off and threw my pillow across the room. "Get moving, *Tesoro.*"

I tossed a few four-letter words his way before finally stumbling toward the closet.

He was already pulling on his coat and sliding his feet into a pair of Ariats. We had gotten them from a local store that was tucked away on Highway 70 while we were on our way to Raleigh to meet with a chocolate supplier.

"Where are we going?" I whined as I pulled on a thick pair of leggings and a chunky sweater.

I only managed to find one of my boots. Thankfully, Luca found the other one while I slipped on a pair of his socks.

It annoyed the hell out of him that I kept a laundry basket full of unmatched socks. Especially when I usually opted to just wear his.

He was anal enough to match his pairs when we were folding laundry.

Those were just some of the little quirks we'd come to begrudgingly love since I moved in.

It had been a month of intense bickering followed by

raunchy make-up sex. Luca always threatened to push me up against the glass that looked out over the water, just like he had that night during the hurricane.

Of course, I always said no. After all, Steve was right across the bay.

I grabbed a salt and pepper hat that my mom had knitted, and shoved it over my bedhead. I ran a toothbrush over my teeth and tried to perk up my tired face with a splash of cold water.

I had stayed up way too late sitting around and drinking wine with Nonna, Luca's mom, Daniella, and Anna-Marie.

"You ready?" Luca asked when he stuck his head into the bathroom.

"You never told me why you have me up at the crack of evil on my day off," I grumbled. "You said you'd get up and take care of the turkey. And even if you needed help, I could've done that in my pajamas. It's my friggin' house. I'll walk around in your boxers if I damn well please."

Luca chuckled at my insolence and leaned in for a chaste kiss. "I love hearing you say that."

Sure, I missed the quirkiness of my houseboat, but I didn't miss the precariousness of living on the water. I had planned to keep it as a rental property for a little extra income to help pay for my mom's care.

That was before I found out that Luca had been paying for it for months.

*Months.*

That had been a fight of epic proportions.

Not because I was mad, but because I was shocked. It was a burden that he had taken from my shoulders, and he did it quietly.

Luca was flashy and outgoing—he had to be to maintain his level of celebrity. What I had fallen more and more in love with was the man he was in secret. The ways he showed that he cared.

It was the big things like taking over the payments to Harlowe Bay Assisted Living.

It was the little things like hosting the poker club here every Monday.

Of course, he was still the reigning champ, and that was infuriating as hell.

He hired a new Jane of all trades to replace Astrid. This time, she was a happily married, sixty-something year old woman who didn't meddle and didn't get her granny panties in a wad if Luca said he was going to lay low.

We tiptoed around his nieces and nephews, who were still sound asleep on the floor, and snuck out to his car.

I kept pestering him about where we were going, but the devilish gleam in his eyes told me that I wasn't finding out.

We settled on talking about the new restaurant concepts that the DeRossi Hospitality Group was working on. The Griffith Brothers deal was finalized last week, and they would start collaborating on Texas's soon-to-be most sought-after steak destination at the beginning of the year.

Luca pulled into the parking lot at Fort Macon and cut the car off. "Let's go on a walk before things get loud."

The beach was deserted at this hour. Then again, it was pre-dawn on Thanksgiving Day. Not even the locals would be out.

We trudged up the hilly beach access and across the soft sand. I smiled as the rock jetty came into view. It was one of my favorite spots on the entire coast.

It was the first place I took Luca when he finally convinced me to take a full day off just for us.

He took my hand and we started on our way out to the

edge of the jagged boulders that jutted into the roaring ocean.

The water was gray and ruthless, spraying us with a salty shower with each crash against the jetty. We finally made it out to the very tip and Luca wrapped his arms around me from behind. A wave broke against the rocks at my feet, and I shrieked as ice water clung to me with a death grip.

Luca let out a hearty laugh, but when I whipped around to nag him for laughing at my misfortune, he was down on one knee with a white box in his hands. "Madeline," he began.

*Oh my God. He was—he was doing the thing.*

*It was happening.*

*Luca was—and I saw the*

I clasped my freezing hands over my mouth and did my best to stay upright while my head spun.

"Do you know why I brought you here today?"

I gave my head a pathetic shake. I barely knew what my name was. If a cop came by and gave me a sobriety test, I would have failed miserably. Seeing Luca down on his knee rendered me completely stupid.

"The day you first brought me here was the day that I realized that I wanted a life here—A life that included you. *Tesoro,* you are everything to me."

He reached up and held my hand, his thumb brushing over the knot bracelet he'd given to me the first time he took me to New York. I only took it off for work.

"You're my treasure. When I first talked to Rob about buying Revanche, he told me the history behind the name. He always liked the folklore of Blackbeard wrecking the *Queen Anne's Revenge* off the coast of Beaufort. He liked the idea that treasure could be buried in the water here, so he named his restaurant *revenge* in French after Blackbeard's ship." Luca shook his head with a ridiculous smile on his face. "Thing is—the treasure isn't in the water. It's right here. It's you, Maddie. *It's always been you.*"

He opened the little box, and my eyes widened when I saw the ring.

"Is that—" I would have recognized that ring anywhere. I spent hours staring at it as a little girl.

Luca nodded. "It is. Your mom gave it to me to give to you with her blessing."

Tears flooded my eyes, and I sobbed into my cupped hands. "Luca—"

"Madeline Lee Dorsey." He grinned while he paused for dramatic effect. "Will you marry me?"

"God, yes!" I exclaimed as he slid the ring onto my shaking finger. Luca rose to his feet and planted a hard kiss on my mouth.

He took my hand and led me back to the car, cranking the heat up as soon as we got in. I was sea-soaked and shivering, but I didn't care one bit.

Luca reached over and popped open the glove box. "One more thing for you."

He handed me a letter that had my mom's handwriting on it. "What is—"

"I dunno. I haven't read it. But, your mom asked me to give it to you after I proposed, so…"

Carefully, I slid my finger along the edge and popped the envelope open. Unfolding the neatly creased paper, I began to read.

*MY DEAR MADDIE LEE,*

.  .  .

*I MAY NOT REMEMBER MUCH, but I remember the important things. I remember that you were seven pounds, seven ounces, and twenty-one and a half inches long when you were born. I remember that you sacrificed your dreams to come back from New York and move back in to take care of your momma. But most of all, I remember what love is.*

*I remember you crying yourself to sleep after your daddy left all those years ago. I cried too. I know it probably would have made it easier on you to hate him, but hate isn't what we're made for.*

*We're made to love big and fierce for all the days of our lives. Sometimes people leave us and hurt us, but that doesn't mean you lose your capacity to love. It just means they weren't worth the love you have to give. It doesn't make it easy, because there's still a hole that's missing love in return. The ones who are worth it will stick. Sometimes they'll leave, but they always come back.*

*I pray every night that you'll find the best kind of love—the kind that sticks when the going gets tough. Love isn't always soft and meek. Sometimes it's loud and knocks you down on your ass from the sheer power of it all. Love fights. It works hard. As you get older, you and your partner will grow as a people. Your love will need to grow too.*

*I know that by the time you read this, I probably won't be the momma you remember, but you'll always be my Maddie Lee.*

*ALL MY LOVE,*
   *Momma*

I LEANED back in the seat, the letter falling to my lap like a leaf.

Luca reached over and laced our fingers together. "You alright, *Tesoro*?"

I wiped the tears away and nodded.

Mom had taken a turn for the worst over the last few weeks. As hard as the visits were, I didn't have to do it alone. Luca was always right beside me. My rock.

After a thorough make-out session in the car that had me feeling like a teenager, we got back to the house and walked straight into an engagement party.

The whole place was awake, and it had me thinking that they knew what Luca had been planning all along.

It wasn't just Luca's family, though. Scott, Carol, Rae, and Javier were there, along with most of the staff from the restaurant. Hannah Jane, Chase, Bridget and Kyle, Steve, Melissa, and Kristin milled around, drinking coffee, and digging into the breakfast spread that Nonna had whipped up.

While the rest of the girls were oohing and aahing over my ring, Hannah Jane was in full wedding planner mode.

"Happy for you, Mad," Steve said when I caught him next to the coffee maker. "Never thought I'd say this, but I actually kinda miss you being a pain in my ass, livin' on that damn houseboat."

Truthfully, I worried about Steve. He'd become somewhat of a recluse. Apart from his shifts with the Beaufort Police Department and poker night, I rarely saw him. None of us did. Luca and Chase had started working out in Steve's garage to make sure he had some company every few days.

That's what we did for each other. We were like a patchwork quilt—different kinds of fabric, different shapes and colors. Some pieces older and some newer, bound together to make something beautiful.

# EPILOGUE
## LUCA

"**W**here the hell did Maddie go?" Hannah Jane hissed as she grabbed the sleeve of my tux and pulled me into a corner by the DJ.

I gave a polite wave to someone who was somehow related to me and, according to my mother, had warranted a wedding invitation.

I chuckled. "You think I know where that woman went?"

"Well, it's almost time to cut the cake," Hannah clipped. "Do not move from this spot until I find your wife. You two are like herding cats. And don't even get me started on your best man."

*Speak of the devil.*

Isaac strutted across the dance floor with a glass of something strong in his hand.

"Well, well, well. If it isn't *Hell Yes Ma'am*," he teased Hannah.

She just rolled her eyes and headed off in search of Maddie.

Isaac's head spun like he needed an exorcism as he watched her walk away.

*Yeah, my man was totally checking her out.*

I should have been mad about that on Maddie's behalf since we were married now. But truth be told, Maddie and Isaac were thick as thieves. Probably because they were both slightly insane.

"So, how's it feel to be a married man, DeRossi?" Isaac asked as he clapped his hand on my shoulder. "You gonna start wearing New Balance sneakers and getting up at seven on Saturday mornings to cut your lawn? Gonna start shopping at the GAP?"

I chuckled and stole his glass, finishing off what little brandy he had left. "I'm married, not over the hill. Besides —you've gotta drive all the way to Wilmington or Raleigh to go to the GAP. Not a whole lot of shopping around here."

I didn't mind. I still had both of my—our—places in LA and New York. If we wanted a taste of city life, we'd just go there.

Isaac grimaced at my obvious adjustment to the quiet life. "Dude, I was kidding. Why the hell did you move out to the middle of nowhere again?"

I spotted Hannah Jane dragging Maddie across the dance floor in a cloud of white tulle.

That was why. Always her.

The DJ faded whatever was playing, and Shania Twain filtered through with her sultry *Let's go girls* blaring over the sound system.

Maddie cheered. "It's my song! Come on, Han! One dance with you, Bee, Kris, and Mel, and *then* we can do the cake."

"Nope," Hannah snapped. "Mad, I love you, but you'll thank me for this when you sober up. Time to cut the cake with your hubby."

I left the spot Hannah had ordered me to stay put at and helped her guide a very tipsy Maddie over to the cake table.

"Where was she?"

Hannah blew a stray piece of hair out of her face and huffed. "Drinking with your grandma at the bar. Fun fact—the lady with one foot in the grave can hold her liquor better than this one." She stabbed a finger toward Maddie, who was all too eagerly looking at the cake.

It had taken Maddie longer to pick a cake designer than it took for her to pick a wedding dress. Or hell, anything else about the wedding. Finally, we decided on a kick-ass pastry chef whose cake samples made Maddie moan the way she did when we were in bed.

*Good to know I ranked just above cake.*

"Nonna's *so* much fun." Maddie giggled as she swayed back and forth. She let out a cute little hiccup and covered her mouth. "She may have convinced me to do *a few* shots."

*Damn that woman.*

Nonna was a feisty one. Maybe that's why she and Maddie got along so well.

I looked around the ballroom at the Taylor Creek Inn and found her cutting up on the dance floor with Chase.

*Because of course she was.*

I couldn't help but laugh. He waltzed around with my Nonna like she was the Queen of England. Next to Chase and Nonna, I saw Bridget and Kyle swaying back and forth.

No wonder Chase was hanging out with my grandma.

Still, they looked like they were having a hell of a time.

We went through the rituals of cutting the cake and tossing the garter and the bouquet.

Isaac caught the garter and, much to her dismay, Hannah Jane caught the bouquet. The DJ coerced them into a quick dance where I saw Hannah intentionally stomp on Isaac's foot at least four times.

If the two of them didn't kill each other by the end of the night, it'd be a miracle.

Things were winding down and Maddie had miraculously sobered up.

"Baby," she whispered as we slow danced while Jon McLaughlin crooned out a love song.

"Yeah, beautiful?"

"Wanna get out of here?"

"Aren't we supposed to do that sparkler thing in a little bit?" I didn't really know. I just caught bits and pieces here and there and showed up on time whenever Hannah Jane gave me a schedule.

Maddie had a naughty gleam in her eye and a wicked smile on her lips. "I have my key to the restaurant with me," she whispered.

I decided to close Revanche for the day so that the staff could have a night off and attend the wedding.

"Oh?" I said with feigned innocence. "And why do you have that with you, Mrs. DeRossi?"

"*Luca*," she soothed in my ear, nibbling on the lobe. "What if I said I wanted a preview of the honeymoon *now*?"

I chuckled low and long. "You're evil, *Tesoro*."

Since the first time we'd had sex in the pastry kitchen at the restaurant, we'd done it there a few more times. *Okay, more than a few.*

"Please?"

*How the hell was I ever supposed to say no to her?*

Heaven help us when we had kids. I'd be a goner if they look anything like Maddie.

She was reckless and wild. She brought out the best in me and pushed me in a way I never knew I needed.

She saw through my poker face—past the punk-ass kid who'd hit on her in the gym, and through the grumpy judge who ragged on her through an entire competition.

She saw through the guy who wanted to have two different lives and somehow managed to mold them into one.

I looked over her shoulder and saw Hannah shaking Isaac off her tail and prancing toward us. "You two ready for your last dance?"

"Then we're out of here?" I asked. *It was more of a desperate plea.*

"Then you're out of here," she promised before giving the DJ the signal to start our final song.

I leaned down and whispered in Maddie's ear. "We'll leave, circle the block, and then sneak in the back door of the restaurant."

Maddie smirked and wrapped her arms around my neck. "I was hoping you'd say that."

# AUTHOR'S NOTE TO THE READER

Dear Reader,

Where to even begin? This book was a freakin' blast to write. I love

Maddie and Luca so much it makes me want to cry, and I think they'll always hold a special place in my heart.

I was a little scared to start writing something other than military romance—that's all I had ever done! I wrote Poker Face because I wanted to share a little bit of my own story and my own experiences—fictitiously, of course!

Some of these things really happened. *Let me tell you: champagne buttercream that's been sitting in the jalapeño bucket is all kinds of nasty!* Maddie and I share the title of pastry chef and it was so much fun to weave her happily ever after together with little threads of my personal experiences.

I loved the world—both fictional and real—of Beaufort, North Carolina. I loved creating the friendships that support Maddie and Luca. I cannot wait to write the other five—yes, FIVE—Beaufort Poker Club novels!

I seriously hope that you love Maddie and Luca as much

as I do! If you do, please leave a review on Amazon or GoodReads!

Thank you for spending your time and hard-earned money on this book. I hope you enjoyed your escape to a wonderful little town of backwoods bars, houseboat jumping, life, and love.

You're a wonderful human being! *Also, you're looking FINE today!* Spread Kindness!

**XO,**

    **—Mags—**

PS. Because you're super cool, let's be friends!

    *Follow me on Instagram @authormaggiegates*

    *Want to spread the love? Tell others what you thought of this book by leaving a review on Amazon and GoodReads!*

    *(I'll do a literal happy dance if you do!)*

# ACKNOWLEDGMENTS

Without the support and expertise of the following people, I would have never been able to bring Maddie and Luca to literary life. These folks are the real MVPs.

**To Mr. Mags:** For being the most amazing husband and cheerleader. For spinning a complex web of lies, convincing me that driving me hours to Fort Macon was a normal Sunday activity, and proposing to me on the rock jetty. It's still my favorite place in the world. You my favorite and I love you more.

**To Alicia:** Thank you for reading every freaking thing I digitally shoved at you over the last few months. You're literally my best friend at this point, and sometime in the future we will meet! Thanks for being the best beta reader and confidant a girl could ask for!

**To My Editor:** Thank you for your editing eagle eyes and graphic design prowess! And for putting up with my virtual temper tantrums when it came to the growing pains of this book! -To my readers, I love you, you know. Thank you for being the coolest hype squad and for getting behind this insane writing venture! Y'all are the best and I freaking love you so much it makes me want to cry!

**To The Pasta Grannies:** thank you for keeping traditions alive.

**To all of my culinary school instructors, colleagues, and co-workers who shall remain nameless and will prob-**

**ably never read this:** We create jobs and memories. That is important and essential work.

**To Scott Conant:** For hating raw onions, thank you for giving me the initial inspiration for the grumpy judge who became Luca De Rossi.

**To Sam Hunt:** For all his awesome music that I jammed to during this write.

**To The Employees at Panera:** Y'all are dope. Sorry for mooching off your wi-fi.

**To Gordon Ramsay and His Daughter:** For endless amusement on TikTok.

**Lastly, to my own Nonna:** I love you and I miss you. No one makes rolls like you do.

# ALSO BY MAGGIE GATES

*What Saves Us: A Small Town Single Mom Romance*

## The Griffith Brothers Series

*Dust Storm: A Single Dad Romance*

*Downpour (Coming 2024)*

*Fire Line (Coming 2024)*

# ABOUT THE AUTHOR
## MAGGIE GATES

Maggie Gates writes raw, relatable romance novels full of heat and humor. She calls North Carolina home. In her spare time, she enjoys daydreaming about her characters, jamming to country music, and eating all the BBQ and tacos she can find! Her Kindle is always within reach due to a love of small-town romances that borders on obsession.

*For future book updates, follow Maggie on social media.*

facebook.com/AuthorMaggieGates

instagram.com/authormaggiegates

tiktok.com/@authormaggiegates

Printed in Great Britain
by Amazon

46583183R00253